POSTAL™

CREATED BY MATT HAWKINS

VOLUME 2

TOP COW
PRODUCTIONS, INC.

PUBLISHED BY TOP COW PRODUCTIONS, INC.
LOS ANGELES

POSTAL™

CREATED BY MATT HAWKINS

BRYAN HILL
MATT HAWKINS
WRITERS

FOR THIS EDITION COVER ART BY
ISAAC GOODHART, LINDA SEJIC,
& BETSY GONIA

ORIGINAL EDITIONS EDITED BY
BETSY GONIA

ISAAC GOODHART
ARTIST

BOOK DESIGN & LAYOUT BY
TRICIA RAMOS

BETSY GONIA
COLORIST & EDITOR

POSTAL: DOSSIER #1 ART BY
ATILIO ROJO

WRITTEN BY
MATT HAWKINS, BRYAN HILL,
& RYAN CADY

TROY PETERI
LETTERER

For Top Cow Productions, Inc.

Marc Silvestri - *CEO* • Matt Hawkins - *President and COO*

Betsy Gonia - *Editor* • Bryan Hill - *Story Editor*

Elena Salcedo - *Operations Manager* • Ryan Cady - *Editorial Assistant*

Vincent Valentine - *Production Assistant*

To find the comic shop
nearest you, call:
1-888-COMICBOOK

Want more info? Check out:
www.topcow.com
for news & exclusive Top Cow merchandi

IMAGE COMICS, INC.
Robert Kirkman – Chief Operating Officer
Erik Larsen – Chief Financial Officer
Todd McFarlane – President
Marc Silvestri – Chief Executive Officer
Jim Valentino – Vice-President

Eric Stephenson – Publisher
Corey Murphy – Director of Sales
Jeff Boison – Director of Publishing Planning & Book Trade Sales
Jeremy Sullivan – Director of Digital Sales
Kat Salazar – Director of PR & Marketing
Emily Miller – Director of Operations
Branwyn Bigglestone – Senior Accounts Manager
Sarah Mello – Accounts Manager
Drew Gill – Art Director
Jonathan Chan – Production Manager
Meredith Wallace – Print Manager
Briah Skelly – Publicity Assistant
Randy Okamura – Marketing Production Designer
David Brothers – Branding Manager
Ally Power – Content Manager
Addison Duke – Production Artist
Vincent Kukua – Production Artist
Sasha Head – Production Artist
Tricia Ramos – Production Artist
Jeff Stang – Direct Market Sales Representative
Emilio Bautista – Digital Sales Associate
Chloe Ramos-Peterson – Administrative Assistant

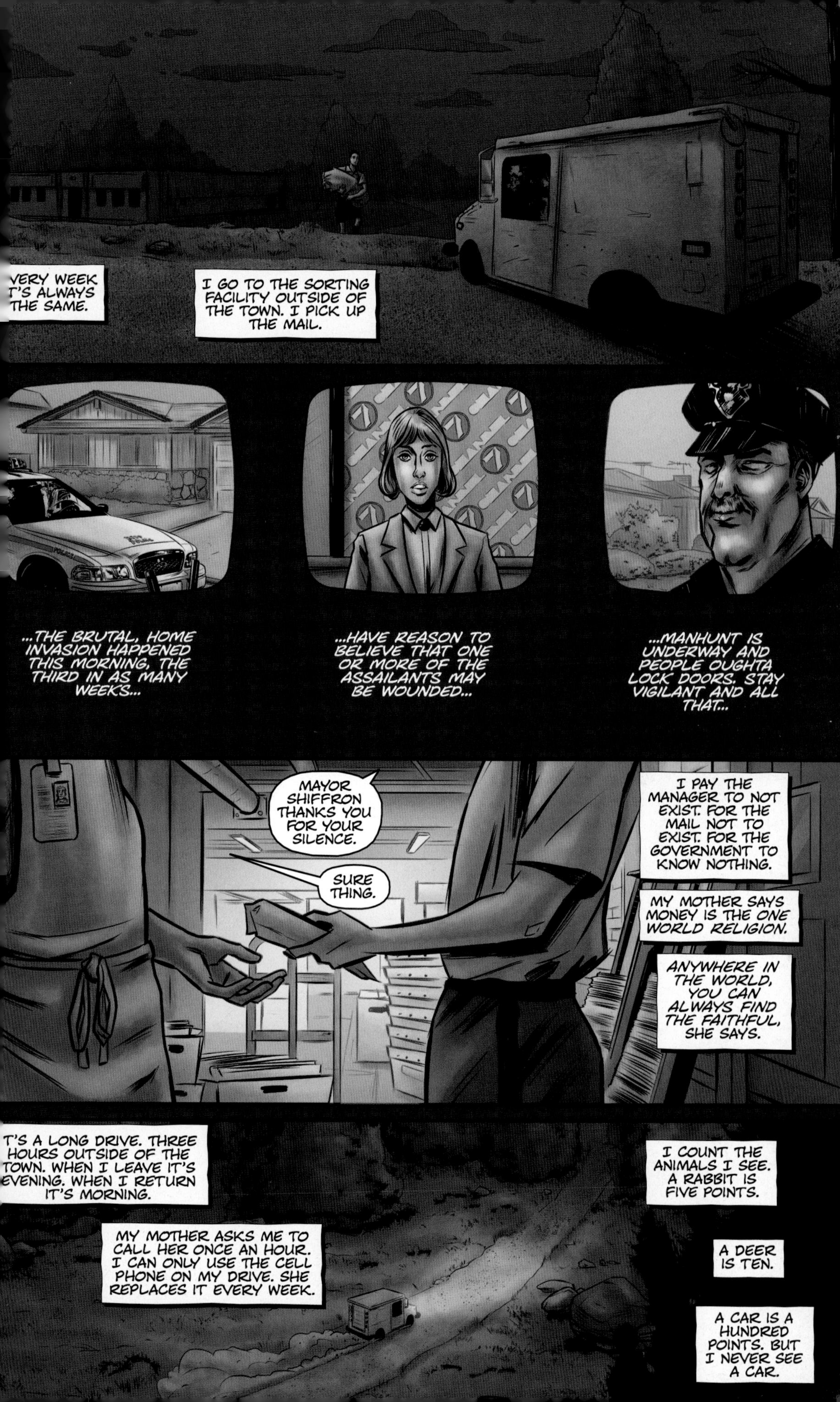
VERY WEEK T'S ALWAYS THE SAME.
I GO TO THE SORTING FACILITY OUTSIDE OF THE TOWN. I PICK UP THE MAIL.
...THE BRUTAL, HOME INVASION HAPPENED THIS MORNING, THE THIRD IN AS MANY WEEKS...
...HAVE REASON TO BELIEVE THAT ONE OR MORE OF THE ASSAILANTS MAY BE WOUNDED...
...MANHUNT IS UNDERWAY AND PEOPLE OUGHTA LOCK DOORS. STAY VIGILANT AND ALL THAT...
MAYOR SHIFFRON THANKS YOU FOR YOUR SILENCE.
SURE THING.
I PAY THE MANAGER TO NOT EXIST. FOR THE MAIL NOT TO EXIST. FOR THE GOVERNMENT TO KNOW NOTHING.
MY MOTHER SAYS MONEY IS THE ONE WORLD RELIGION.
ANYWHERE IN THE WORLD, YOU CAN ALWAYS FIND THE FAITHFUL, SHE SAYS.
T'S A LONG DRIVE. THREE HOURS OUTSIDE OF THE TOWN. WHEN I LEAVE IT'S EVENING. WHEN I RETURN IT'S MORNING.
MY MOTHER ASKS ME TO CALL HER ONCE AN HOUR. I CAN ONLY USE THE CELL PHONE ON MY DRIVE. SHE REPLACES IT EVERY WEEK.
I COUNT THE ANIMALS I SEE. A RABBIT IS FIVE POINTS.
A DEER IS TEN.
A CAR IS A HUNDRED POINTS. BUT I NEVER SEE A CAR.

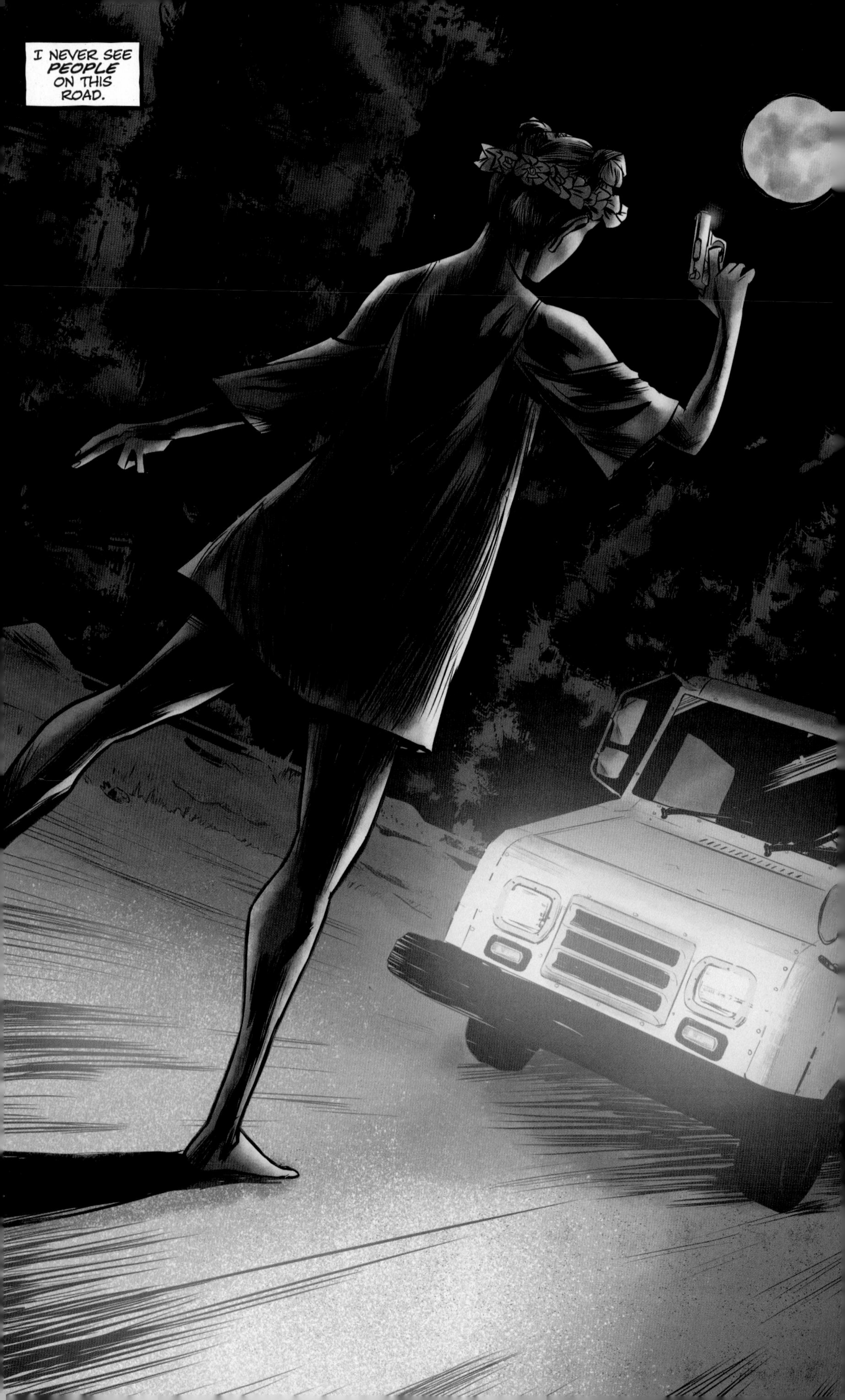
I NEVER SEE *PEOPLE* ON THIS ROAD.

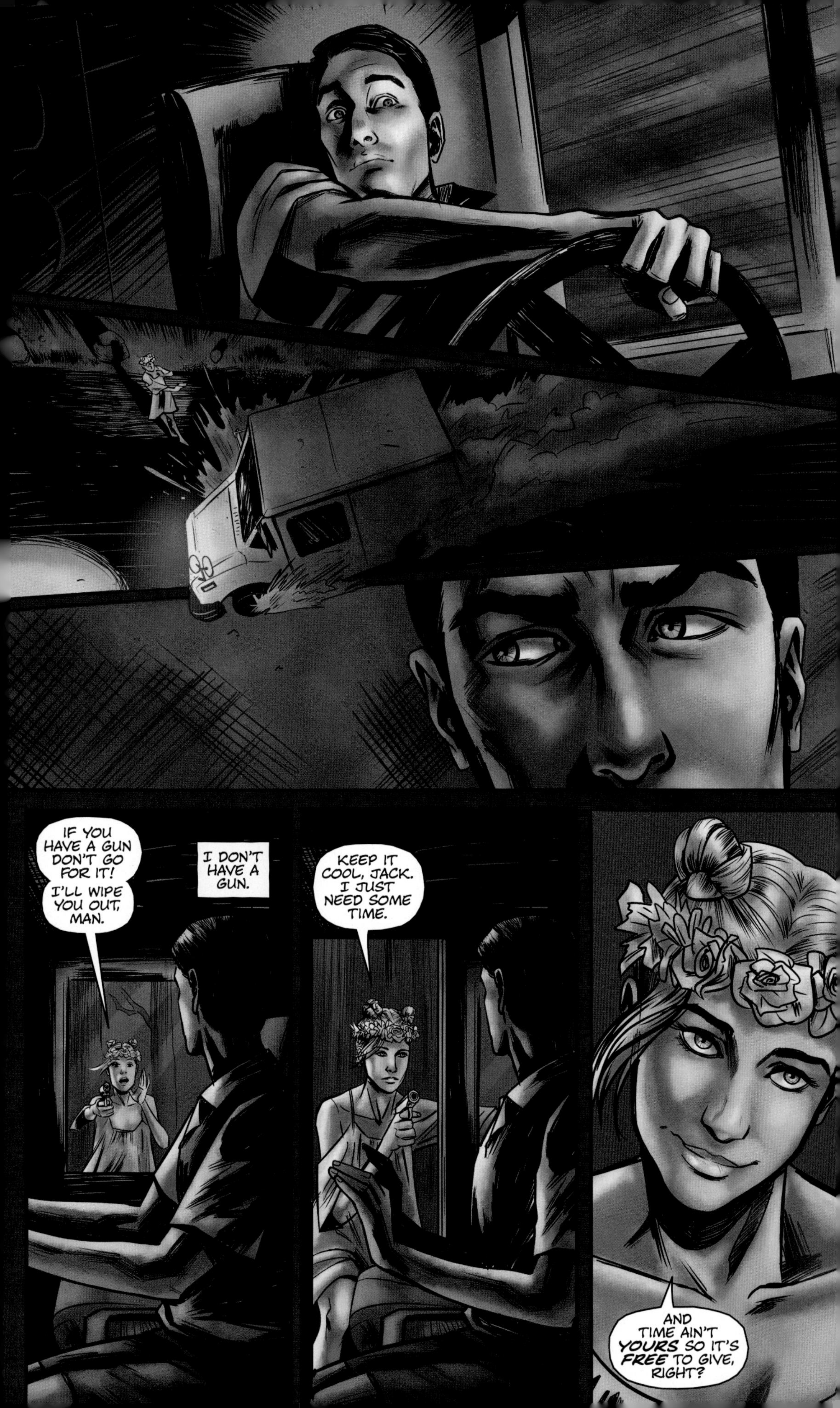
IF YOU HAVE A GUN DON'T GO FOR IT!
I'LL WIPE YOU OUT, MAN.
I DON'T HAVE A GUN.
KEEP IT COOL, JACK. I JUST NEED SOME TIME.
AND TIME AIN'T YOURS SO IT'S FREE TO GIVE, RIGHT?

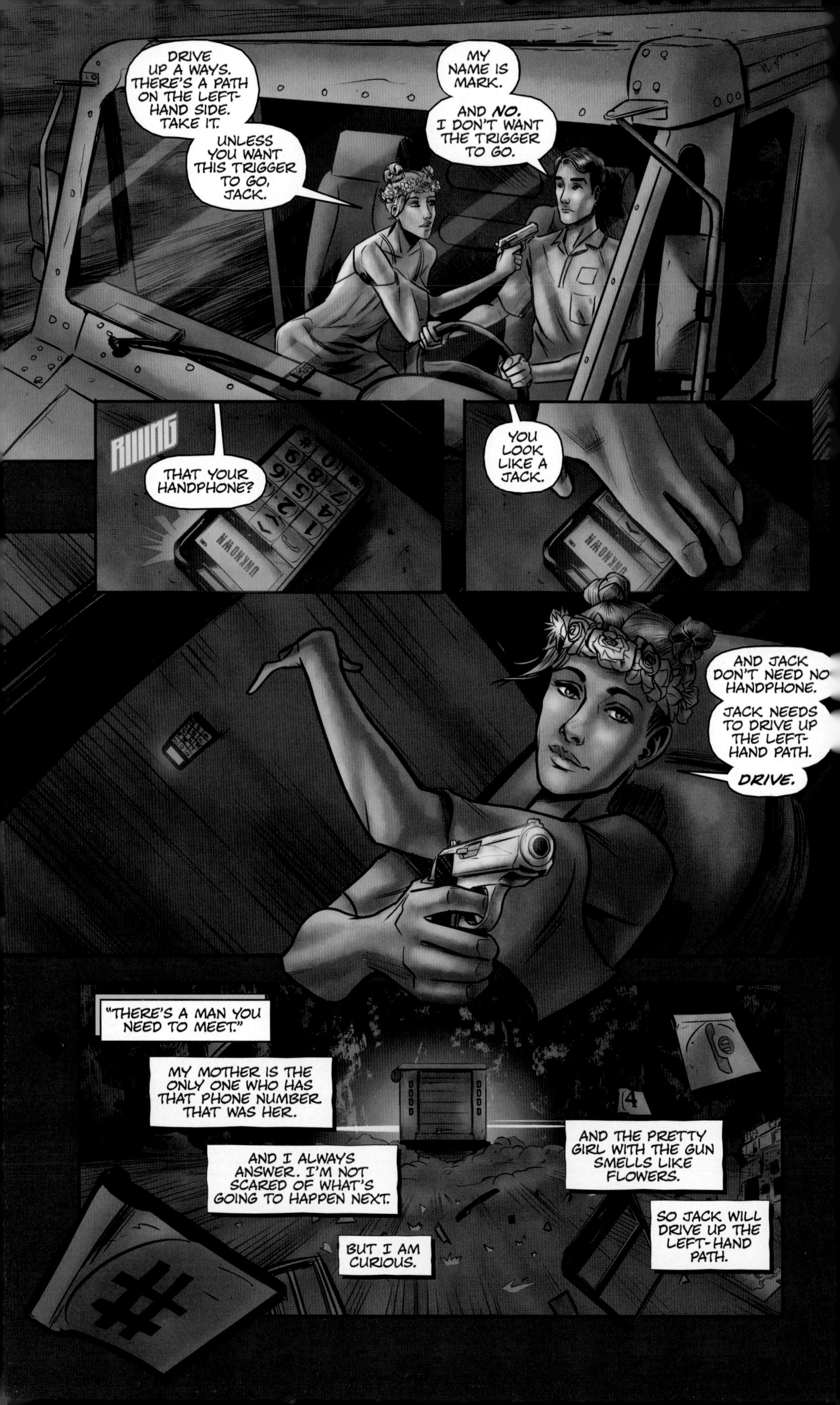
DRIVE UP A WAYS. THERE'S A PATH ON THE LEFT-HAND SIDE. TAKE IT.
UNLESS YOU WANT THIS TRIGGER TO GO, JACK.
MY NAME IS MARK.
AND NO. I DON'T WANT THE TRIGGER TO GO.
RIIIING
THAT YOUR HANDPHONE?
UNKNOWN
YOU LOOK LIKE A JACK.
AND JACK DON'T NEED NO HANDPHONE.
JACK NEEDS TO DRIVE UP THE LEFT-HAND PATH.
DRIVE.
"THERE'S A MAN YOU NEED TO MEET."
MY MOTHER IS THE ONLY ONE WHO HAS THAT PHONE NUMBER THAT WAS HER.
AND I ALWAYS ANSWER. I'M NOT SCARED OF WHAT'S GOING TO HAPPEN NEXT.
BUT I AM CURIOUS.
AND THE PRETTY GIRL WITH THE GUN SMELLS LIKE FLOWERS.
SO JACK WILL DRIVE UP THE LEFT-HAND PATH.

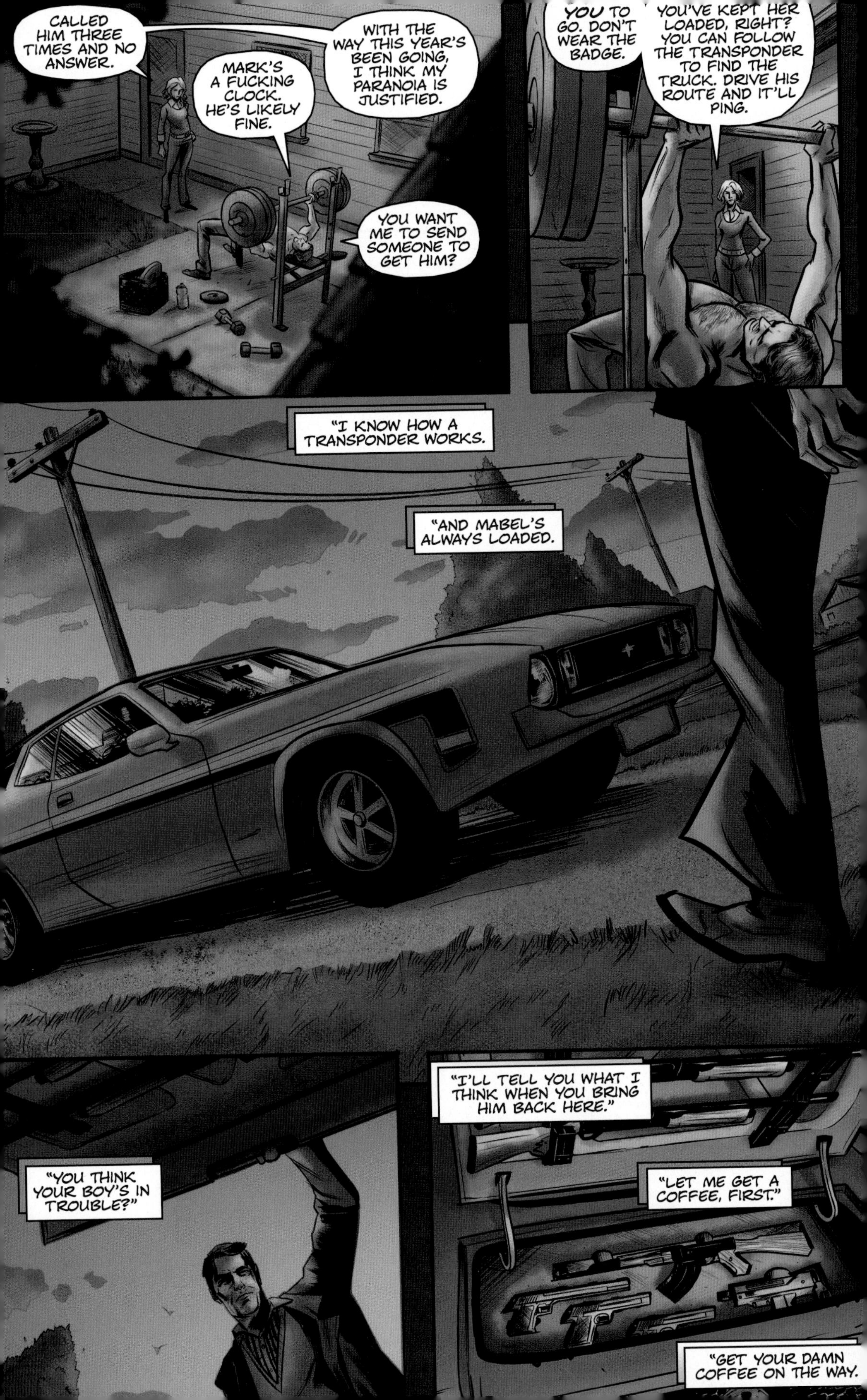

CALLED HIM THREE TIMES AND NO ANSWER.
MARK'S A FUCKING CLOCK. HE'S LIKELY FINE.
WITH THE WAY THIS YEAR'S BEEN GOING, I THINK MY PARANOIA IS JUSTIFIED.
YOU WANT ME TO SEND SOMEONE TO GET HIM?
YOU TO GO. DON'T WEAR THE BADGE.
YOU'VE KEPT HER LOADED, RIGHT? YOU CAN FOLLOW THE TRANSPONDER TO FIND THE TRUCK. DRIVE HIS ROUTE AND IT'LL PING.
"I KNOW HOW A TRANSPONDER WORKS.
"AND MABEL'S ALWAYS LOADED.
"YOU THINK YOUR BOY'S IN TROUBLE?"
"I'LL TELL YOU WHAT I THINK WHEN YOU BRING HIM BACK HERE."
"LET ME GET A COFFEE, FIRST."
"GET YOUR DAMN COFFEE ON THE WAY.

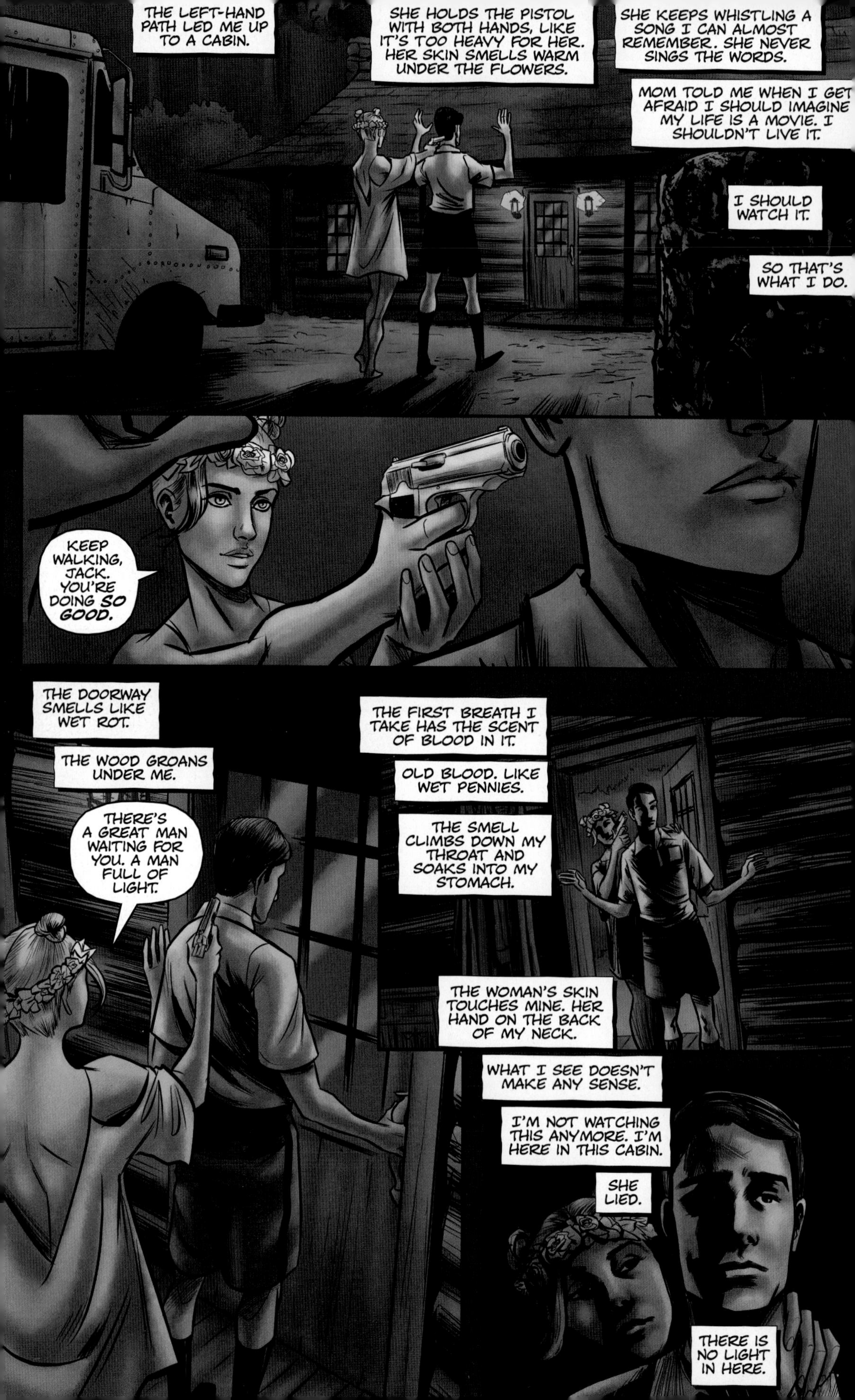
THE LEFT-HAND PATH LED ME UP TO A CABIN.
SHE HOLDS THE PISTOL WITH BOTH HANDS, LIKE IT'S TOO HEAVY FOR HER. HER SKIN SMELLS WARM UNDER THE FLOWERS.
SHE KEEPS WHISTLING A SONG I CAN ALMOST REMEMBER. SHE NEVER SINGS THE WORDS.
MOM TOLD ME WHEN I GET AFRAID I SHOULD IMAGINE MY LIFE IS A MOVIE. I SHOULDN'T LIVE IT.
I SHOULD WATCH IT.
SO THAT'S WHAT I DO.
KEEP WALKING, JACK. YOU'RE DOING SO GOOD.
THE DOORWAY SMELLS LIKE WET ROT.
THE WOOD GROANS UNDER ME.
THERE'S A GREAT MAN WAITING FOR YOU. A MAN FULL OF LIGHT.
THE FIRST BREATH I TAKE HAS THE SCENT OF BLOOD IN IT.
OLD BLOOD. LIKE WET PENNIES.
THE SMELL CLIMBS DOWN MY THROAT AND SOAKS INTO MY STOMACH.
THE WOMAN'S SKIN TOUCHES MINE. HER HAND ON THE BACK OF MY NECK.
WHAT I SEE DOESN'T MAKE ANY SENSE.
I'M NOT WATCHING THIS ANYMORE. I'M HERE IN THIS CABIN.
SHE LIED.
THERE IS NO LIGHT IN HERE.

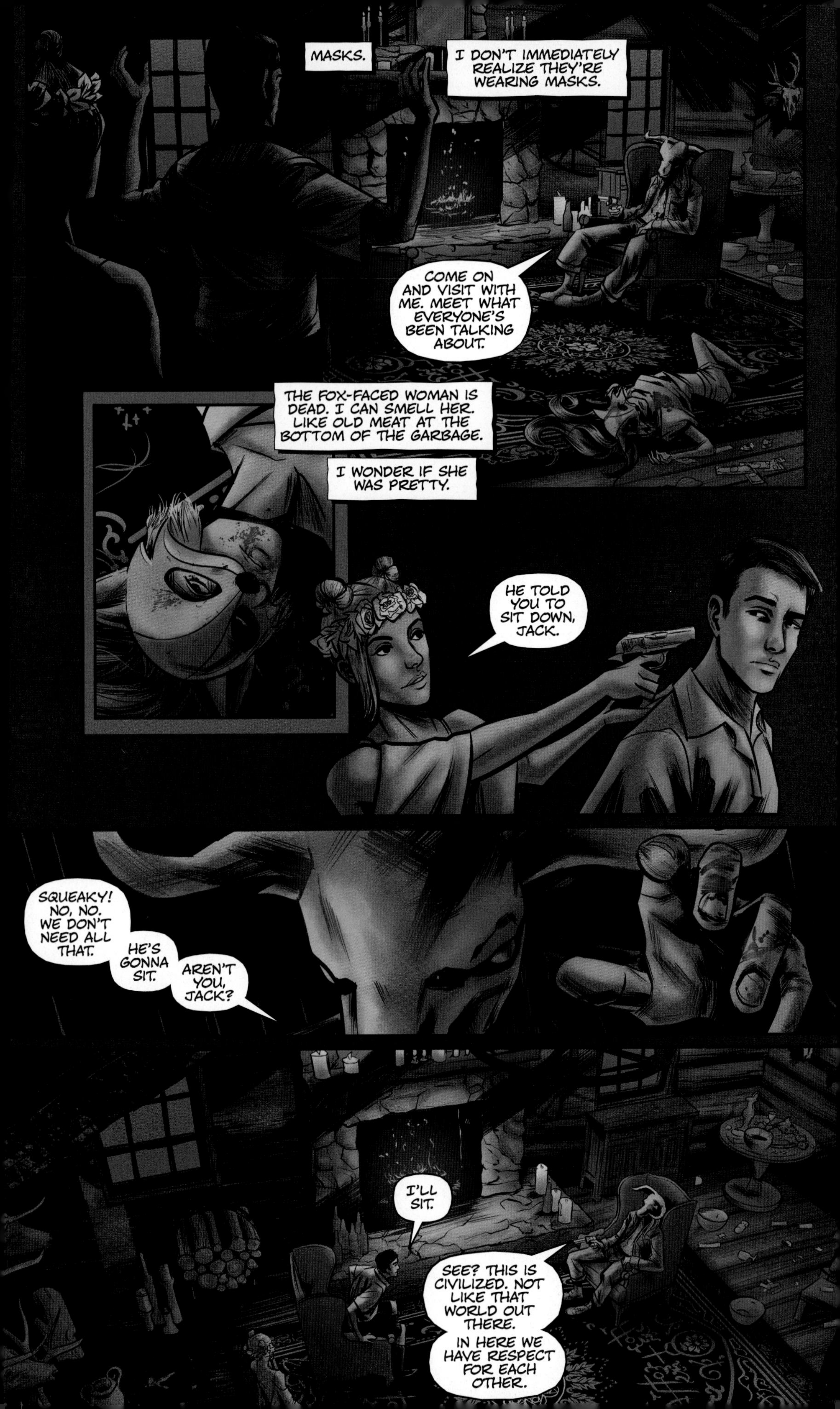
MASKS.
I DON'T IMMEDIATELY REALIZE THEY'RE WEARING MASKS.
COME ON AND VISIT WITH ME. MEET WHAT EVERYONE'S BEEN TALKING ABOUT.
THE FOX-FACED WOMAN IS DEAD. I CAN SMELL HER. LIKE OLD MEAT AT THE BOTTOM OF THE GARBAGE.
I WONDER IF SHE WAS PRETTY.
HE TOLD YOU TO SIT DOWN, JACK.
SQUEAKY! NO, NO. WE DON'T NEED ALL THAT.
HE'S GONNA SIT.
AREN'T YOU, JACK?
I'LL SIT.
SEE? THIS IS CIVILIZED. NOT LIKE THAT WORLD OUT THERE.
IN HERE WE HAVE RESPECT FOR EACH OTHER.

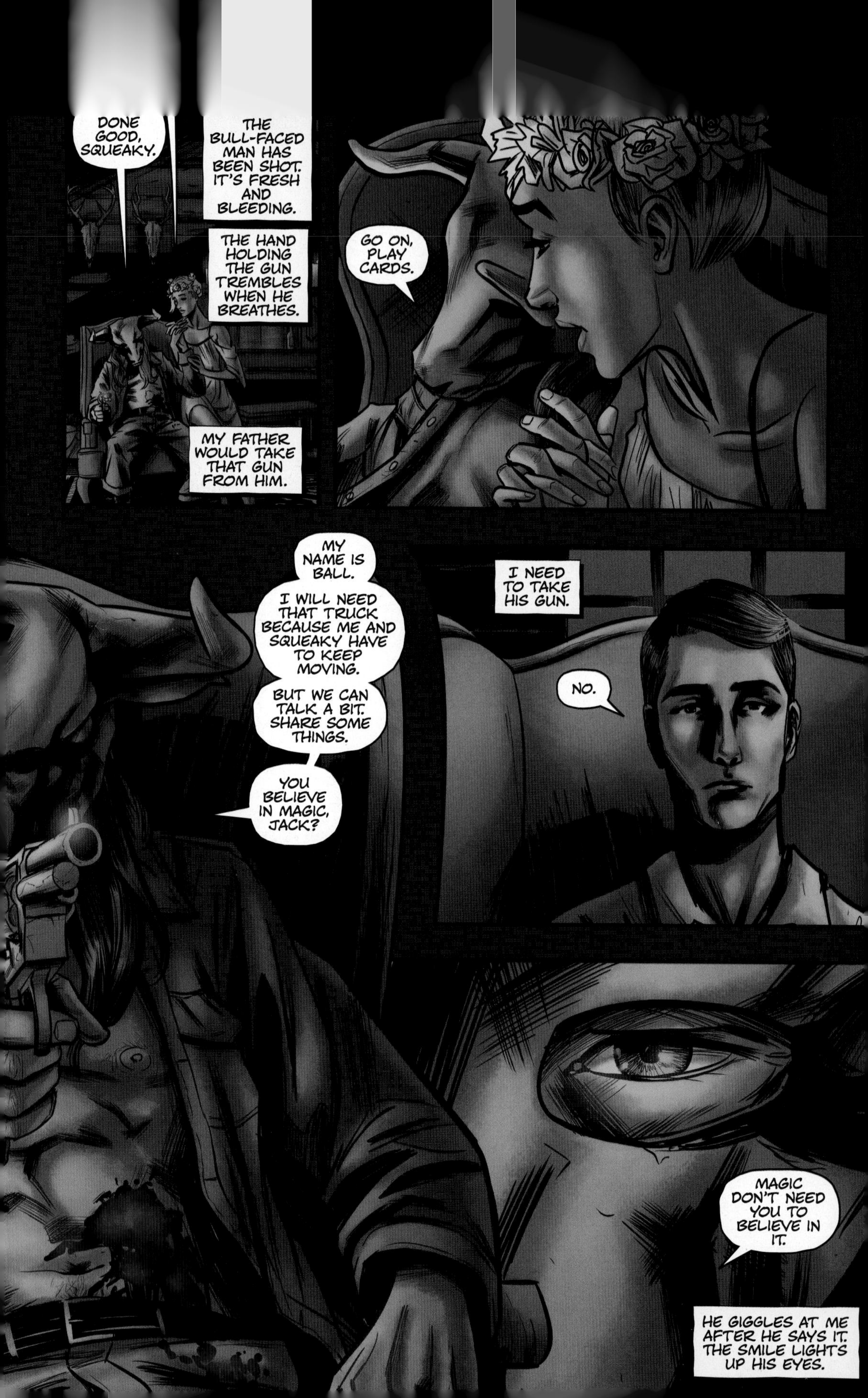
DONE GOOD, SQUEAKY.
THE BULL-FACED MAN HAS BEEN SHOT. IT'S FRESH AND BLEEDING.
THE HAND HOLDING THE GUN TREMBLES WHEN HE BREATHES.
MY FATHER WOULD TAKE THAT GUN FROM HIM.
GO ON, PLAY CARDS.
MY NAME IS BALL.
I WILL NEED THAT TRUCK BECAUSE ME AND SQUEAKY HAVE TO KEEP MOVING.
BUT WE CAN TALK A BIT. SHARE SOME THINGS.
YOU BELIEVE IN MAGIC, JACK?
I NEED TO TAKE HIS GUN.
NO.
MAGIC DON'T NEED YOU TO BELIEVE IN IT.
HE GIGGLES AT ME AFTER HE SAYS IT. THE SMILE LIGHTS UP HIS EYES.

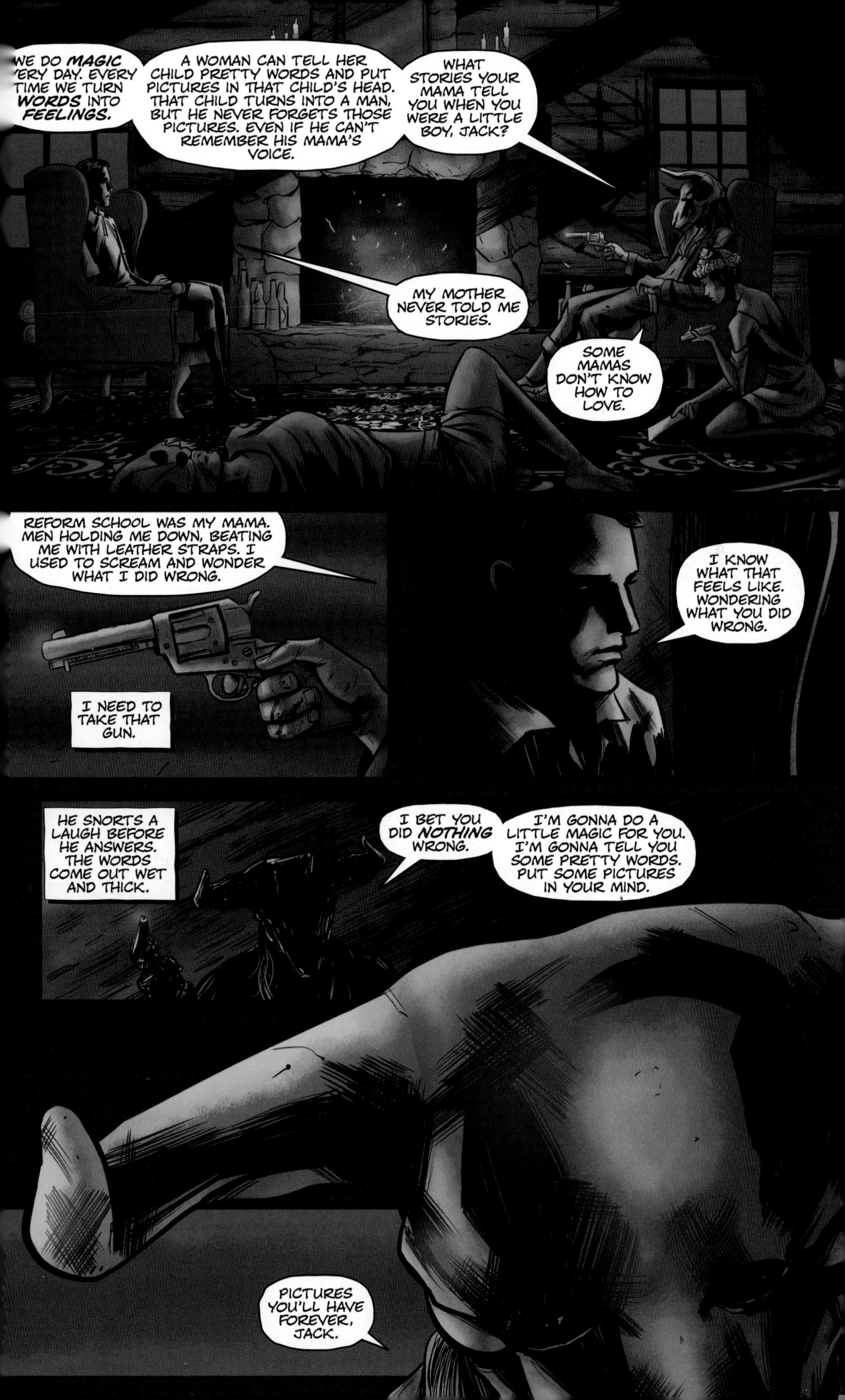
WE DO **MAGIC** EVERY DAY. EVERY TIME WE TURN **WORDS** INTO **FEELINGS.**
A WOMAN CAN TELL HER CHILD PRETTY WORDS AND PUT PICTURES IN THAT CHILD'S HEAD. THAT CHILD TURNS INTO A MAN, BUT HE NEVER FORGETS THOSE PICTURES. EVEN IF HE CAN'T REMEMBER HIS MAMA'S VOICE.
WHAT STORIES YOUR MAMA TELL YOU WHEN YOU WERE A LITTLE BOY, JACK?
MY MOTHER NEVER TOLD ME STORIES.
SOME MAMAS DON'T KNOW HOW TO LOVE.
REFORM SCHOOL WAS MY MAMA. MEN HOLDING ME DOWN, BEATING ME WITH LEATHER STRAPS. I USED TO SCREAM AND WONDER WHAT I DID WRONG.
I NEED TO TAKE THAT GUN.
I KNOW WHAT THAT FEELS LIKE. WONDERING WHAT YOU DID WRONG.
HE SNORTS A LAUGH BEFORE HE ANSWERS. THE WORDS COME OUT WET AND THICK.
I BET YOU DID **NOTHING** WRONG.
I'M GONNA DO A LITTLE MAGIC FOR YOU. I'M GONNA TELL YOU SOME PRETTY WORDS. PUT SOME PICTURES IN YOUR MIND.
PICTURES YOU'LL HAVE FOREVER, JACK.

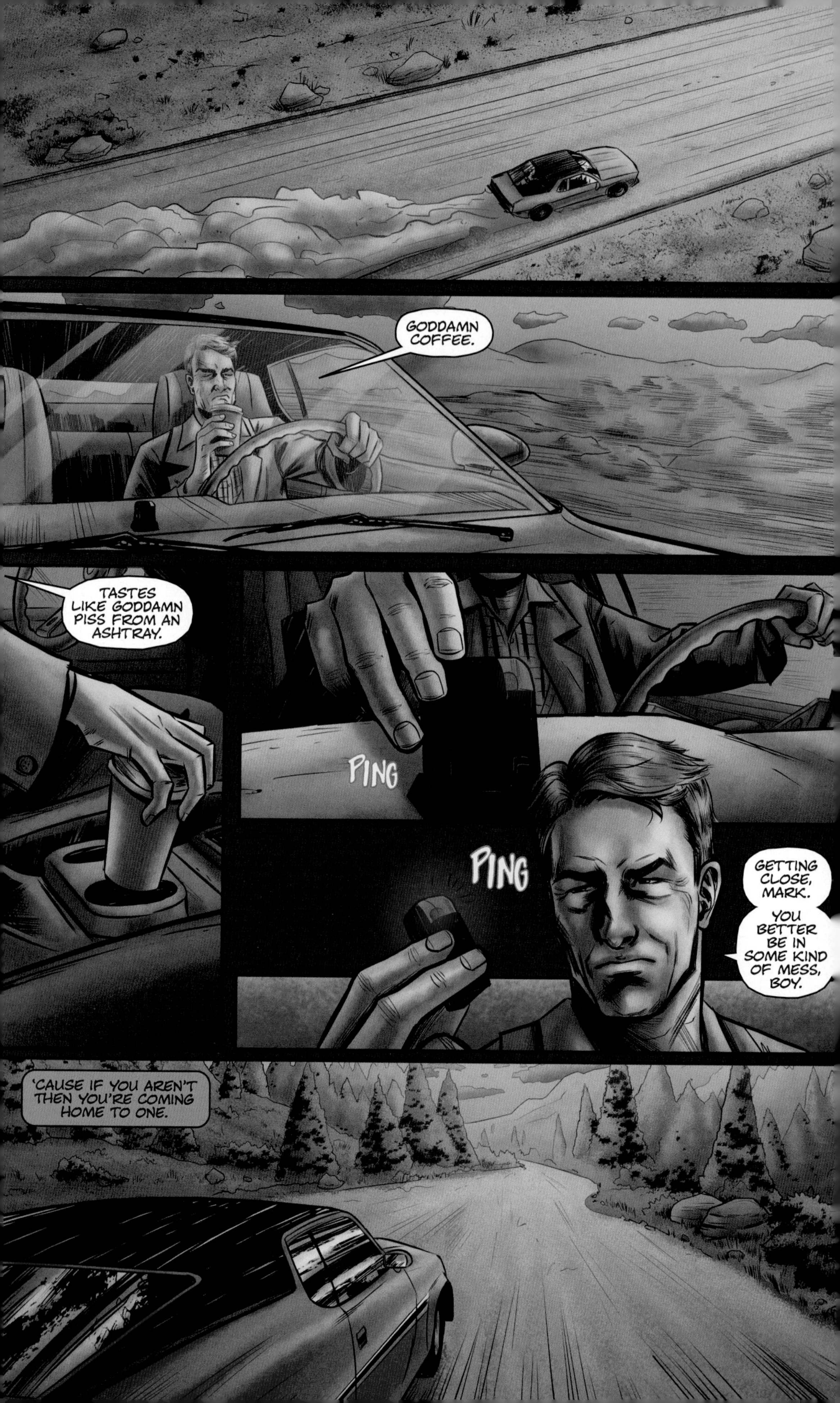
GODDAMN COFFEE.
TASTES LIKE GODDAMN PISS FROM AN ASHTRAY.
PING
PING
GETTING CLOSE, MARK.
YOU BETTER BE IN SOME KIND OF MESS, BOY.
'CAUSE IF YOU AREN'T THEN YOU'RE COMING HOME TO ONE.

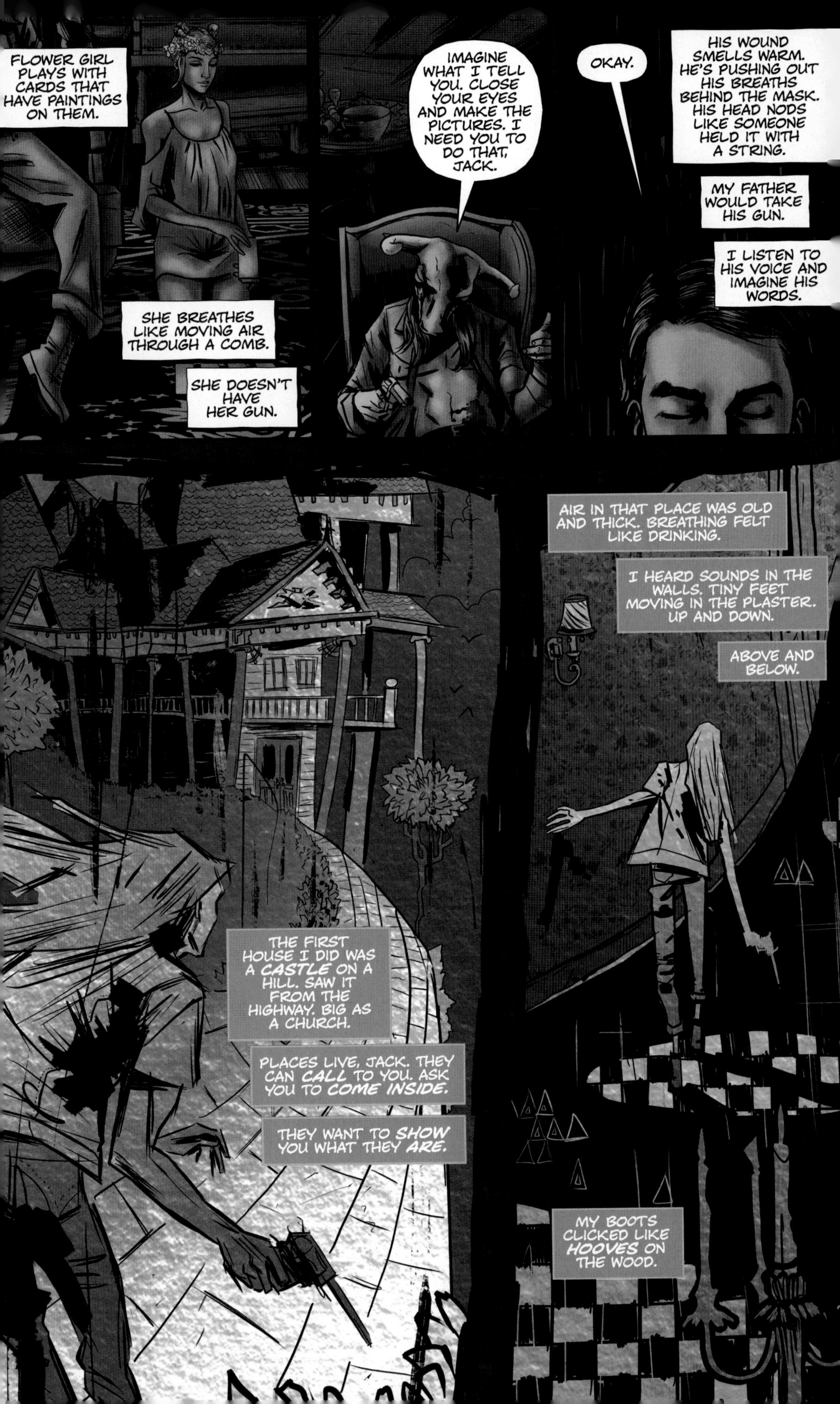
FLOWER GIRL PLAYS WITH CARDS THAT HAVE PAINTINGS ON THEM.
SHE BREATHES LIKE MOVING AIR THROUGH A COMB.
SHE DOESN'T HAVE HER GUN.
IMAGINE WHAT I TELL YOU. CLOSE YOUR EYES AND MAKE THE PICTURES. I NEED YOU TO DO THAT, JACK.
OKAY.
HIS WOUND SMELLS WARM. HE'S PUSHING OUT HIS BREATHS BEHIND THE MASK. HIS HEAD NODS LIKE SOMEONE HELD IT WITH A STRING.
MY FATHER WOULD TAKE HIS GUN.
I LISTEN TO HIS VOICE AND IMAGINE HIS WORDS.
THE FIRST HOUSE I DID WAS A CASTLE ON A HILL. SAW IT FROM THE HIGHWAY. BIG AS A CHURCH.
PLACES LIVE, JACK. THEY CAN CALL TO YOU. ASK YOU TO COME INSIDE.
THEY WANT TO SHOW YOU WHAT THEY ARE.
AIR IN THAT PLACE WAS OLD AND THICK. BREATHING FELT LIKE DRINKING.
I HEARD SOUNDS IN THE WALLS. TINY FEET MOVING IN THE PLASTER. UP AND DOWN.
ABOVE AND BELOW.
MY BOOTS CLICKED LIKE HOOVES ON THE WOOD.

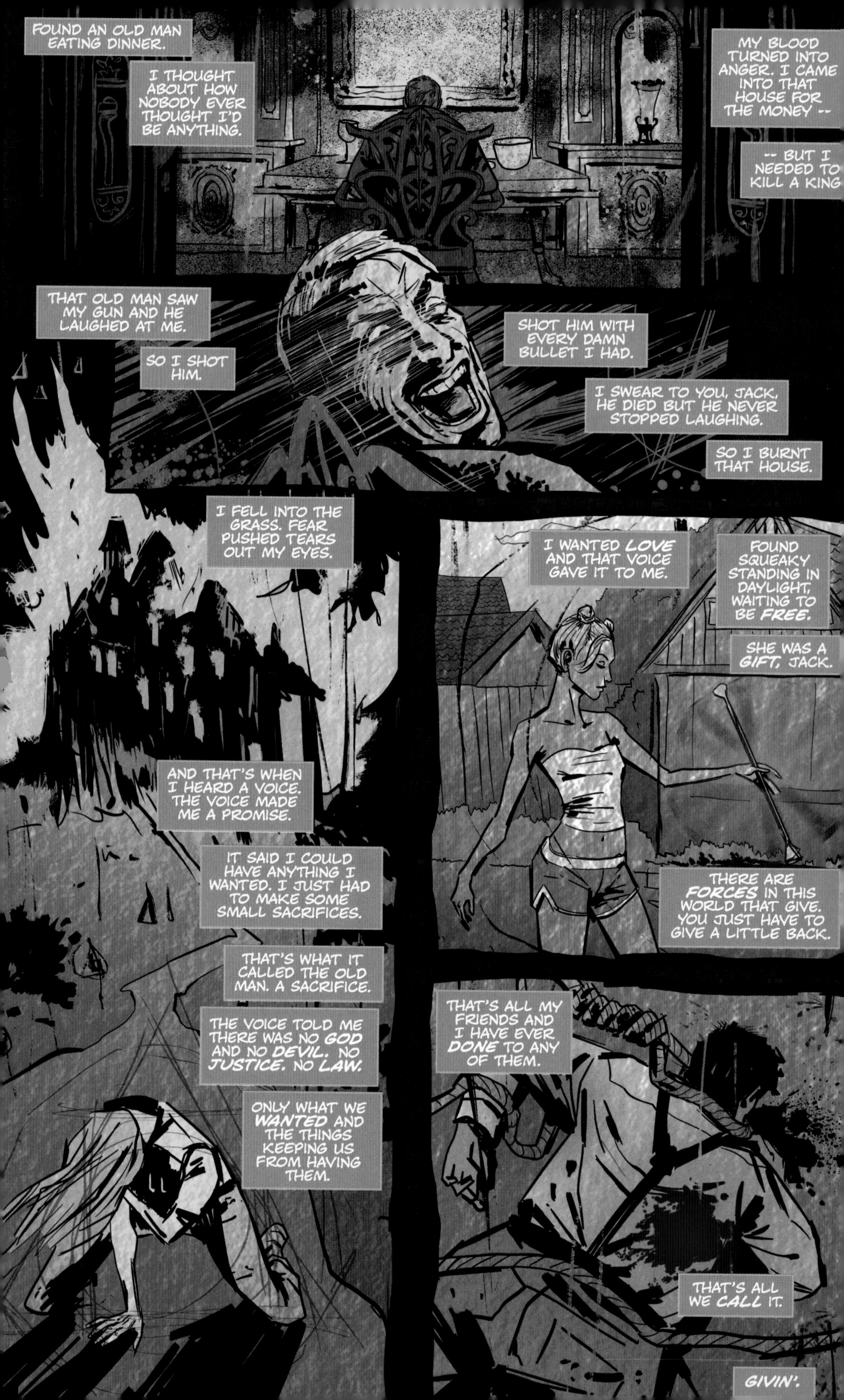

FOUND AN OLD MAN EATING DINNER.
I THOUGHT ABOUT HOW NOBODY EVER THOUGHT I'D BE ANYTHING.
MY BLOOD TURNED INTO ANGER. I CAME INTO THAT HOUSE FOR THE MONEY --
-- BUT I NEEDED TO KILL A KING
THAT OLD MAN SAW MY GUN AND HE LAUGHED AT ME.
SO I SHOT HIM.
SHOT HIM WITH EVERY DAMN BULLET I HAD.
I SWEAR TO YOU, JACK, HE DIED BUT HE NEVER STOPPED LAUGHING.
SO I BURNT THAT HOUSE.
I FELL INTO THE GRASS. FEAR PUSHED TEARS OUT MY EYES.
AND THAT'S WHEN I HEARD A VOICE. THE VOICE MADE ME A PROMISE.
IT SAID I COULD HAVE ANYTHING I WANTED. I JUST HAD TO MAKE SOME SMALL SACRIFICES.
THAT'S WHAT IT CALLED THE OLD MAN. A SACRIFICE.
THE VOICE TOLD ME THERE WAS NO GOD AND NO DEVIL. NO JUSTICE. NO LAW.
ONLY WHAT WE WANTED AND THE THINGS KEEPING US FROM HAVING THEM.
I WANTED LOVE AND THAT VOICE GAVE IT TO ME.
FOUND SQUEAKY STANDING IN DAYLIGHT, WAITING TO BE FREE.
SHE WAS A GIFT, JACK.
THERE ARE FORCES IN THIS WORLD THAT GIVE. YOU JUST HAVE TO GIVE A LITTLE BACK.
THAT'S ALL MY FRIENDS AND I HAVE EVER DONE TO ANY OF THEM.
THAT'S ALL WE CALL IT.
GIVIN'.

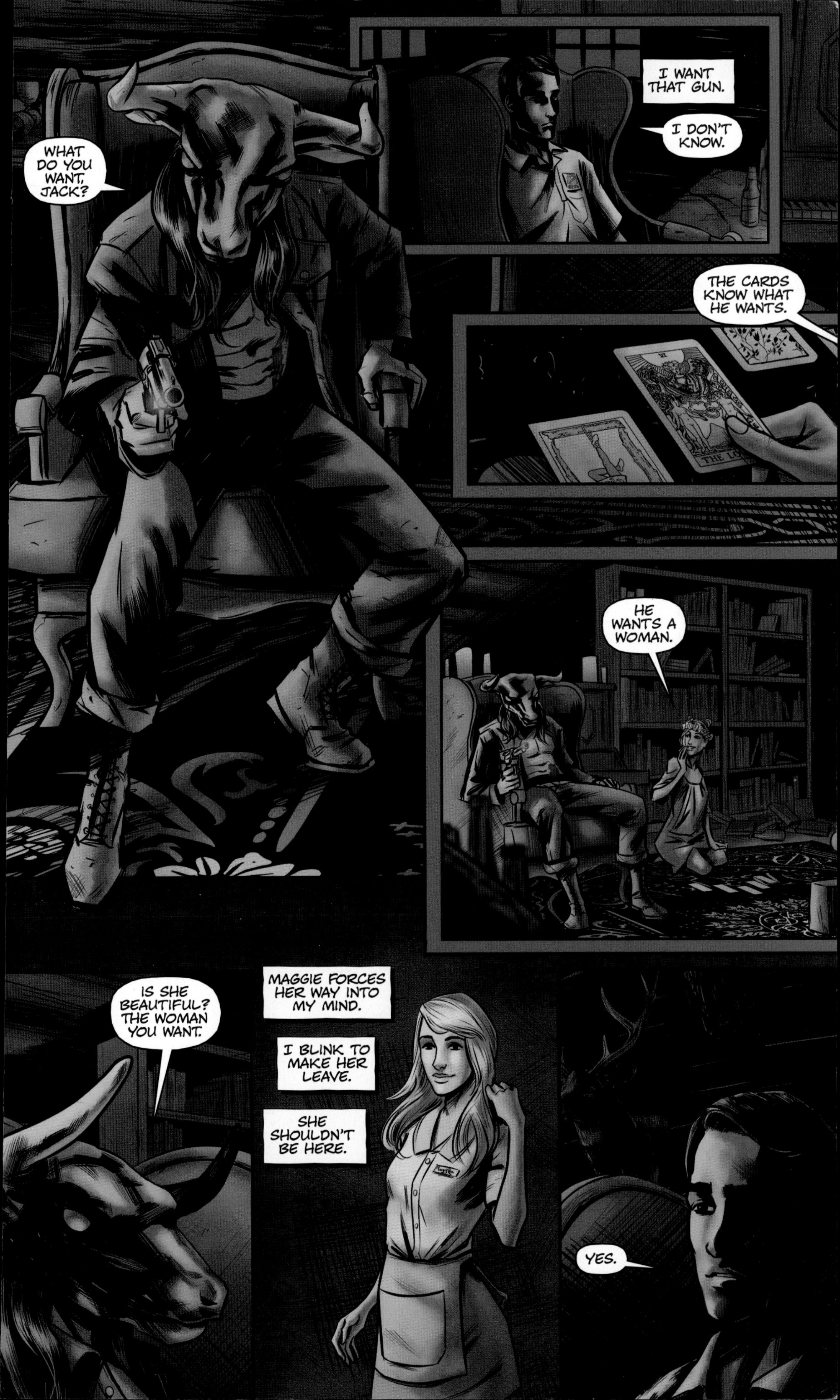
WHAT DO YOU WANT, JACK?
I WANT THAT GUN.
I DON'T KNOW.
THE CARDS KNOW WHAT HE WANTS.
HE WANTS A WOMAN.
IS SHE BEAUTIFUL? THE WOMAN YOU WANT.
MAGGIE FORCES HER WAY INTO MY MIND.
I BLINK TO MAKE HER LEAVE.
SHE SHOULDN'T BE HERE.
YES.

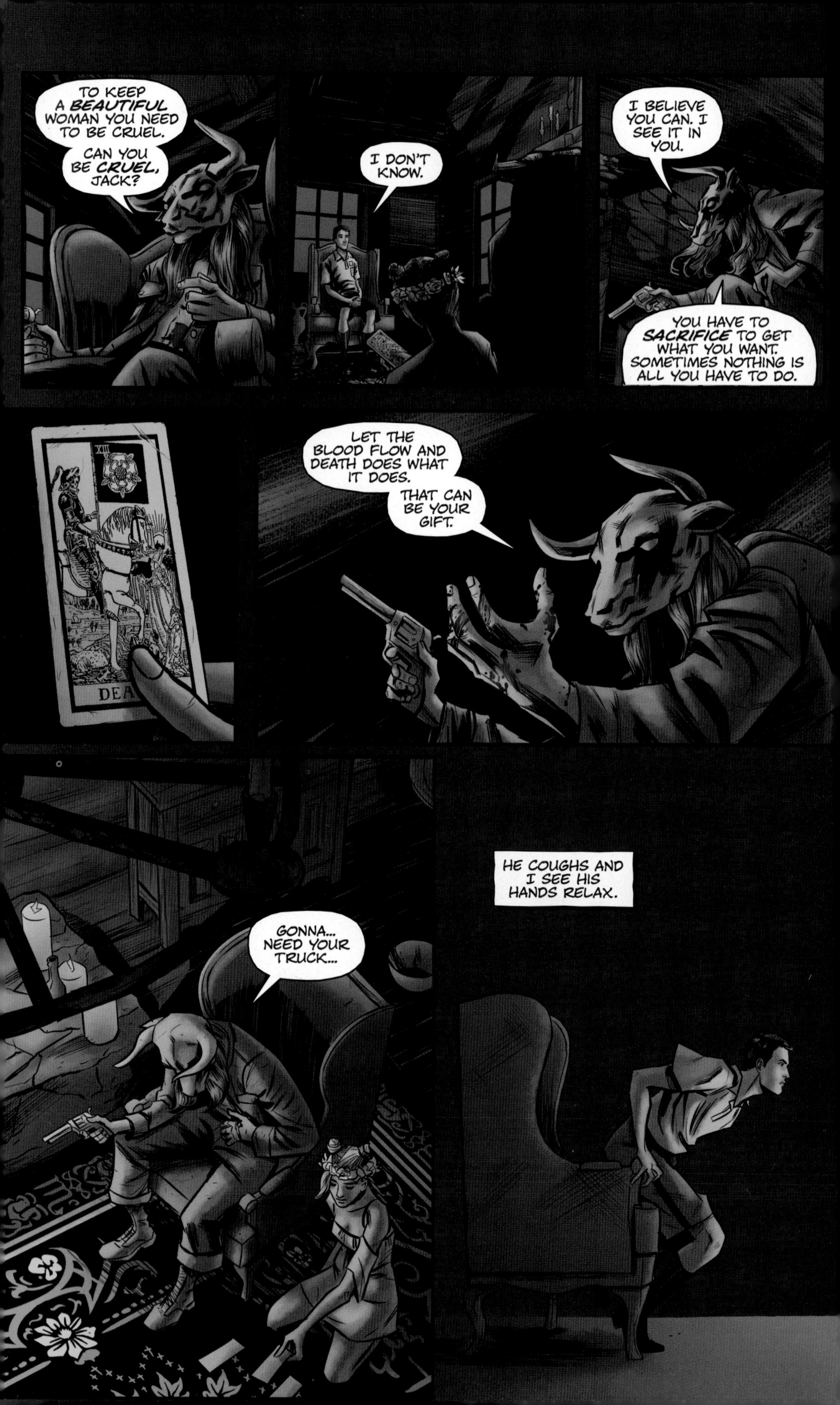
TO KEEP A BEAUTIFUL WOMAN YOU NEED TO BE CRUEL.
CAN YOU BE CRUEL, JACK?
I DON'T KNOW.
I BELIEVE YOU CAN. I SEE IT IN YOU.
YOU HAVE TO SACRIFICE TO GET WHAT YOU WANT. SOMETIMES NOTHING IS ALL YOU HAVE TO DO.
XIII
LET THE BLOOD FLOW AND DEATH DOES WHAT IT DOES.
THAT CAN BE YOUR GIFT.
GONNA... NEED YOUR TRUCK...
HE COUGHS AND I SEE HIS HANDS RELAX.

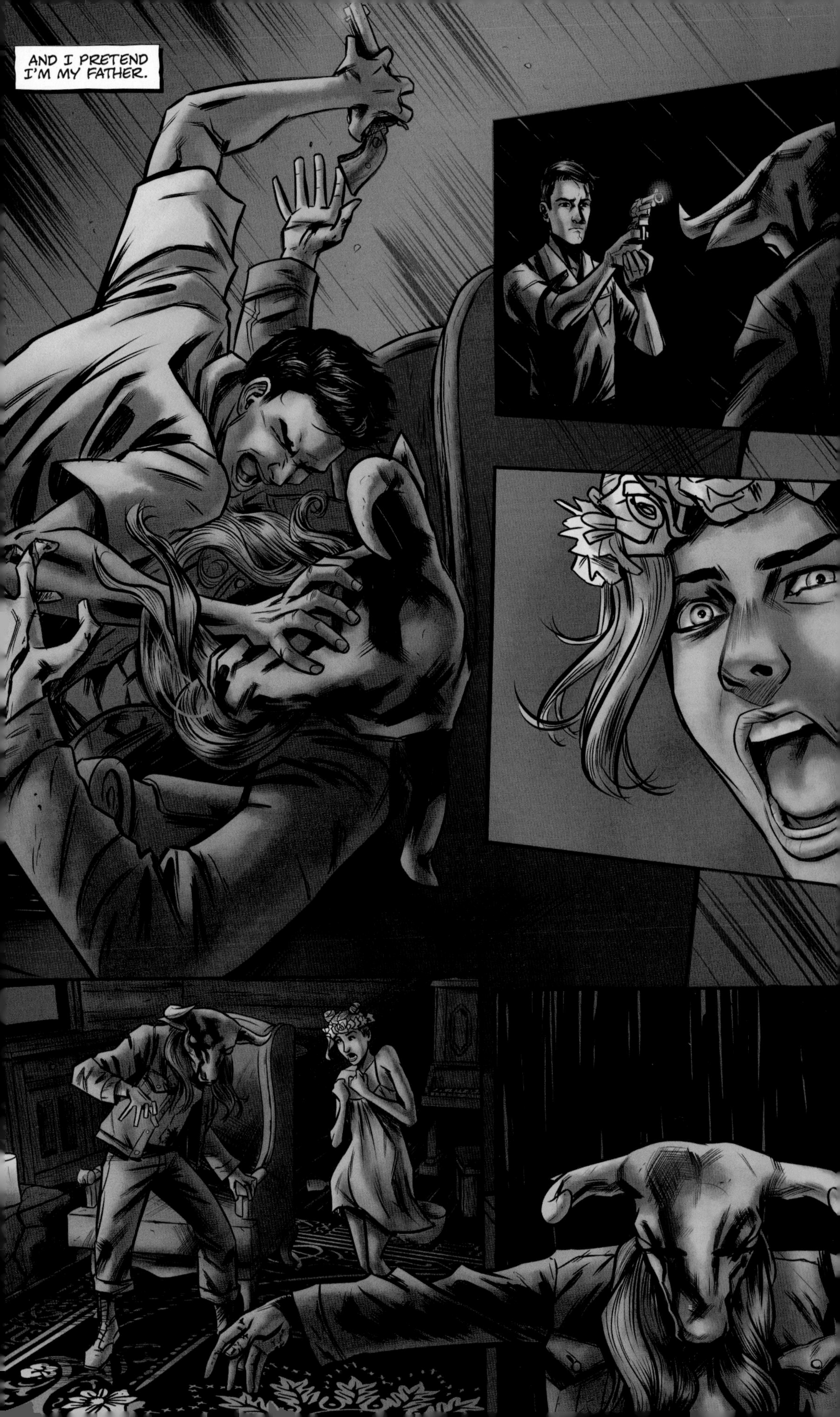
AND I PRETEND I'M MY FATHER.

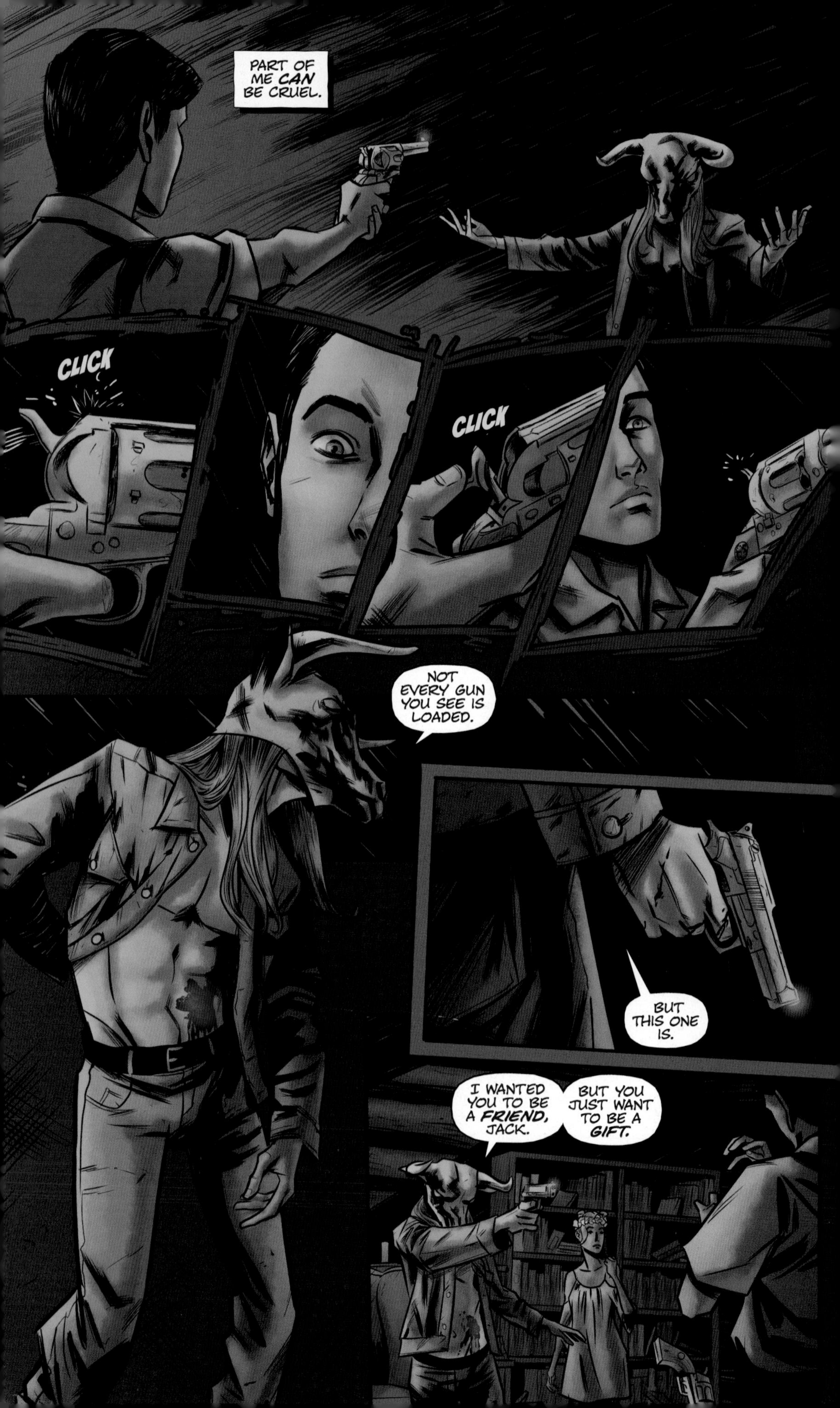
PART OF ME *CAN* BE CRUEL.
CLICK
CLICK
NOT EVERY GUN YOU SEE IS LOADED.
BUT THIS ONE IS.
I WANTED YOU TO BE A *FRIEND,* JACK.
BUT YOU JUST WANT TO BE A *GIFT.*

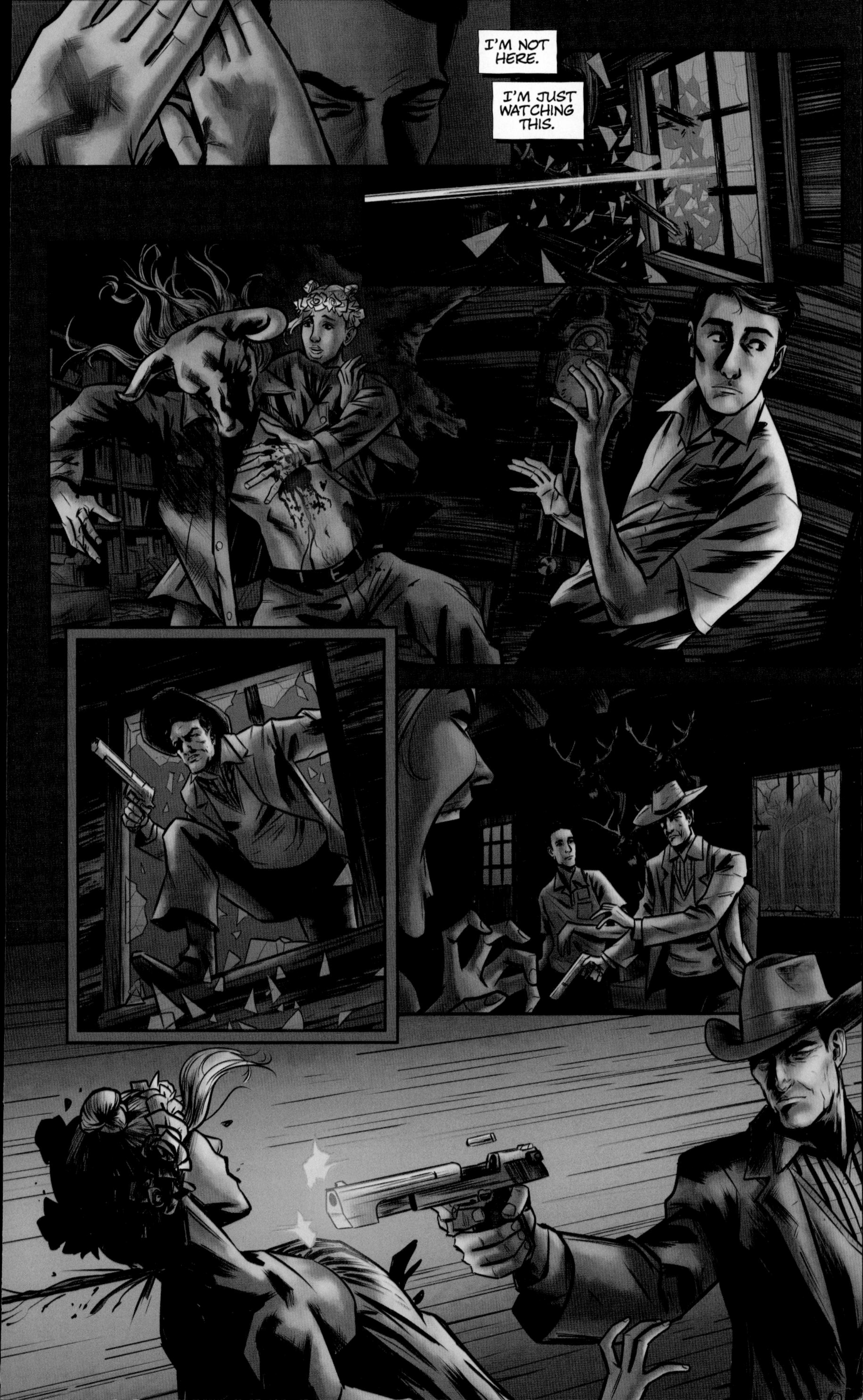
I'M NOT HERE.
I'M JUST WATCHING THIS.

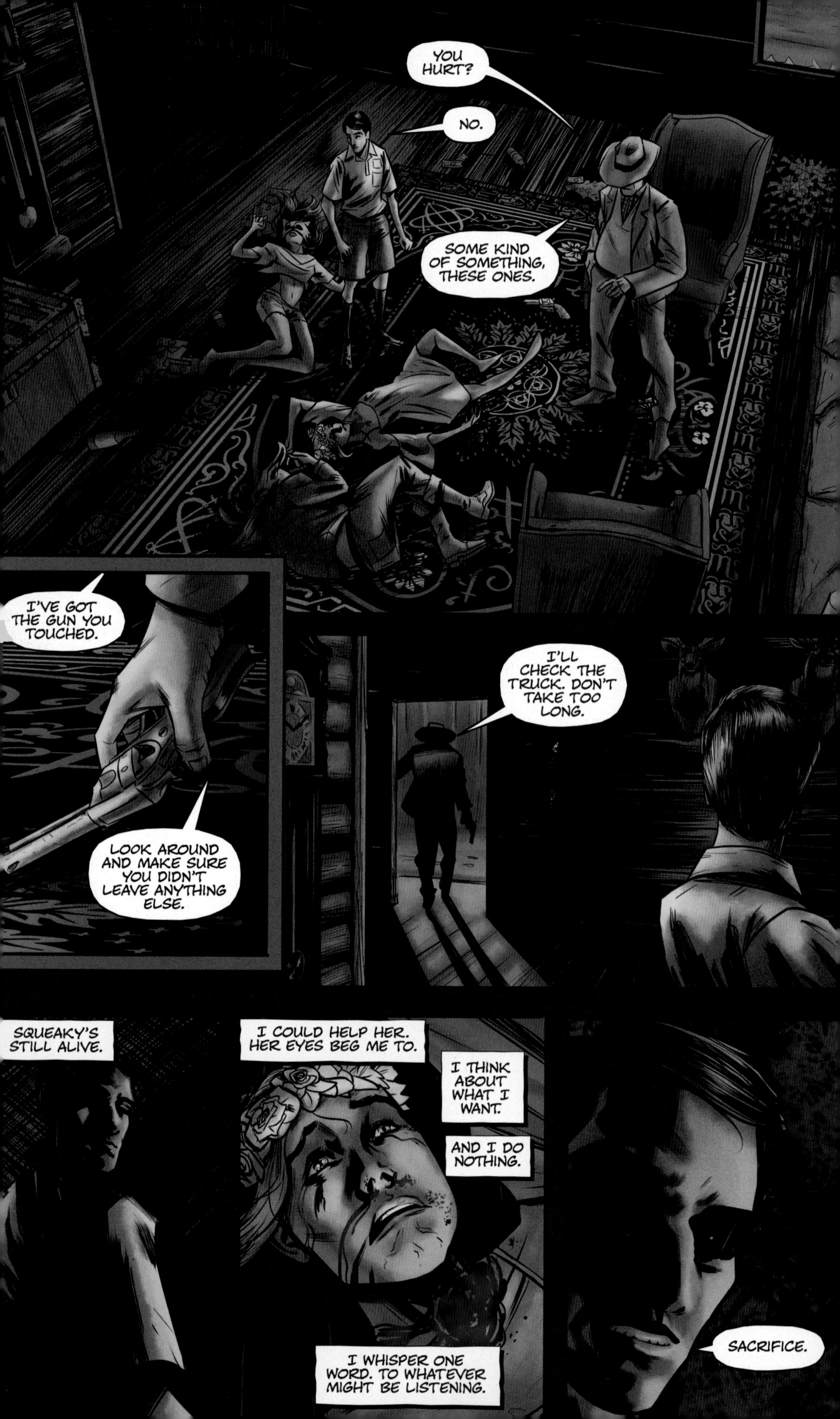
YOU HURT?
NO.
SOME KIND OF SOMETHING, THESE ONES.
I'VE GOT THE GUN YOU TOUCHED.
LOOK AROUND AND MAKE SURE YOU DIDN'T LEAVE ANYTHING ELSE.
I'LL CHECK THE TRUCK. DON'T TAKE TOO LONG.
SQUEAKY'S STILL ALIVE.
I COULD HELP HER. HER EYES BEG ME TO.
I THINK ABOUT WHAT I WANT.
AND I DO NOTHING.
I WHISPER ONE WORD. TO WHATEVER MIGHT BE LISTENING.
SACRIFICE.

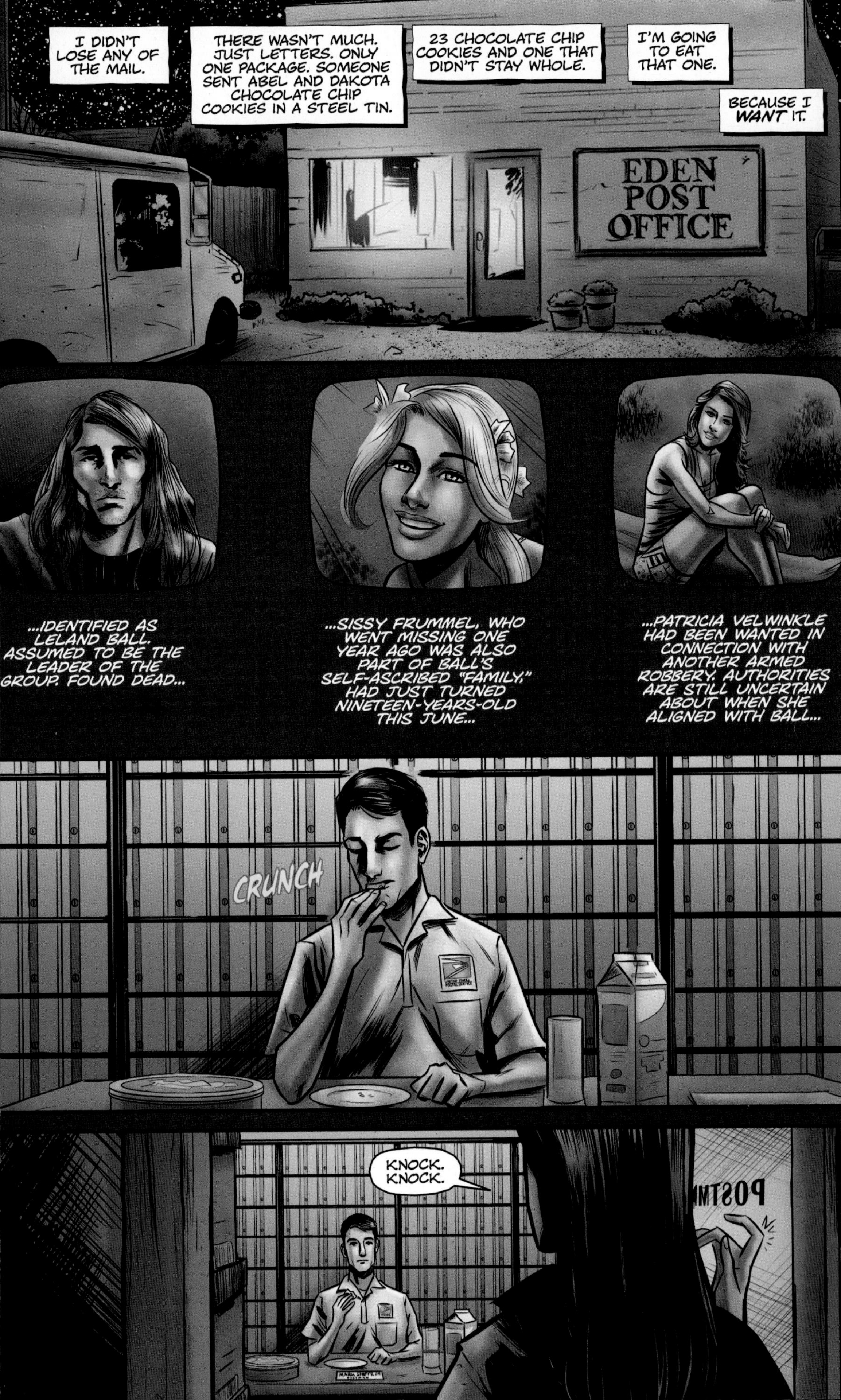
I DIDN'T LOSE ANY OF THE MAIL.
THERE WASN'T MUCH. JUST LETTERS. ONLY ONE PACKAGE. SOMEONE SENT ABEL AND DAKOTA CHOCOLATE CHIP COOKIES IN A STEEL TIN.
23 CHOCOLATE CHIP COOKIES AND ONE THAT DIDN'T STAY WHOLE.
I'M GOING TO EAT THAT ONE.
BECAUSE I *WANT* IT.
EDEN POST OFFICE
...IDENTIFIED AS LELAND BALL. ASSUMED TO BE THE LEADER OF THE GROUP. FOUND DEAD...
...SISSY FRUMMEL, WHO WENT MISSING ONE YEAR AGO WAS ALSO PART OF BALL'S SELF-ASCRIBED "FAMILY," HAD JUST TURNED NINETEEN-YEARS-OLD THIS JUNE...
...PATRICIA VELWINKLE HAD BEEN WANTED IN CONNECTION WITH ANOTHER ARMED ROBBERY. AUTHORITIES ARE STILL UNCERTAIN ABOUT WHEN SHE ALIGNED WITH BALL...
CRUNCH
KNOCK. KNOCK.

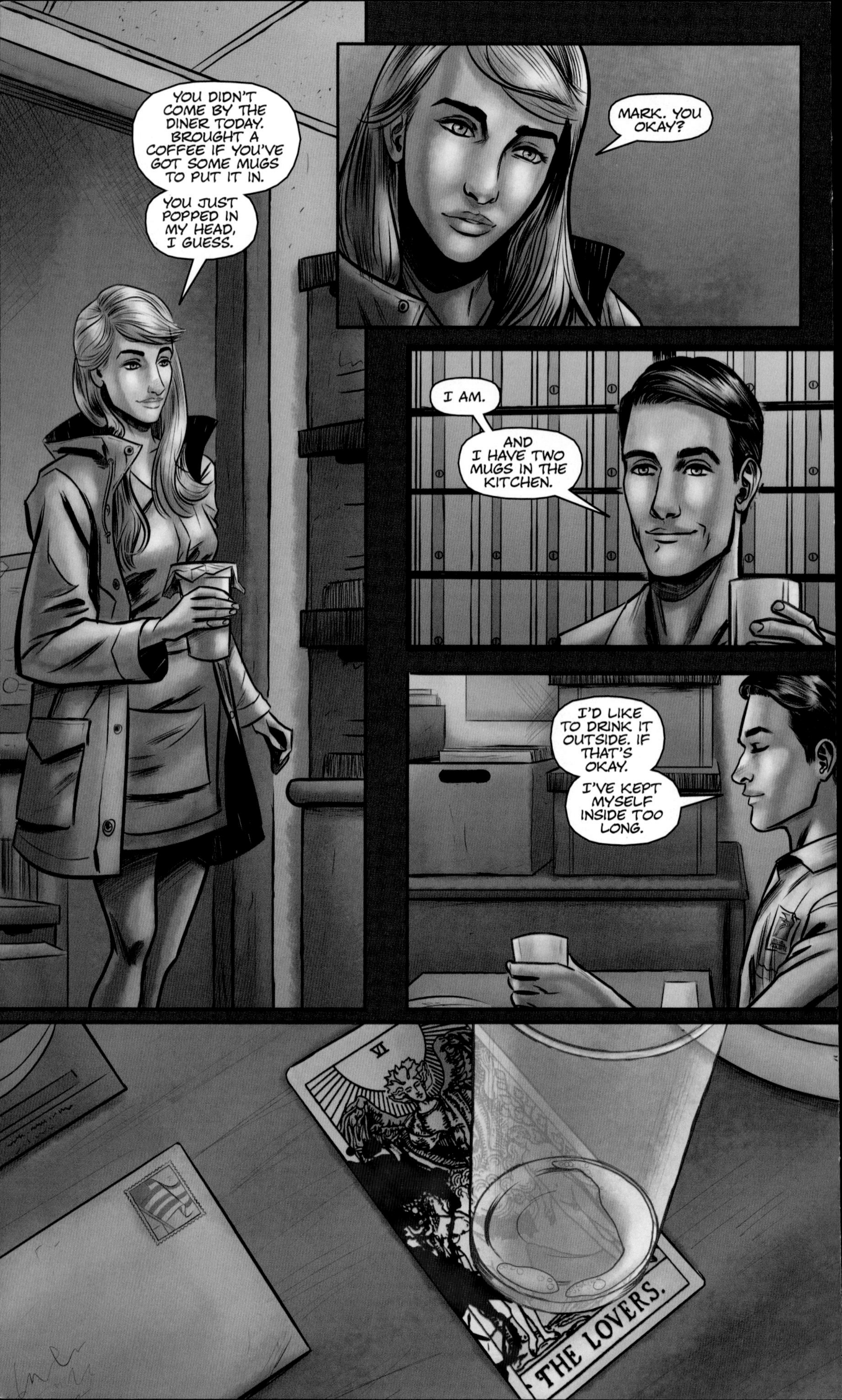

YOU DIDN'T COME BY THE DINER TODAY. BROUGHT A COFFEE IF YOU'VE GOT SOME MUGS TO PUT IT IN.
YOU JUST POPPED IN MY HEAD, I GUESS.
MARK. YOU OKAY?
I AM.
AND I HAVE TWO MUGS IN THE KITCHEN.
I'D LIKE TO DRINK IT OUTSIDE. IF THAT'S OKAY.
I'VE KEPT MYSELF INSIDE TOO LONG.
VI
THE LOVERS.

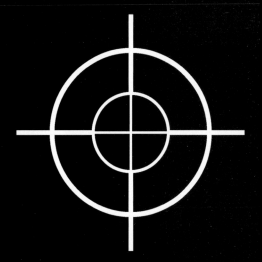

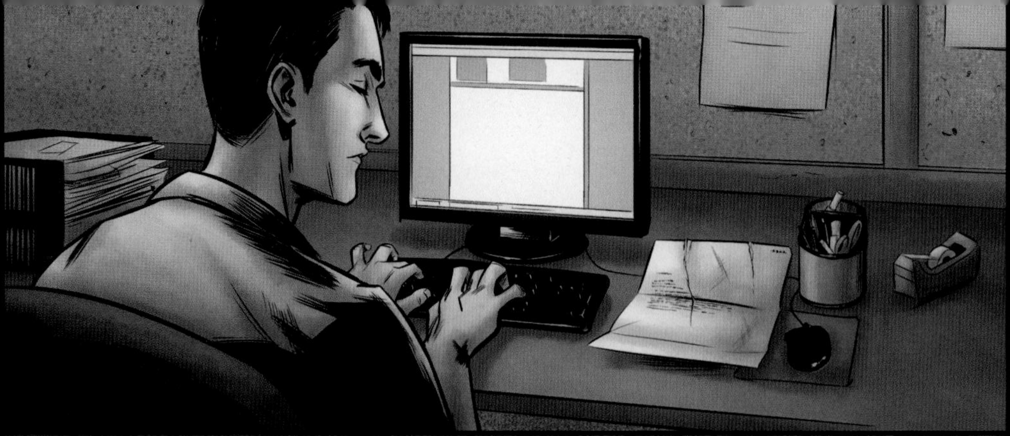

I transcribe all the mail now. I take the letters and postcards in different fonts and sizes and make them all the same. Times New Roman, 12-point font, 8 ½" x 11", bright white paper. I file them away for my mother.

Except for these three. These three are just for me.

Letter from Leland Ball, to Sissy "Squeaky" Frummel:

You wanna know what I see in you? What makes you special? You're a blossom, Squeaky. When I first came down from my pilgrimage of blood, I bore witness to your spectacle – a preparation for transformation. A display of potential. You showed me, with a twirl of baton, with the alchemic circle, symbol upon symbol, you proved your worth.

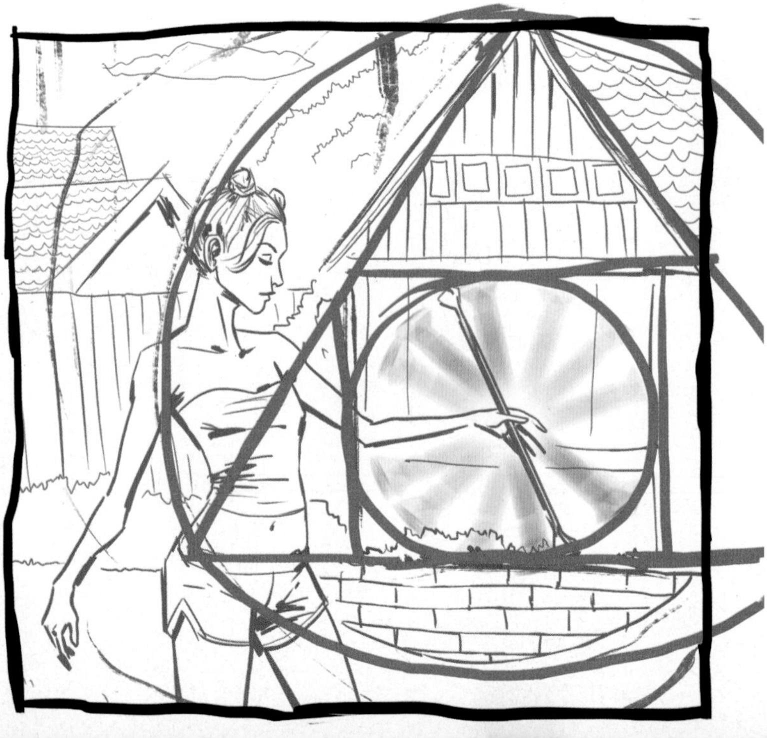

Letter from Sissy Frummel, to her parents:

Let your daughter teach you, for you do not understand as I do. I have read your letters, childish scrawl, unlearned, concerned with the world I have abandoned. I ain't your "Sissy," I ain't your anything. I'm about something new. I'm about Ball, now, and His great work. He called me a "gift."

Watch me walking in the path of Jupiter, garland of flowers, guided by Him. When He found me, He saw the potential in me to become something more, to transform. And I have transformed and am still transforming. I'm prettier for Him than I was for you.

When I was with you I understood as a child, but I have set aside childish things – Ball has shown me better. Ball has shown me that truth is not a farmhouse or a high school dance or a lifetime working paycheck to paycheck. The truth is not my Sunday dress or the misunderstandings of the false prophets in your liar's churches. The truth, the real truth…that's a truth I can dig. Ball's truth. Your whole world was all show and no go. Ball's gonna teach me to tune it all out.

When you catch sight of me next, it will be as He sees me. Holy, wholly, light, and free – of the air and the beyond. It's gonna take blood to show me and to show you. It always does.

Letter from Leland Ball, to Patricia Velwinkle:

That's a load of bull. Here's the heavy, friend – you can have anything you want if you're willing to give up what's necessary.

I can show you something more, if you want. I can show you a place where all the castles are kingless and all the moats are full of blood. I can teach you all about how they went and fucked the world with bombs and books. There was an old way of doing things. A right way. A path colored carmine, firelit, where a man made his own way and only hurt those that needed hurting.

Let me help you walk it. It ain't easy, but I can help you, if you'll let me. Won't you let me be a friend?

Patricia Velwinkle's Final Diary Entry

You know foxes eat their young? Ball taught me that. Ball taught me all kinds of stuff.

It's weird, ya know? I've been watching us on the news, folks always talking about us and what we do. I watched some chrome dome with a bad mustache asking you questions on the tube, and you said how you were just so afraid for me, and you were afraid I was gonna eat it once and for all.

But that's what you don't get – there's no such thing as once and for all. Permanency, transience, diamonds are forever – it's all bullshit. There's no start and no stop, and that's why it's okay. I saw you crying and I wanted to wipe off those tears and tell you that it was okay, no, better than okay.

It was good.

It was good when we broke into those people's homes and it was good when we gathered them and their families and cut them up and let them bleed. It was good of us to do that because that's how the cycle works. Ball taught me that, too, and at least we tried to teach those people before they bit it.

This body's hurting pretty bad. Ball says that the MEDIA will call this a suicide note, but that's so ignorant. That's so jacked and wrong. Because I'm not gonna die, man, I'm never gonna die. That's not what any of this is. There's blood everywhere but it's a good thing, because I'm not dying.

I'm being born. Maybe as something new. Maybe as a fox – wouldn't that be rad? My new mama would eat me and I'd start fresh right away. Far out. I love you, Mama. I love you, Dad. Almost as much as I loved Him.

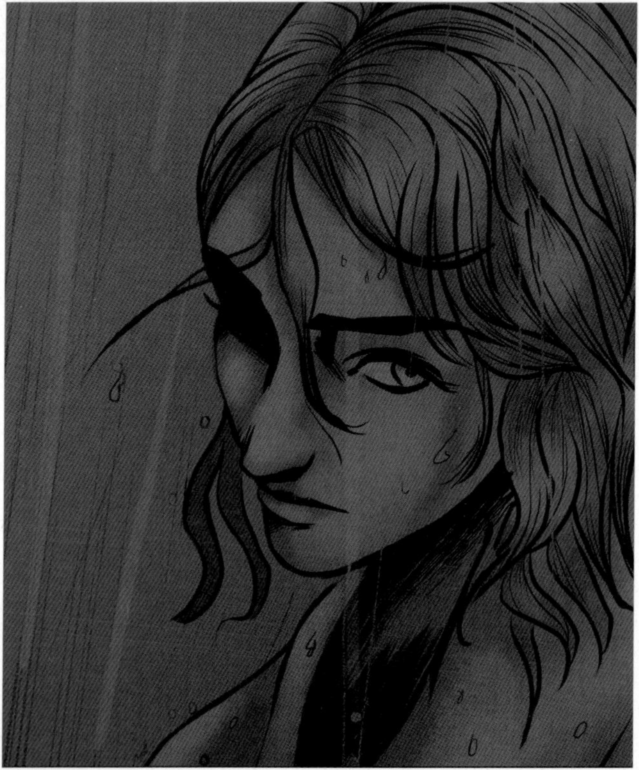

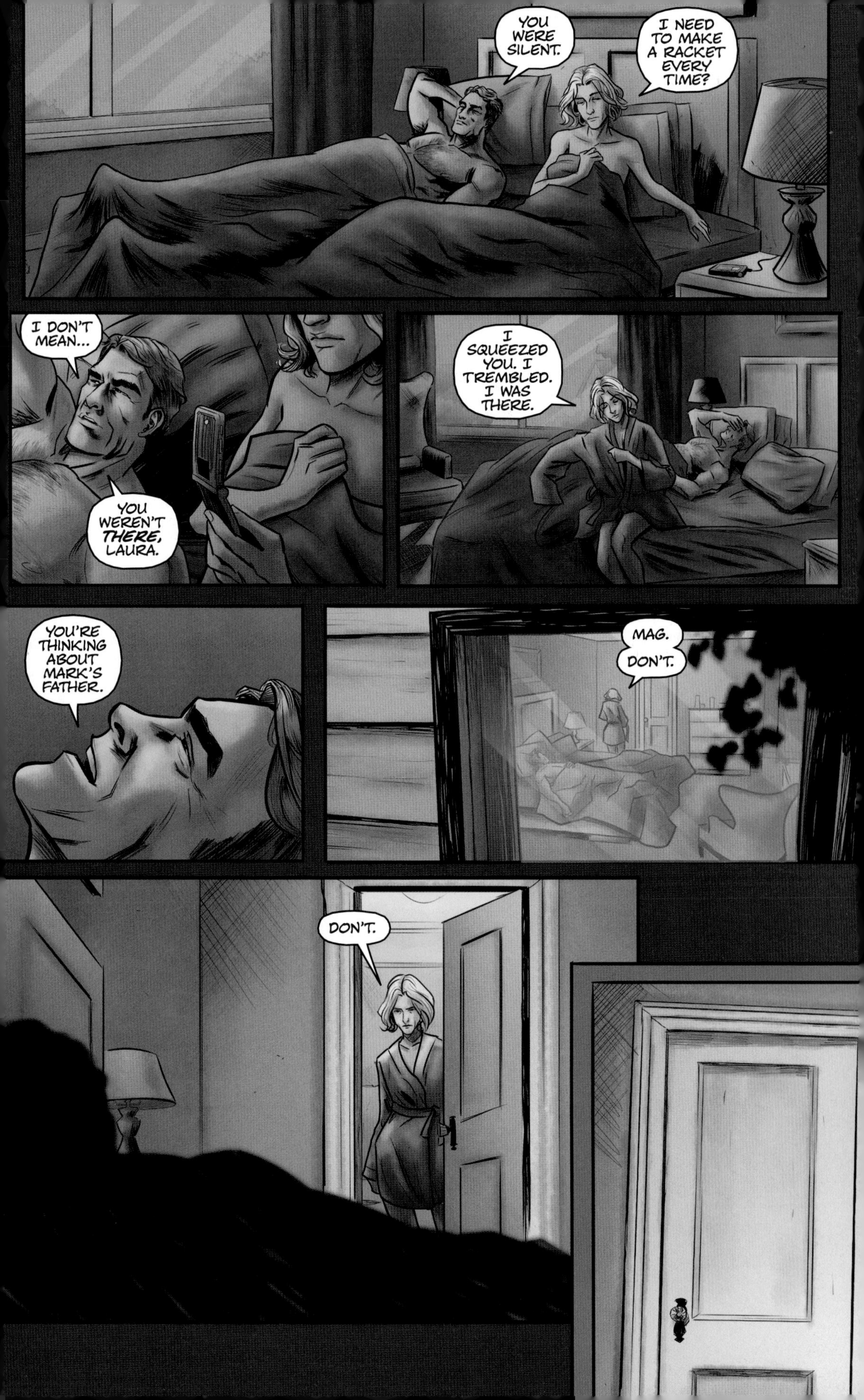
YOU WERE SILENT.
I NEED TO MAKE A RACKET EVERY TIME?
I DON'T MEAN...
YOU WEREN'T *THERE*, LAURA.
I SQUEEZED YOU. I TREMBLED. I WAS THERE.
YOU'RE THINKING ABOUT MARK'S FATHER.
MAG.
DON'T.
DON'T.

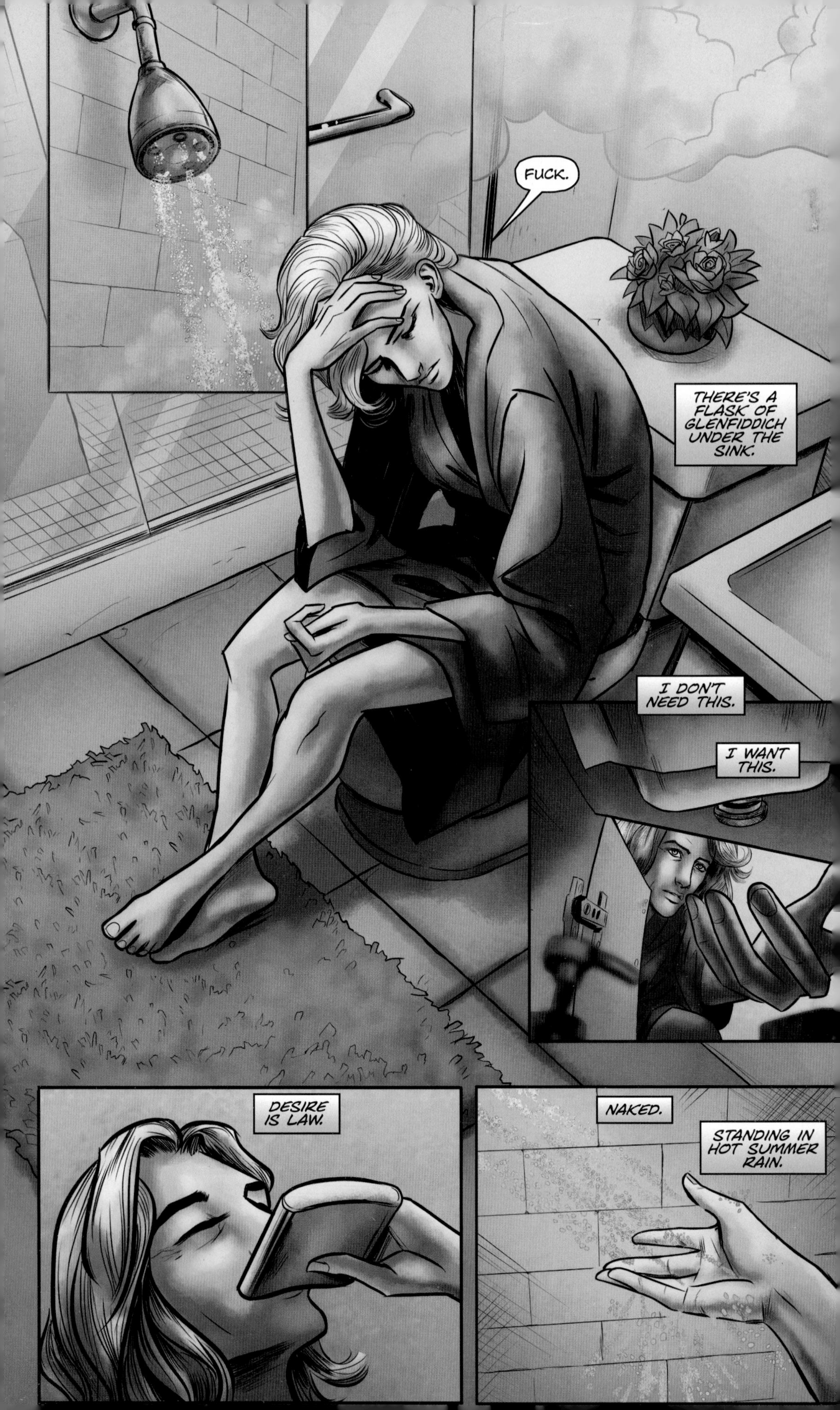
FUCK.
THERE'S A FLASK OF GLENFIDDICH UNDER THE SINK.
I DON'T NEED THIS.
I WANT THIS.
DESIRE IS LAW.
NAKED.
STANDING IN HOT SUMMER RAIN.

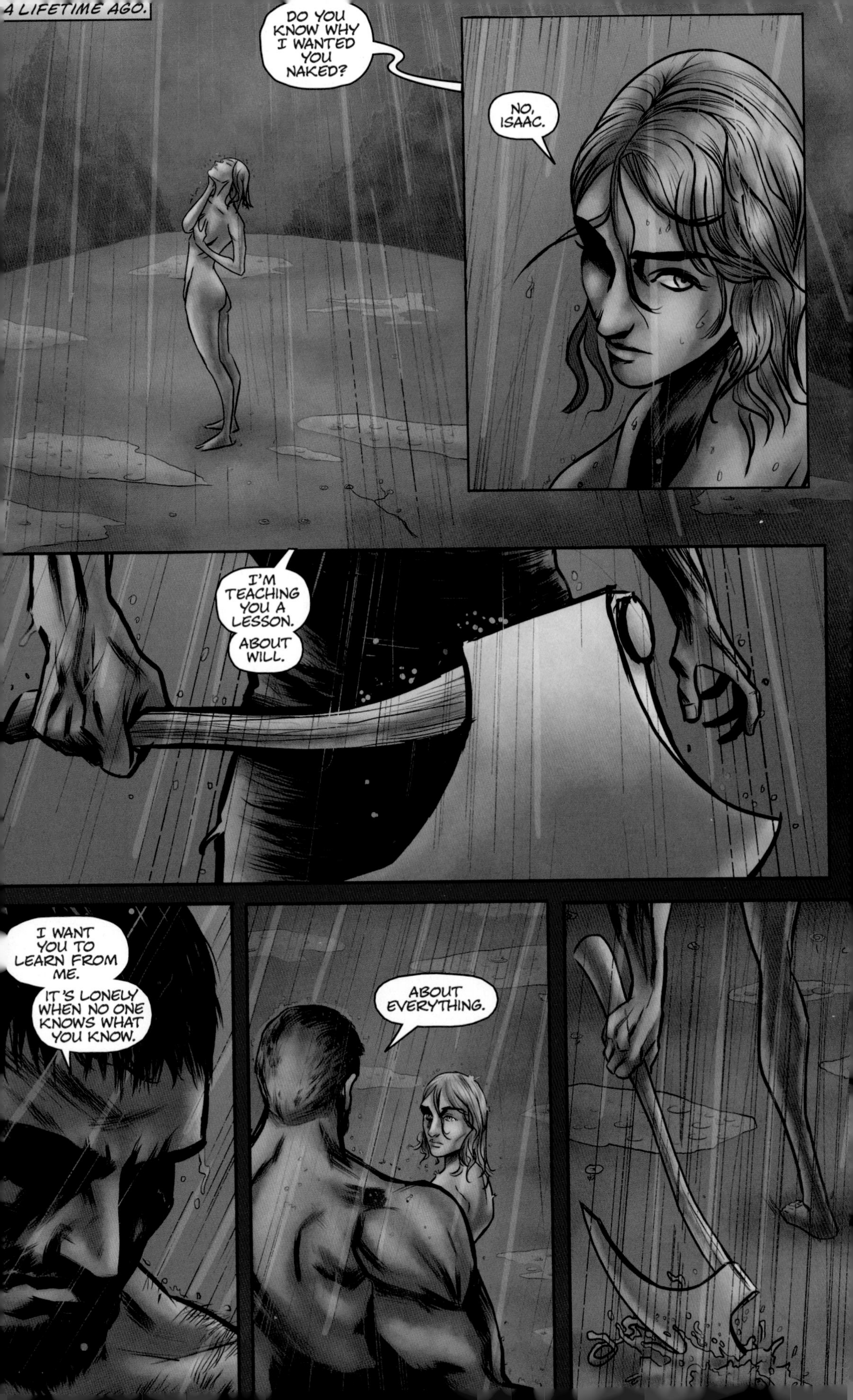
A LIFETIME AGO.
DO YOU KNOW WHY I WANTED YOU NAKED?
NO, ISAAC.
I'M TEACHING YOU A LESSON.
ABOUT WILL.
I WANT YOU TO LEARN FROM ME.
IT'S LONELY WHEN NO ONE KNOWS WHAT YOU KNOW.
ABOUT EVERYTHING.

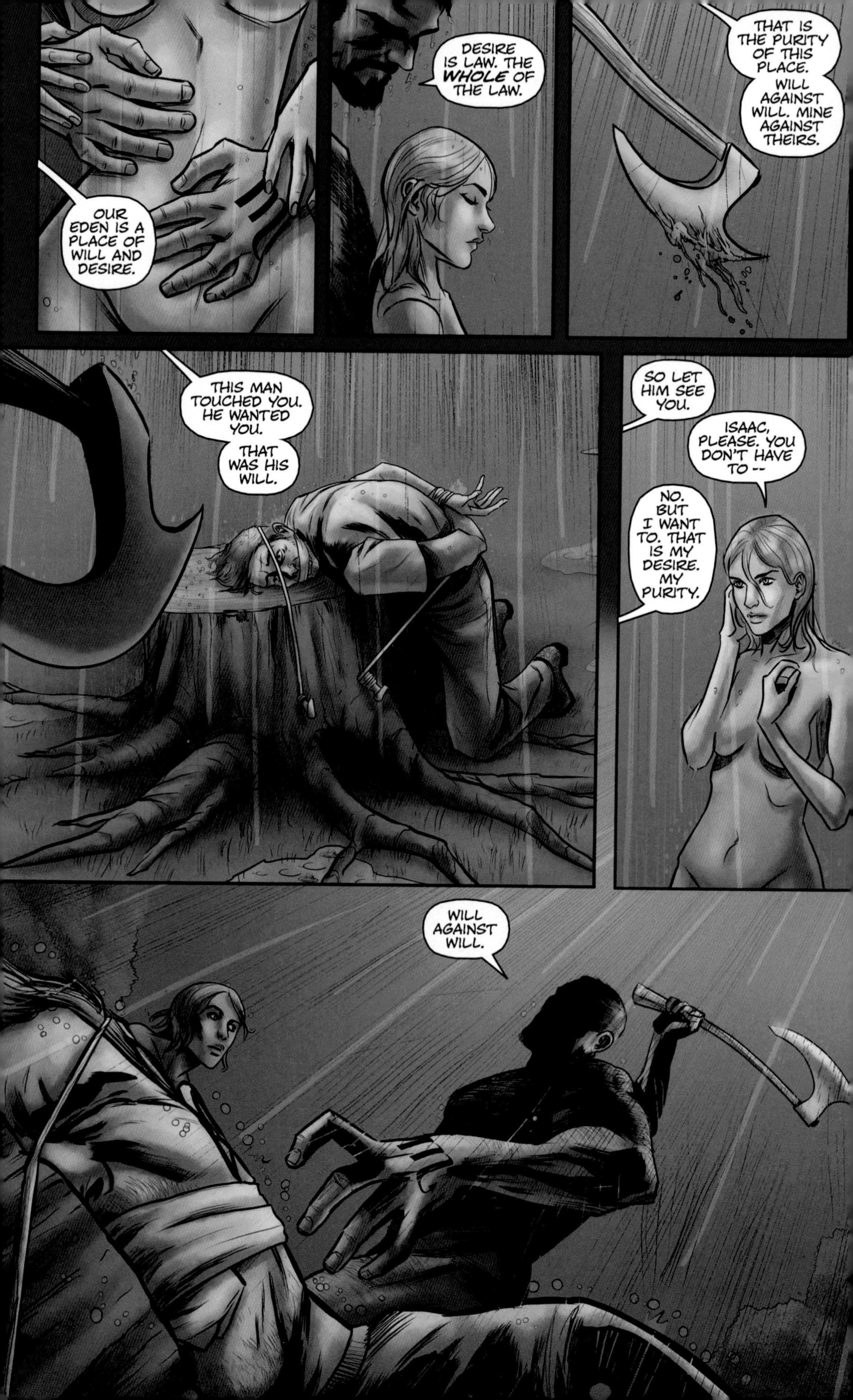
OUR EDEN IS A PLACE OF WILL AND DESIRE.
DESIRE IS LAW. THE WHOLE OF THE LAW.
THAT IS THE PURITY OF THIS PLACE.
WILL AGAINST WILL. MINE AGAINST THEIRS.
THIS MAN TOUCHED YOU. HE WANTED YOU.
THAT WAS HIS WILL.
SO LET HIM SEE YOU.
ISAAC, PLEASE. YOU DON'T HAVE TO --
NO. BUT I WANT TO. THAT IS MY DESIRE. MY PURITY.
WILL AGAINST WILL.

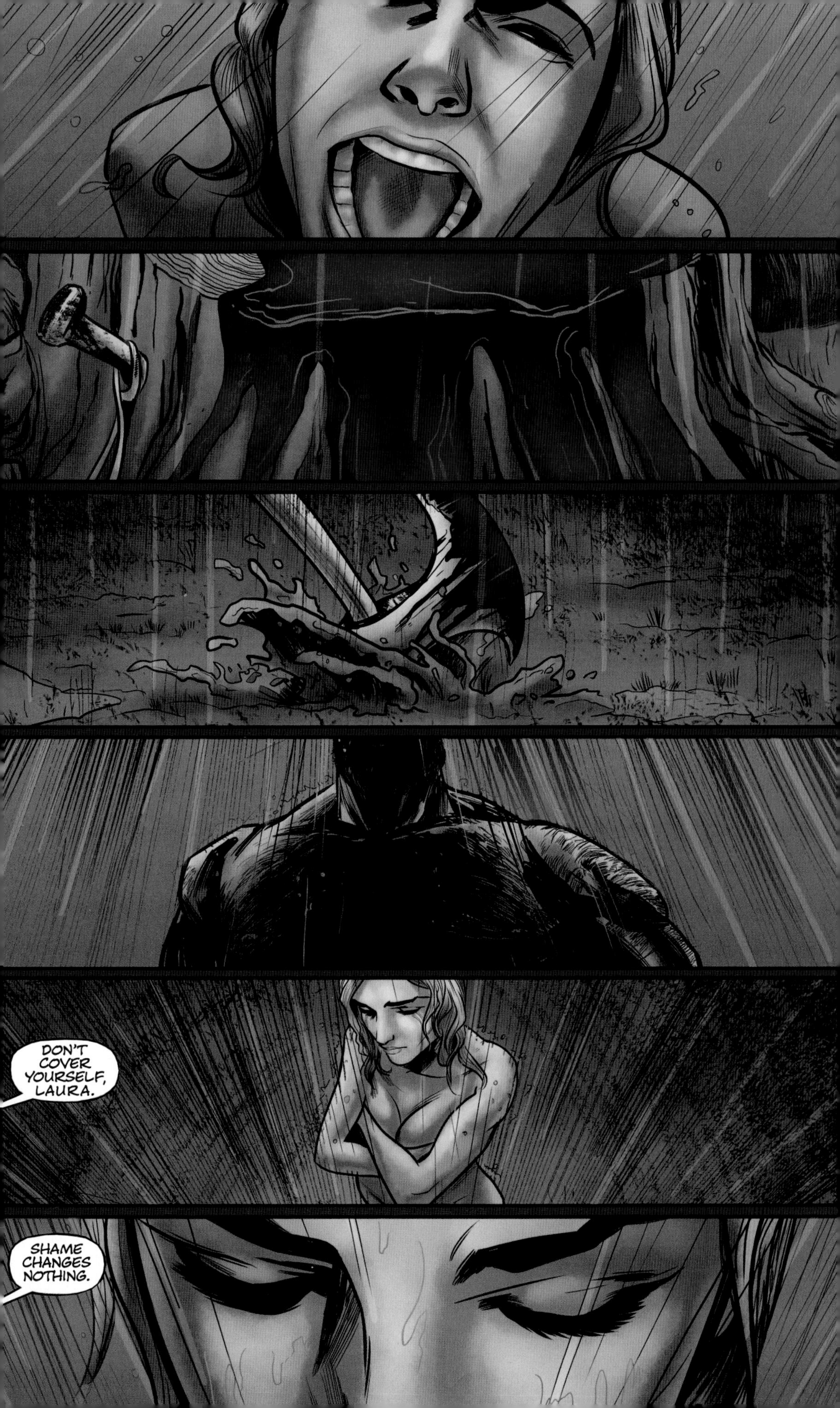
DON'T COVER YOURSELF, LAURA.
SHAME CHANGES NOTHING.

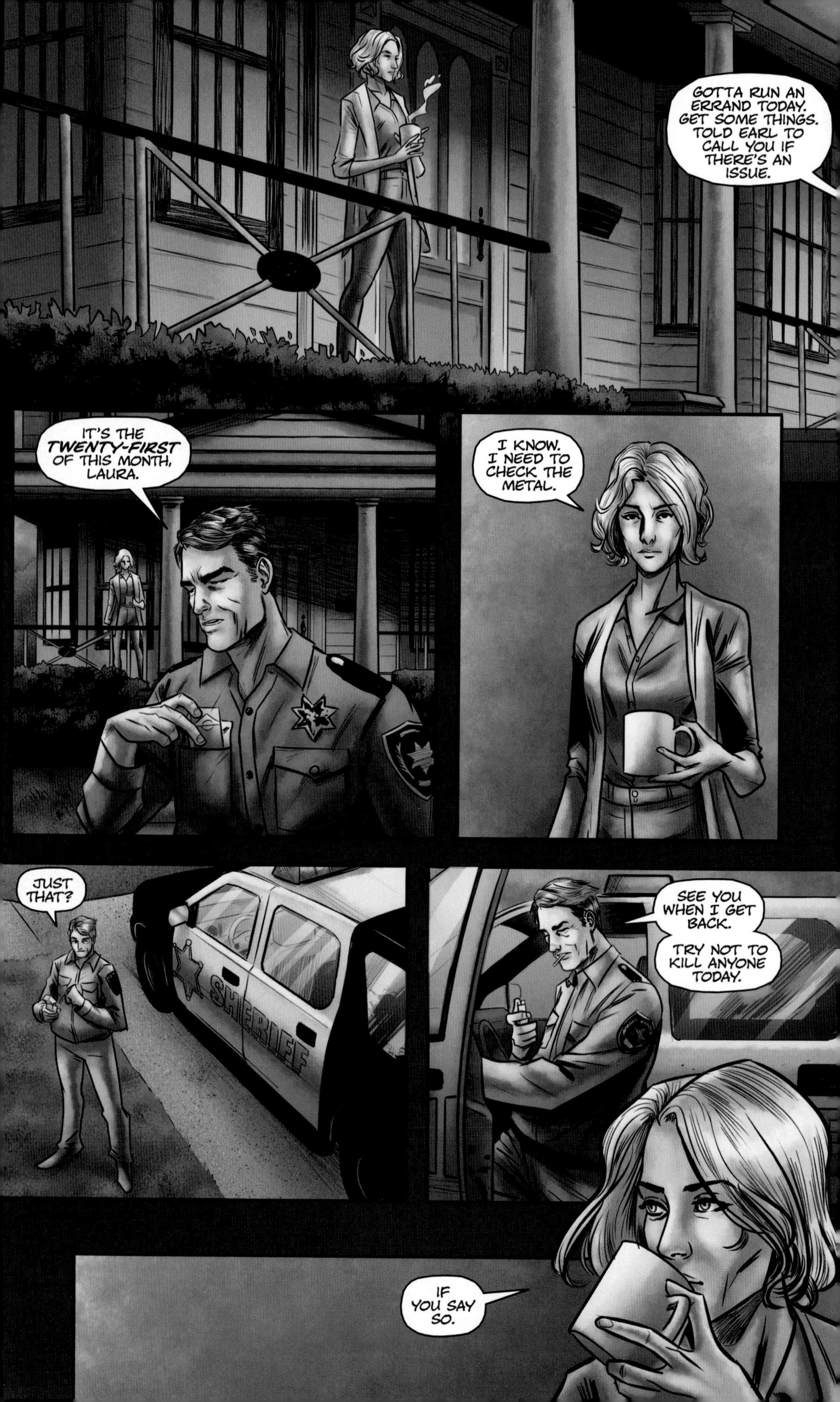
GOTTA RUN AN ERRAND TODAY. GET SOME THINGS. TOLD EARL TO CALL YOU IF THERE'S AN ISSUE.
IT'S THE *TWENTY-FIRST* OF THIS MONTH, LAURA.
I KNOW. I NEED TO CHECK THE METAL.
JUST THAT?
SHERIFF
SEE YOU WHEN I GET BACK.
TRY NOT TO KILL ANYONE TODAY.
IF YOU SAY SO.

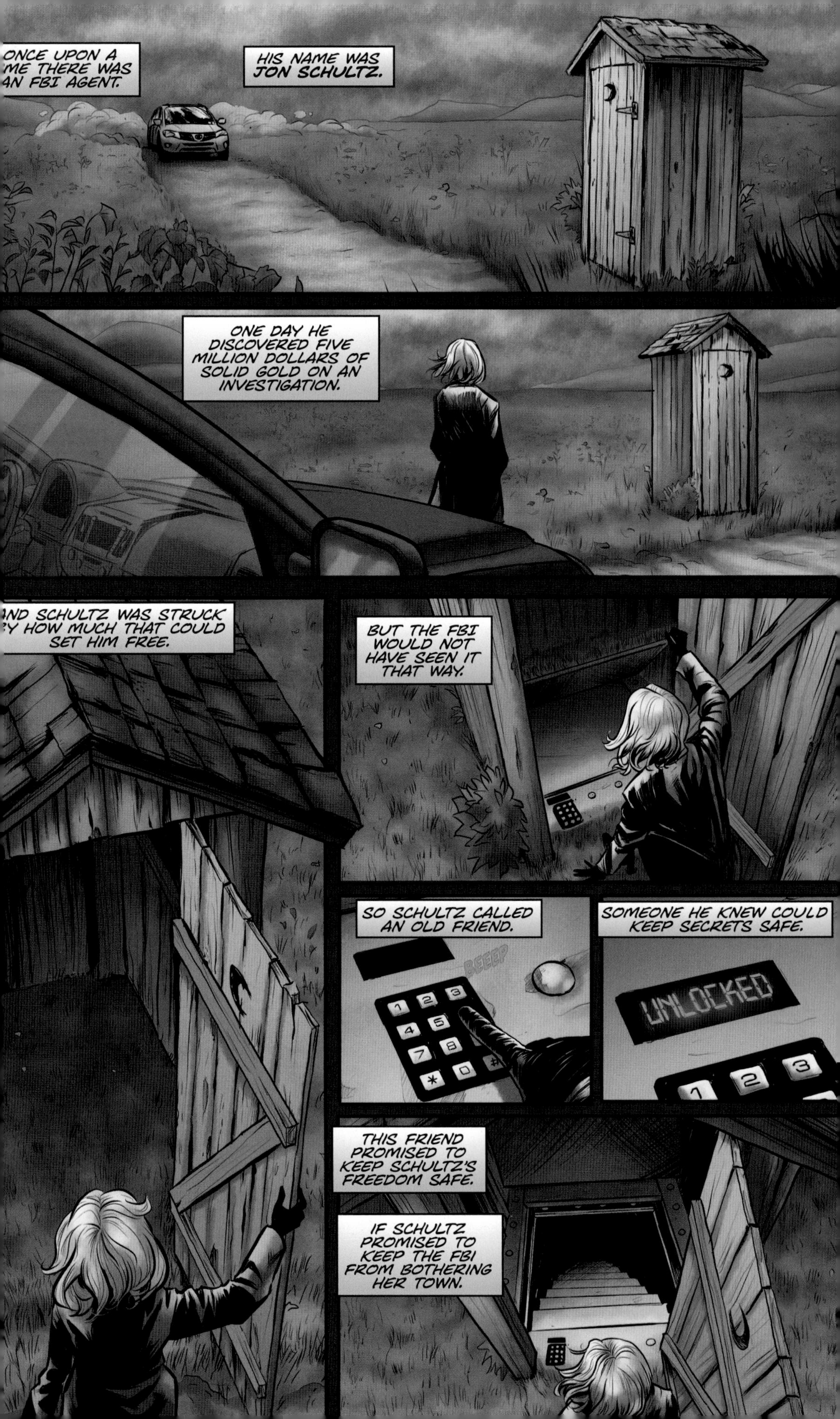
ONCE UPON A
ME THERE WAS
AN FBI AGENT.
HIS NAME WAS
JON SCHULTZ.
ONE DAY HE DISCOVERED FIVE MILLION DOLLARS OF SOLID GOLD ON AN INVESTIGATION.
ND SCHULTZ WAS STRUCK
Y HOW MUCH THAT COULD
SET HIM FREE.
BUT THE FBI WOULD NOT HAVE SEEN IT THAT WAY.
SO SCHULTZ CALLED AN OLD FRIEND.
BEEEP
SOMEONE HE KNEW COULD KEEP SECRETS SAFE.
UNLOCKED
THIS FRIEND PROMISED TO KEEP SCHULTZ'S FREEDOM SAFE.
IF SCHULTZ PROMISED TO KEEP THE FBI FROM BOTHERING HER TOWN.

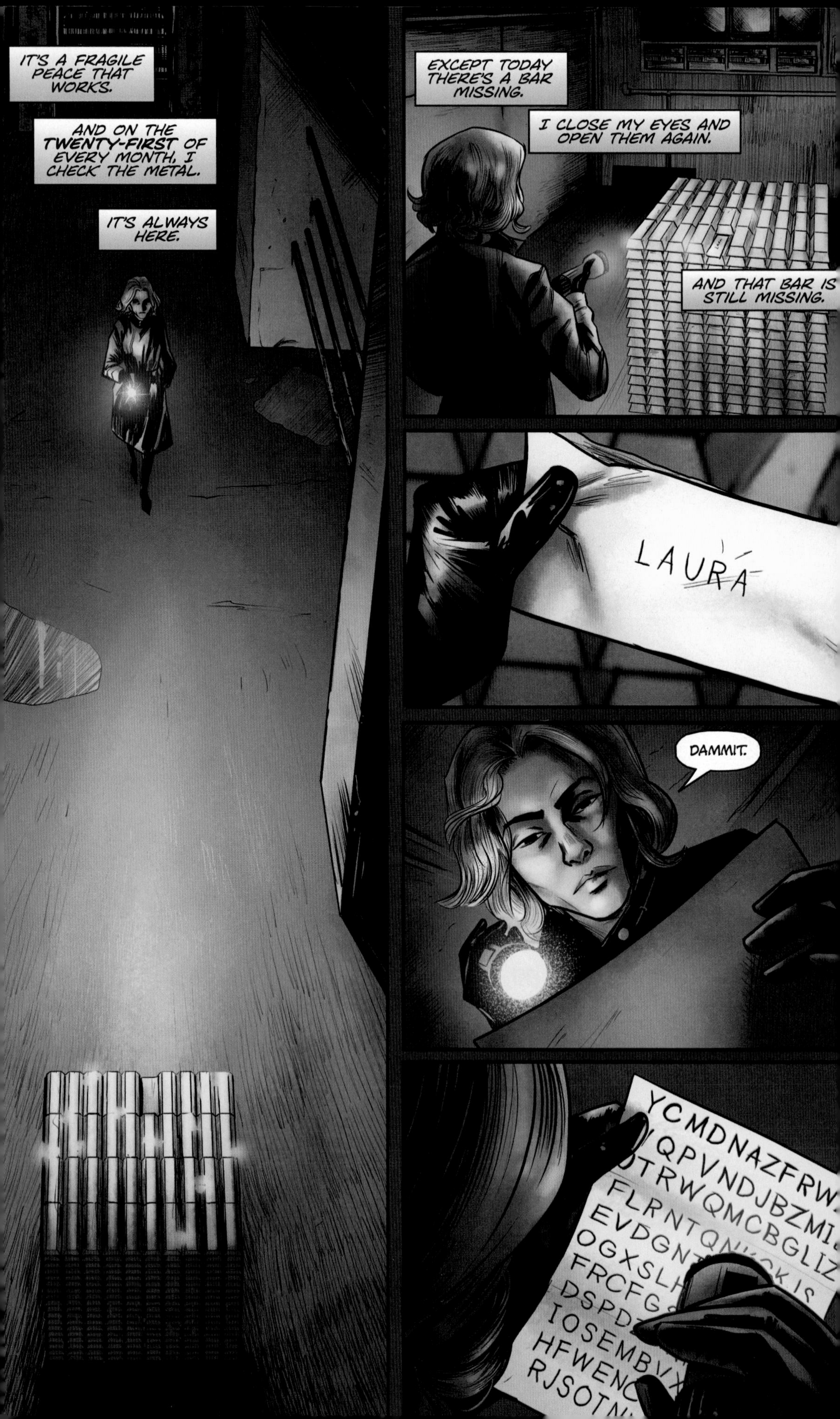

IT'S A FRAGILE PEACE THAT WORKS.
AND ON THE TWENTY-FIRST OF EVERY MONTH, I CHECK THE METAL.
IT'S ALWAYS HERE.
EXCEPT TODAY THERE'S A BAR MISSING.
I CLOSE MY EYES AND OPEN THEM AGAIN.
AND THAT BAR IS STILL MISSING.
LAURA
DAMMIT.

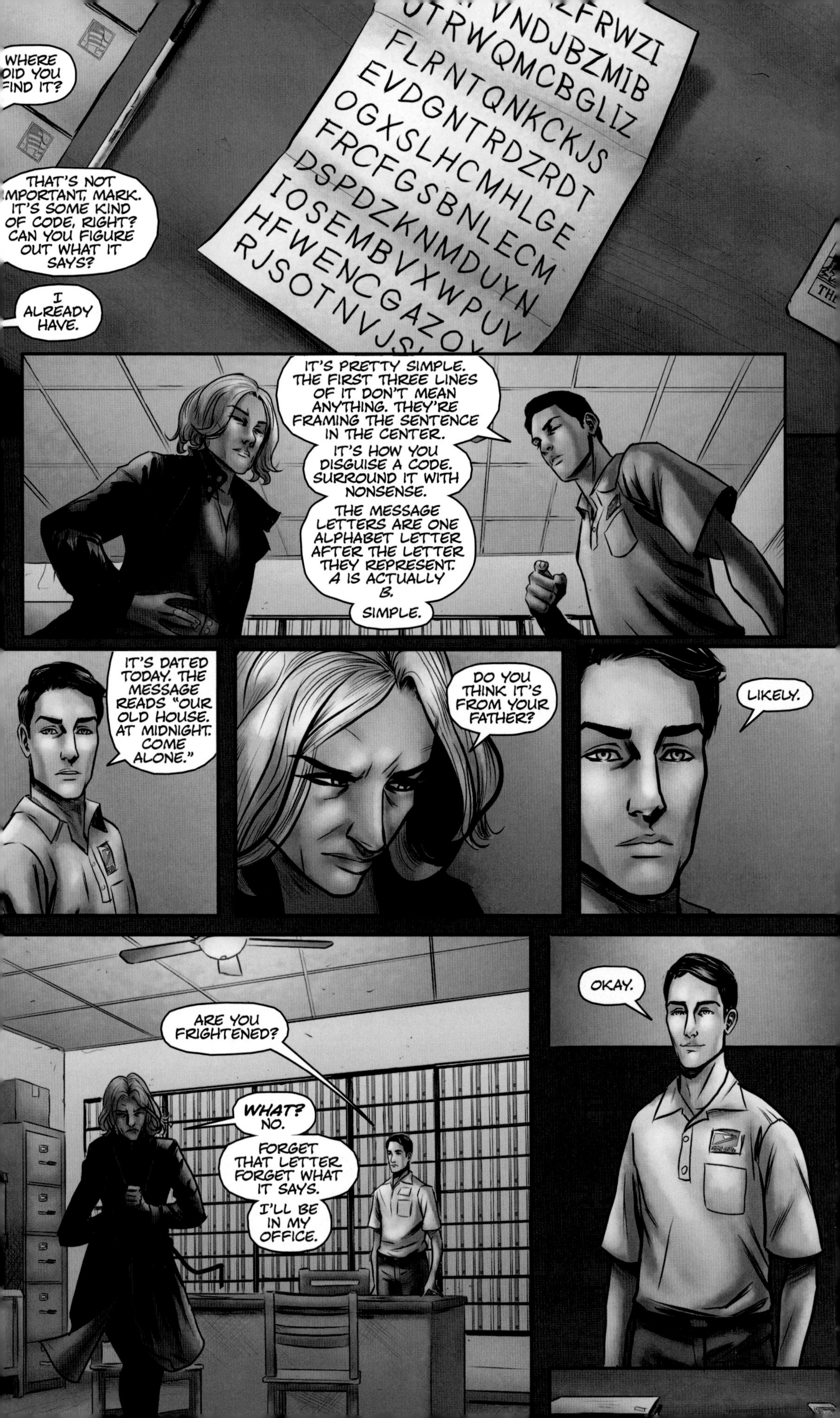
WHERE DID YOU FIND IT?
THAT'S NOT IMPORTANT, MARK. IT'S SOME KIND OF CODE, RIGHT? CAN YOU FIGURE OUT WHAT IT SAYS?
I ALREADY HAVE.
IT'S PRETTY SIMPLE. THE FIRST THREE LINES OF IT DON'T MEAN ANYTHING. THEY'RE FRAMING THE SENTENCE IN THE CENTER.
IT'S HOW YOU DISGUISE A CODE. SURROUND IT WITH NONSENSE.
THE MESSAGE LETTERS ARE ONE ALPHABET LETTER AFTER THE LETTER THEY REPRESENT. A IS ACTUALLY B.
SIMPLE.
IT'S DATED TODAY. THE MESSAGE READS "OUR OLD HOUSE. AT MIDNIGHT. COME ALONE."
DO YOU THINK IT'S FROM YOUR FATHER?
LIKELY.
ARE YOU FRIGHTENED?
WHAT? NO.
FORGET THAT LETTER. FORGET WHAT IT SAYS.
I'LL BE IN MY OFFICE.
OKAY.

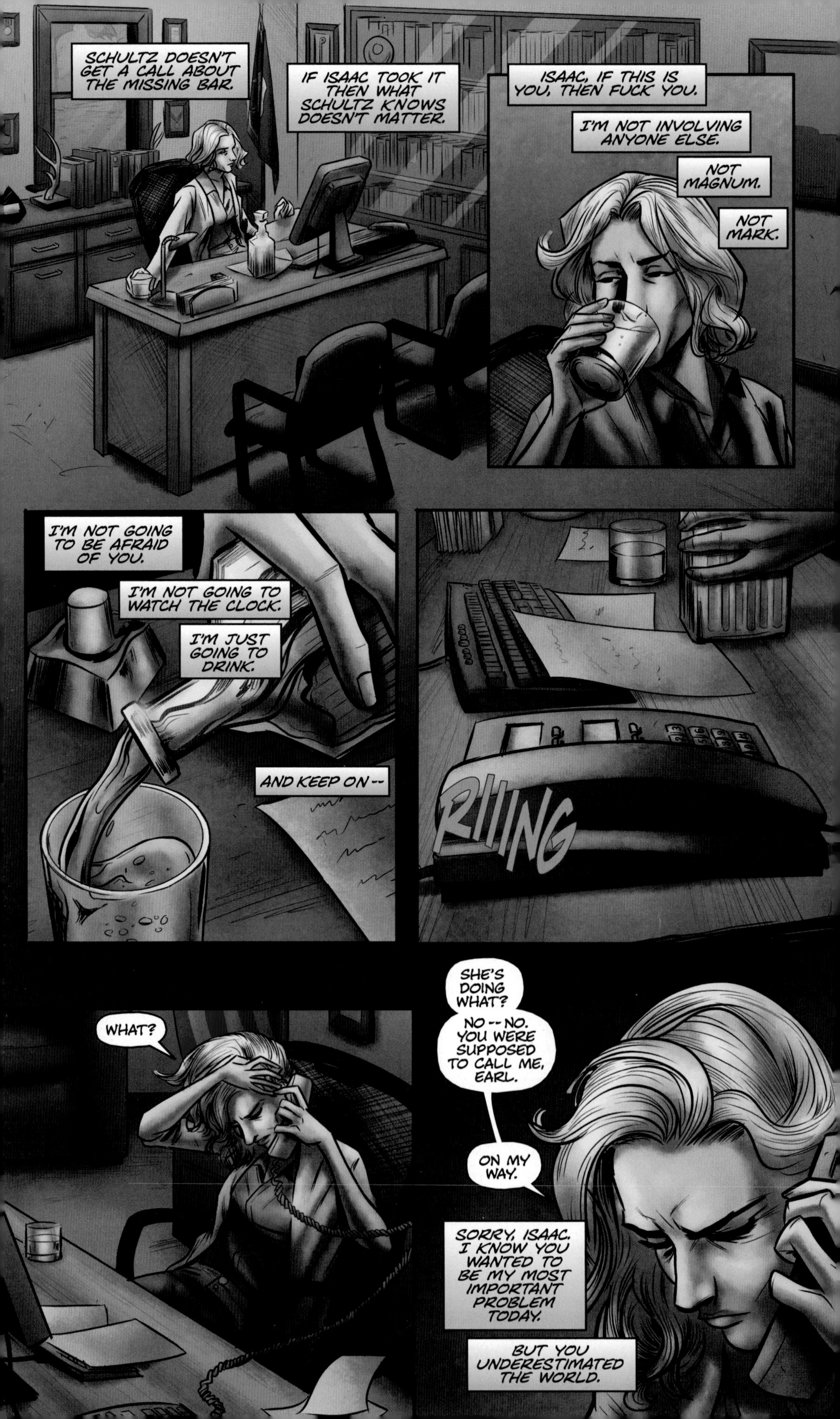
SCHULTZ DOESN'T GET A CALL ABOUT THE MISSING BAR.
IF ISAAC TOOK IT THEN WHAT SCHULTZ KNOWS DOESN'T MATTER.
ISAAC, IF THIS IS YOU, THEN FUCK YOU.
I'M NOT INVOLVING ANYONE ELSE.
NOT MAGNUM.
NOT MARK.
I'M NOT GOING TO BE AFRAID OF YOU.
I'M NOT GOING TO WATCH THE CLOCK.
I'M JUST GOING TO DRINK.
AND KEEP ON --
RIIING
WHAT?
SHE'S DOING WHAT?
NO -- NO. YOU WERE SUPPOSED TO CALL ME, EARL.
ON MY WAY.
SORRY, ISAAC. I KNOW YOU WANTED TO BE MY MOST IMPORTANT PROBLEM TODAY.
BUT YOU UNDERESTIMATED THE WORLD.

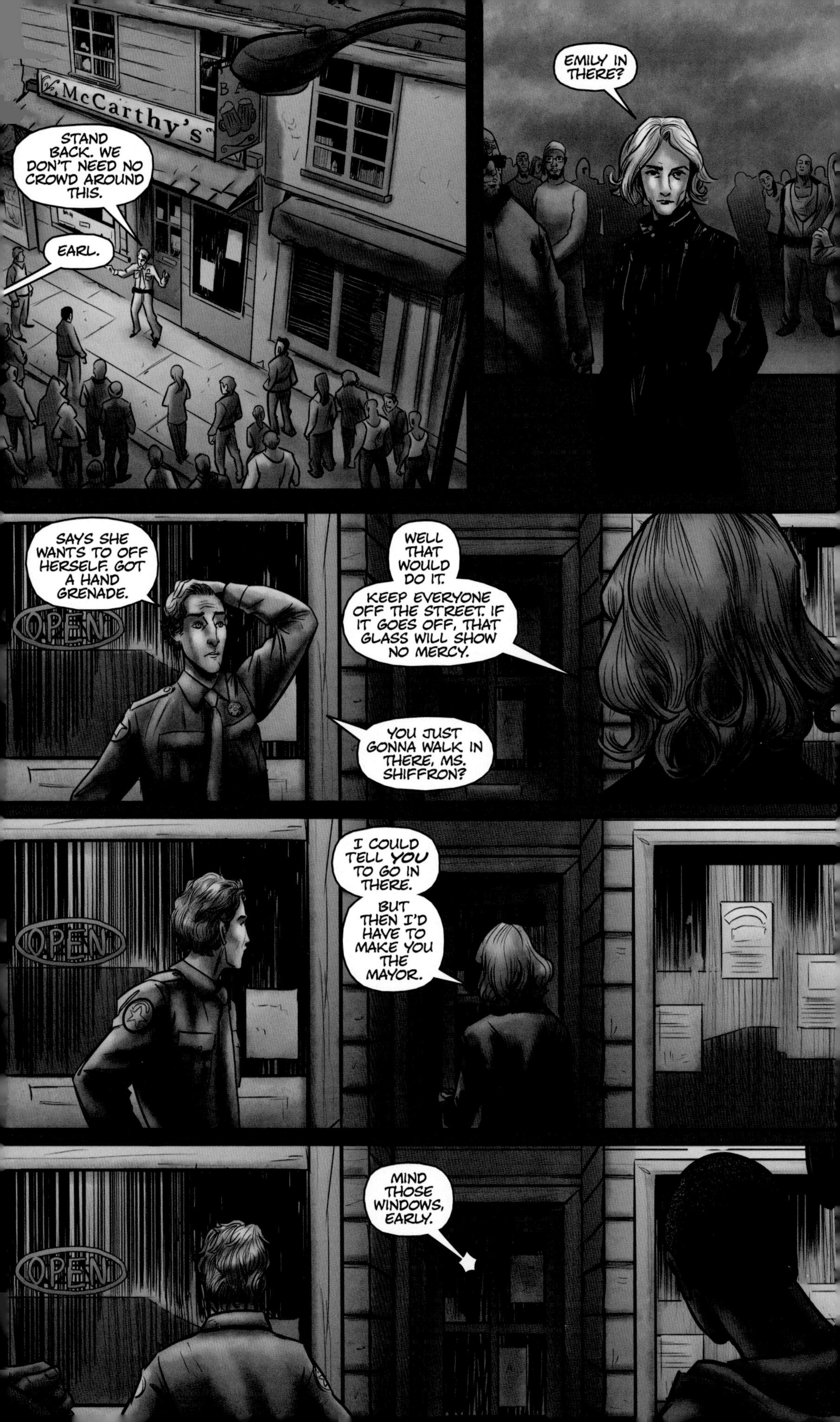
McCarthy's
STAND BACK. WE DON'T NEED NO CROWD AROUND THIS.
EARL.
EMILY IN THERE?
SAYS SHE WANTS TO OFF HERSELF. GOT A HAND GRENADE.
OPEN
WELL THAT WOULD DO IT.
KEEP EVERYONE OFF THE STREET. IF IT GOES OFF, THAT GLASS WILL SHOW NO MERCY.
YOU JUST GONNA WALK IN THERE, MS. SHIFFRON?
OPEN
I COULD TELL YOU TO GO IN THERE.
BUT THEN I'D HAVE TO MAKE YOU THE MAYOR.
OPEN
MIND THOSE WINDOWS, EARLY.

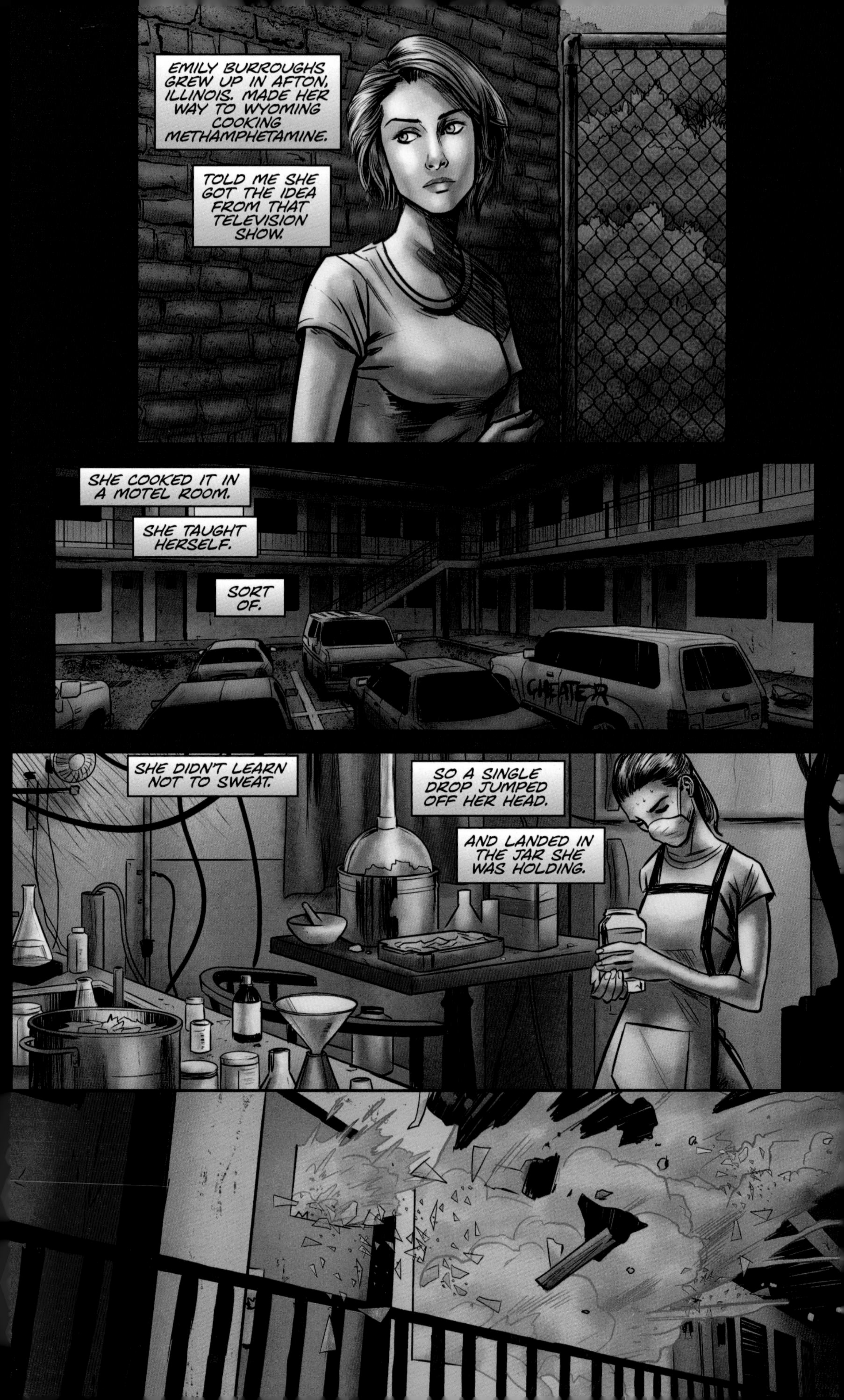
EMILY BURROUGHS GREW UP IN AFTON, ILLINOIS. MADE HER WAY TO WYOMING COOKING METHAMPHETAMINE.
TOLD ME SHE GOT THE IDEA FROM THAT TELEVISION SHOW.
SHE COOKED IT IN A MOTEL ROOM.
SHE TAUGHT HERSELF.
SORT OF.
CHEATER
SHE DIDN'T LEARN NOT TO SWEAT.
SO A SINGLE DROP JUMPED OFF HER HEAD.
AND LANDED IN THE JAR SHE WAS HOLDING.

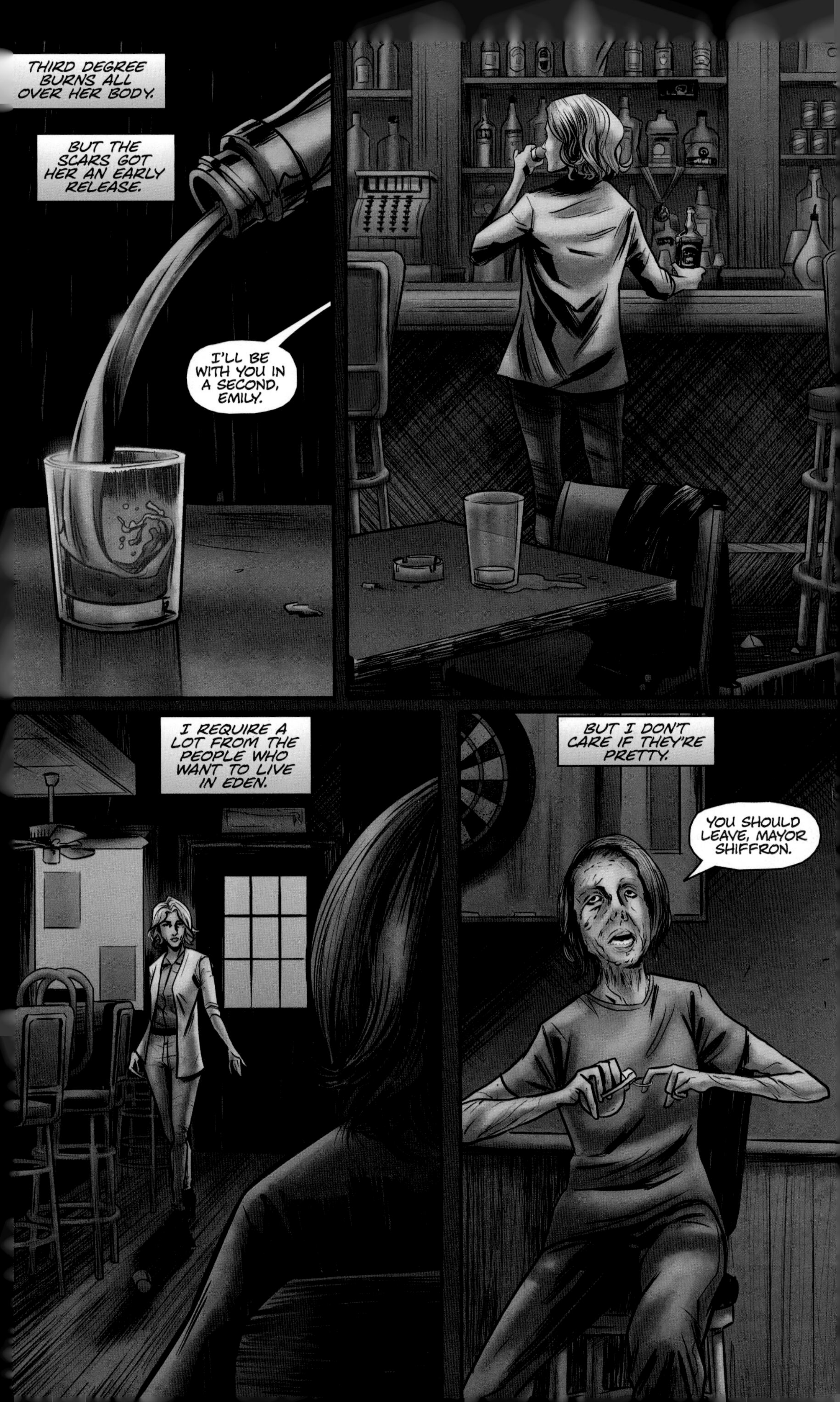
THIRD DEGREE BURNS ALL OVER HER BODY.
BUT THE SCARS GOT HER AN EARLY RELEASE.
I'LL BE WITH YOU IN A SECOND, EMILY.
I REQUIRE A LOT FROM THE PEOPLE WHO WANT TO LIVE IN EDEN.
BUT I DON'T CARE IF THEY'RE PRETTY.
YOU SHOULD LEAVE, MAYOR SHIFFRON.

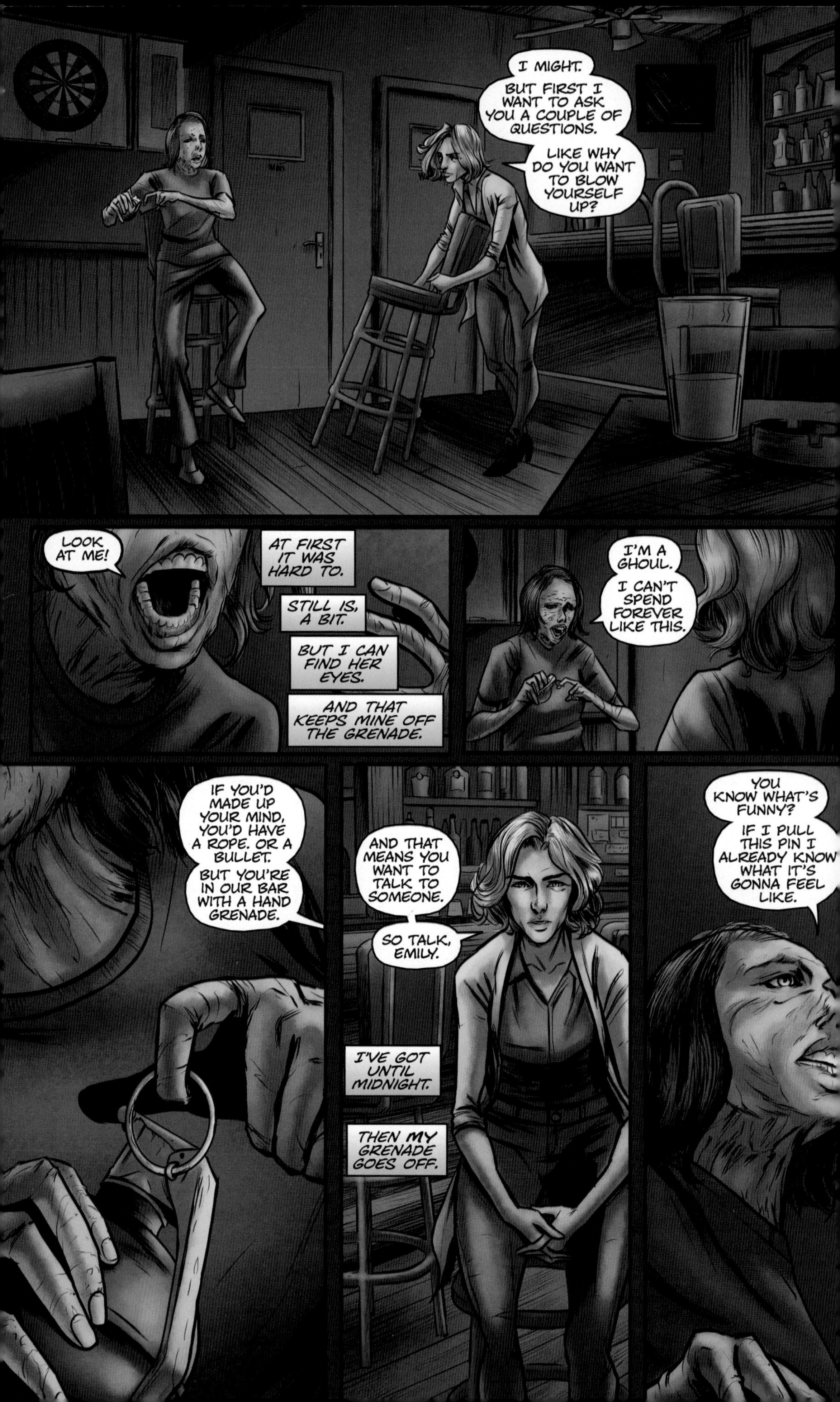
I MIGHT.
BUT FIRST I WANT TO ASK YOU A COUPLE OF QUESTIONS.
LIKE WHY DO YOU WANT TO BLOW YOURSELF UP?
LOOK AT ME!
AT FIRST IT WAS HARD TO.
STILL IS, A BIT.
BUT I CAN FIND HER EYES.
AND THAT KEEPS MINE OFF THE GRENADE.
I'M A GHOUL.
I CAN'T SPEND FOREVER LIKE THIS.
IF YOU'D MADE UP YOUR MIND, YOU'D HAVE A ROPE. OR A BULLET.
BUT YOU'RE IN OUR BAR WITH A HAND GRENADE.
AND THAT MEANS YOU WANT TO TALK TO SOMEONE.
SO TALK, EMILY.
I'VE GOT UNTIL MIDNIGHT.
THEN MY GRENADE GOES OFF.
YOU KNOW WHAT'S FUNNY?
IF I PULL THIS PIN I ALREADY KNOW WHAT IT'S GONNA FEEL LIKE.

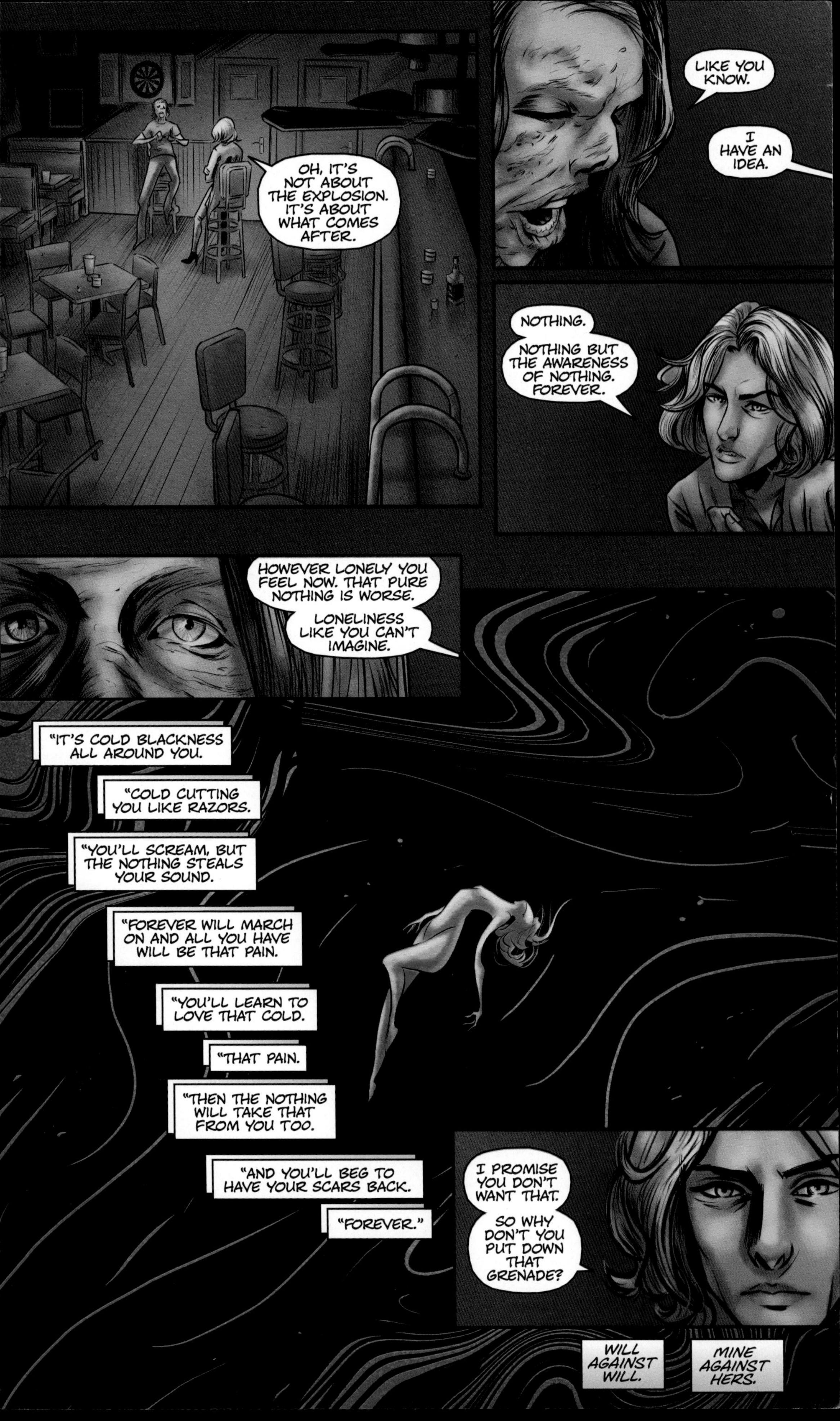
OH, IT'S NOT ABOUT THE EXPLOSION. IT'S ABOUT WHAT COMES AFTER.
LIKE YOU KNOW.
I HAVE AN IDEA.
NOTHING.
NOTHING BUT THE AWARENESS OF NOTHING. FOREVER.
HOWEVER LONELY YOU FEEL NOW. THAT PURE NOTHING IS WORSE.
LONELINESS LIKE YOU CAN'T IMAGINE.
"IT'S COLD BLACKNESS ALL AROUND YOU.
"COLD CUTTING YOU LIKE RAZORS.
"YOU'LL SCREAM, BUT THE NOTHING STEALS YOUR SOUND.
"FOREVER WILL MARCH ON AND ALL YOU HAVE WILL BE THAT PAIN.
"YOU'LL LEARN TO LOVE THAT COLD.
"THAT PAIN.
"THEN THE NOTHING WILL TAKE THAT FROM YOU TOO.
"AND YOU'LL BEG TO HAVE YOUR SCARS BACK.
"FOREVER."
I PROMISE YOU DON'T WANT THAT.
SO WHY DON'T YOU PUT DOWN THAT GRENADE?
WILL AGAINST WILL.
MINE AGAINST HERS.

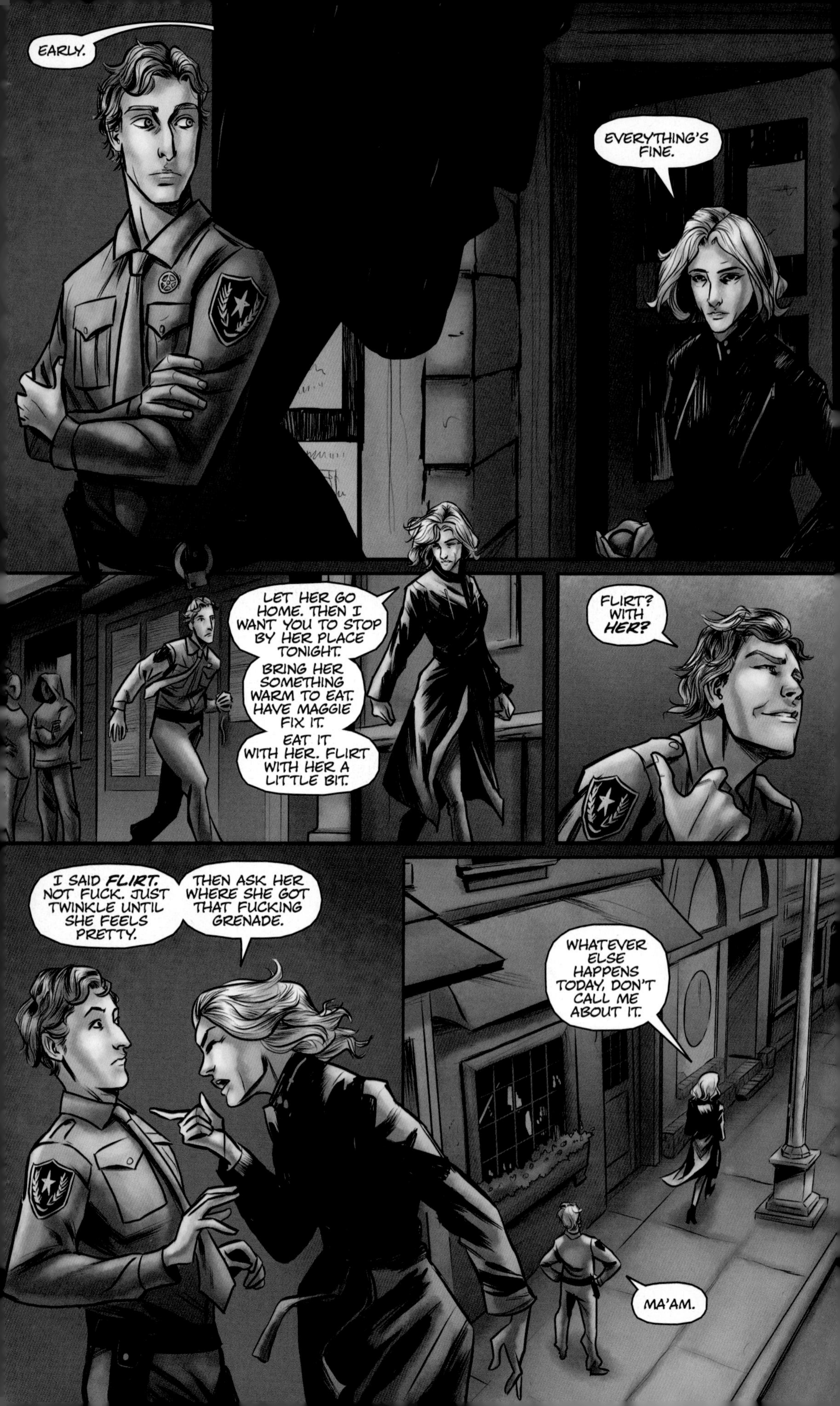
EARLY.
EVERYTHING'S FINE.
LET HER GO HOME. THEN I WANT YOU TO STOP BY HER PLACE TONIGHT.
BRING HER SOMETHING WARM TO EAT. HAVE MAGGIE FIX IT.
EAT IT WITH HER. FLIRT WITH HER A LITTLE BIT.
FLIRT? WITH ***HER?***
I SAID ***FLIRT.*** NOT FUCK. JUST TWINKLE UNTIL SHE FEELS PRETTY.
THEN ASK HER WHERE SHE GOT THAT FUCKING GRENADE.
WHATEVER ELSE HAPPENS TODAY, DON'T CALL ME ABOUT IT.
MA'AM.

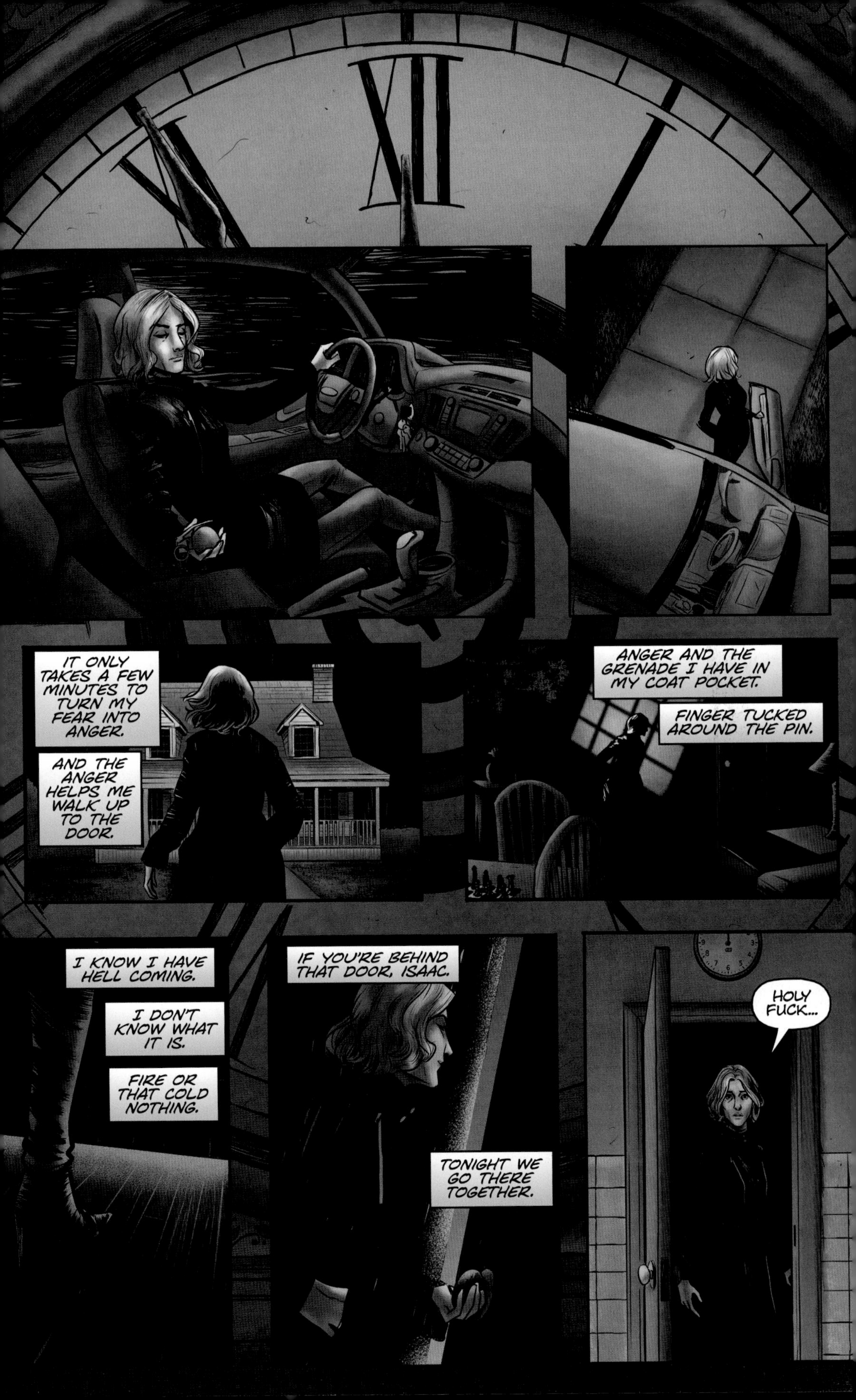
IT ONLY TAKES A FEW MINUTES TO TURN MY FEAR INTO ANGER.
AND THE ANGER HELPS ME WALK UP TO THE DOOR.
ANGER AND THE GRENADE I HAVE IN MY COAT POCKET.
FINGER TUCKED AROUND THE PIN.
I KNOW I HAVE HELL COMING.
I DON'T KNOW WHAT IT IS.
FIRE OR THAT COLD NOTHING.
IF YOU'RE BEHIND THAT DOOR, ISAAC.
TONIGHT WE GO THERE TOGETHER.
HOLY FUCK...

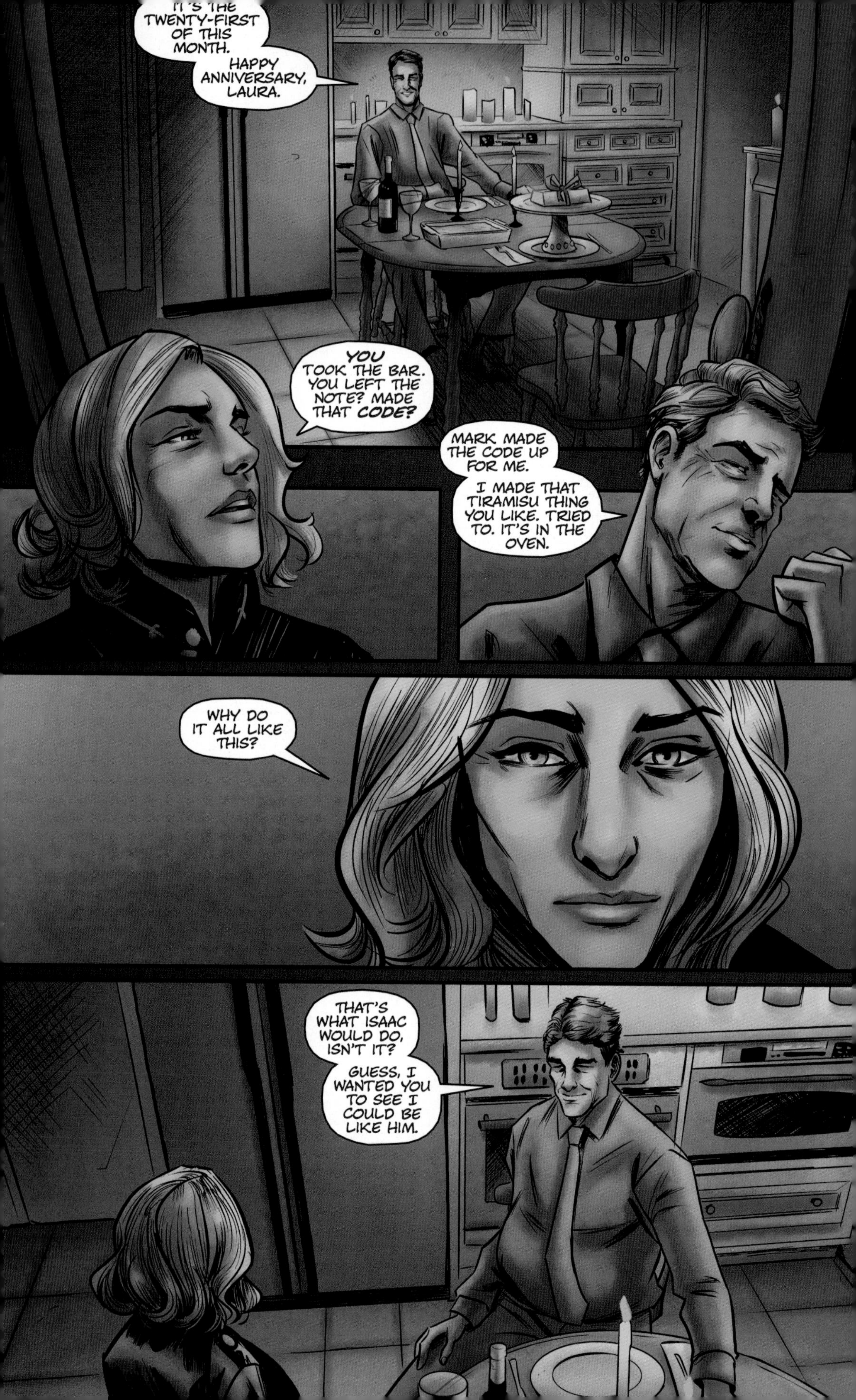
IT'S THE TWENTY-FIRST OF THIS MONTH.
HAPPY ANNIVERSARY, LAURA.
YOU TOOK THE BAR. YOU LEFT THE NOTE? MADE THAT CODE?
MARK MADE THE CODE UP FOR ME.
I MADE THAT TIRAMISU THING YOU LIKE. TRIED TO. IT'S IN THE OVEN.
WHY DO IT ALL LIKE THIS?
THAT'S WHAT ISAAC WOULD DO, ISN'T IT?
GUESS, I WANTED YOU TO SEE I COULD BE LIKE HIM.

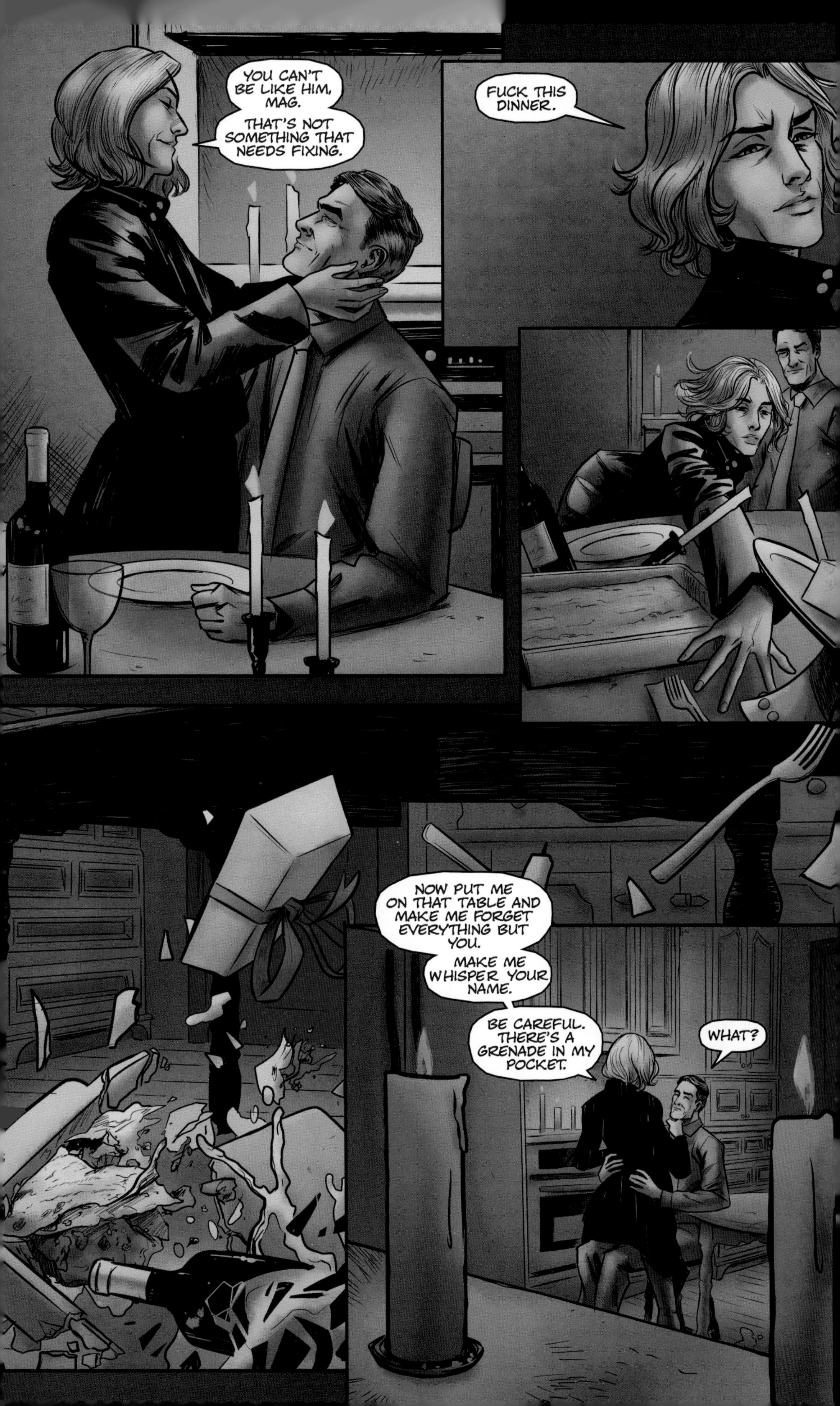
YOU CAN'T BE LIKE HIM, MAG.
THAT'S NOT SOMETHING THAT NEEDS FIXING.
FUCK THIS DINNER.
NOW PUT ME ON THAT TABLE AND MAKE ME FORGET EVERYTHING BUT YOU.
MAKE ME WHISPER YOUR NAME.
BE CAREFUL. THERE'S A GRENADE IN MY POCKET.
WHAT?

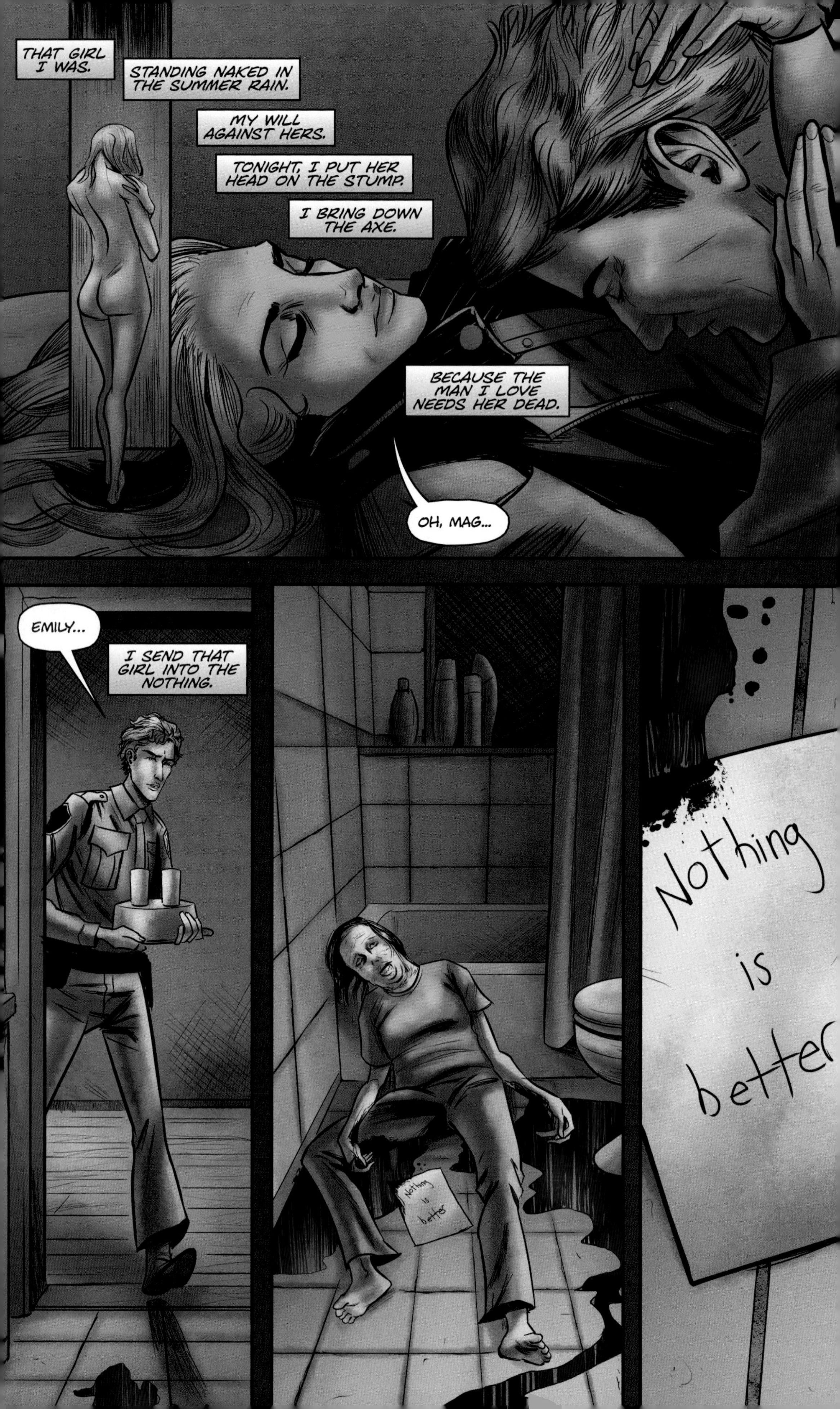
THAT GIRL I WAS.
STANDING NAKED IN THE SUMMER RAIN.
MY WILL AGAINST HERS.
TONIGHT, I PUT HER HEAD ON THE STUMP.
I BRING DOWN THE AXE.
BECAUSE THE MAN I LOVE NEEDS HER DEAD.
OH, MAG...
EMILY...
I SEND THAT GIRL INTO THE NOTHING.
Nothing is better
Nothing is better

CHAPTER 7

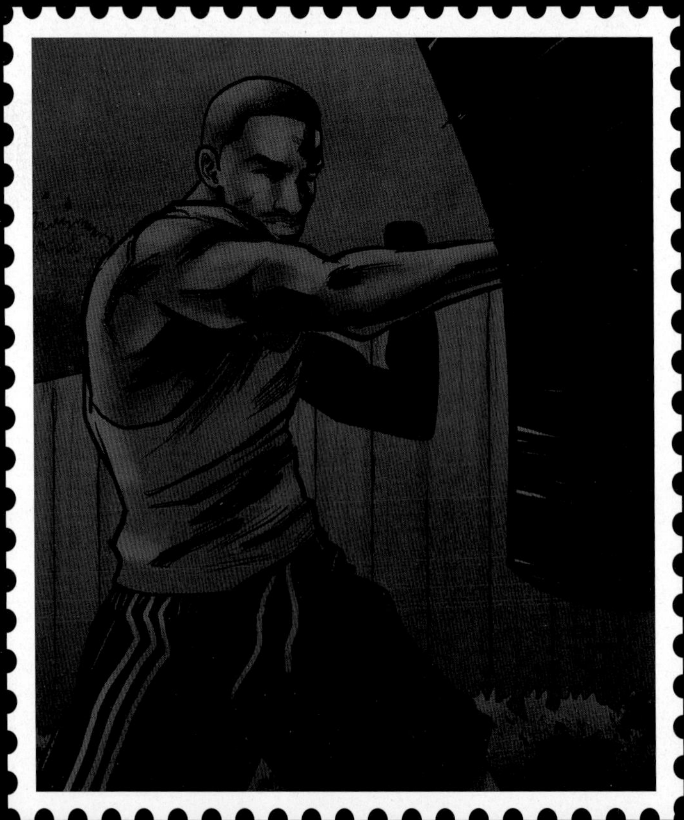

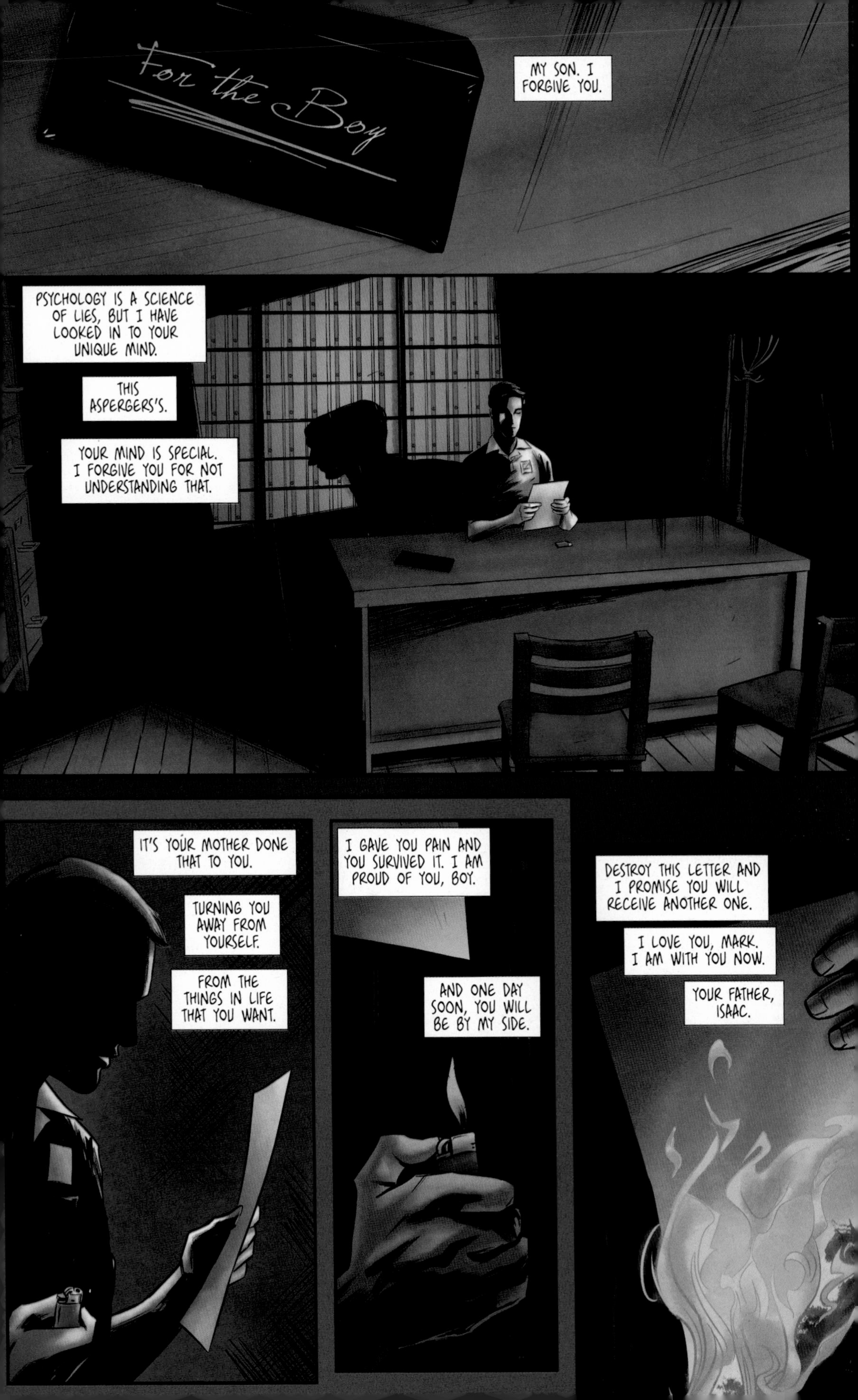
For the Boy
MY SON. I FORGIVE YOU.
PSYCHOLOGY IS A SCIENCE OF LIES, BUT I HAVE LOOKED IN TO YOUR UNIQUE MIND.
THIS ASPERGERS'S.
YOUR MIND IS SPECIAL. I FORGIVE YOU FOR NOT UNDERSTANDING THAT.
IT'S YOUR MOTHER DONE THAT TO YOU.
TURNING YOU AWAY FROM YOURSELF.
FROM THE THINGS IN LIFE THAT YOU WANT.
I GAVE YOU PAIN AND YOU SURVIVED IT. I AM PROUD OF YOU, BOY.
AND ONE DAY SOON, YOU WILL BE BY MY SIDE.
DESTROY THIS LETTER AND I PROMISE YOU WILL RECEIVE ANOTHER ONE.
I LOVE YOU, MARK. I AM WITH YOU NOW.
YOUR FATHER, ISAAC.

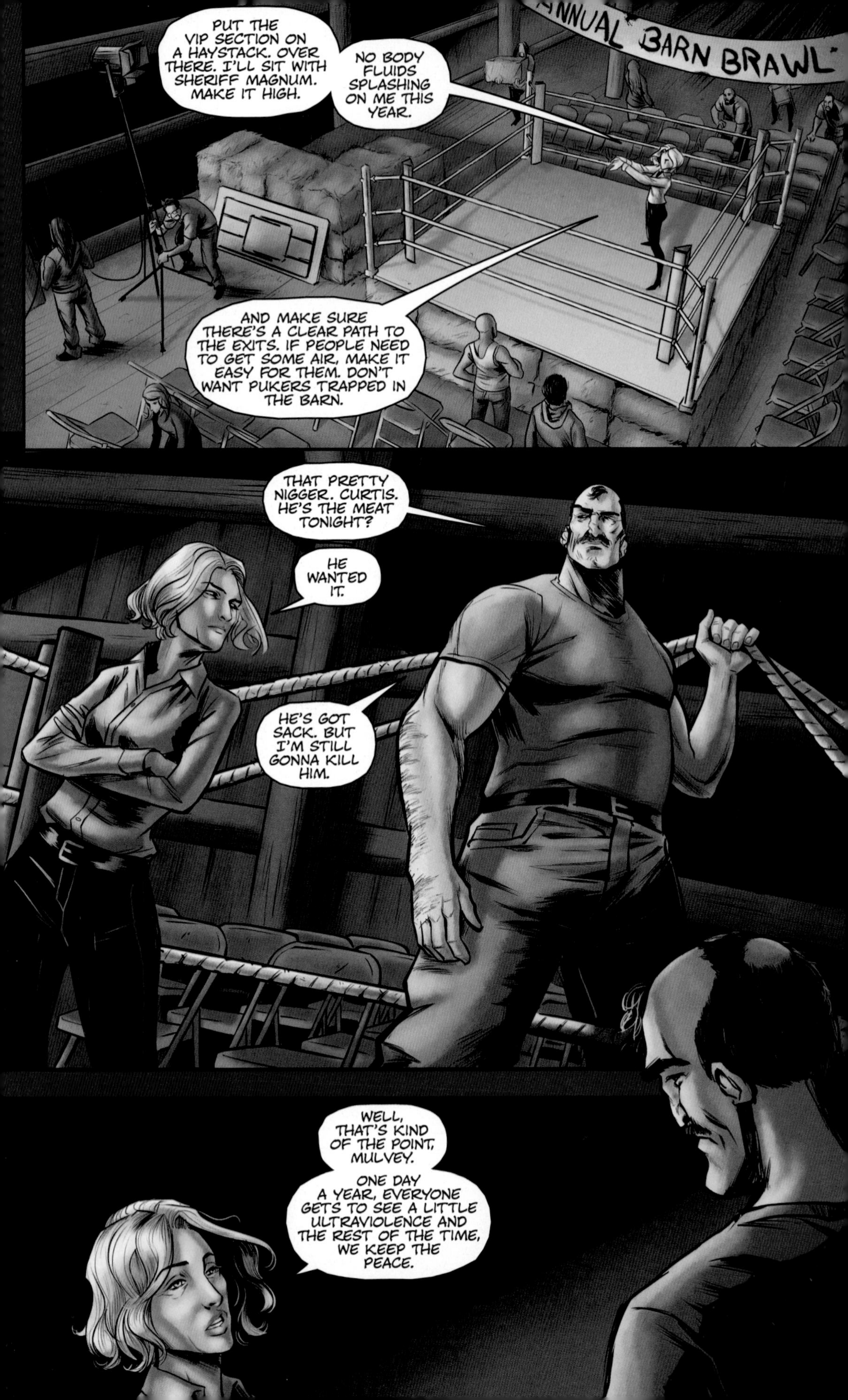

ANNUAL BARN BRAWL
PUT THE VIP SECTION ON A HAYSTACK. OVER THERE. I'LL SIT WITH SHERIFF MAGNUM. MAKE IT HIGH.
NO BODY FLUIDS SPLASHING ON ME THIS YEAR.
AND MAKE SURE THERE'S A CLEAR PATH TO THE EXITS. IF PEOPLE NEED TO GET SOME AIR, MAKE IT EASY FOR THEM. DON'T WANT PUKERS TRAPPED IN THE BARN.
THAT PRETTY NIGGER. CURTIS. HE'S THE MEAT TONIGHT?
HE WANTED IT.
HE'S GOT SACK. BUT I'M STILL GONNA KILL HIM.
WELL, THAT'S KIND OF THE POINT, MULVEY.
ONE DAY A YEAR, EVERYONE GETS TO SEE A LITTLE ULTRAVIOLENCE AND THE REST OF THE TIME, WE KEEP THE PEACE.

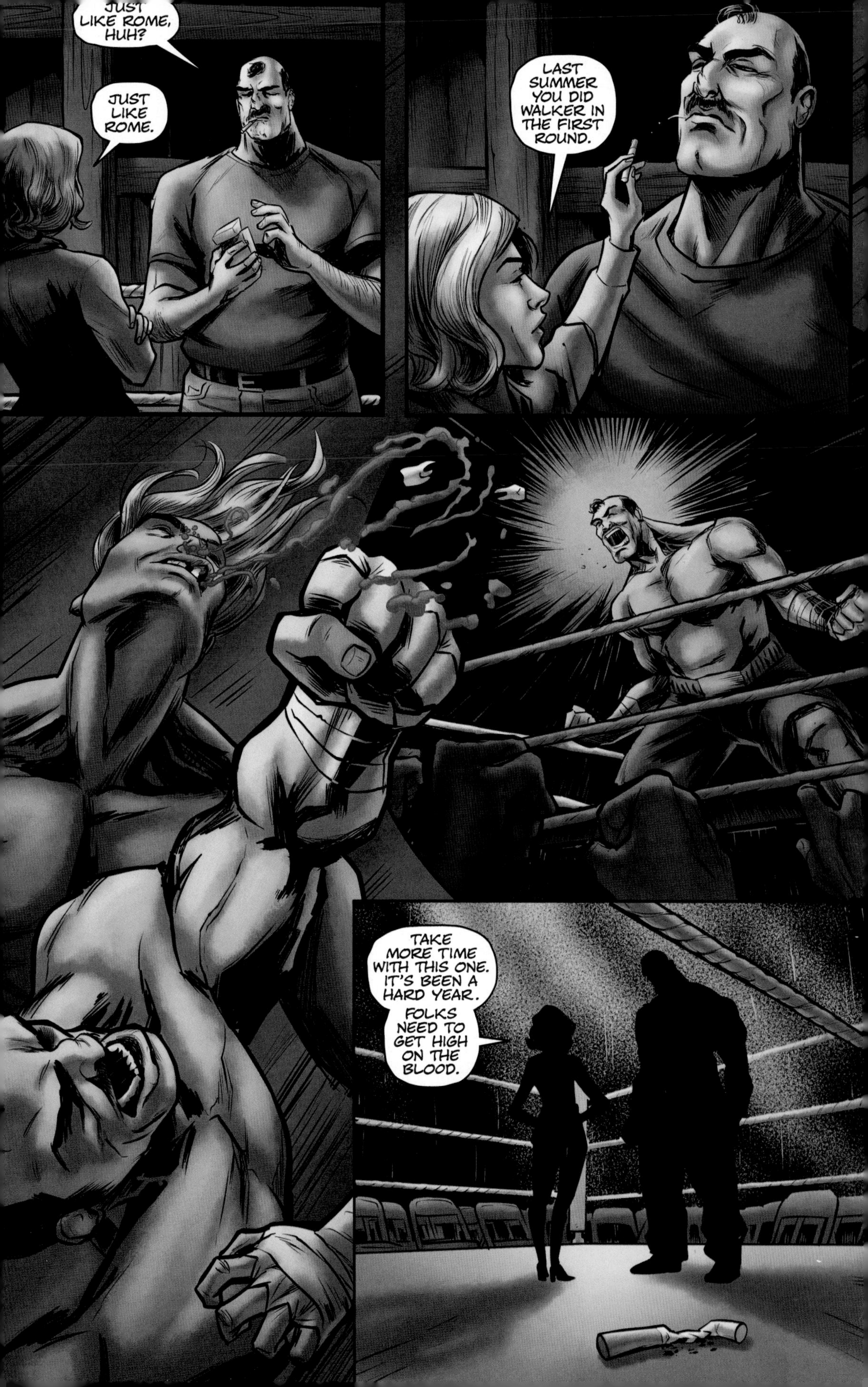
JUST LIKE ROME, HUH?
JUST LIKE ROME.
LAST SUMMER YOU DID WALKER IN THE FIRST ROUND.
TAKE MORE TIME WITH THIS ONE. IT'S BEEN A HARD YEAR.
FOLKS NEED TO GET HIGH ON THE BLOOD.

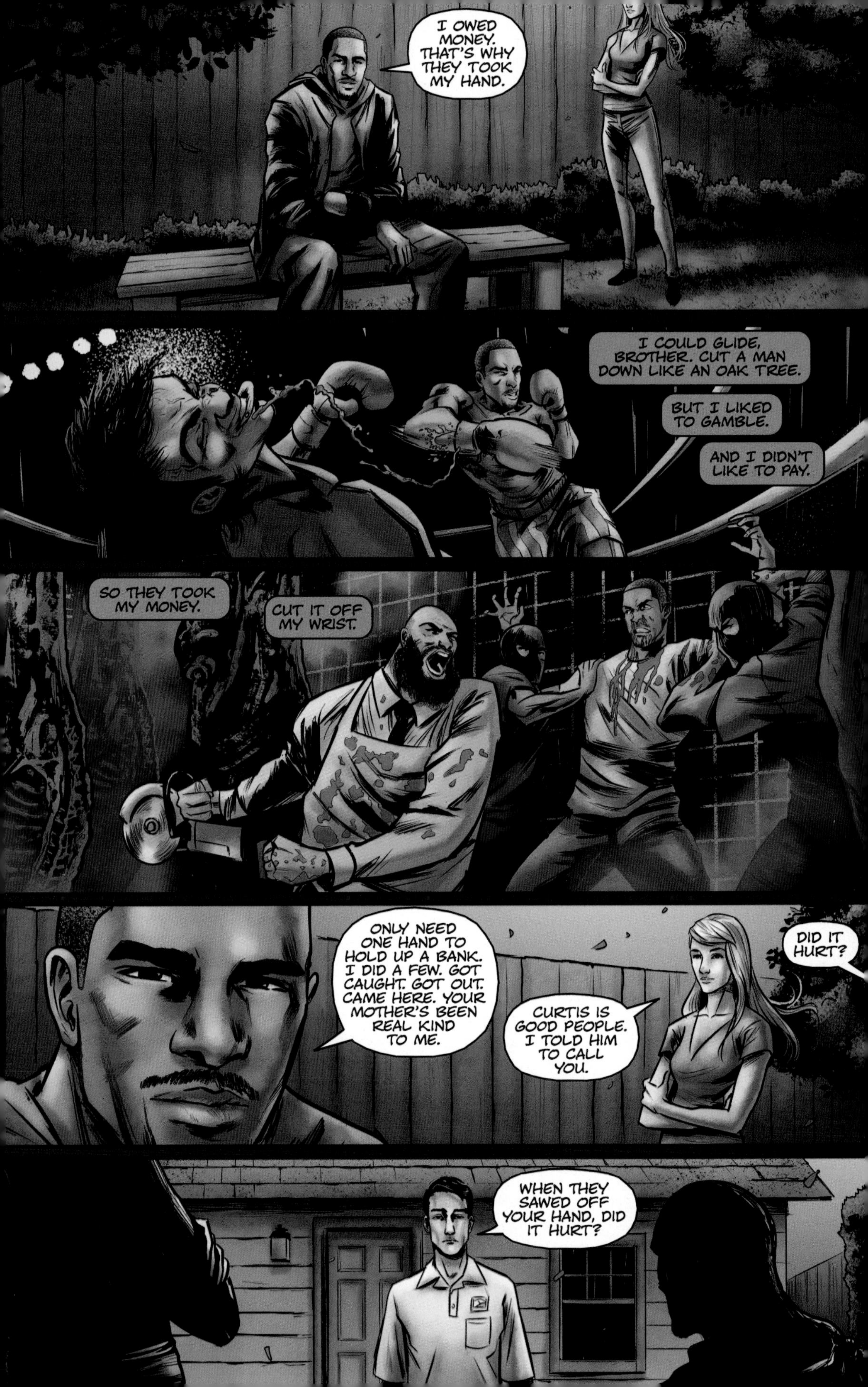
I OWED MONEY. THAT'S WHY THEY TOOK MY HAND.
I COULD GLIDE, BROTHER. CUT A MAN DOWN LIKE AN OAK TREE.
BUT I LIKED TO GAMBLE.
AND I DIDN'T LIKE TO PAY.
SO THEY TOOK MY MONEY.
CUT IT OFF MY WRIST.
ONLY NEED ONE HAND TO HOLD UP A BANK. I DID A FEW. GOT CAUGHT. GOT OUT. CAME HERE. YOUR MOTHER'S BEEN REAL KIND TO ME.
CURTIS IS GOOD PEOPLE. I TOLD HIM TO CALL YOU.
DID IT HURT?
WHEN THEY SAWED OFF YOUR HAND, DID IT HURT?

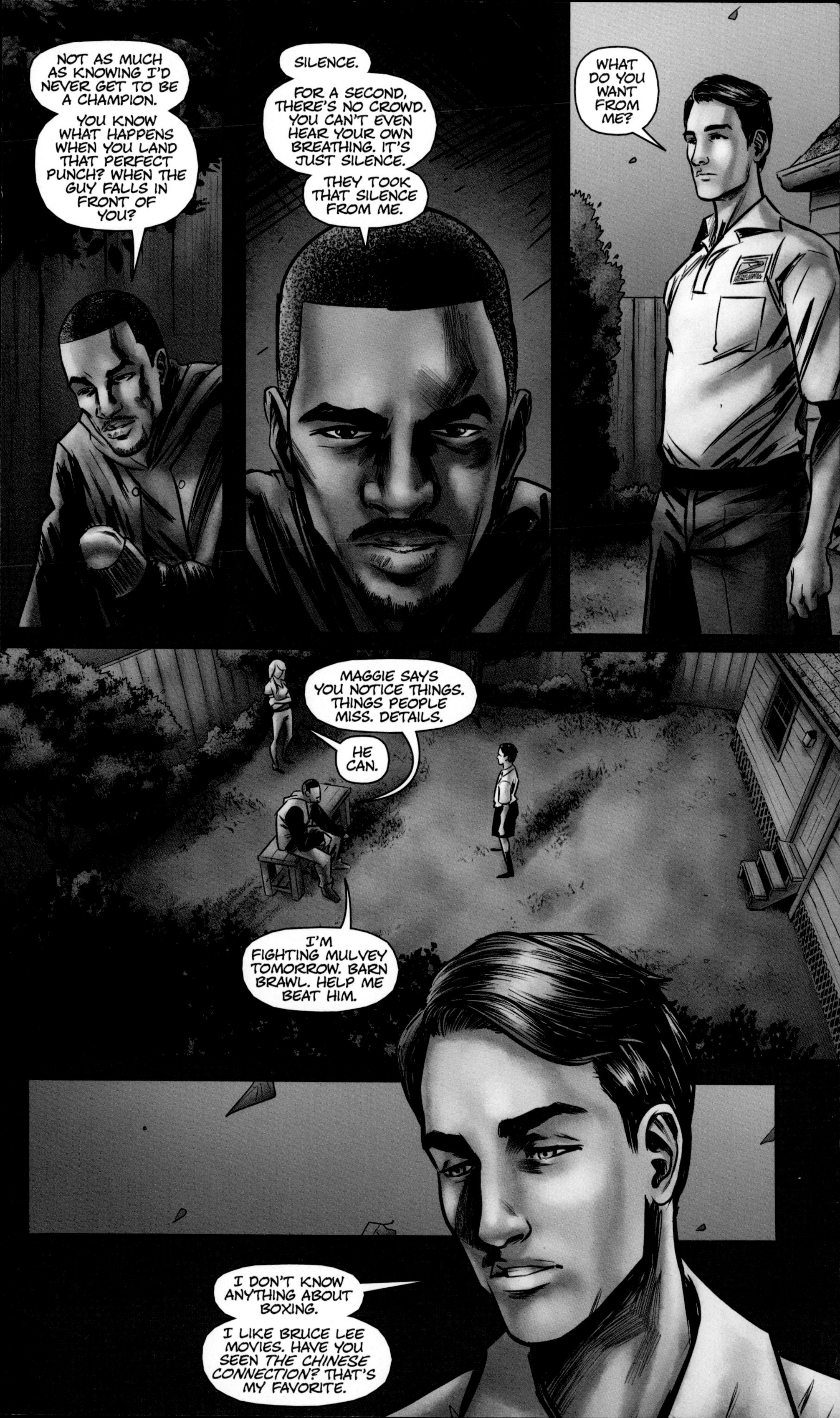
NOT AS MUCH AS KNOWING I'D NEVER GET TO BE A CHAMPION.
YOU KNOW WHAT HAPPENS WHEN YOU LAND THAT PERFECT PUNCH? WHEN THE GUY FALLS IN FRONT OF YOU?
SILENCE.
FOR A SECOND, THERE'S NO CROWD. YOU CAN'T EVEN HEAR YOUR OWN BREATHING. IT'S JUST SILENCE.
THEY TOOK THAT SILENCE FROM ME.
WHAT DO YOU WANT FROM ME?
MAGGIE SAYS YOU NOTICE THINGS. THINGS PEOPLE MISS. DETAILS.
HE CAN.
I'M FIGHTING MULVEY TOMORROW. BARN BRAWL. HELP ME BEAT HIM.
I DON'T KNOW ANYTHING ABOUT BOXING.
I LIKE BRUCE LEE MOVIES. HAVE YOU SEEN *THE CHINESE CONNECTION*? THAT'S MY FAVORITE.

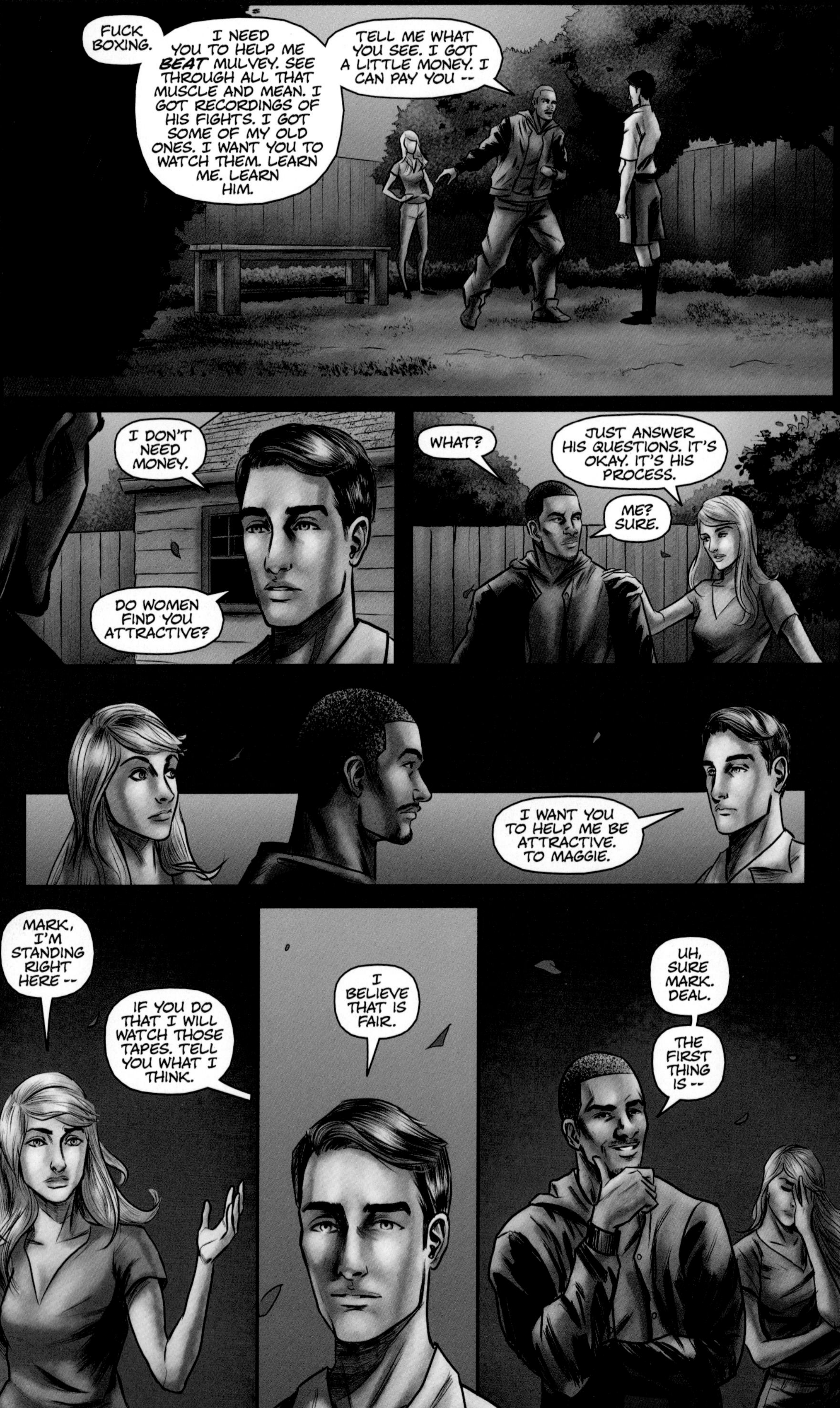
FUCK BOXING.
I NEED YOU TO HELP ME BEAT MULVEY. SEE THROUGH ALL THAT MUSCLE AND MEAN. I GOT RECORDINGS OF HIS FIGHTS. I GOT SOME OF MY OLD ONES. I WANT YOU TO WATCH THEM. LEARN ME. LEARN HIM.
TELL ME WHAT YOU SEE. I GOT A LITTLE MONEY. I CAN PAY YOU --
I DON'T NEED MONEY.
DO WOMEN FIND YOU ATTRACTIVE?
WHAT?
JUST ANSWER HIS QUESTIONS. IT'S OKAY. IT'S HIS PROCESS.
ME? SURE.
I WANT YOU TO HELP ME BE ATTRACTIVE. TO MAGGIE.
MARK, I'M STANDING RIGHT HERE --
IF YOU DO THAT I WILL WATCH THOSE TAPES. TELL YOU WHAT I THINK.
I BELIEVE THAT IS FAIR.
UH, SURE MARK. DEAL.
THE FIRST THING IS --

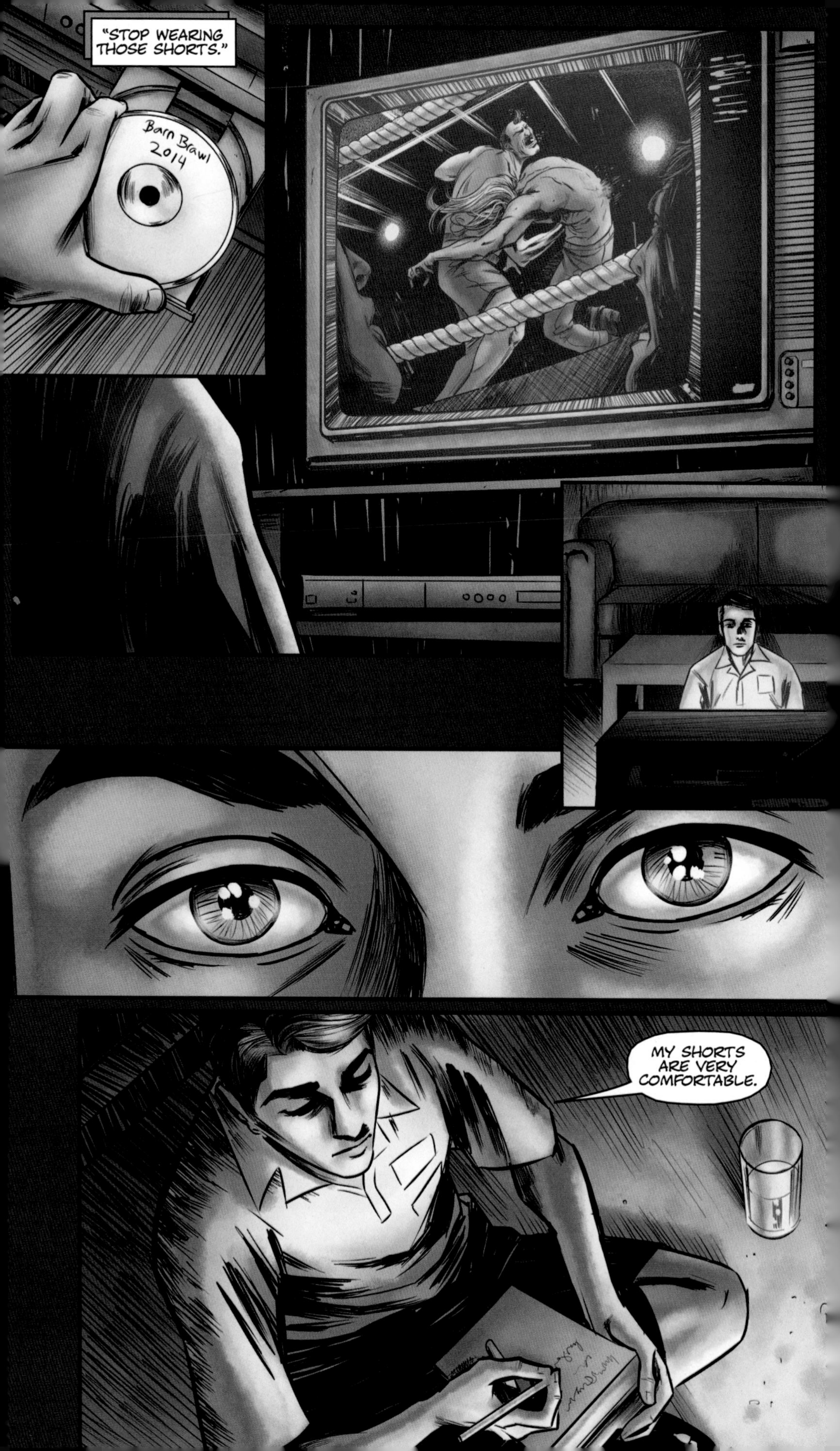
"STOP WEARING THOSE SHORTS."
Barn Brawl 2014
MY SHORTS ARE VERY COMFORTABLE.

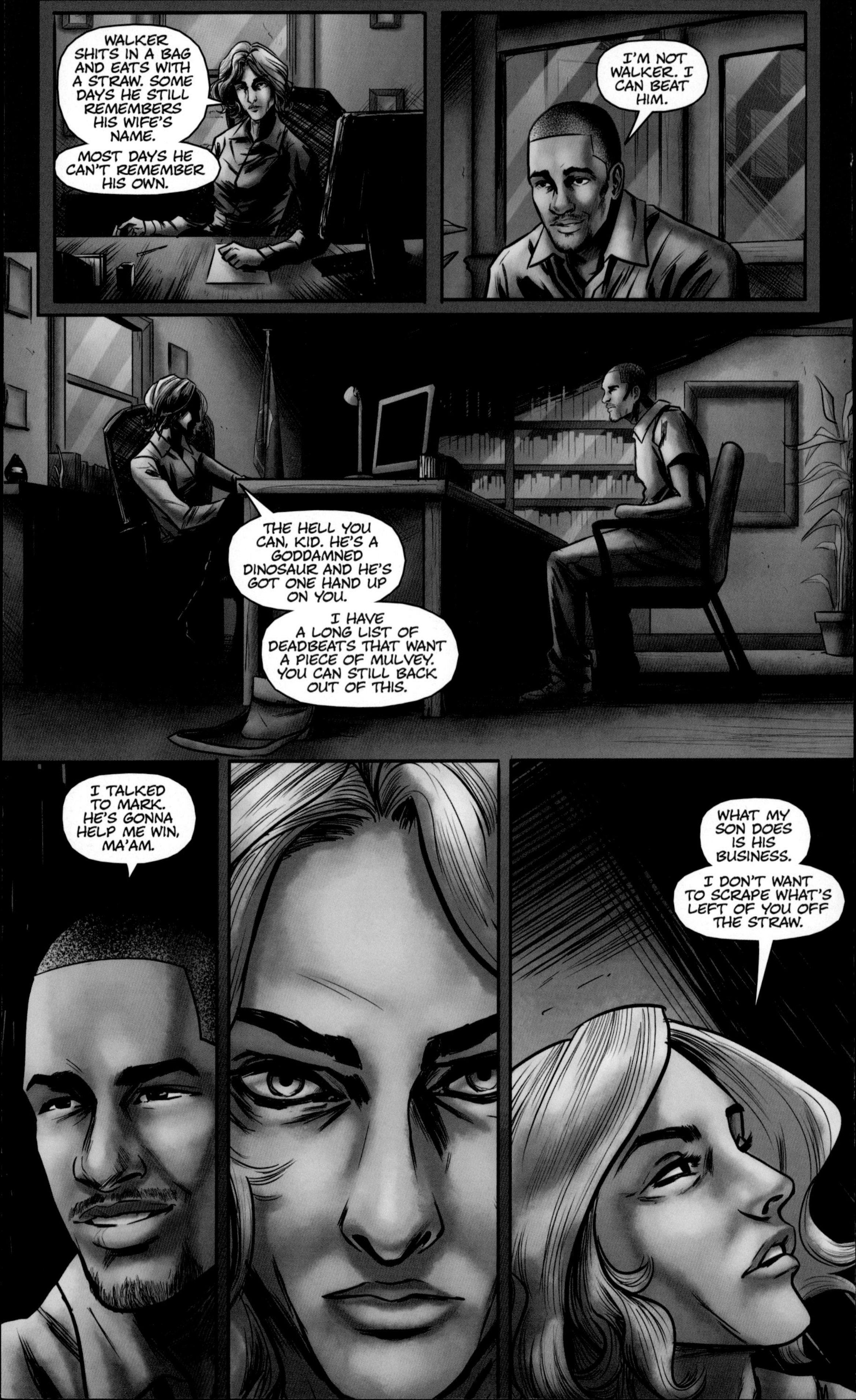
WALKER SHITS IN A BAG AND EATS WITH A STRAW. SOME DAYS HE STILL REMEMBERS HIS WIFE'S NAME.
MOST DAYS HE CAN'T REMEMBER HIS OWN.
I'M NOT WALKER. I CAN BEAT HIM.
THE HELL YOU CAN, KID. HE'S A GODDAMNED DINOSAUR AND HE'S GOT ONE HAND UP ON YOU.
I HAVE A LONG LIST OF DEADBEATS THAT WANT A PIECE OF MULVEY. YOU CAN STILL BACK OUT OF THIS.
I TALKED TO MARK. HE'S GONNA HELP ME WIN, MA'AM.
WHAT MY SON DOES IS HIS BUSINESS.
I DON'T WANT TO SCRAPE WHAT'S LEFT OF YOU OFF THE STRAW.

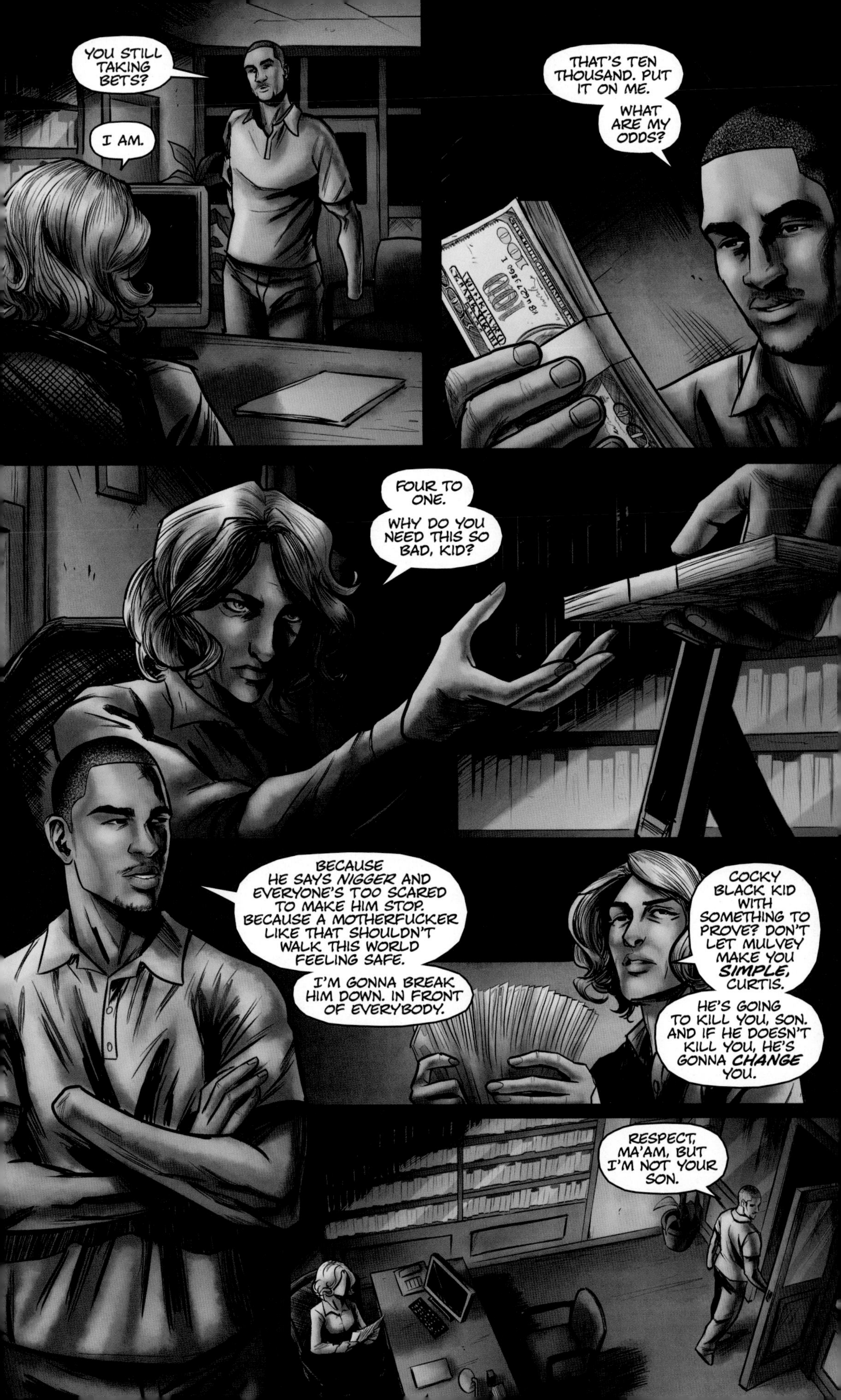
YOU STILL TAKING BETS?
I AM.
THAT'S TEN THOUSAND. PUT IT ON ME.
WHAT ARE MY ODDS?
FOUR TO ONE.
WHY DO YOU NEED THIS SO BAD, KID?
BECAUSE HE SAYS *NIGGER* AND EVERYONE'S TOO SCARED TO MAKE HIM STOP. BECAUSE A MOTHERFUCKER LIKE THAT SHOULDN'T WALK THIS WORLD FEELING SAFE.
I'M GONNA BREAK HIM DOWN. IN FRONT OF EVERYBODY.
COCKY BLACK KID WITH SOMETHING TO PROVE? DON'T LET MULVEY MAKE YOU ***SIMPLE,*** CURTIS.
HE'S GOING TO KILL YOU, SON. AND IF HE DOESN'T KILL YOU, HE'S GONNA ***CHANGE*** YOU.
RESPECT, MA'AM, BUT I'M NOT YOUR SON.

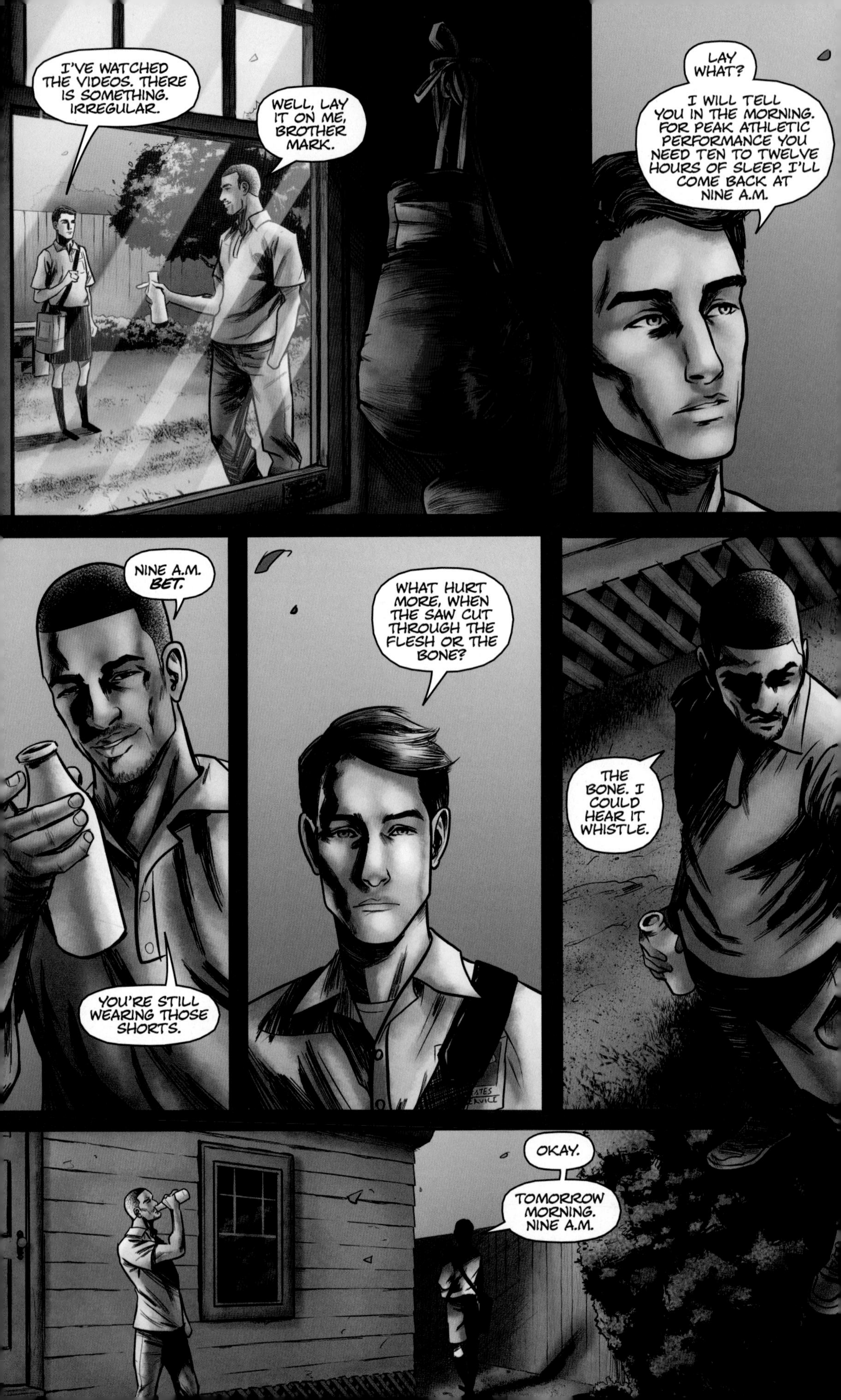
I'VE WATCHED THE VIDEOS. THERE IS SOMETHING. IRREGULAR.
WELL, LAY IT ON ME, BROTHER MARK.
LAY WHAT?
I WILL TELL YOU IN THE MORNING. FOR PEAK ATHLETIC PERFORMANCE YOU NEED TEN TO TWELVE HOURS OF SLEEP. I'LL COME BACK AT NINE A.M.
NINE A.M. *BET.*
YOU'RE STILL WEARING THOSE SHORTS.
WHAT HURT MORE, WHEN THE SAW CUT THROUGH THE FLESH OR THE BONE?
THE BONE. I COULD HEAR IT WHISTLE.
OKAY.
TOMORROW MORNING. NINE A.M.

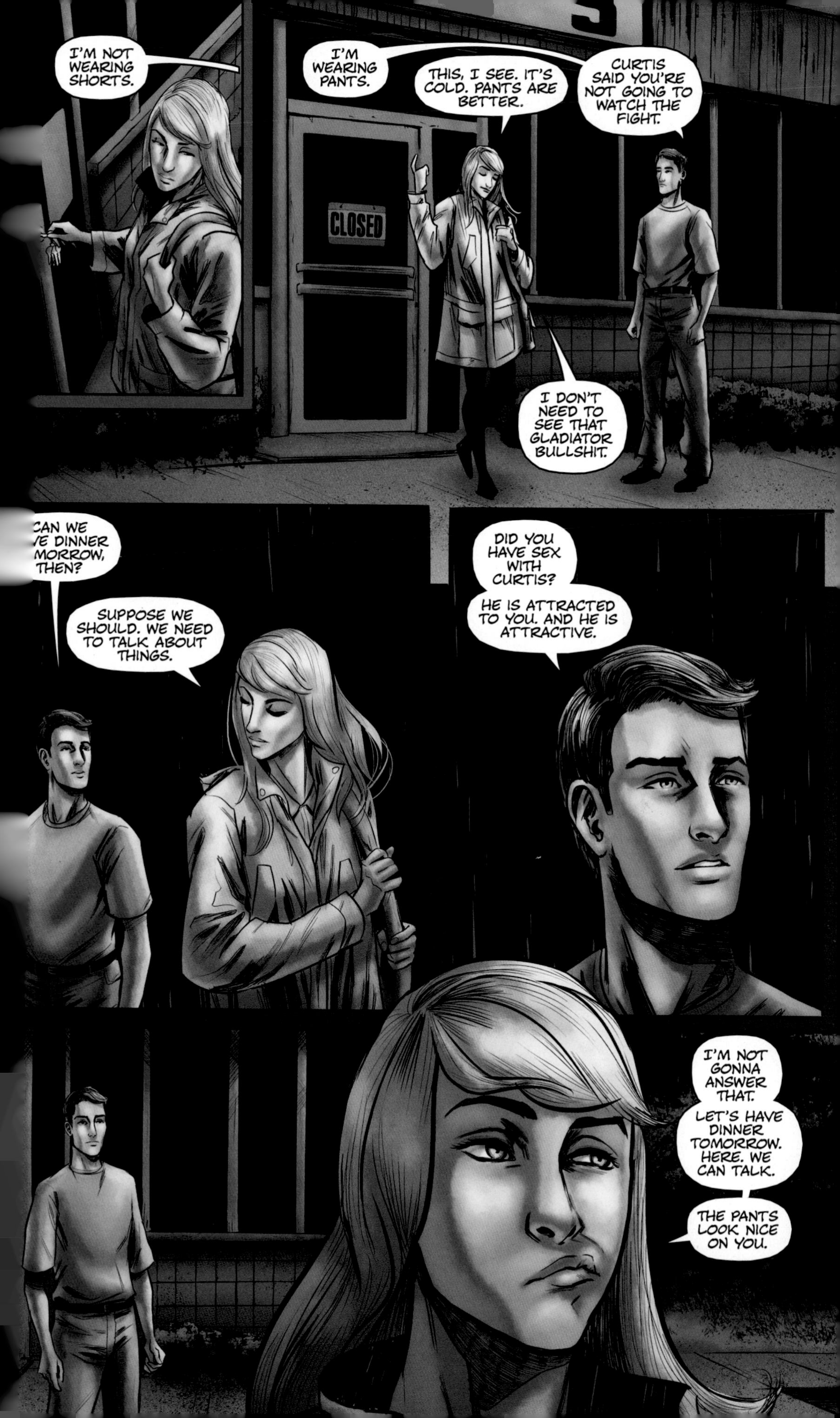
I'M NOT WEARING SHORTS.
I'M WEARING PANTS.
THIS, I SEE. IT'S COLD. PANTS ARE BETTER.
CURTIS SAID YOU'RE NOT GOING TO WATCH THE FIGHT.
CLOSED
I DON'T NEED TO SEE THAT GLADIATOR BULLSHIT.
CAN WE VE DINNER MORROW, THEN?
SUPPOSE WE SHOULD. WE NEED TO TALK ABOUT THINGS.
DID YOU HAVE SEX WITH CURTIS?
HE IS ATTRACTED TO YOU. AND HE IS ATTRACTIVE.
I'M NOT GONNA ANSWER THAT.
LET'S HAVE DINNER TOMORROW. HERE. WE CAN TALK.
THE PANTS LOOK NICE ON YOU.

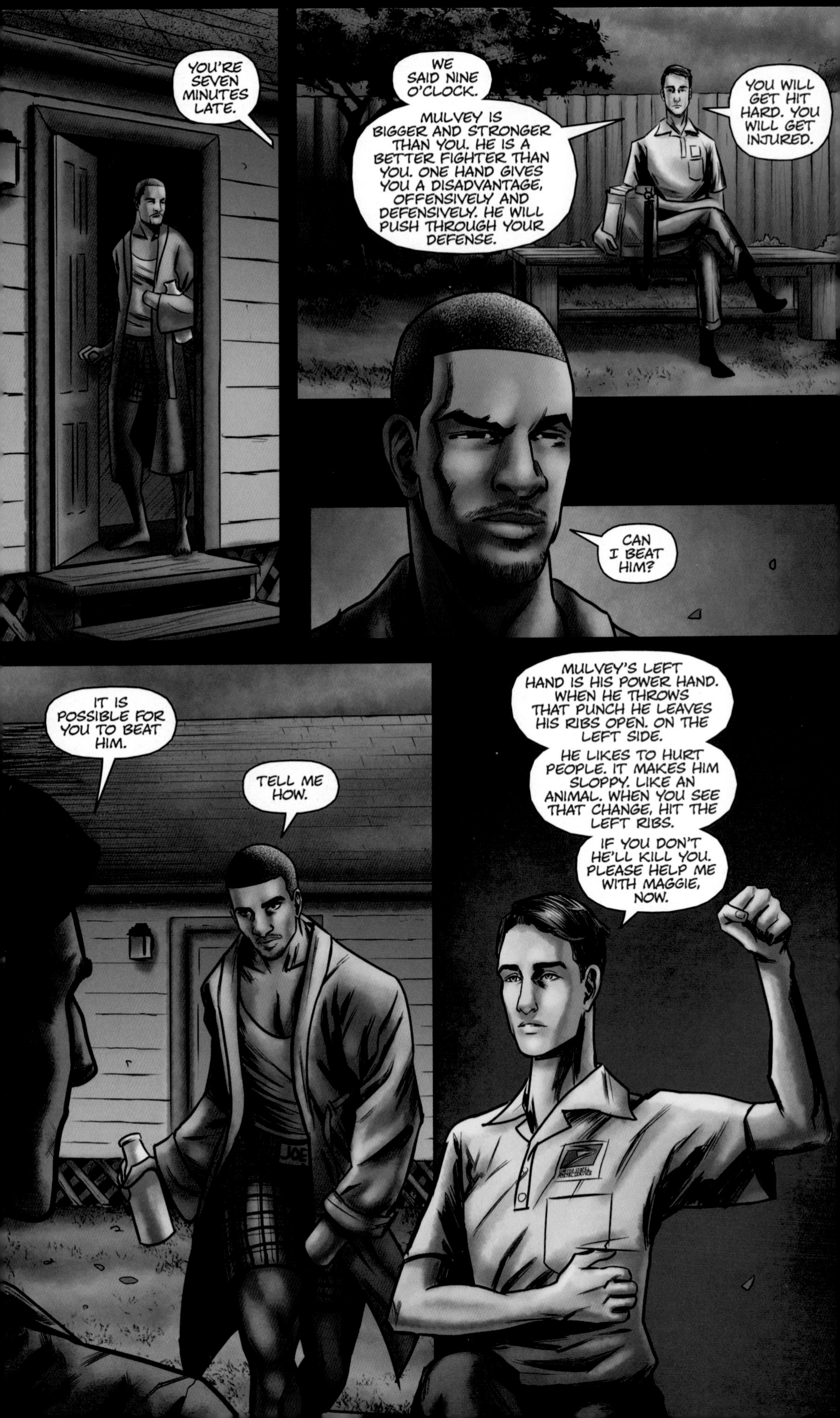
YOU'RE SEVEN MINUTES LATE.
WE SAID NINE O'CLOCK.
MULVEY IS BIGGER AND STRONGER THAN YOU. HE IS A BETTER FIGHTER THAN YOU. ONE HAND GIVES YOU A DISADVANTAGE, OFFENSIVELY AND DEFENSIVELY. HE WILL PUSH THROUGH YOUR DEFENSE.
YOU WILL GET HIT HARD. YOU WILL GET INJURED.
CAN I BEAT HIM?
IT IS POSSIBLE FOR YOU TO BEAT HIM.
TELL ME HOW.
MULVEY'S LEFT HAND IS HIS POWER HAND. WHEN HE THROWS THAT PUNCH HE LEAVES HIS RIBS OPEN. ON THE LEFT SIDE.
HE LIKES TO HURT PEOPLE. IT MAKES HIM SLOPPY. LIKE AN ANIMAL. WHEN YOU SEE THAT CHANGE, HIT THE LEFT RIBS.
IF YOU DON'T HE'LL KILL YOU. PLEASE HELP ME WITH MAGGIE, NOW.

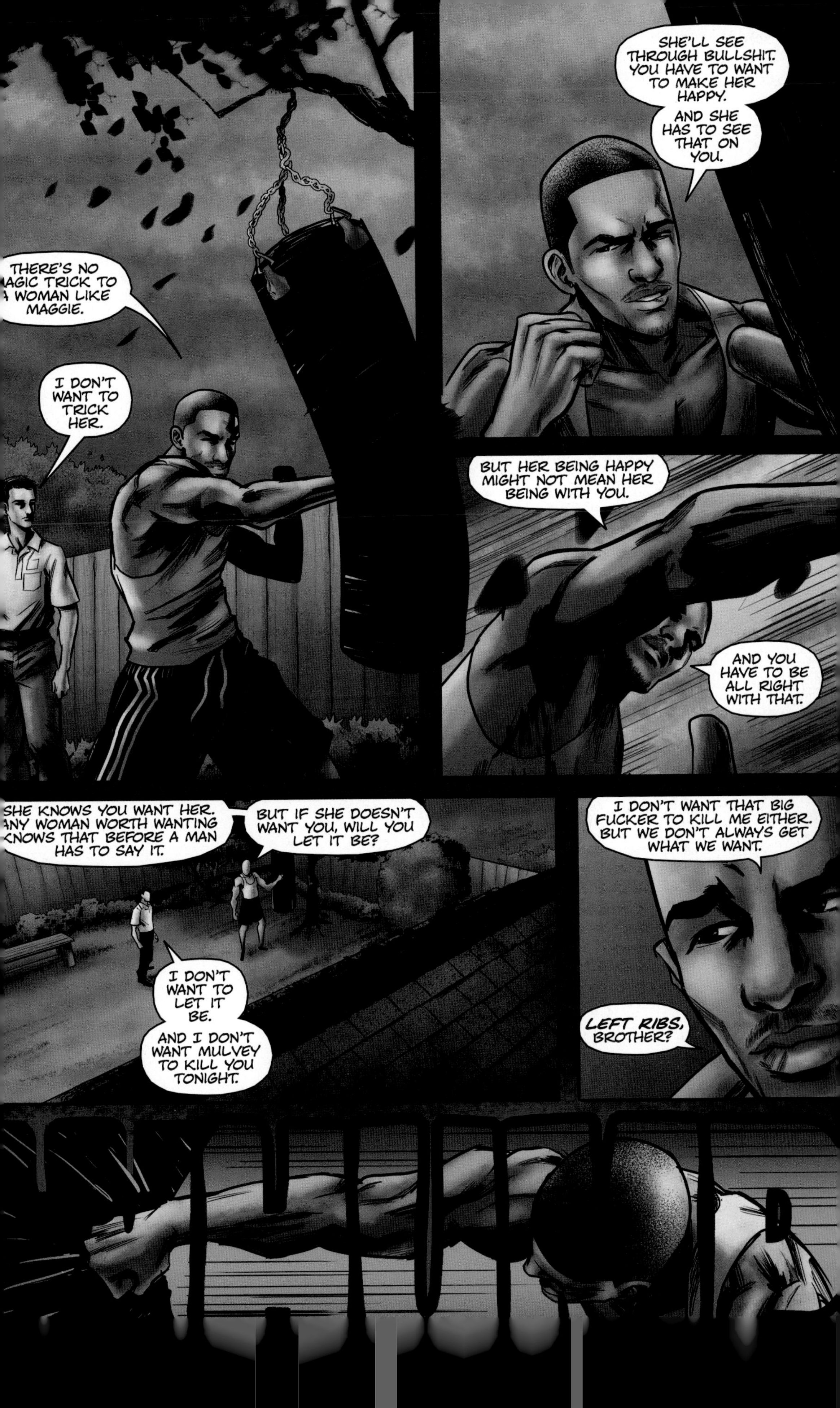

THERE'S NO MAGIC TRICK TO A WOMAN LIKE MAGGIE.
I DON'T WANT TO TRICK HER.
SHE'LL SEE THROUGH BULLSHIT. YOU HAVE TO WANT TO MAKE HER HAPPY.
AND SHE HAS TO SEE THAT ON YOU.
BUT HER BEING HAPPY MIGHT NOT MEAN HER BEING WITH YOU.
AND YOU HAVE TO BE ALL RIGHT WITH THAT.
SHE KNOWS YOU WANT HER. ANY WOMAN WORTH WANTING KNOWS THAT BEFORE A MAN HAS TO SAY IT.
BUT IF SHE DOESN'T WANT YOU, WILL YOU LET IT BE?
I DON'T WANT TO LET IT BE.
AND I DON'T WANT MULVEY TO KILL YOU TONIGHT.
I DON'T WANT THAT BIG FUCKER TO KILL ME EITHER. BUT WE DON'T ALWAYS GET WHAT WE WANT.
LEFT RIBS, BROTHER?

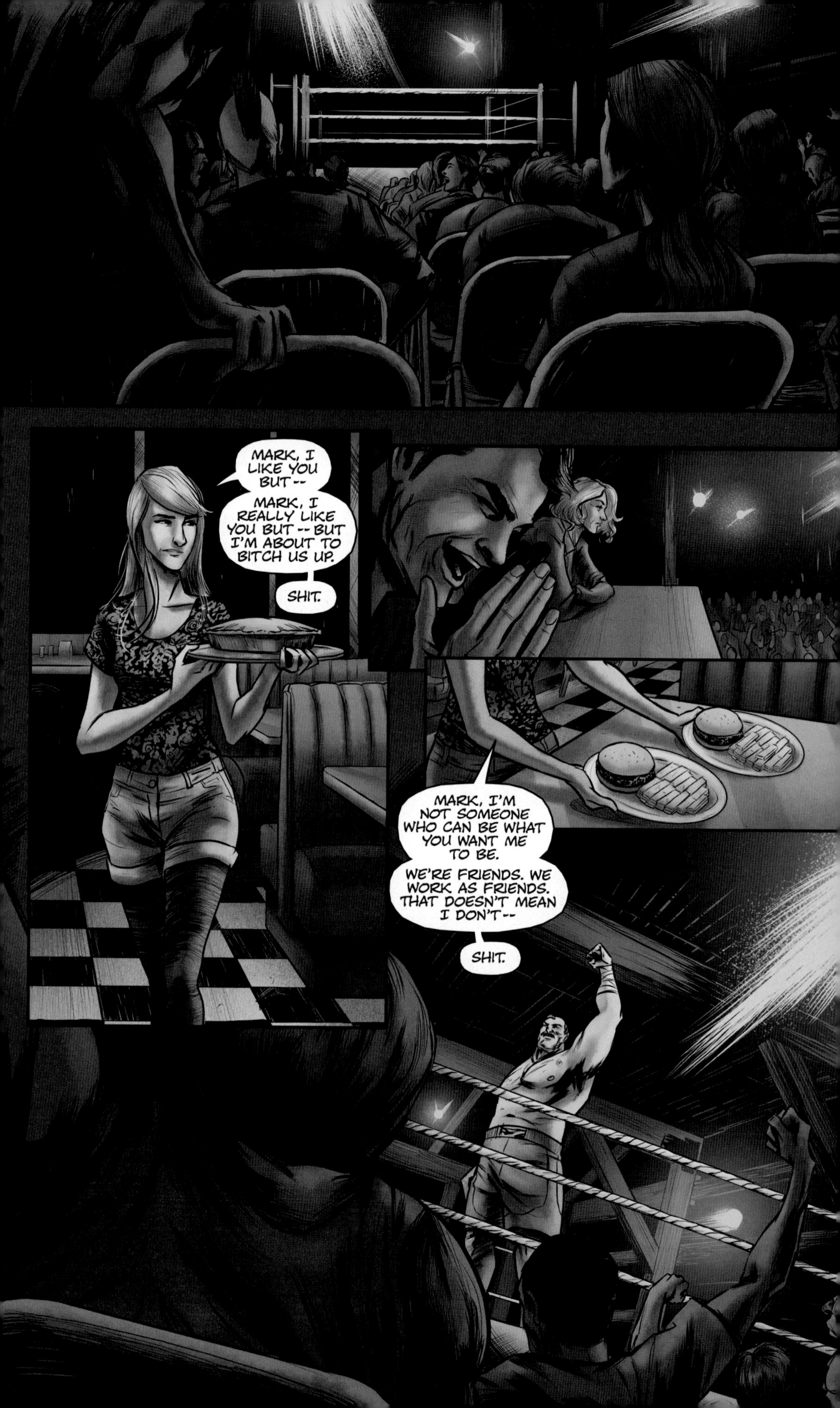
MARK, I LIKE YOU BUT --
MARK, I REALLY LIKE YOU BUT -- BUT I'M ABOUT TO BITCH US UP.
SHIT.
MARK, I'M NOT SOMEONE WHO CAN BE WHAT YOU WANT ME TO BE.
WE'RE FRIENDS. WE WORK AS FRIENDS. THAT DOESN'T MEAN I DON'T --
SHIT.

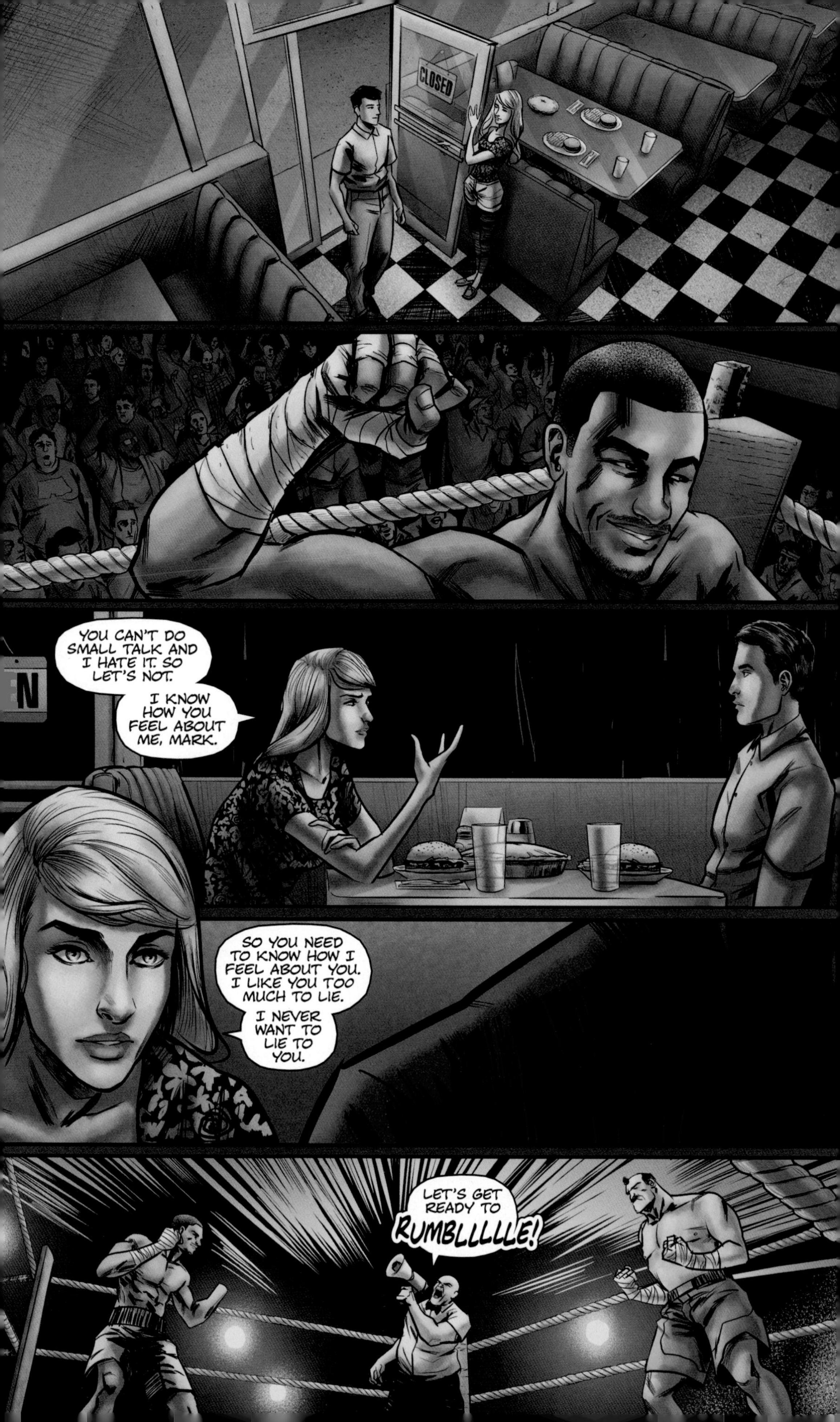
CLOSED
YOU CAN'T DO SMALL TALK AND I HATE IT. SO LET'S NOT.
I KNOW HOW YOU FEEL ABOUT ME, MARK.
SO YOU NEED TO KNOW HOW I FEEL ABOUT YOU. I LIKE YOU TOO MUCH TO LIE.
I NEVER WANT TO LIE TO YOU.
LET'S GET READY TO RUMBLLLLLE!

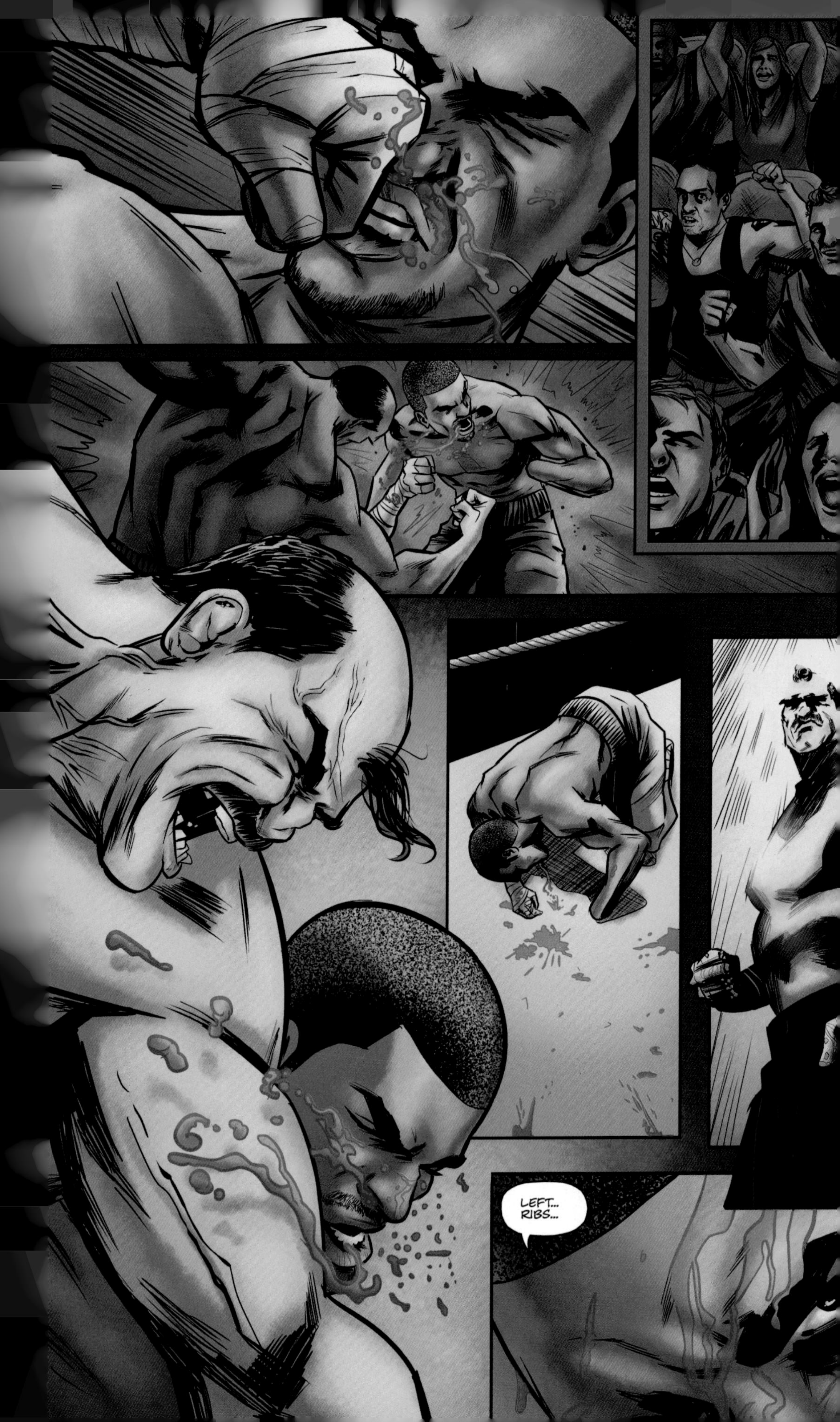
LEFT... RIBS...

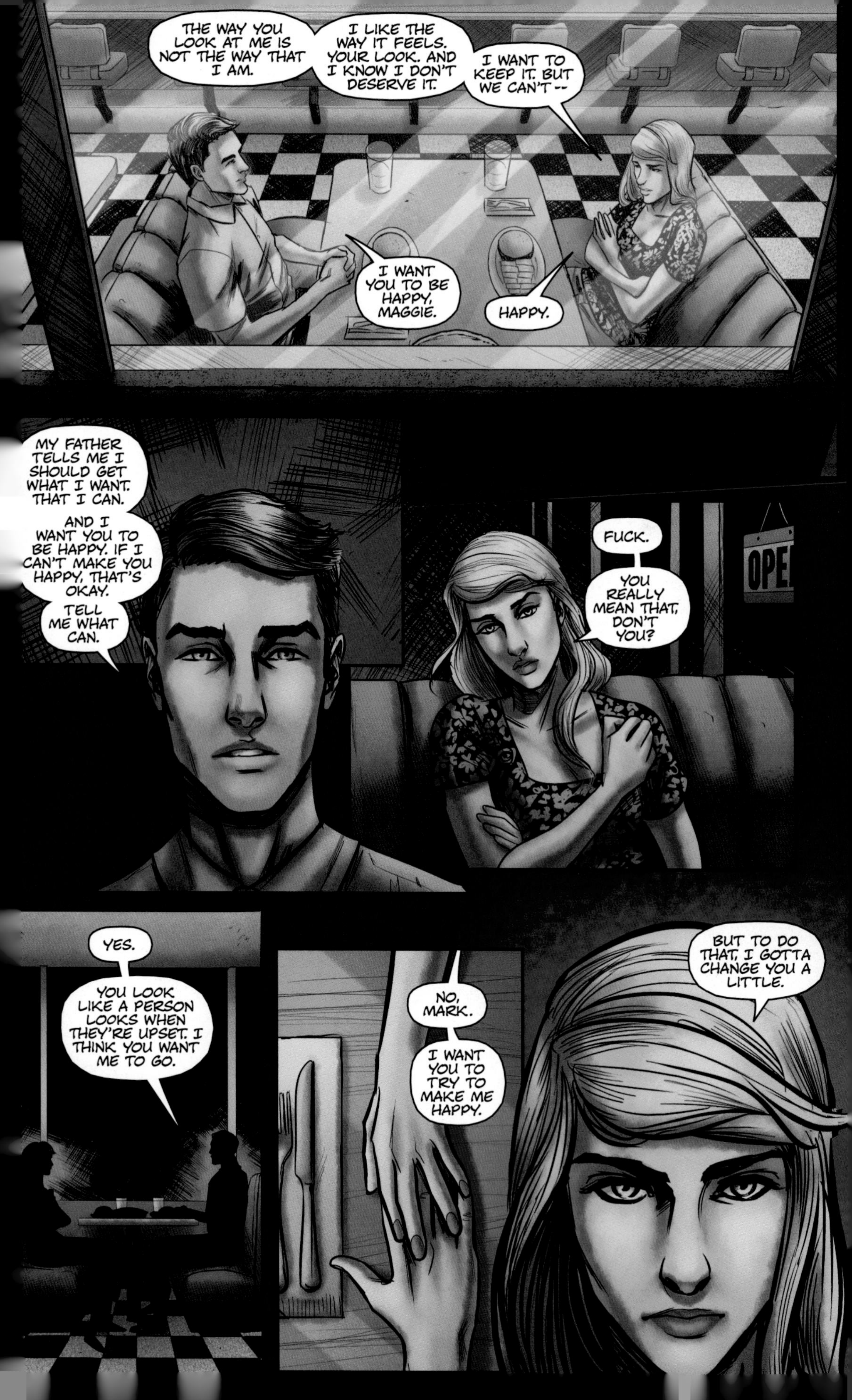
THE WAY YOU LOOK AT ME IS NOT THE WAY THAT I AM.
I LIKE THE WAY IT FEELS. YOUR LOOK. AND I KNOW I DON'T DESERVE IT.
I WANT TO KEEP IT. BUT WE CAN'T --
I WANT YOU TO BE HAPPY, MAGGIE.
HAPPY.
MY FATHER TELLS ME I SHOULD GET WHAT I WANT. THAT I CAN.
AND I WANT YOU TO BE HAPPY. IF I CAN'T MAKE YOU HAPPY, THAT'S OKAY.
TELL ME WHAT CAN.
FUCK.
YOU REALLY MEAN THAT, DON'T YOU?
OPE
YES.
YOU LOOK LIKE A PERSON LOOKS WHEN THEY'RE UPSET. I THINK YOU WANT ME TO GO.
NO, MARK.
I WANT YOU TO TRY TO MAKE ME HAPPY.
BUT TO DO THAT, I GOTTA CHANGE YOU A LITTLE.

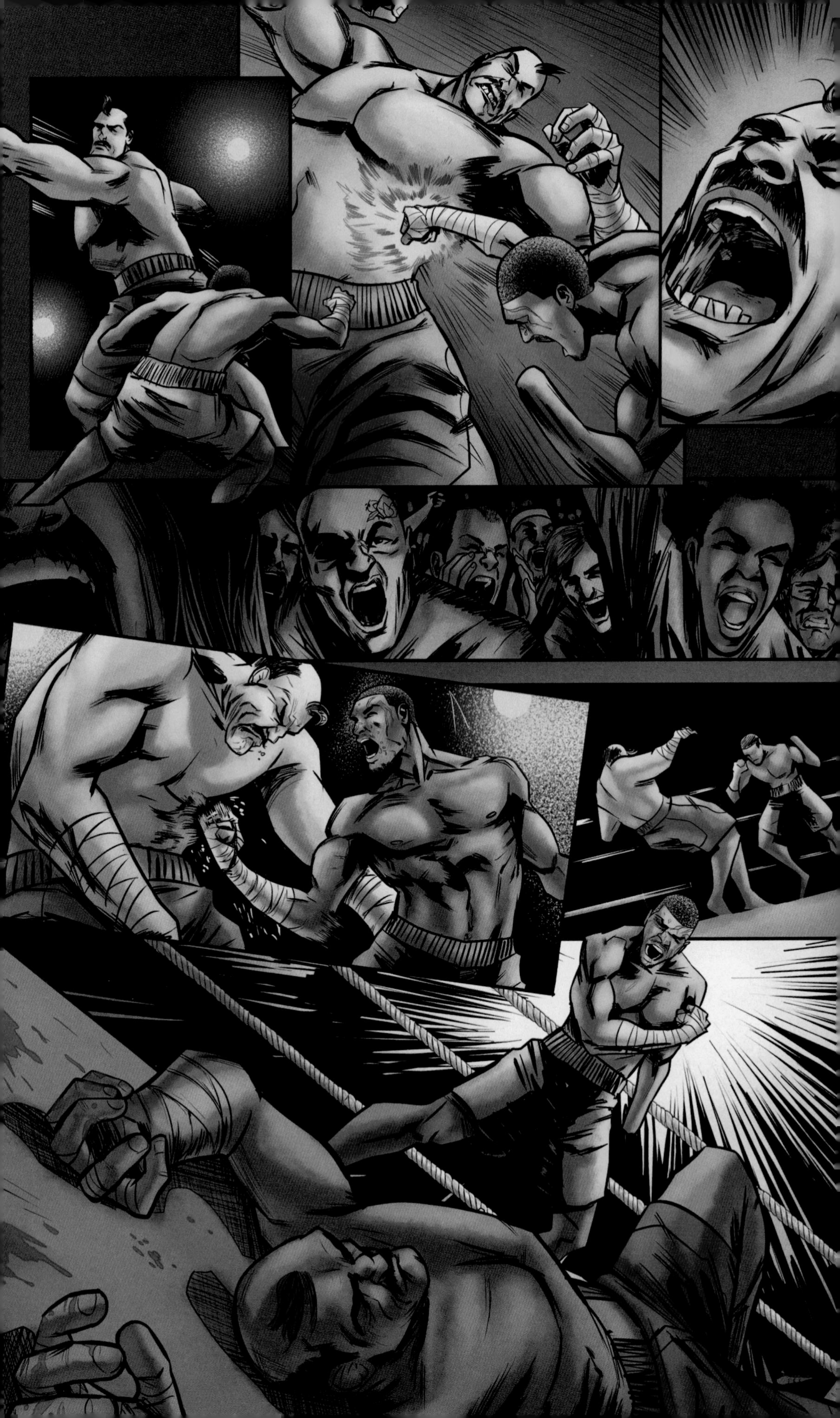

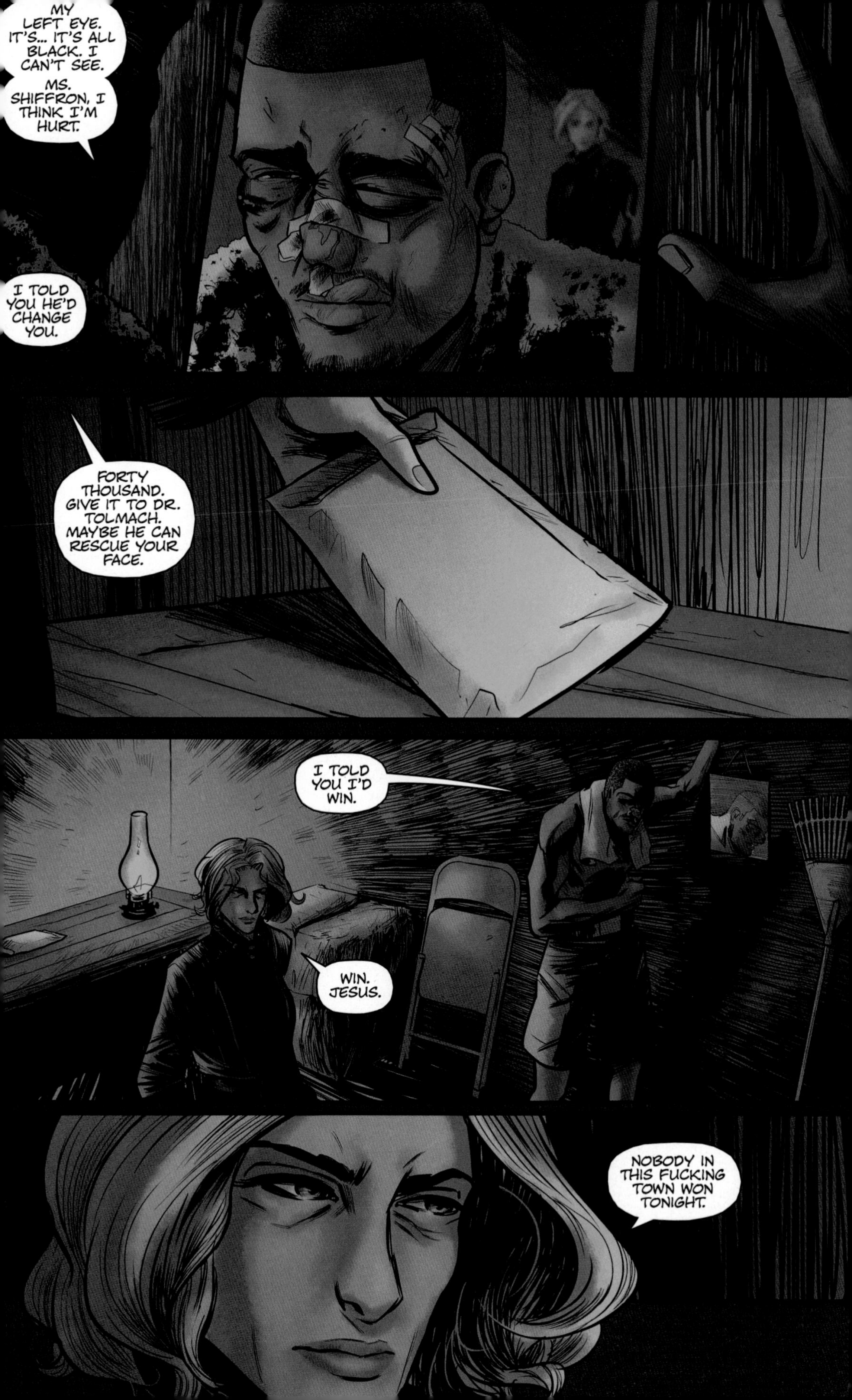
MY LEFT EYE. IT'S... IT'S ALL BLACK. I CAN'T SEE.
MS. SHIFFRON, I THINK I'M HURT.
I TOLD YOU HE'D CHANGE YOU.
FORTY THOUSAND. GIVE IT TO DR. TOLMACH. MAYBE HE CAN RESCUE YOUR FACE.
I TOLD YOU I'D WIN.
WIN. JESUS.
NOBODY IN THIS FUCKING TOWN WON TONIGHT.

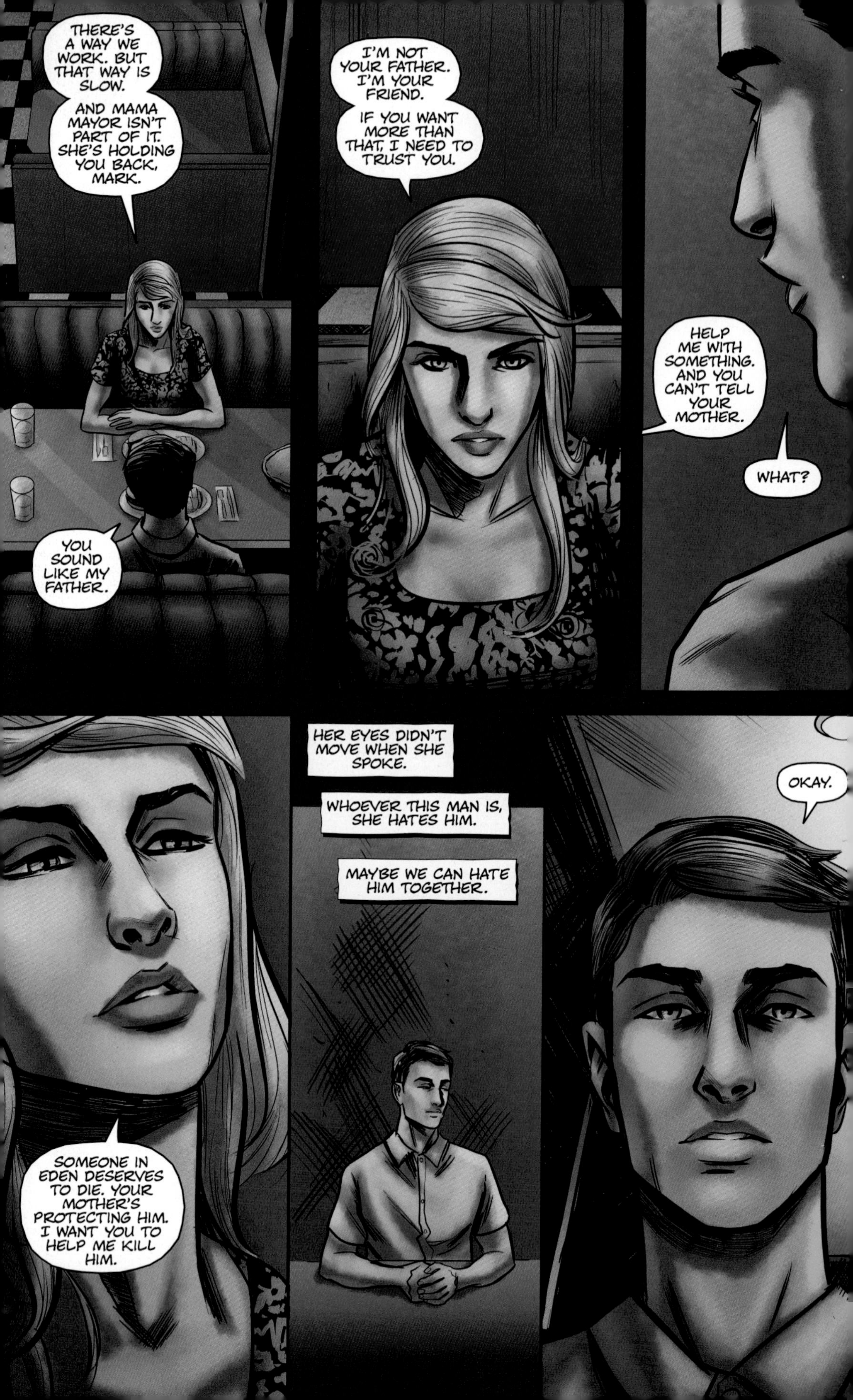
THERE'S A WAY WE WORK. BUT THAT WAY IS SLOW.
AND MAMA MAYOR ISN'T PART OF IT. SHE'S HOLDING YOU BACK, MARK.
YOU SOUND LIKE MY FATHER.
I'M NOT YOUR FATHER. I'M YOUR FRIEND.
IF YOU WANT MORE THAN THAT, I NEED TO TRUST YOU.
HELP ME WITH SOMETHING. AND YOU CAN'T TELL YOUR MOTHER.
WHAT?
SOMEONE IN EDEN DESERVES TO DIE. YOUR MOTHER'S PROTECTING HIM. I WANT YOU TO HELP ME KILL HIM.
HER EYES DIDN'T MOVE WHEN SHE SPOKE.
WHOEVER THIS MAN IS, SHE HATES HIM.
MAYBE WE CAN HATE HIM TOGETHER.
OKAY.

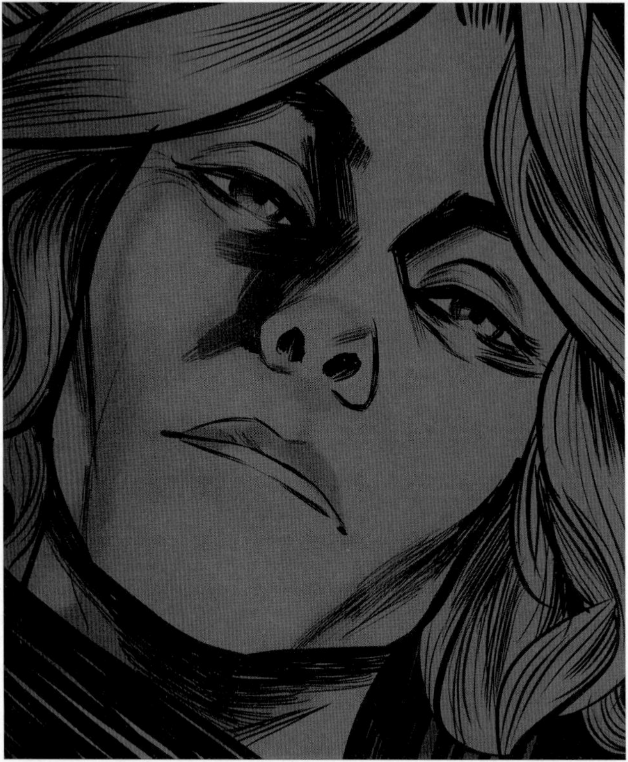

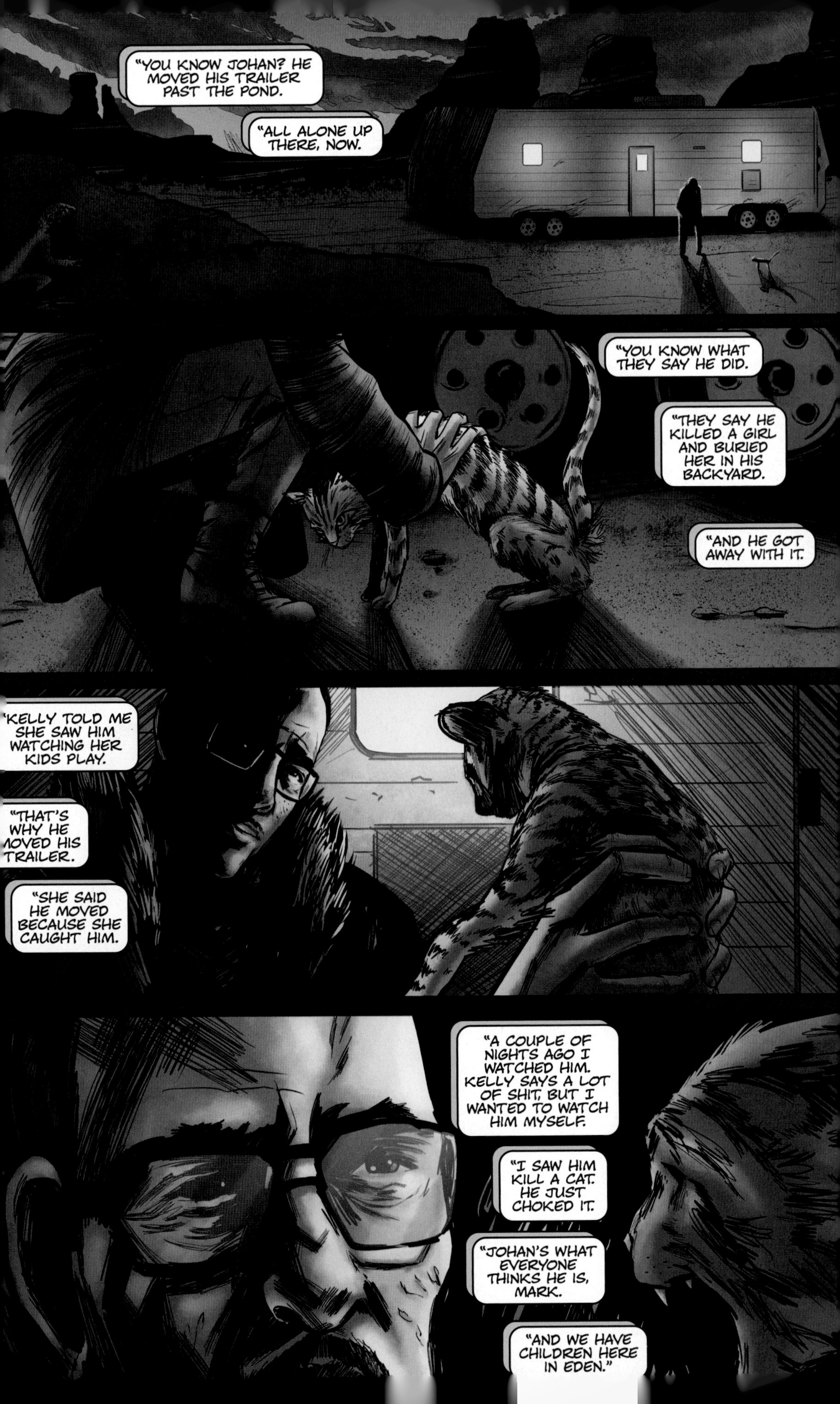
"YOU KNOW JOHAN? HE MOVED HIS TRAILER PAST THE POND.
"ALL ALONE UP THERE, NOW.
"YOU KNOW WHAT THEY SAY HE DID.
"THEY SAY HE KILLED A GIRL AND BURIED HER IN HIS BACKYARD.
"AND HE GOT AWAY WITH IT.
"KELLY TOLD ME SHE SAW HIM WATCHING HER KIDS PLAY.
"THAT'S WHY HE MOVED HIS TRAILER.
"SHE SAID HE MOVED BECAUSE SHE CAUGHT HIM.
"A COUPLE OF NIGHTS AGO I WATCHED HIM. KELLY SAYS A LOT OF SHIT, BUT I WANTED TO WATCH HIM MYSELF.
"I SAW HIM KILL A CAT. HE JUST CHOKED IT.
"JOHAN'S WHAT EVERYONE THINKS HE IS, MARK.
"AND WE HAVE CHILDREN HERE IN EDEN."

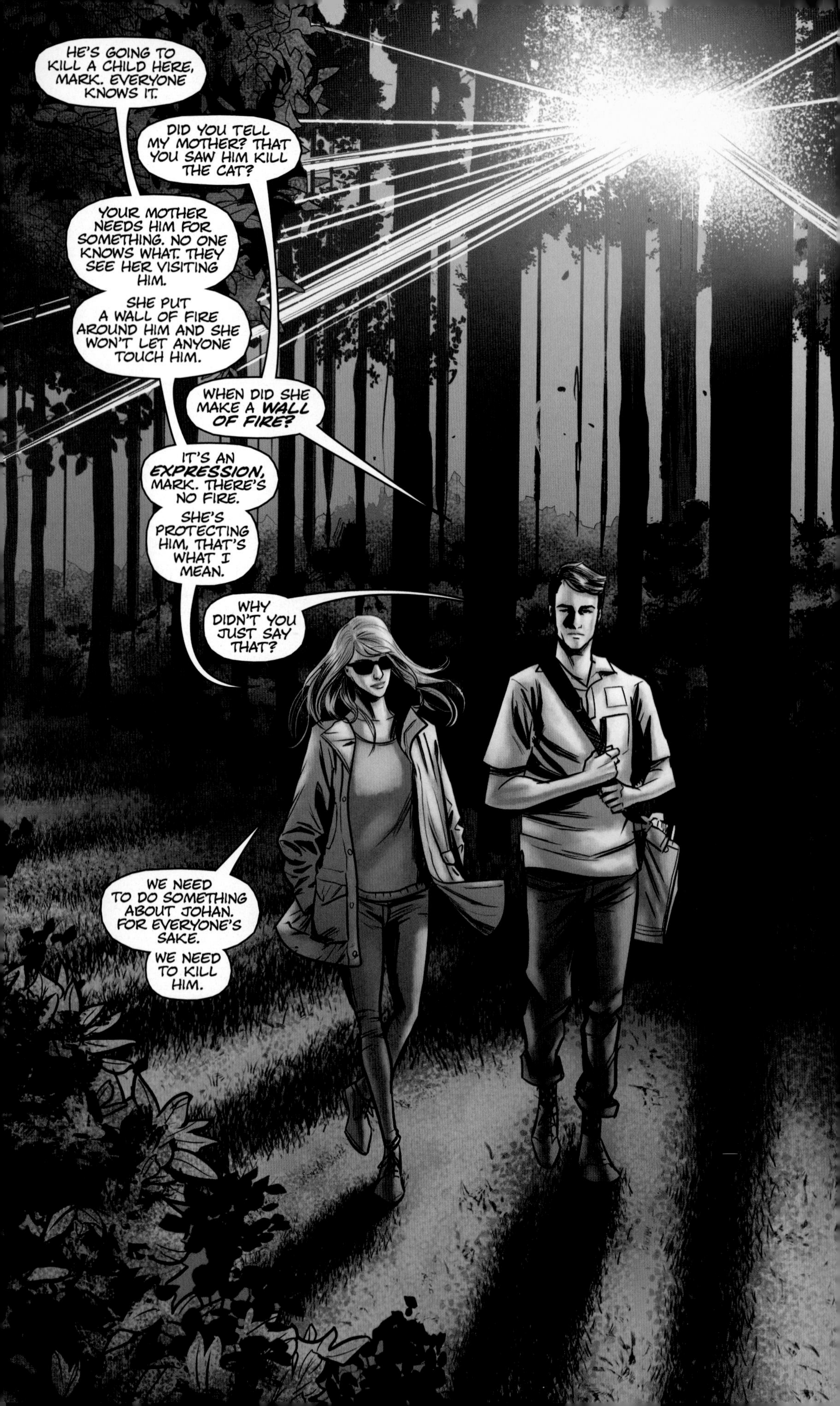

HE'S GOING TO KILL A CHILD HERE, MARK. EVERYONE KNOWS IT.
DID YOU TELL MY MOTHER? THAT YOU SAW HIM KILL THE CAT?
YOUR MOTHER NEEDS HIM FOR SOMETHING. NO ONE KNOWS WHAT. THEY SEE HER VISITING HIM.
SHE PUT A WALL OF FIRE AROUND HIM AND SHE WON'T LET ANYONE TOUCH HIM.
WHEN DID SHE MAKE A WALL OF FIRE?
IT'S AN EXPRESSION, MARK. THERE'S NO FIRE.
SHE'S PROTECTING HIM, THAT'S WHAT I MEAN.
WHY DIDN'T YOU JUST SAY THAT?
WE NEED TO DO SOMETHING ABOUT JOHAN. FOR EVERYONE'S SAKE.
WE NEED TO KILL HIM.

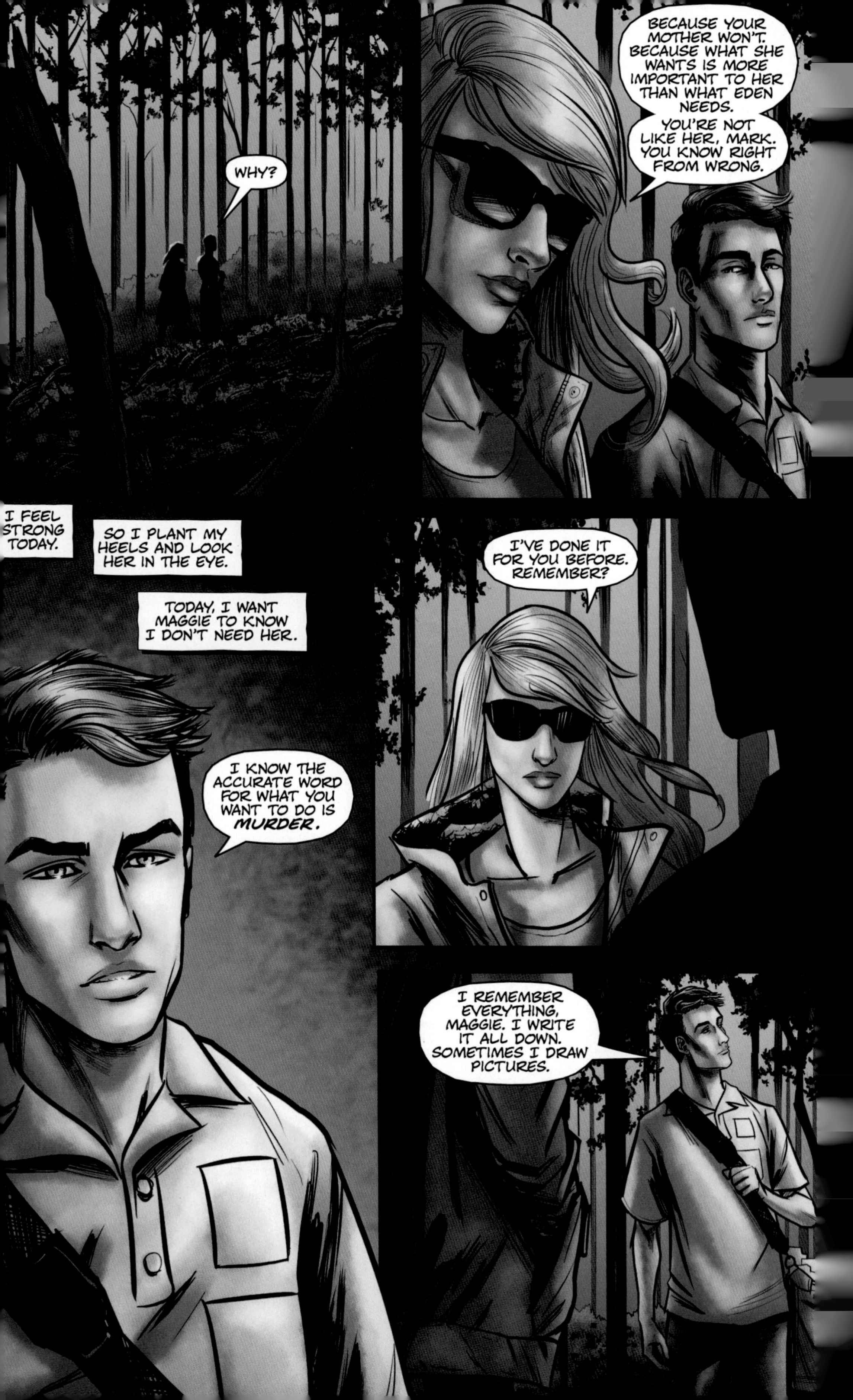
WHY?
BECAUSE YOUR MOTHER WON'T. BECAUSE WHAT SHE WANTS IS MORE IMPORTANT TO HER THAN WHAT EDEN NEEDS.
YOU'RE NOT LIKE HER, MARK. YOU KNOW RIGHT FROM WRONG.
I FEEL STRONG TODAY.
SO I PLANT MY HEELS AND LOOK HER IN THE EYE.
TODAY, I WANT MAGGIE TO KNOW I DON'T NEED HER.
I KNOW THE ACCURATE WORD FOR WHAT YOU WANT TO DO IS MURDER.
I'VE DONE IT FOR YOU BEFORE. REMEMBER?
I REMEMBER EVERYTHING, MAGGIE. I WRITE IT ALL DOWN. SOMETIMES I DRAW PICTURES.

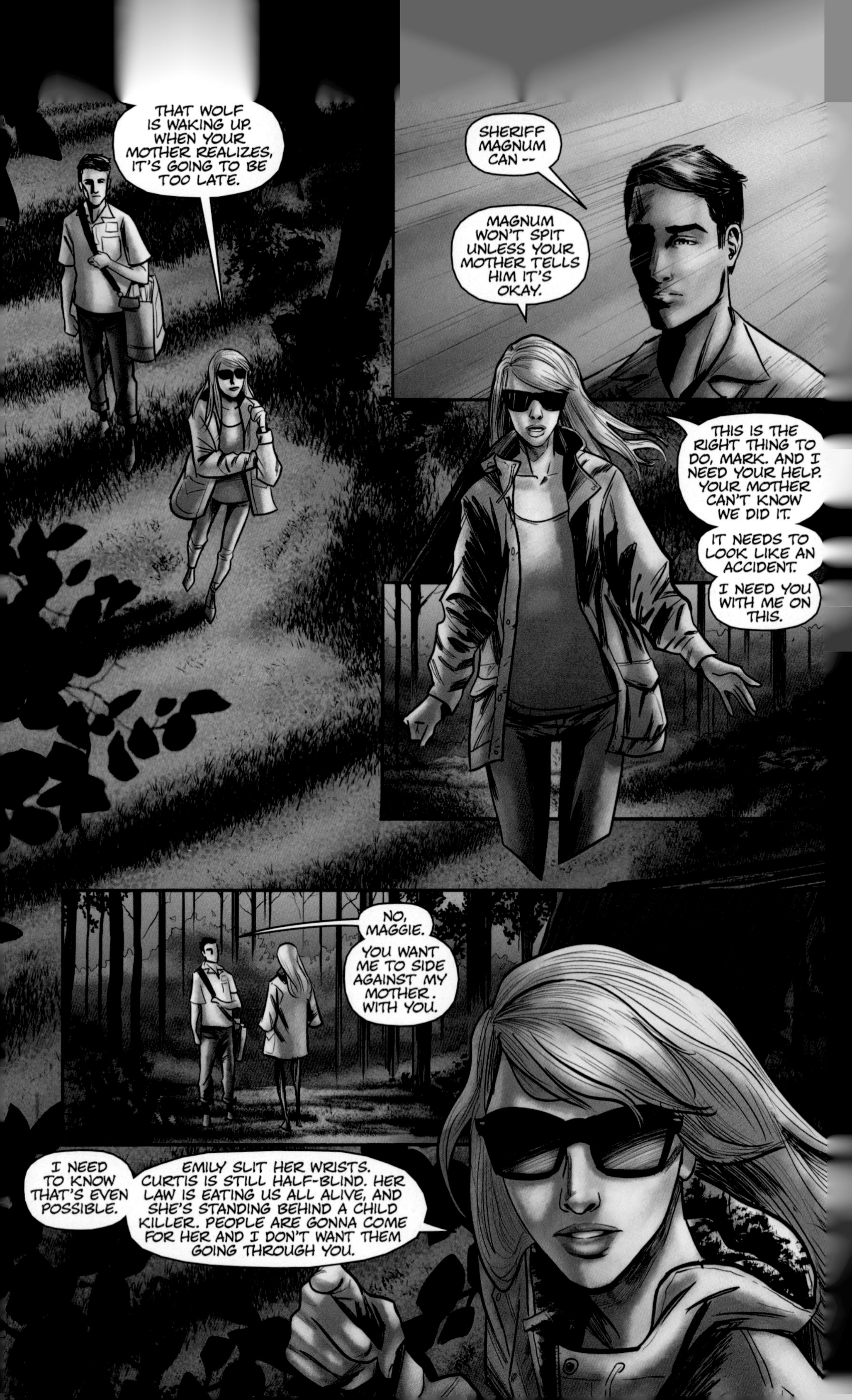
THAT WOLF IS WAKING UP. WHEN YOUR MOTHER REALIZES, IT'S GOING TO BE TOO LATE.
SHERIFF MAGNUM CAN --
MAGNUM WON'T SPIT UNLESS YOUR MOTHER TELLS HIM IT'S OKAY.
THIS IS THE RIGHT THING TO DO, MARK. AND I NEED YOUR HELP. YOUR MOTHER CAN'T KNOW WE DID IT.
IT NEEDS TO LOOK LIKE AN ACCIDENT.
I NEED YOU WITH ME ON THIS.
NO, MAGGIE.
YOU WANT ME TO SIDE AGAINST MY MOTHER. WITH YOU.
I NEED TO KNOW THAT'S EVEN POSSIBLE.
EMILY SLIT HER WRISTS. CURTIS IS STILL HALF-BLIND. HER LAW IS EATING US ALL ALIVE, AND SHE'S STANDING BEHIND A CHILD KILLER. PEOPLE ARE GONNA COME FOR HER AND I DON'T WANT THEM GOING THROUGH YOU.

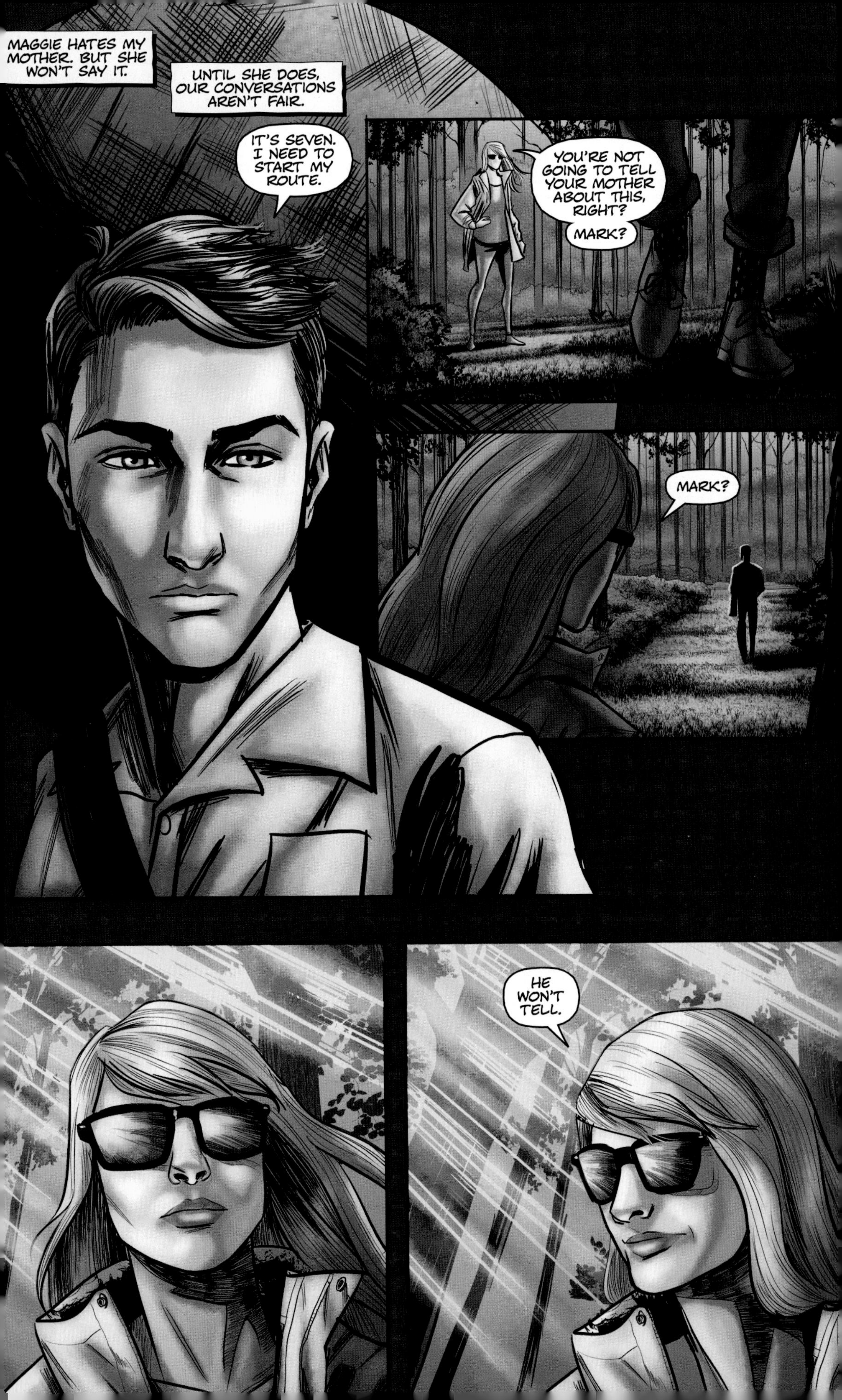
MAGGIE HATES MY MOTHER. BUT SHE WON'T SAY IT.
UNTIL SHE DOES, OUR CONVERSATIONS AREN'T FAIR.
IT'S SEVEN. I NEED TO START MY ROUTE.
YOU'RE NOT GOING TO TELL YOUR MOTHER ABOUT THIS, RIGHT?
MARK?
MARK?
HE WON'T TELL.

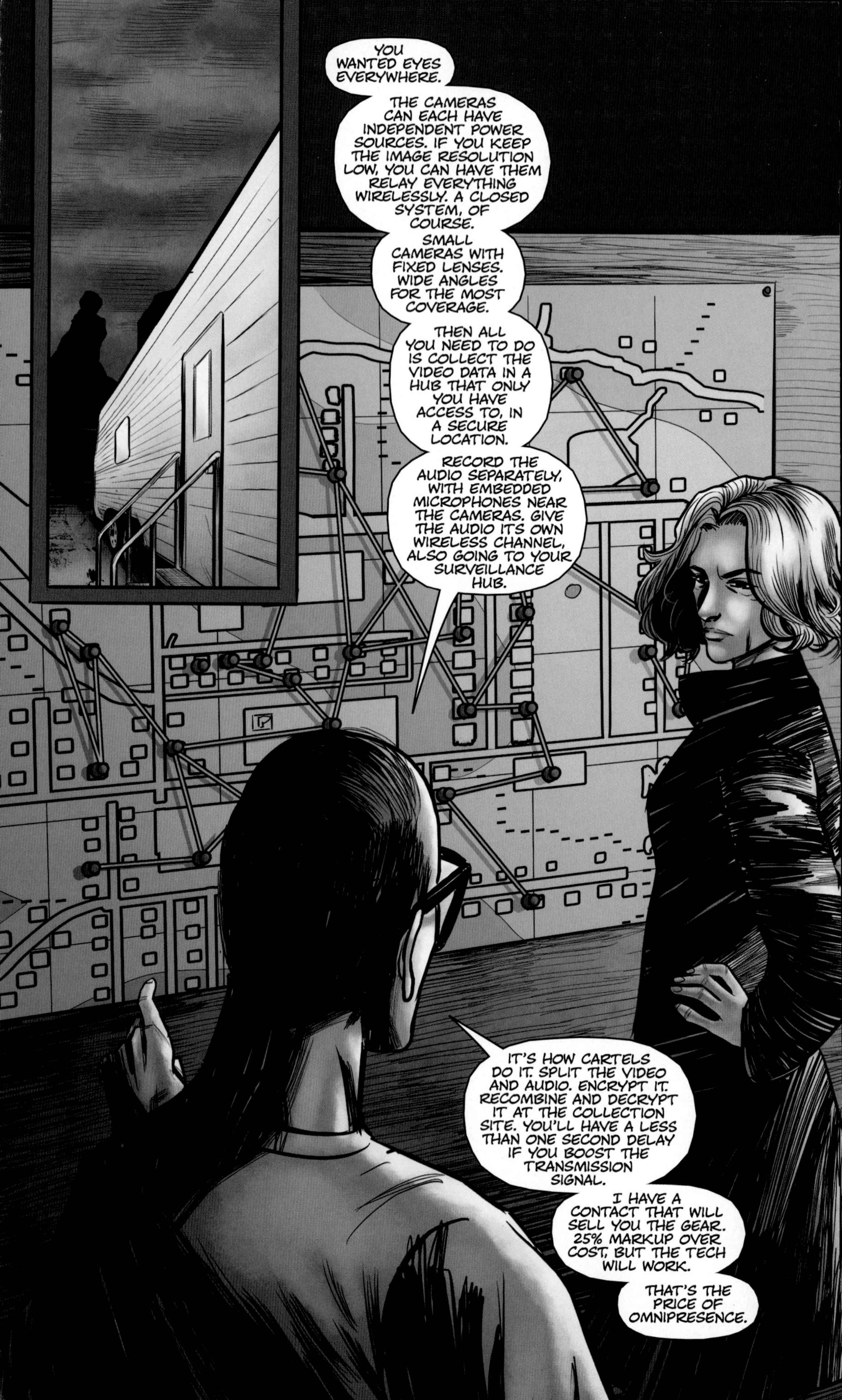

YOU WANTED EYES EVERYWHERE.
THE CAMERAS CAN EACH HAVE INDEPENDENT POWER SOURCES. IF YOU KEEP THE IMAGE RESOLUTION LOW, YOU CAN HAVE THEM RELAY EVERYTHING WIRELESSLY. A CLOSED SYSTEM, OF COURSE.
SMALL CAMERAS WITH FIXED LENSES. WIDE ANGLES FOR THE MOST COVERAGE.
THEN ALL YOU NEED TO DO IS COLLECT THE VIDEO DATA IN A HUB THAT ONLY YOU HAVE ACCESS TO, IN A SECURE LOCATION.
RECORD THE AUDIO SEPARATELY, WITH EMBEDDED MICROPHONES NEAR THE CAMERAS. GIVE THE AUDIO ITS OWN WIRELESS CHANNEL, ALSO GOING TO YOUR SURVEILLANCE HUB.
IT'S HOW CARTELS DO IT. SPLIT THE VIDEO AND AUDIO. ENCRYPT IT. RECOMBINE AND DECRYPT IT AT THE COLLECTION SITE. YOU'LL HAVE A LESS THAN ONE SECOND DELAY IF YOU BOOST THE TRANSMISSION SIGNAL.
I HAVE A CONTACT THAT WILL SELL YOU THE GEAR. 25% MARKUP OVER COST, BUT THE TECH WILL WORK.
THAT'S THE PRICE OF OMNIPRESENCE.

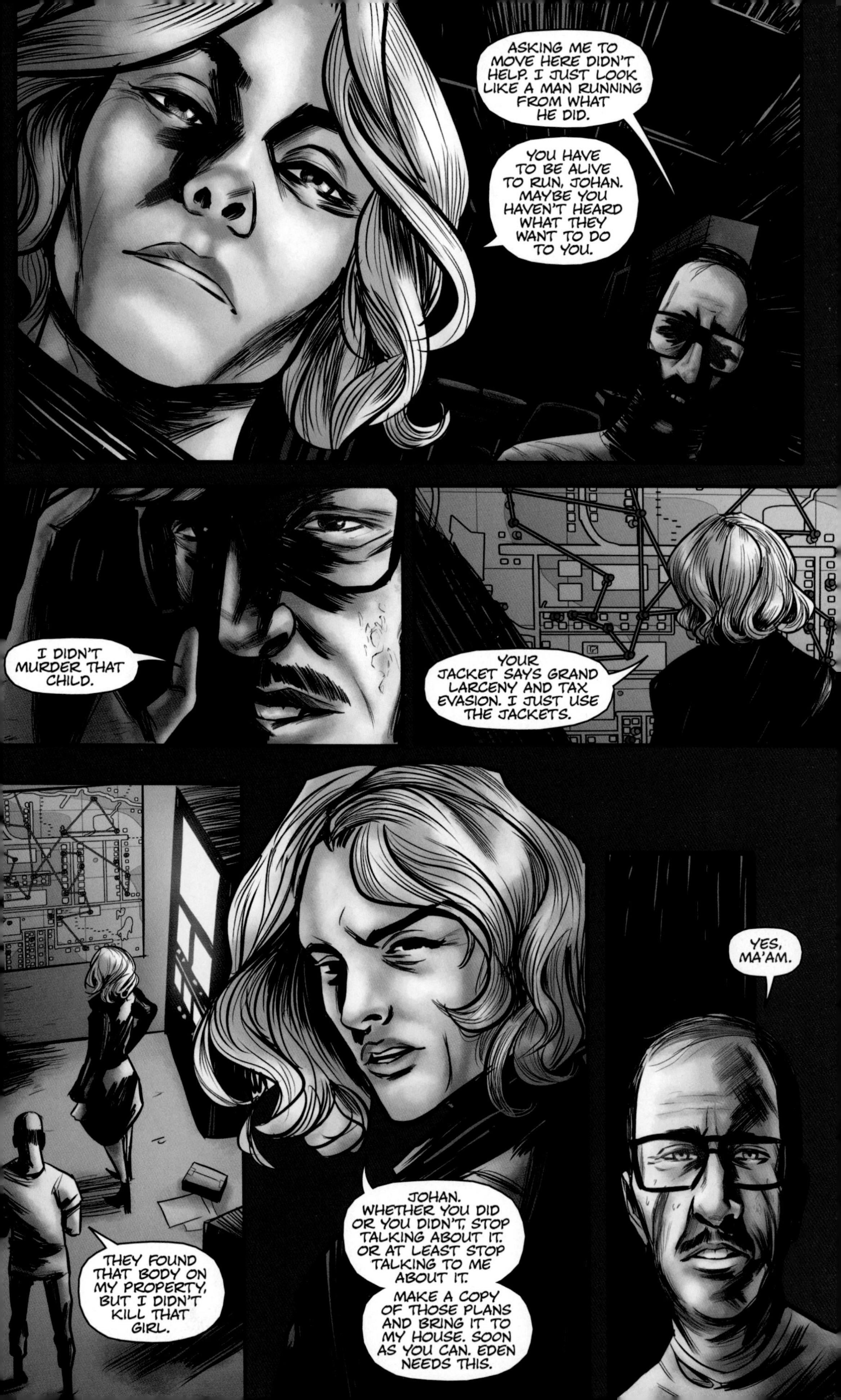

ASKING ME TO MOVE HERE DIDN'T HELP. I JUST LOOK LIKE A MAN RUNNING FROM WHAT HE DID.
YOU HAVE TO BE ALIVE TO RUN, JOHAN. MAYBE YOU HAVEN'T HEARD WHAT THEY WANT TO DO TO YOU.
I DIDN'T MURDER THAT CHILD.
YOUR JACKET SAYS GRAND LARCENY AND TAX EVASION. I JUST USE THE JACKETS.
THEY FOUND THAT BODY ON MY PROPERTY, BUT I DIDN'T KILL THAT GIRL.
JOHAN. WHETHER YOU DID OR YOU DIDN'T, STOP TALKING ABOUT IT. OR AT LEAST STOP TALKING TO ME ABOUT IT.
MAKE A COPY OF THOSE PLANS AND BRING IT TO MY HOUSE. SOON AS YOU CAN. EDEN NEEDS THIS.
YES, MA'AM.

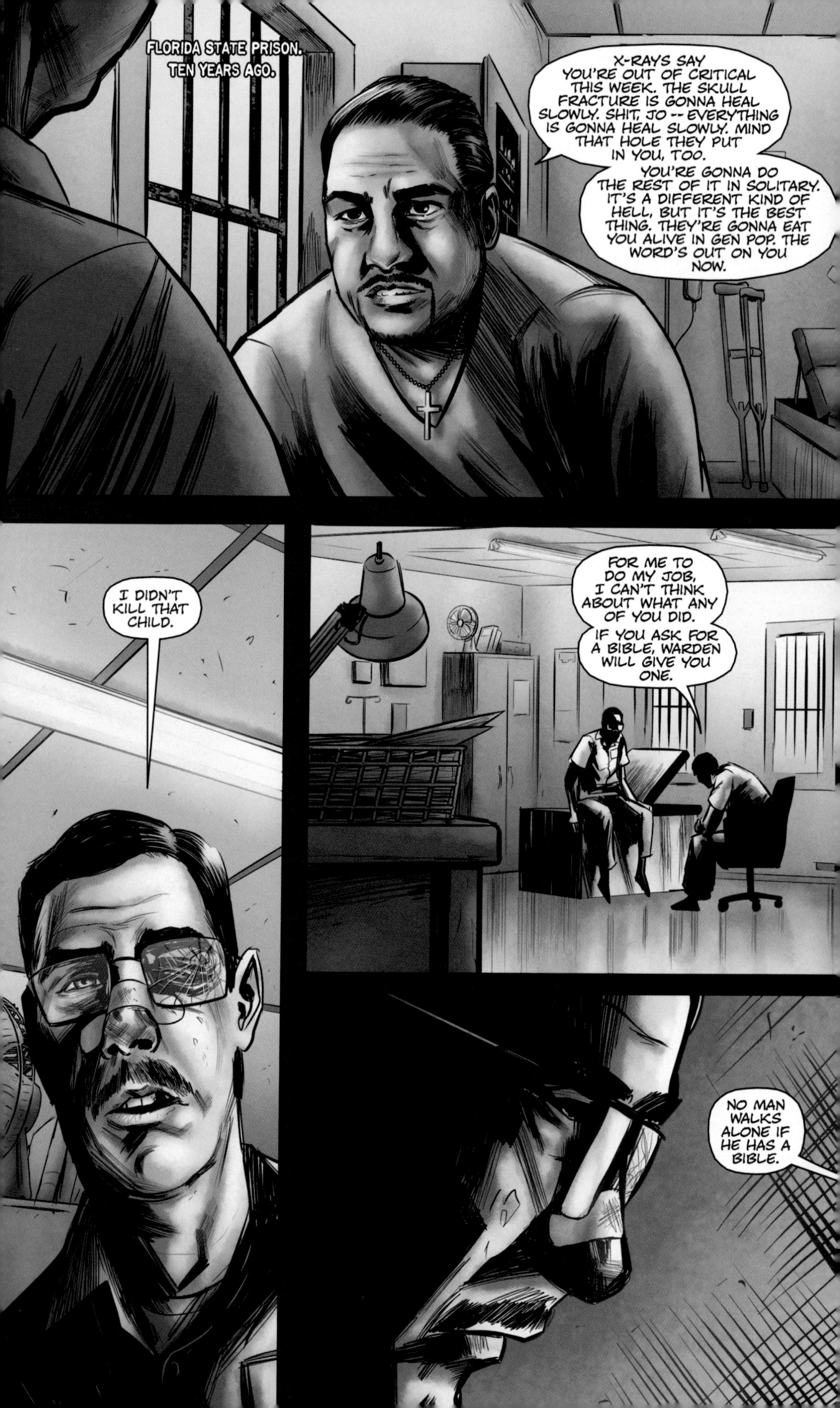
FLORIDA STATE PRISON. TEN YEARS AGO.
X-RAYS SAY YOU'RE OUT OF CRITICAL THIS WEEK. THE SKULL FRACTURE IS GONNA HEAL SLOWLY. SHIT, JO -- EVERYTHING IS GONNA HEAL SLOWLY. MIND THAT HOLE THEY PUT IN YOU, TOO.
YOU'RE GONNA DO THE REST OF IT IN SOLITARY. IT'S A DIFFERENT KIND OF HELL, BUT IT'S THE BEST THING. THEY'RE GONNA EAT YOU ALIVE IN GEN POP. THE WORD'S OUT ON YOU NOW.
I DIDN'T KILL THAT CHILD.
FOR ME TO DO MY JOB, I CAN'T THINK ABOUT WHAT ANY OF YOU DID.
IF YOU ASK FOR A BIBLE, WARDEN WILL GIVE YOU ONE.
NO MAN WALKS ALONE IF HE HAS A BIBLE.

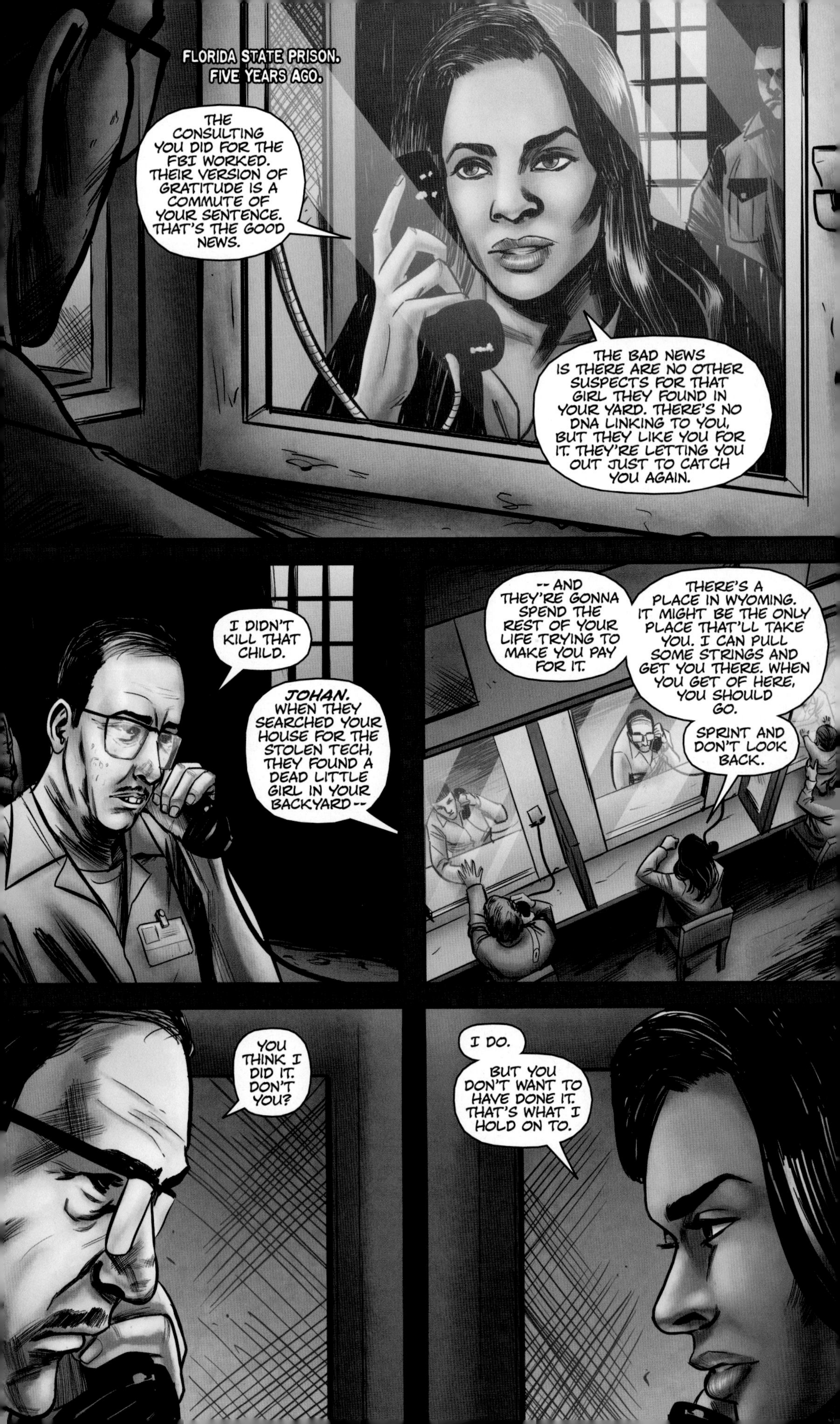
FLORIDA STATE PRISON. FIVE YEARS AGO.
THE CONSULTING YOU DID FOR THE FBI WORKED. THEIR VERSION OF GRATITUDE IS A COMMUTE OF YOUR SENTENCE. THAT'S THE GOOD NEWS.
THE BAD NEWS IS THERE ARE NO OTHER SUSPECTS FOR THAT GIRL THEY FOUND IN YOUR YARD. THERE'S NO DNA LINKING TO YOU, BUT THEY LIKE YOU FOR IT. THEY'RE LETTING YOU OUT JUST TO CATCH YOU AGAIN.
I DIDN'T KILL THAT CHILD.
JOHAN. WHEN THEY SEARCHED YOUR HOUSE FOR THE STOLEN TECH, THEY FOUND A DEAD LITTLE GIRL IN YOUR BACKYARD--
-- AND THEY'RE GONNA SPEND THE REST OF YOUR LIFE TRYING TO MAKE YOU PAY FOR IT.
THERE'S A PLACE IN WYOMING. IT MIGHT BE THE ONLY PLACE THAT'LL TAKE YOU. I CAN PULL SOME STRINGS AND GET YOU THERE. WHEN YOU GET OF HERE, YOU SHOULD GO.
SPRINT AND DON'T LOOK BACK.
YOU THINK I DID IT. DON'T YOU?
I DO.
BUT YOU DON'T WANT TO HAVE DONE IT. THAT'S WHAT I HOLD ON TO.

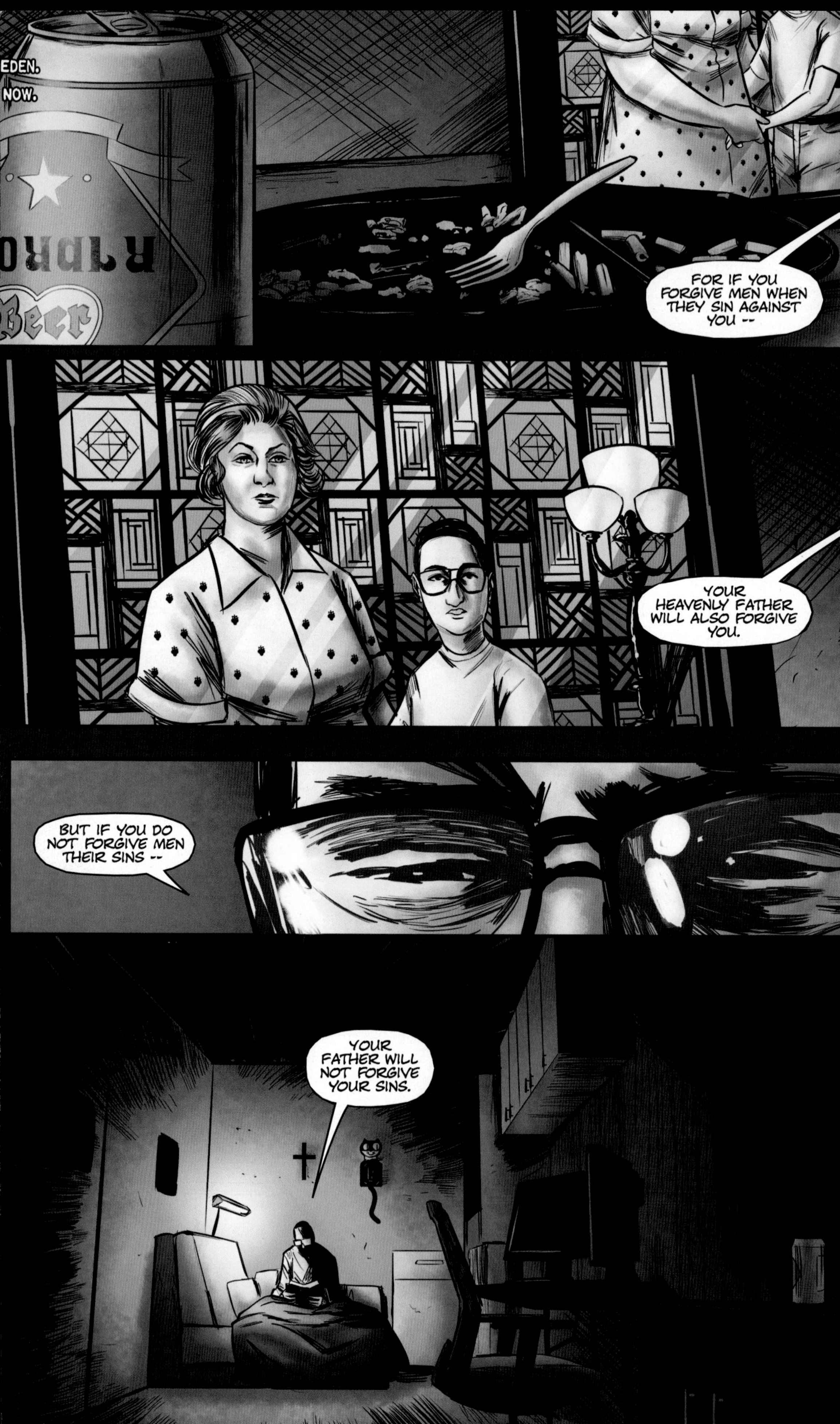
EDEN.
NOW.
FOR IF YOU FORGIVE MEN WHEN THEY SIN AGAINST YOU --
YOUR HEAVENLY FATHER WILL ALSO FORGIVE YOU.
BUT IF YOU DO NOT FORGIVE MEN THEIR SINS --
YOUR FATHER WILL NOT FORGIVE YOUR SINS.

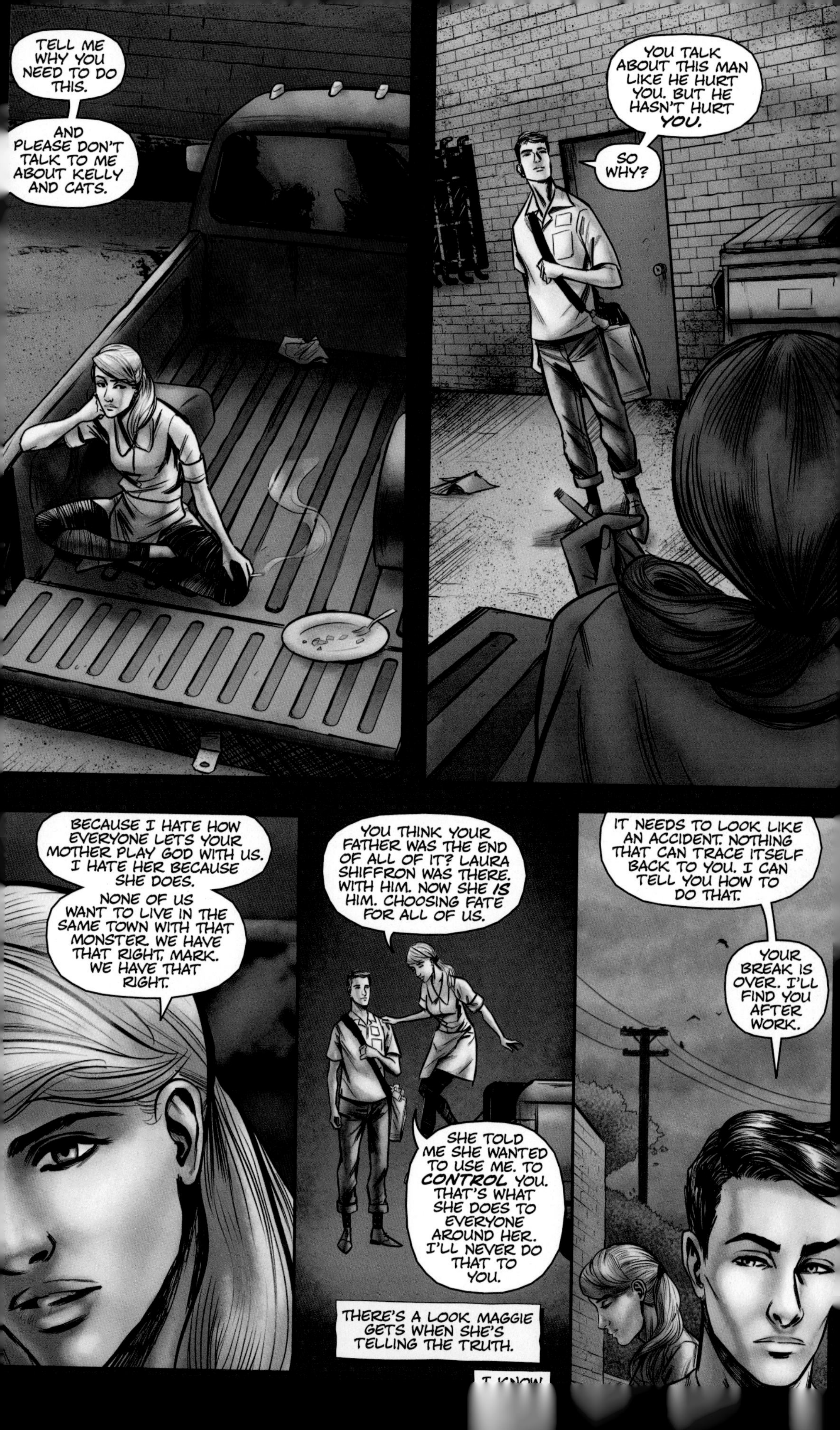
TELL ME WHY YOU NEED TO DO THIS.
AND PLEASE DON'T TALK TO ME ABOUT KELLY AND CATS.
YOU TALK ABOUT THIS MAN LIKE HE HURT YOU. BUT HE HASN'T HURT YOU.
SO WHY?
BECAUSE I HATE HOW EVERYONE LETS YOUR MOTHER PLAY GOD WITH US. I HATE HER BECAUSE SHE DOES.
NONE OF US WANT TO LIVE IN THE SAME TOWN WITH THAT MONSTER. WE HAVE THAT RIGHT, MARK. WE HAVE THAT RIGHT.
YOU THINK YOUR FATHER WAS THE END OF ALL OF IT? LAURA SHIFFRON WAS THERE. WITH HIM. NOW SHE IS HIM. CHOOSING FATE FOR ALL OF US.
SHE TOLD ME SHE WANTED TO USE ME. TO CONTROL YOU. THAT'S WHAT SHE DOES TO EVERYONE AROUND HER. I'LL NEVER DO THAT TO YOU.
THERE'S A LOOK MAGGIE GETS WHEN SHE'S TELLING THE TRUTH.
IT NEEDS TO LOOK LIKE AN ACCIDENT. NOTHING THAT CAN TRACE ITSELF BACK TO YOU. I CAN TELL YOU HOW TO DO THAT.
YOUR BREAK IS OVER. I'LL FIND YOU AFTER WORK.

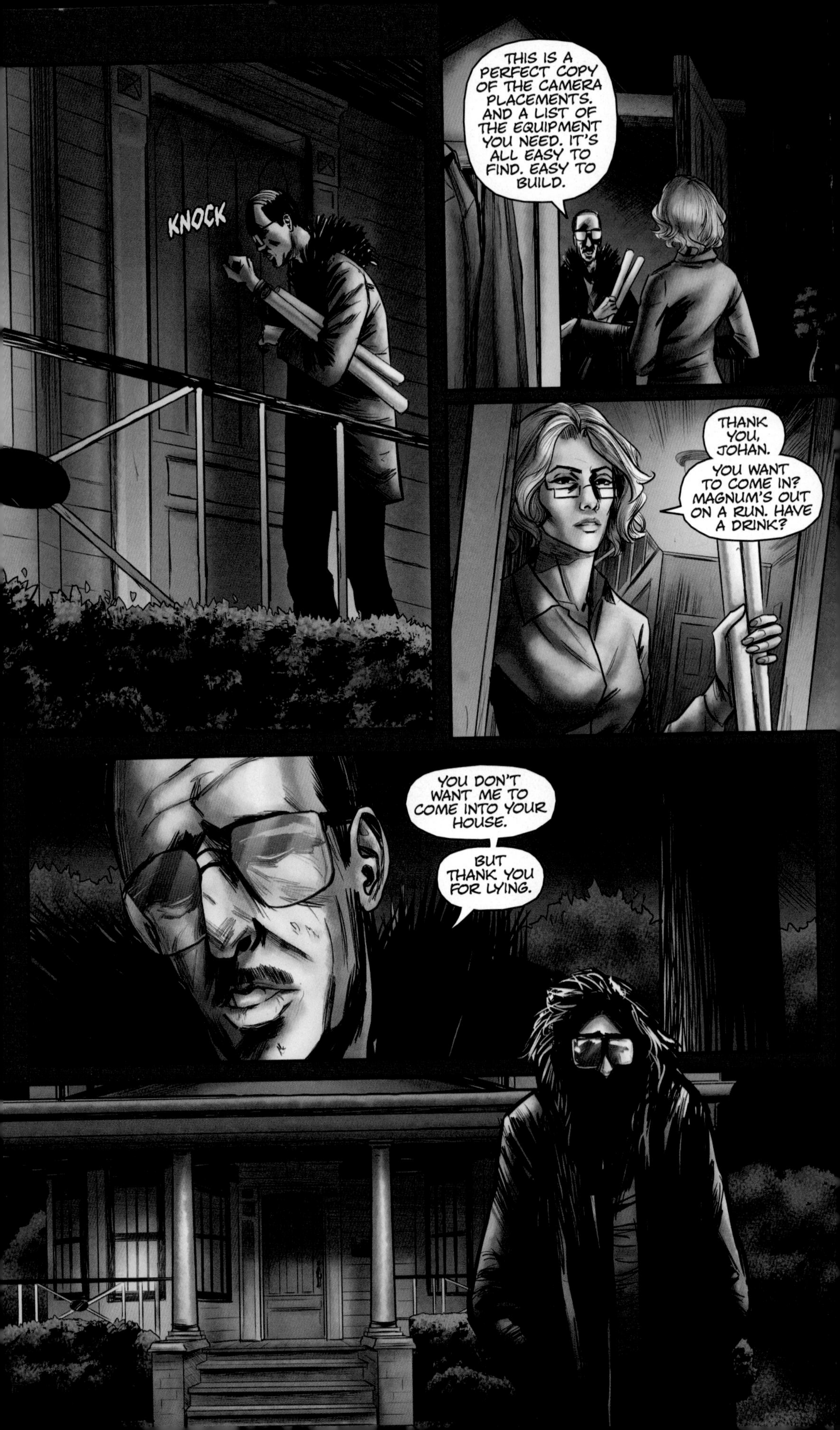
KNOCK
THIS IS A PERFECT COPY OF THE CAMERA PLACEMENTS. AND A LIST OF THE EQUIPMENT YOU NEED. IT'S ALL EASY TO FIND. EASY TO BUILD.
THANK YOU, JOHAN.
YOU WANT TO COME IN? MAGNUM'S OUT ON A RUN. HAVE A DRINK?
YOU DON'T WANT ME TO COME INTO YOUR HOUSE.
BUT THANK YOU FOR LYING.

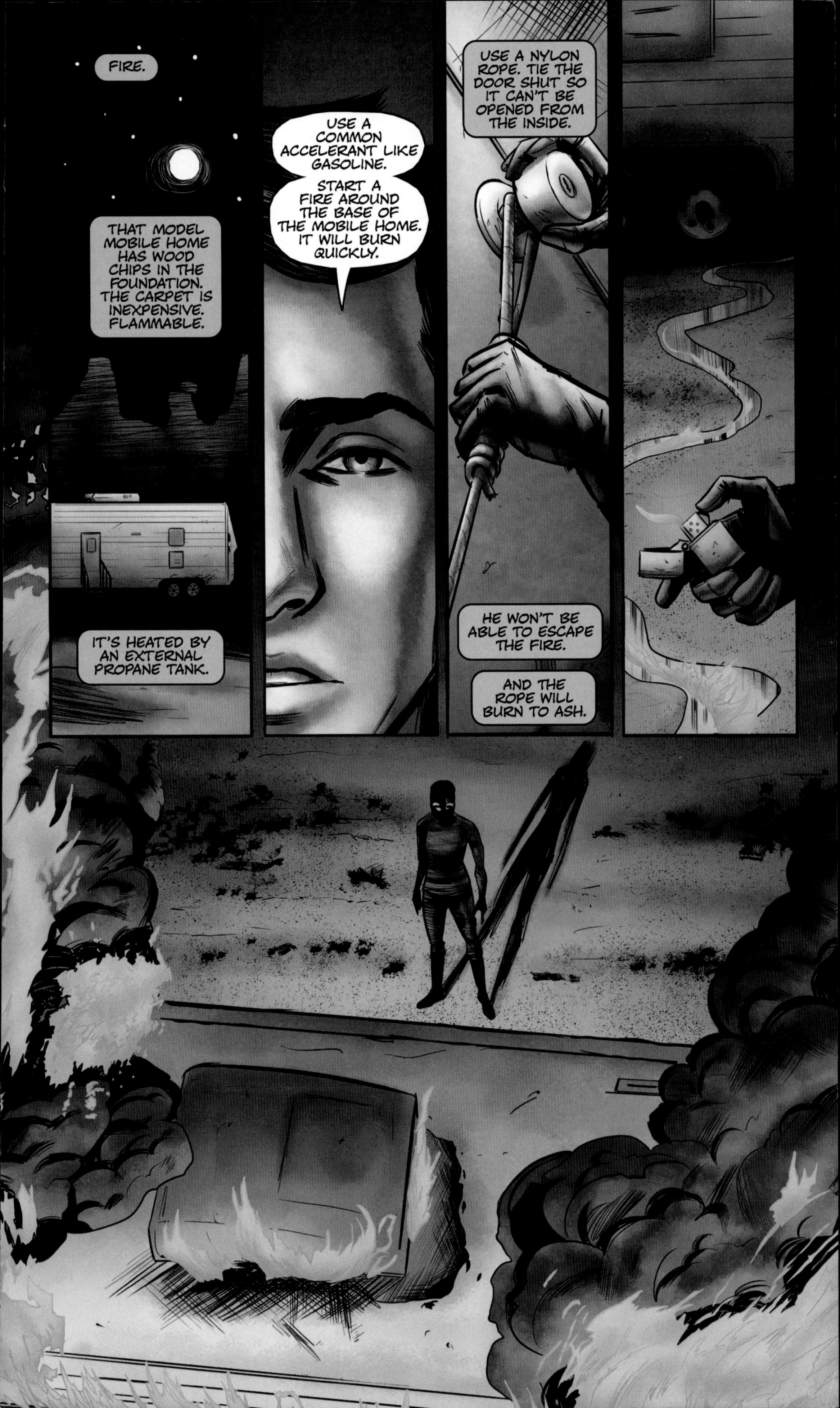
FIRE.
THAT MODEL MOBILE HOME HAS WOOD CHIPS IN THE FOUNDATION. THE CARPET IS INEXPENSIVE. FLAMMABLE.
IT'S HEATED BY AN EXTERNAL PROPANE TANK.
USE A COMMON ACCELERANT LIKE GASOLINE.
START A FIRE AROUND THE BASE OF THE MOBILE HOME. IT WILL BURN QUICKLY.
USE A NYLON ROPE. TIE THE DOOR SHUT SO IT CAN'T BE OPENED FROM THE INSIDE.
HE WON'T BE ABLE TO ESCAPE THE FIRE.
AND THE ROPE WILL BURN TO ASH.

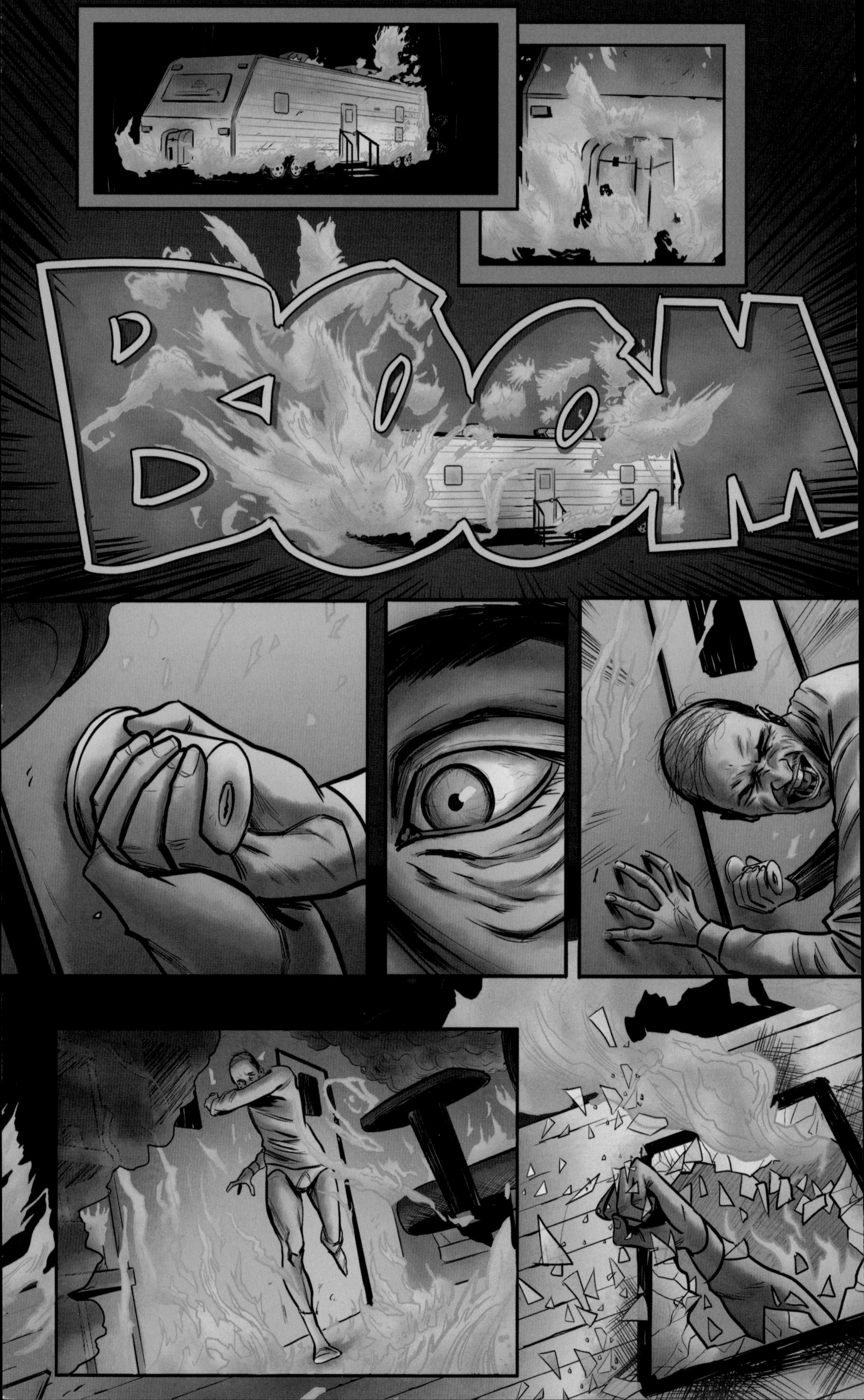
BOOM

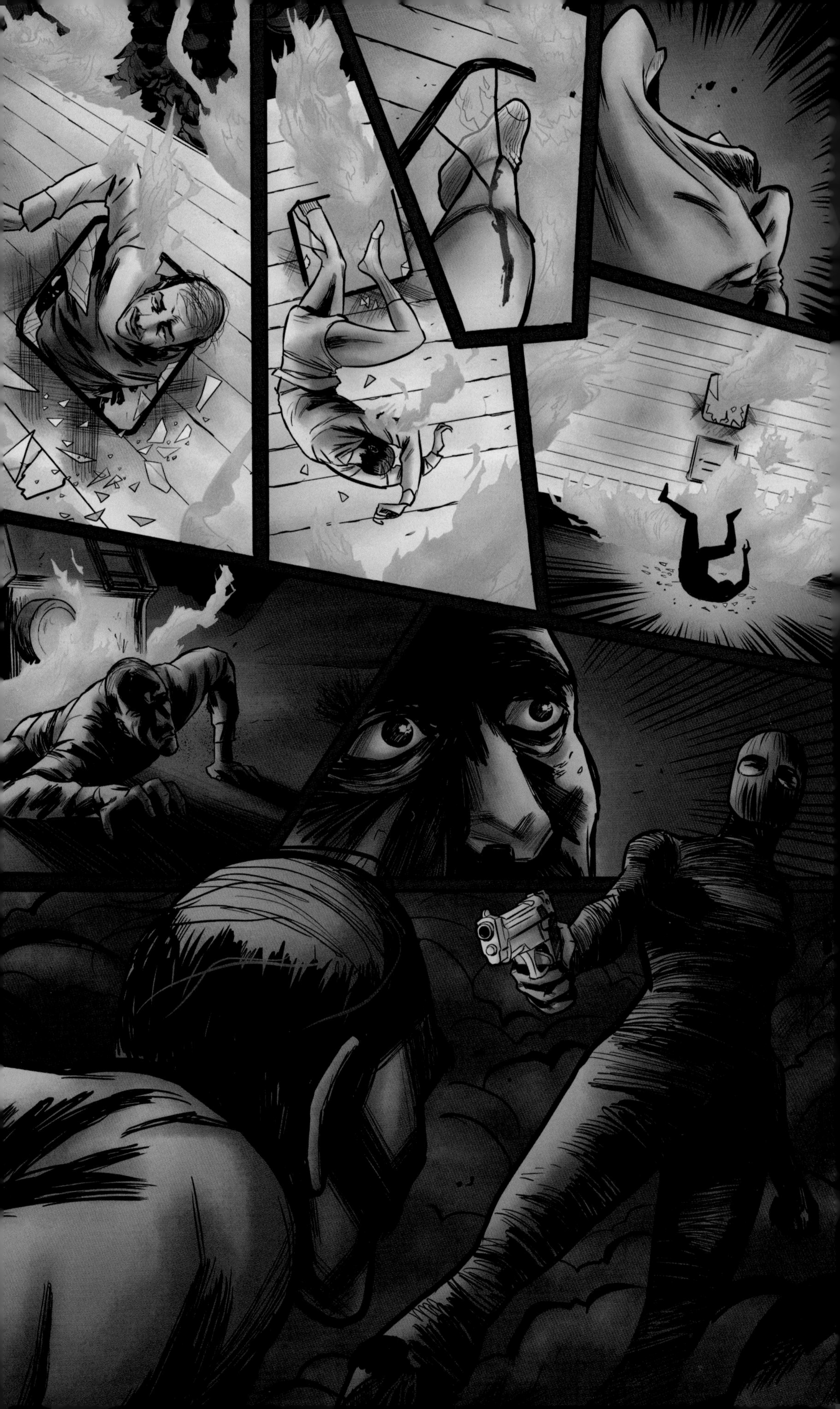

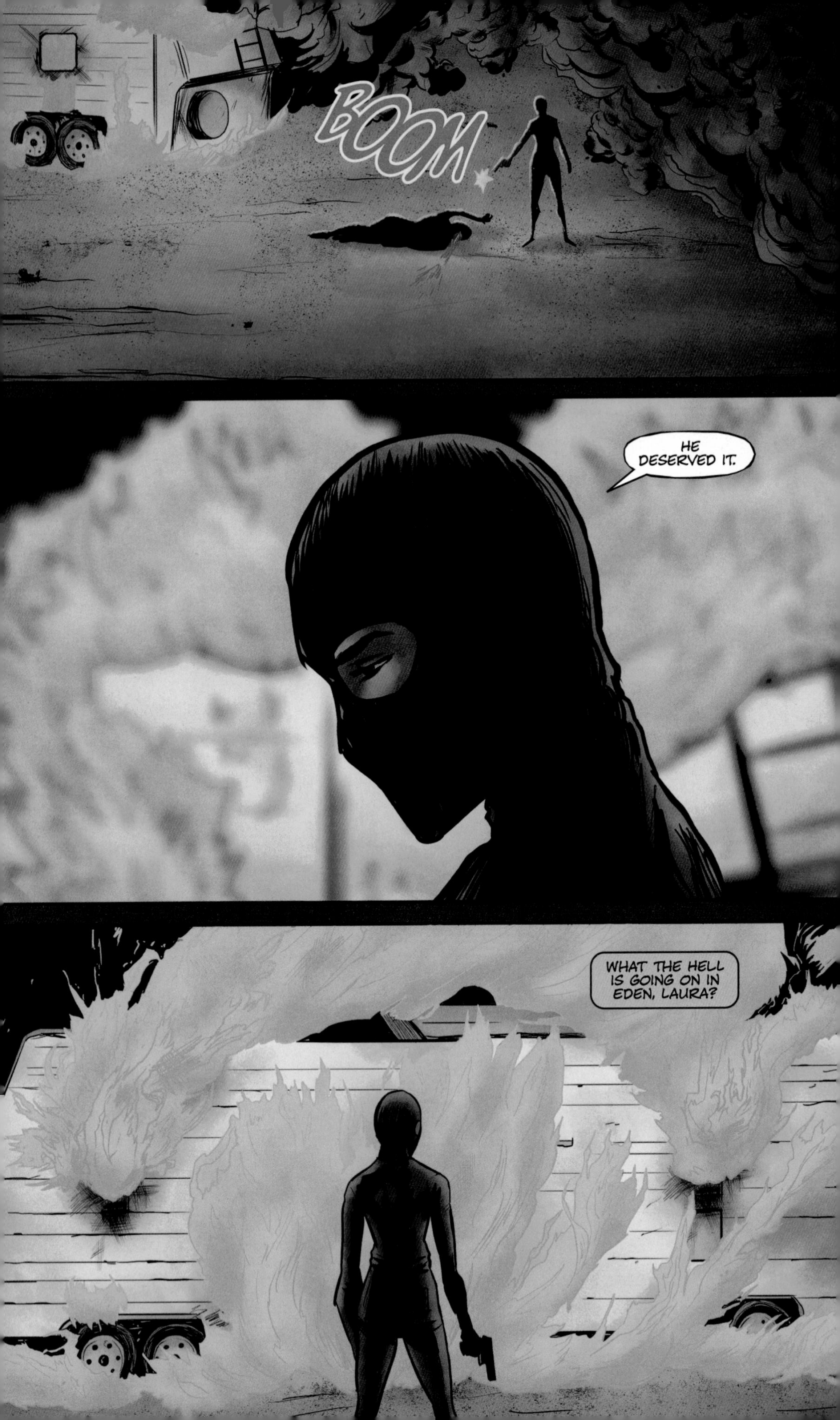
BOOM
HE DESERVED IT.
WHAT THE HELL IS GOING ON IN EDEN, LAURA?

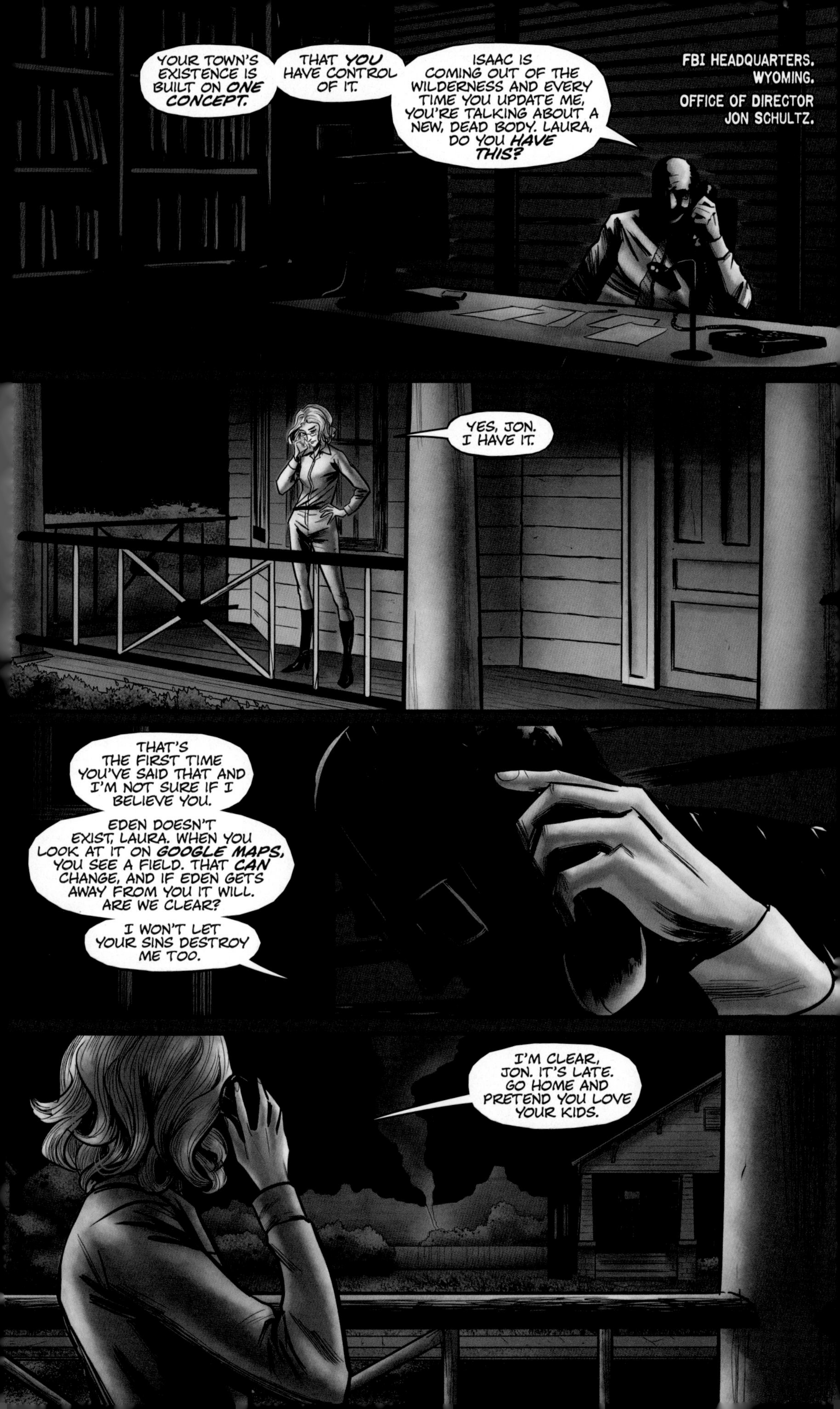
FBI HEADQUARTERS.
WYOMING.
OFFICE OF DIRECTOR JON SCHULTZ.
YOUR TOWN'S EXISTENCE IS BUILT ON ONE CONCEPT.
THAT YOU HAVE CONTROL OF IT.
ISAAC IS COMING OUT OF THE WILDERNESS AND EVERY TIME YOU UPDATE ME, YOU'RE TALKING ABOUT A NEW, DEAD BODY. LAURA, DO YOU HAVE THIS?
YES, JON. I HAVE IT.
THAT'S THE FIRST TIME YOU'VE SAID THAT AND I'M NOT SURE IF I BELIEVE YOU.
EDEN DOESN'T EXIST, LAURA. WHEN YOU LOOK AT IT ON GOOGLE MAPS, YOU SEE A FIELD. THAT CAN CHANGE, AND IF EDEN GETS AWAY FROM YOU IT WILL. ARE WE CLEAR?
I WON'T LET YOUR SINS DESTROY ME TOO.
I'M CLEAR, JON. IT'S LATE. GO HOME AND PRETEND YOU LOVE YOUR KIDS.

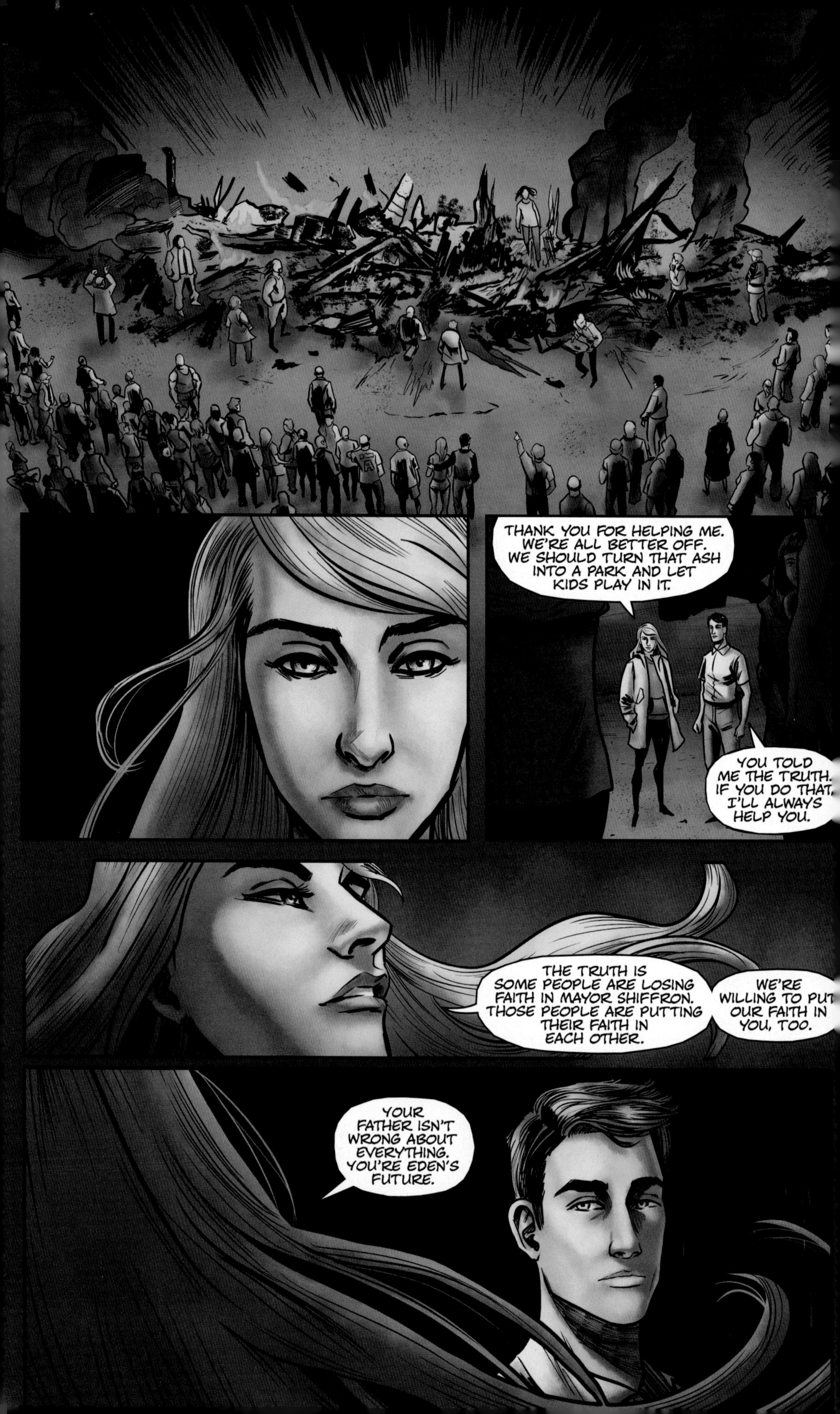
THANK YOU FOR HELPING ME. WE'RE ALL BETTER OFF. WE SHOULD TURN THAT ASH INTO A PARK AND LET KIDS PLAY IN IT.
YOU TOLD ME THE TRUTH. IF YOU DO THAT, I'LL ALWAYS HELP YOU.
THE TRUTH IS SOME PEOPLE ARE LOSING FAITH IN MAYOR SHIFFRON. THOSE PEOPLE ARE PUTTING THEIR FAITH IN EACH OTHER.
WE'RE WILLING TO PUT OUR FAITH IN YOU, TOO.
YOUR FATHER ISN'T WRONG ABOUT EVERYTHING. YOU'RE EDEN'S FUTURE.

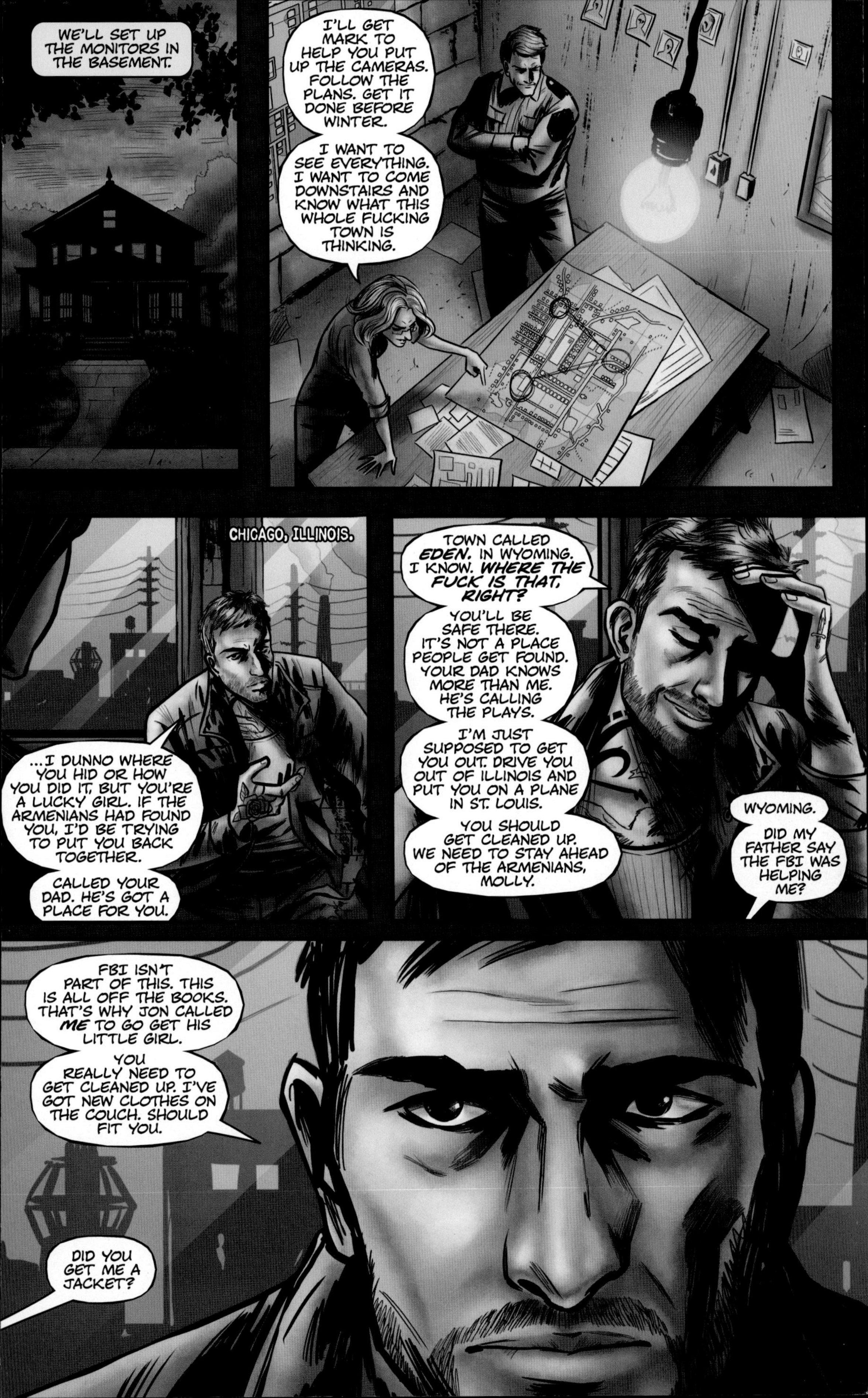
WE'LL SET UP THE MONITORS IN THE BASEMENT.
I'LL GET MARK TO HELP YOU PUT UP THE CAMERAS. FOLLOW THE PLANS. GET IT DONE BEFORE WINTER.
I WANT TO SEE EVERYTHING. I WANT TO COME DOWNSTAIRS AND KNOW WHAT THIS WHOLE FUCKING TOWN IS THINKING.
CHICAGO, ILLINOIS.
...I DUNNO WHERE YOU HID OR HOW YOU DID IT, BUT YOU'RE A LUCKY GIRL. IF THE ARMENIANS HAD FOUND YOU, I'D BE TRYING TO PUT YOU BACK TOGETHER.
CALLED YOUR DAD. HE'S GOT A PLACE FOR YOU.
TOWN CALLED EDEN. IN WYOMING. I KNOW. WHERE THE FUCK IS THAT, RIGHT?
YOU'LL BE SAFE THERE. IT'S NOT A PLACE PEOPLE GET FOUND. YOUR DAD KNOWS MORE THAN ME. HE'S CALLING THE PLAYS.
I'M JUST SUPPOSED TO GET YOU OUT. DRIVE YOU OUT OF ILLINOIS AND PUT YOU ON A PLANE IN ST. LOUIS.
YOU SHOULD GET CLEANED UP. WE NEED TO STAY AHEAD OF THE ARMENIANS, MOLLY.
WYOMING.
DID MY FATHER SAY THE FBI WAS HELPING ME?
FBI ISN'T PART OF THIS. THIS IS ALL OFF THE BOOKS. THAT'S WHY JON CALLED ME TO GO GET HIS LITTLE GIRL.
YOU REALLY NEED TO GET CLEANED UP. I'VE GOT NEW CLOTHES ON THE COUCH. SHOULD FIT YOU.
DID YOU GET ME A JACKET?

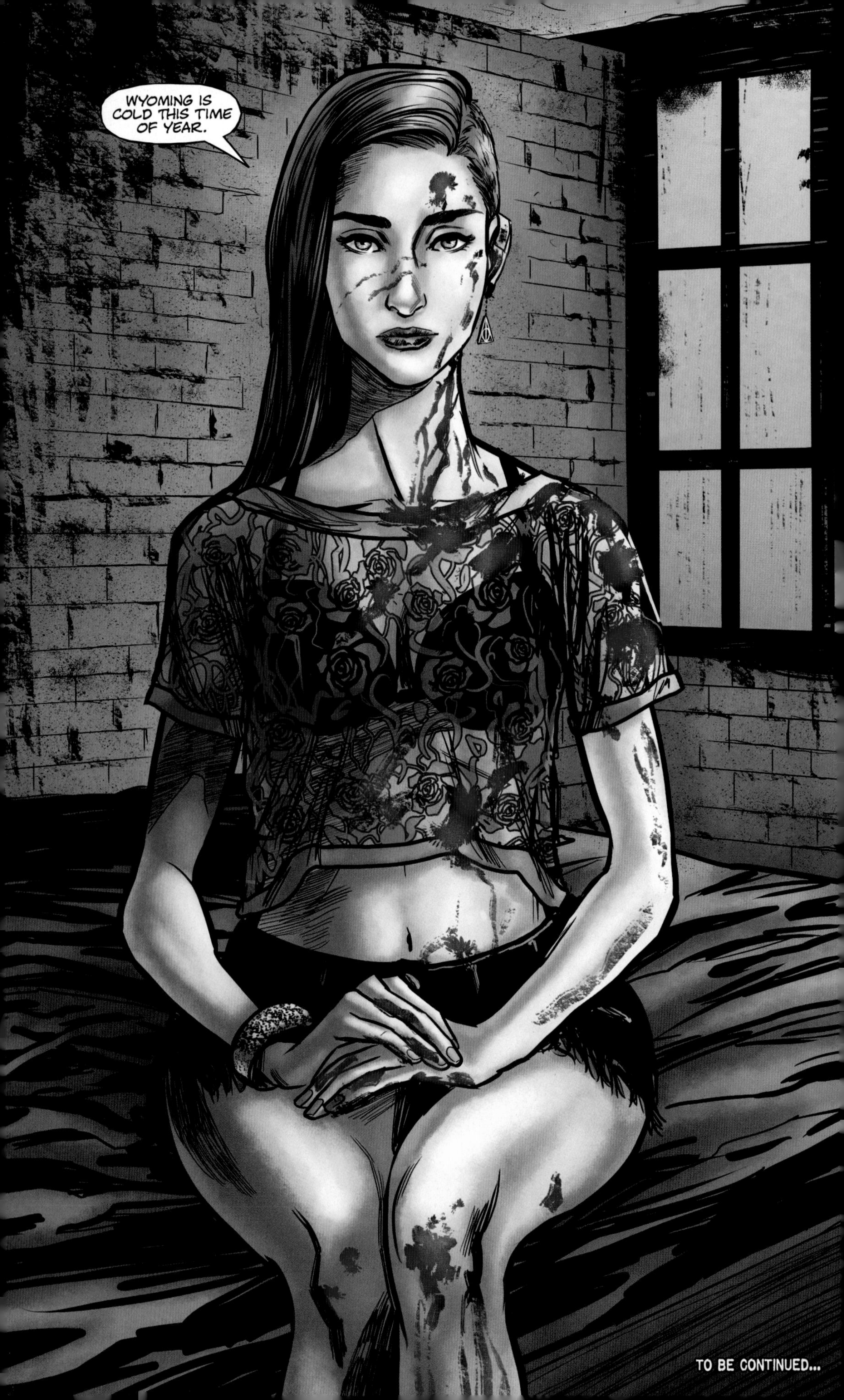
WYOMING IS COLD THIS TIME OF YEAR.
TO BE CONTINUED...

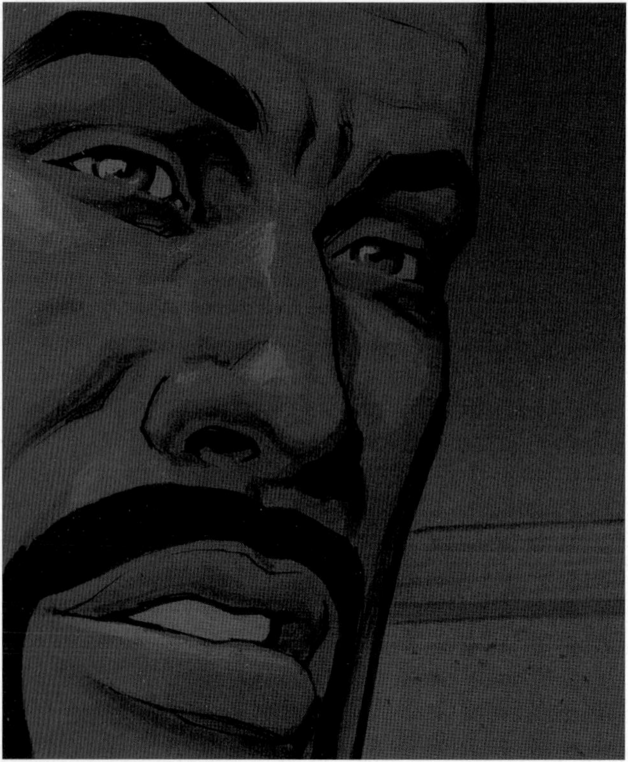

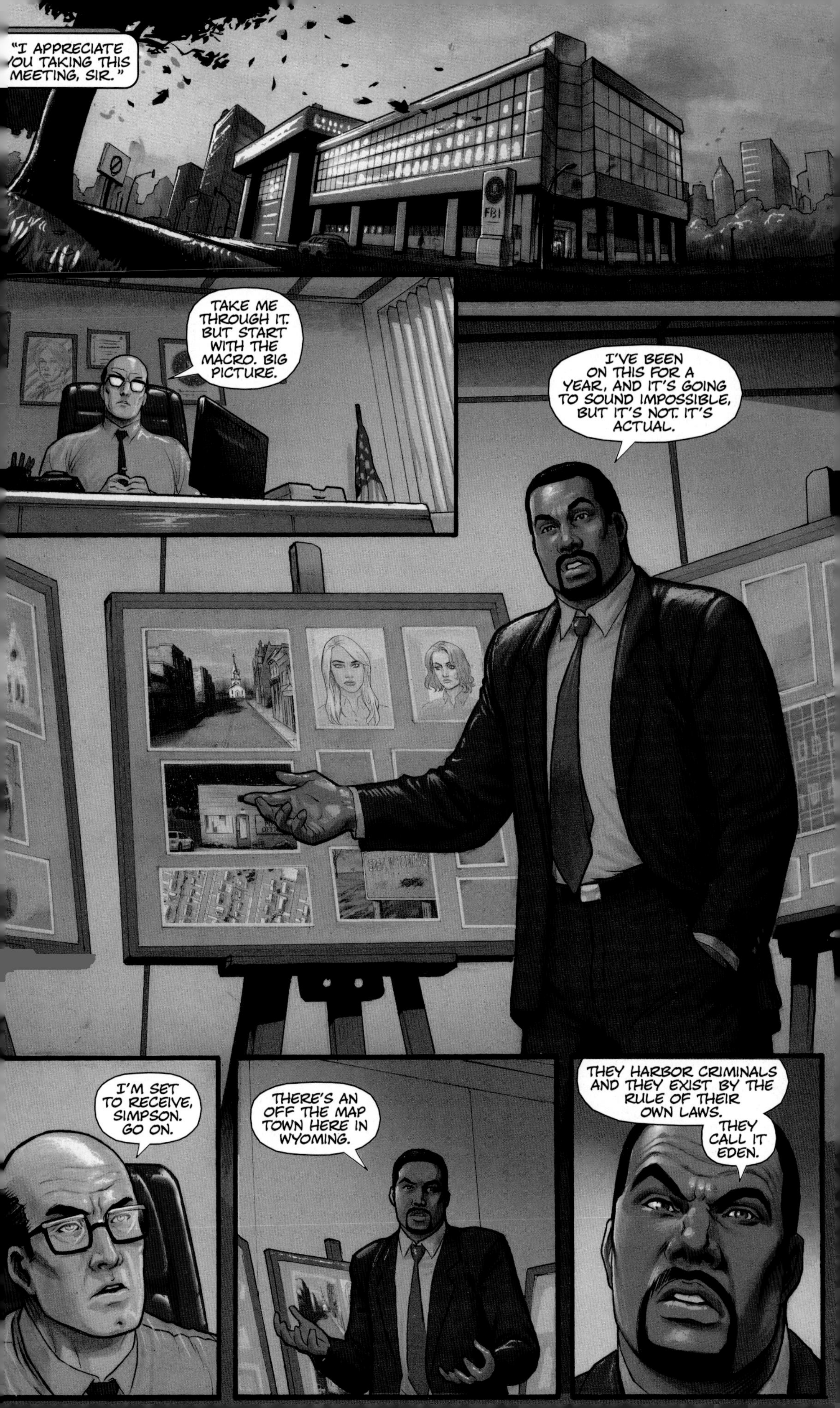
"I APPRECIATE YOU TAKING THIS MEETING, SIR."
FBI
TAKE ME THROUGH IT. BUT START WITH THE MACRO. BIG PICTURE.
I'VE BEEN ON THIS FOR A YEAR, AND IT'S GOING TO SOUND IMPOSSIBLE, BUT IT'S NOT. IT'S ACTUAL.
I'M SET TO RECEIVE, SIMPSON. GO ON.
THERE'S AN OFF THE MAP TOWN HERE IN WYOMING.
THEY HARBOR CRIMINALS AND THEY EXIST BY THE RULE OF THEIR OWN LAWS.
THEY CALL IT EDEN.

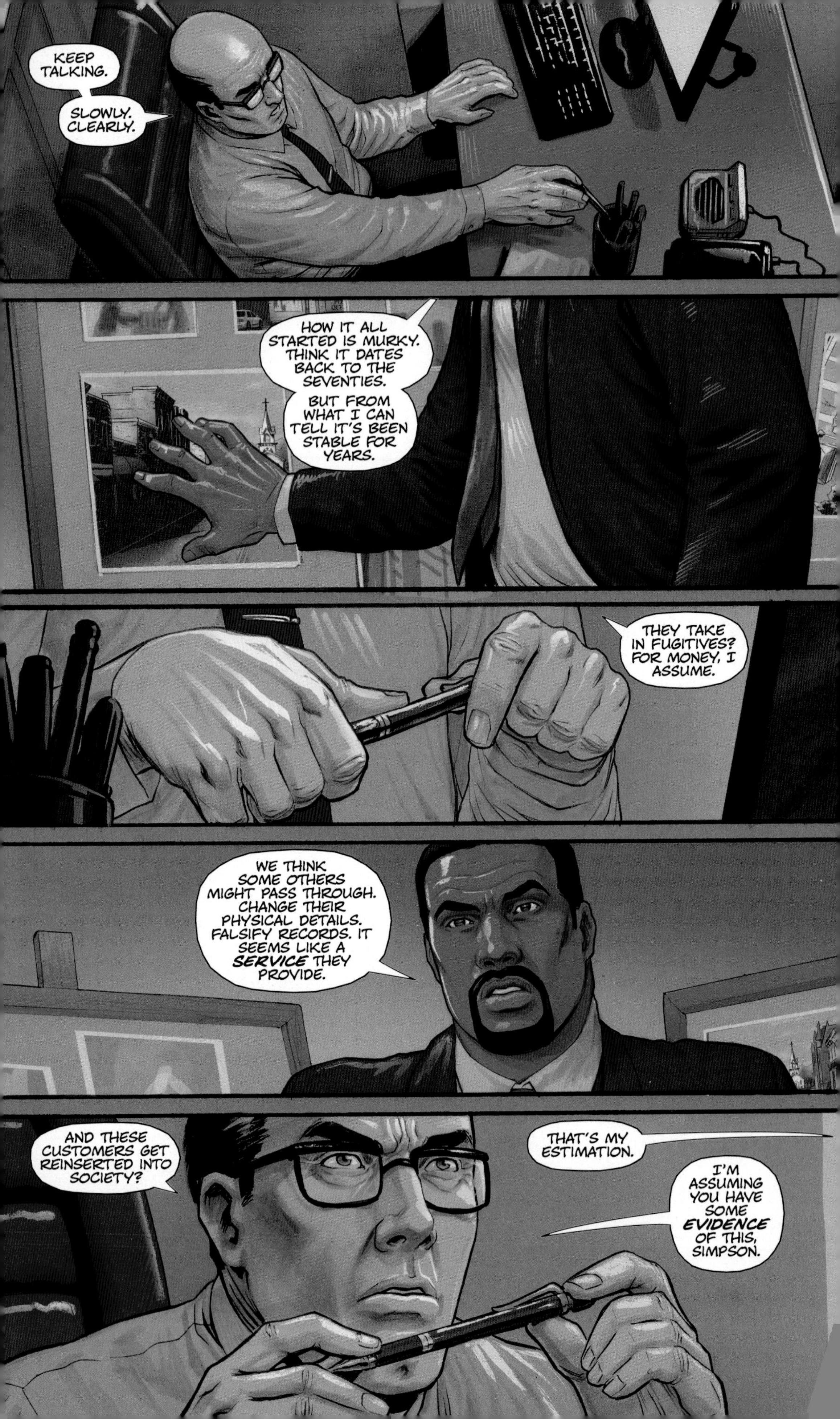
KEEP TALKING.
SLOWLY. CLEARLY.
HOW IT ALL STARTED IS MURKY. THINK IT DATES BACK TO THE SEVENTIES.
BUT FROM WHAT I CAN TELL IT'S BEEN STABLE FOR YEARS.
THEY TAKE IN FUGITIVES? FOR MONEY, I ASSUME.
WE THINK SOME OTHERS MIGHT PASS THROUGH. CHANGE THEIR PHYSICAL DETAILS. FALSIFY RECORDS. IT SEEMS LIKE A SERVICE THEY PROVIDE.
AND THESE CUSTOMERS GET REINSERTED INTO SOCIETY?
THAT'S MY ESTIMATION.
I'M ASSUMING YOU HAVE SOME EVIDENCE OF THIS, SIMPSON.

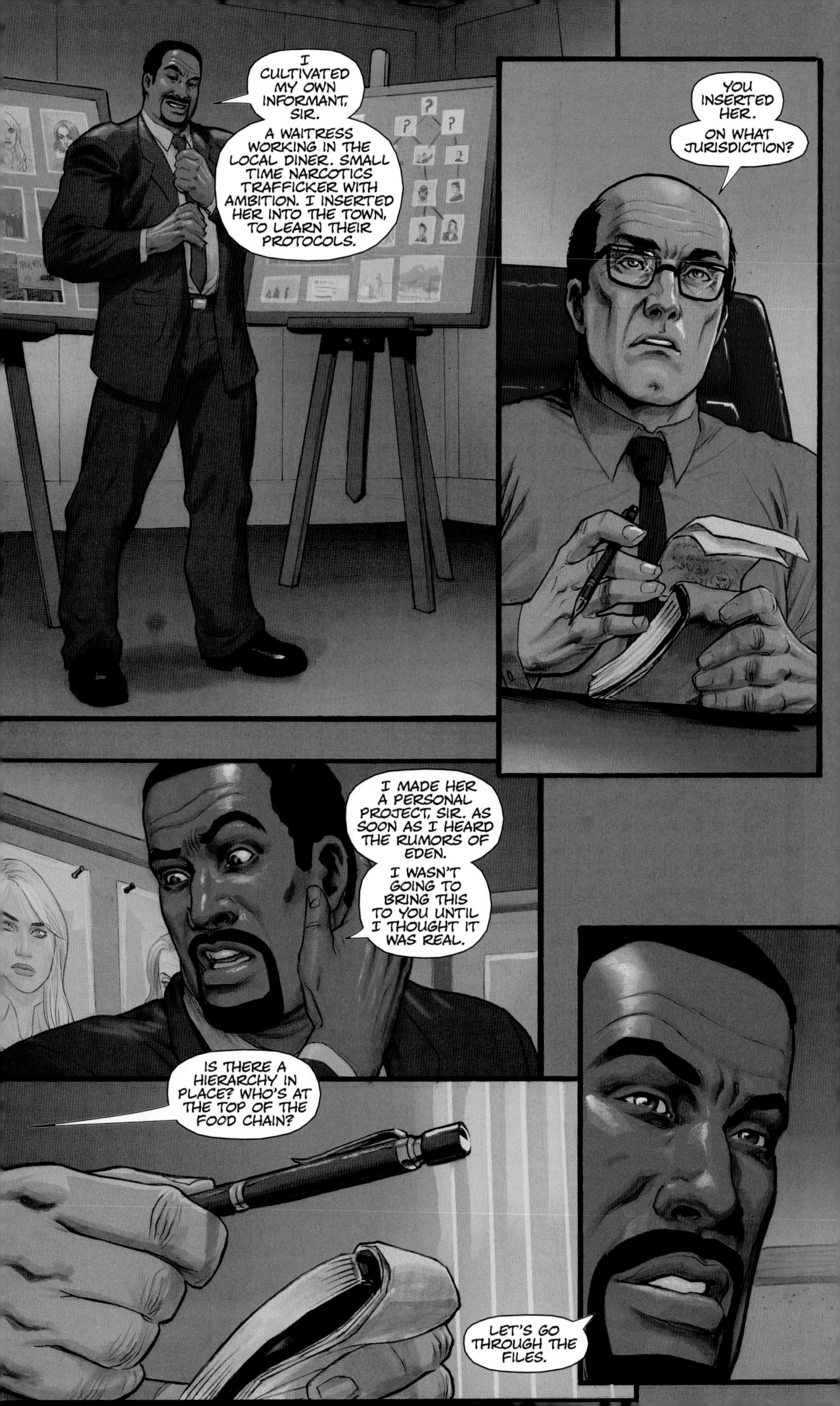
I CULTIVATED MY OWN INFORMANT, SIR.
A WAITRESS WORKING IN THE LOCAL DINER. SMALL TIME NARCOTICS TRAFFICKER WITH AMBITION. I INSERTED HER INTO THE TOWN, TO LEARN THEIR PROTOCOLS.
YOU INSERTED HER.
ON WHAT JURISDICTION?
I MADE HER A PERSONAL PROJECT, SIR. AS SOON AS I HEARD THE RUMORS OF EDEN.
I WASN'T GOING TO BRING THIS TO YOU UNTIL I THOUGHT IT WAS REAL.
IS THERE A HIERARCHY IN PLACE? WHO'S AT THE TOP OF THE FOOD CHAIN?
LET'S GO THROUGH THE FILES.

EDEN, WYOMING

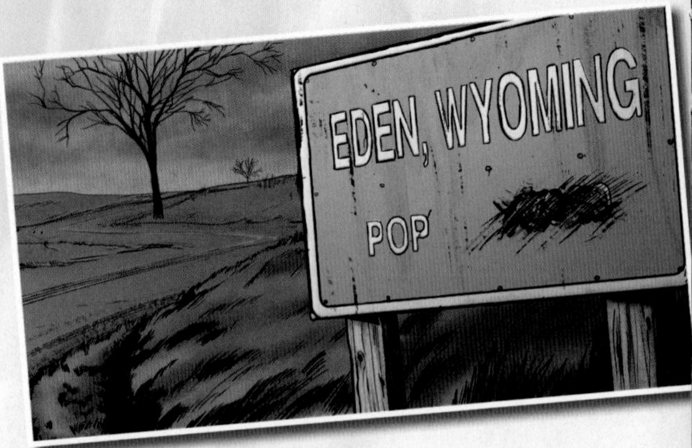
EDEN, WYOMING
POP

POPULATION: 2,190 (Approximate)

FOUNDED: 1979

FOUNDED BY: Isaac [REDACTED]

DMS Lat: 40 - 48° ?' ????" N

DMS Long: 105 - 109?° ??' ????" W

LOCAL GOVERNMENT:
Laura Shiffron – Mayor
Roy Magnum (alias) – Sheriff
Mark Shiffron – Postmaster (unofficial)

NOTES ON STATISTICS: Data for ethnic makeup, crime rate (ha!), birth rate, death rate, state and federal civic participation, and local economy are effectively unavailable – and, this agent would argue, irrelevant.

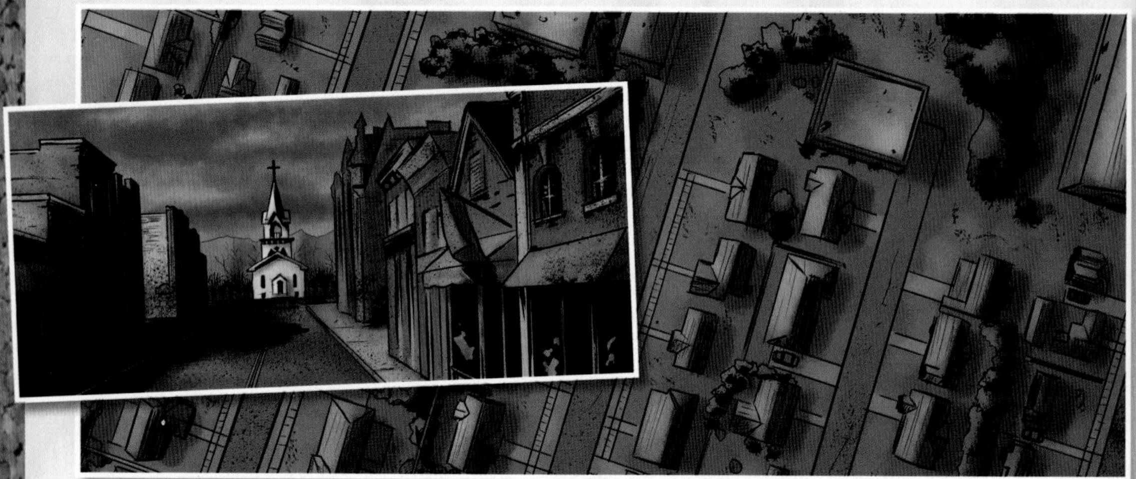

"This is a place that wants to be quiet."

A town like Eden doesn't have an official motto, but I heard one of the townspeople say that once, during surveillance, and it stuck with me. Eden doesn't have an official anything – even the sign posted at the town limits isn't DOT official, trust me – I checked.

You won't find it on a map, and you won't find it on satellite imaging. There's no cellphone towers, no open internet usage, no cable TV, no state infrastructure – not even the road that runs through it. Eden doesn't apply for any state or federal funding, doesn't submit tax records, and – in spite of the evidence I am presenting to you in this report – doesn't have a zip code or designation.

The Department of Water and Power, the State Comptroller's office, the United States Postal Service, any relevant branch of the federal government – including the FBI and the CIA, I've checked – and even the congressmen chomping at the bit to gerrymander the state every chance they can get. Not a single trace or record of the town anywhere. How is that possible?

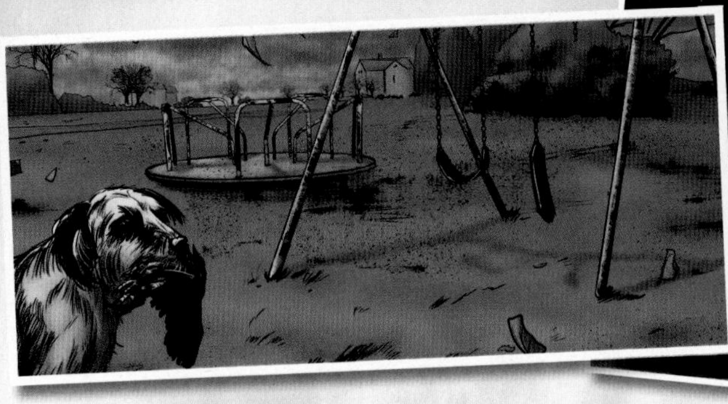

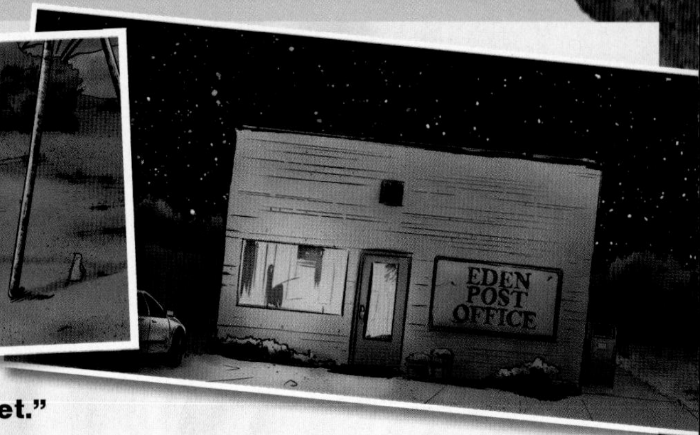
EDEN
POST
OFFICE

"This is a place that wants to be quiet."

They take it to heart out here, and for good reason, because with a handful of exceptions – most of them children – every single individual within the town limits is a person of interest in a criminal investigation. Most that I've identified are convicted felons, adjusting to society following release from security facilities. Others are witnesses, or individuals wanted for questioning…or people who've never been brought up on formal charges but have, in all likelihood, committed felonies of their own.

Some of Eden's residents, however – and this is where it gets troubling – appear to be wanted criminals on the run, men and women who have performed heinous acts and violent crimes and may never be brought to justice.

This town shelters them, some of them temporarily, some of them permanently, but either way it ensures that they elude our grasp. Some of the intel gathered even suggests that Eden employs a skilled plastic surgeon – someone by the name of Tolmach, though no records of interest matching that name could be found – who painstakingly reconstructs their faces to mask their appearance. I can even confirm that Eden employs a highly skilled technician (likely Johan Richter, see file) to systematically delete and replace records of the town's individuals, allowing them to transition back into society with no repercussions. (Having consulted with Southwest Branch's Agent James Miller, Badge no. [REDACTED], I can confirm the plausibility of such a scenario.)

To get down to the rub – Eden operates like a twisted version of the Federal Witness Protection Program, keeping the scum of the earth out of sight and out of the justice system. This is a maximum priority investigation, and if even half of the hearsay I've come across about the town's founder, Isaac, is true, then Eden could become a hotbed for the kind of violence that alters a nation irrevocably.

Admittedly, I have been conducting an off-the-books investigation of my own on Eden, which I've denoted in my own files as OPERATION: FORBIDDEN FRUIT. I understand the potential legal pitfalls I've placed the Bureau in, but I was careful not to violate any individual rights or clauses, and I've not disclosed my identity or blown my cover to anyone within the town – barring, of course, my single undercover informant.

This is the kind of bust that goes down in the history books, the kind of bust that makes careers – more importantly, the town of Eden flies in the face of everything that this country, and the Federal Bureau of Investigation, stands for.

I consider it my civic duty as an American to eliminate this hidden threat, and look forward to pressing forward with OPERATION: FORBIDDEN FRUIT in a more official capacity, with the full force of the Bureau behind me.

Simpson

OFFICIAL REQUISITIONS AND ACQUISITIONS DISCLOSURE FORM

Federal Bureau of Investigation

Operation: "Forbidden Fruit"
Location of Operation: Eden, Wyoming
Lead Operative: Simpson
Relevant Director of Operations: Jon Schultz

Equipment Logged:
 -Binoculars [QUANTITY: 1 Pair]
 -9mm Rounds [QUANTITY: 50]
 -Parabolic Microphone [QUANTITY: 1]

Vehicle(s) Logged:
Make: Ford
Model: Taurus
Year: 2002
Color: Burnt Sienna
Was this vehicle returned in an unaltered condition: Mostly.
If not, describe alterations: Dents in back fender

Expenses Logged:

Travel (including, but not limited to, gasoline, airfare, public transportation): $467
Lodging: $245
Food/Necessities: $580
Misc. (please provide detailed receipts): $1,189

Human Resources Logged: Informant Established

Name of Informant: Margaret [REDACTED] (alias surname of "Prendowski")

Occupation of Informant: Food Services, Waitress

Brief Description of Informant: Blonde Hair, Blue Eyes, Mid-20s, svelte

Is this Informant applicable for consideration as a "Criminal Informant" (If so, please complete and attach FORM NO. 88-C): Yes.

Brief Description of Informant's Prior Offenses: Narcotics Distribution, Assault, Tax Evasion

Brief Description of Informant's Role: Observes much of the criminal activity in and around the town of Eden. May be romantically involved with one MARK SHIFFRON, town postmaster and son of the town's mayor.

STATEMENT OF INTENT TO PURSUE CRIMINAL CHARGES

Federal Bureau of Investigation

CHARGES WILL BE LEVIED AGAINST:

-The Town of Eden, Wyoming (see previous report on success of the Racketeer Influenced and Corrupt Organizations Act)

-Laura Shiffron

AT THE TIME OF THIS FORM'S COMPLETION, IS THERE EVIDENCE SIGNIFICANT ENOUGH TO LEVY THE AFOREMENTIONED CHARGES: No.

IF NO, HAS A FOLLOW-UP OPERATION BEEN REQUESTED: Yes.

IF YES, LIST THE FOLLOW-UP OPERATION'S DESIGNATION HERE:
Operation: Forbidden Fruit.

LIST OF CHARGES TO BE PURSUED:

-Conspiracy to Commit Murder in the First Degree
-Murder in the First Degree
-Murder in the Second Degree
-Murder in the Third Degree
-Manslaughter
-Resisting Arrest
-Obstructing Justice
-Treason
-Racketeering
-Terrorist Activities
-Tax Evasion
-Tax Fraud

MINIMUM NUMBER OF PERSONS TO BE CHARGED: 2,190

SPECIAL NOTES: Utilizing RICO, I believe that we can successfully charge the town of Eden with its many crimes – it's happened before. Read my previous report on the successful implementation of RICO in small town racketeering cases, and against these so-called homegrown mafias.

Simpson

To: Deputy Director Jon Schultz
Federal Bureau of Investigation

The following profiles represent the most significant intelligence I've gathered on the residents of the town of Eden, Wyoming. After reading through my report on the town itself, and considering the evidence in support of my discoveries, I've whittled down my surveillance footage and notes, my full psychological profiles on the town's residents, and my opinion on its functions into the following single page profiles.

The proceeding files are succinct, and to the point, and have avoided unnecessary idle speculation – although in some cases speculation was necessary, as you will see. Still, I have avoided discussing the nonsensical or the irrelevant.

For example, while I have dozens of pages and hours of recorded surveillance on the Chef at the Eden Diner, who is almost certainly the same "Chef" made infamous in the violent socioanarcho demonstrations in France during the '90s, I have not included this information. I have not included the town's lone Native American resident, affectionately (or hatefully, depending on the speaker) nicknamed "Big Injun," in the following report, because some of my research suggest that the Comanche may in fact have been innocent of the previous charges held against him.

Most importantly, I have not included the vast amount of speculation, hearsay, and near myth associated with the town's co-founder, Isaac - former husband to Laura Shiffron and father of Mark. I have not listed his frequent association with the quasioccult criminal sprees of the late 1980s – although, in the attached miscellany, I have attached a newsprint article from the mid-80s that may allude to one of his crimes. But I will not waste time digging around for the possible real life identity of this legend of a man. Isaac is dead. Eden's residents hanged him from a tree well over a decade ago.

There are enough monsters in Eden without my needing to bring back a dead man, Director Schultz.

See for yourself.

Simpson

LEGAL NAME: SHIFFRON, LAURA

KNOWN ALIAS(ES): N/A

BIRTH DATE: 23 SEPTEMBER 1965
STATE/NATION OF ORIGIN: Hartford, CT
HEIGHT/WEIGHT: 5' 6", 120 LBS
OCCUPATION: Mayor of Eden

PRIOR OFFENSES: Fraud, Racketeering, Distribution of Narcotics, Distribution of Firearms, Conspiracy to Commit Murder in the First Degree
KNOWN CRIMINAL AFFILIATIONS: N/A
KNOWN NONCRIMINAL AFFILIATIONS: N/A

PSYCHOLOGICAL PROFILE: I've read the profiles the Bureau has on record, from back when Shiffron first started associating with Isaac. It's not pretty stuff, but it's inaccurate, in my opinion – I don't think Shiffron is a sociopath.
Rather, I classify her as an amateur autocrat – there's an inherent Narcissism to a person who sees the violence and chaos at work in the world and thinks they can chain it up, make it a pet. You can't domesticate a place like Eden, with its people, but Laura seems to think that, given an iron first, a surveillance grid, and the occasional "Barn Brawl" that she can keep the pressure from boiling over. She's brilliant, cruel, and runs Eden as well as it could've been run, I believe – but she's either blind to, or in denial of, the carnage that's building up in that place.

SURVEILLANCE LOG (MARCH 29th, 2015):

6:00 AM – Subject rises. Engages in a 4 mile run around and through Eden.

7:00 AM – Subject returns to discover MARK SHIFFRON at her residence. The two enter and emerge several minutes later, heading for town.

7:30 AM – 9:00 AM – Subject, MARK SHIFFRON, and ROY MAGNUM meet in Sheriff's Office. DEPUTY EARLE is not present.

12:00 PM – Town hall meeting at CHURCH. Over 500 residents in attendance. (Surveillance note: Parabolic mic encounters extraordinary interference. Could not discern topics of discussion at meeting, but can guess – when the residents emerge, they are carrying the body of one DANIEL MESSERSMITH.)

1:00 PM – At some point while my surveillance was occupied on the church itself, the body of a young, white female was placed in the church's parking lot. At no point did I hear or see an automobile, or a suspect.

2:00 – 5:00 PM – Subject and SHERIFF canvas Eden and outskirts. SHERIFF and DEPUTY begin interrogating residents, as Subject returns home.

7:00 PM – Subject stands on porch, drinking from a mug and watching.
(Surveillance note: it's not possible, but I feel like she's looking right at me. Like she can see me, sitting in my dark car, parked in the woods, no one else around.)

LEGAL NAME: LAFLEUR, RORY

KNOWN ALIAS(ES): ROY MAGNUM

BIRTH DATE: 14 MARCH (A previously obtained record claims "1972" as Magnum's birth year – this seems unlikely, and may have been included by Magnum to obfuscate…or flatter himself.)
STATE/NATION OF ORIGIN: SAN FRANCISCO, CA
HEIGHT/WEIGHT: 6' 1", 203 LBS
OCCUPATION: Sheriff of Eden

PRIOR OFFENSES: Fraud, Petty Theft, Vandalism, Possession of an Unregistered Firearm, Assault and Battery
KNOWN CRIMINAL AFFILIATIONS: Hell's Angels (Inconsequential)
KNOWN NONCRIMINAL AFFILIATIONS: U.S. Army Rangers (Dishonorable Discharge), Gold's Gym (Membership Expired)

PSYCHOLOGICAL PROFILE: Profiles created before Magnum's association with Eden were scant, and many of them seemed to focus on Magnum's perceived overcompensation and nigh-obsession with North American standards of masculinity. These, I believe, may be in error – after detailed examination of intelligence, both new and old, it is this agent's opinion that Roy Magnum is neither an angry, closeted homosexual, nor a hotbed of toxic masculinity evolving into a homegrown terrorist. Rather, I would contend that Magnum is just as he appears – fatherly, but stern, capable of extreme action but not extreme planning. He is, in a word, simple. That, of course, makes him dangerous.

SURVEILLANCE LOG (MARCH 28th, 2015):

8:15 AM – Subject wakes, prepares and consumes breakfast of bacon, eggs, and milk.

9:03 AM – Subject finishes showering, shaving, and dressing – exits home in uniform.

9:30 AM – 5:06 PM – Subject patrols EDEN, both on foot and in vehicle. Nothing of consequence occurs. Subject samples muffins at grocery store, greets citizens, and partakes of meals at the EDEN DINER. Subject returns home, and removes uniform.

5:30 PM – 6:00 PM – Subject lifts weights and performs limited cardiovascular exercise. Music playlist comprised of "The Eagles" tunes plays at high volume.

7:00 PM – Subject travels to home of Mayor Laura Shiffron. Subject does not leave Shiffron's home until the following morning. A romantic relationship can be inferred.

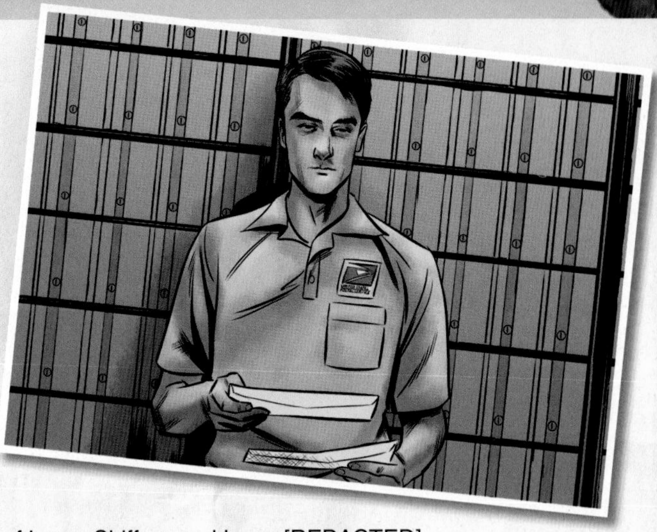

LEGAL NAME: SHIFFRON, MARK

KNOWN ALIAS(ES): N/A

BIRTH DATE: 11 NOVEMBER 1985
STATE/NATION OF ORIGIN: EDEN, WY
HEIGHT/WEIGHT: 6' 0", 175 LBS
OCCUPATION: Eden Postmaster

PRIOR OFFENSES: N/A

KNOWN CRIMINAL AFFILIATIONS: Son of Laura Shiffron and Isaac [REDACTED]

KNOWN NONCRIMINAL AFFILIATIONS: United States Postal Service (Unofficial)

PSYCHOLOGICAL PROFILE: Examining my own earlier psych profiles of Mark, I discovered that I had been lax in my analysis, simplifying the man into little more than a Forrest Gump analog. I should've known better – nothing in Eden is simple.
Mark is, assuredly, a textbook case of Asperger's Syndrome. Given the information from my own in-town source, and what I've observed, Mark can be brusque, fails to read social cues, and often displays behavior and reasoning we've come to associate with individuals stuck in Piaget's "Concrete Operational" state.
Still, Mark has his father in him – and his mother. He has been raised by criminals and sociopaths, murderers and monsters, and where once I suspected a weak link I now fear may manifest an avatar of the violence in Eden, an heir to the bloody throne that Isaac and Laura have built.
To put it plainly – I believe that Mark could become something very, very dangerous.

SURVEILLANCE LOG (JULY 8th, 2015):
(Surveillance note – subject is meticulous and slow in his actions. What might take an average person five minutes to do can take Mark up to half an hour.)

8:15 AM – Subject wakes late. Prepares and eats breakfast. (Surveillance note: Subject returned to town late last evening following his weekly pickup run, escorted by SHERIFF MAGNUM. He appears to be wounded. I have been unable to tail Mark on these excursions, which I believe involve him retrieving parcels and letters.)

9:30 AM – 12:00 PM – Subject sorts and transcribes mail.

12:30 – 2:30 PM – Subject breaks usual routine and eats lunch with MAYOR SHIFFRON and SHERIFF MAGNUM, presumably to debrief.

3:00 PM – 6:00 PM – Subject delivers mail and parcels.

7:00 PM – MAGGIE PRENDOWSKI arrives, with food from the diner. The two, presumably, share a meal. (Surveillance note – romantic connection? MAGGIE was exceedingly cagey on this particular topic.)

LEGAL NAME: MARGARET [REDACTED]

KNOWN ALIAS(ES): "Margaret Prendowski" (Bureau-established false identity)

BIRTH DATE: 9 January 1985
STATE/NATION OF ORIGIN: Los Angeles, CA
HEIGHT/WEIGHT: 5' 7", 120 LBS
OCCUPATION: Food Service

PRIOR OFFENSES: Distribution of Narcotics, Assault, Manslaughter, Possession of an Illegal Firearm
KNOWN CRIMINAL AFFILIATIONS: MS-13 (The cartel has standing orders to kill Margaret on sight)
KNOWN NONCRIMINAL AFFILIATIONS: N/A

PSYCHOLOGICAL PROFILE: Now that I'm no longer fluffing up her profile with fake information about "Margaret Prendowski," I can be honest about Maggie.
Here is a person capable of great moral sacrifice, and I mean that in the worst possible way. Maggie is ambitious, fatally so – a pretty little white girl from Los Angeles tried to cut in on the heroin trade…and almost succeeded, until she got on the bad side of MS-13 and got her boyfriend gunned down in front of her.
But that didn't phase her. Not remotely.
I only happened upon Maggie because she was begging for deals, she knew the Guatemalans would gut her in federal, and I had friends looking for criminals that fit a certain profile. In that respect, Maggie was perfect.
But that experience in her life didn't quell the violence in her, and neither did Eden. Every time she and I met up to exchange information, she became more hostile. In our last meeting, there was an incident. She seems to have eyes on taking control of the town – I think she may be slipping from my grasp. It might not be the worst thing for the op if, with the Deputy Director's permission, of course, her time as an informant was terminated. With extreme prejudice.

SURVEILLANCE LOG (SEPTEMBER 1st, 2015):

9:00 AM – 5:00 PM – Subject serves guests at the EDEN DINER. Among them: "BIG INJUN," SHERIFF MAGNUM, MARK SHIFFRON, and DEPUTY EARLE.

6:00 – 8:00 PM – Subject engages in a series of (presumably clandestine) meetings with town residents, most notably ROWAN, CURTIS, and "BIG INJUN."
(Surveillance note: I don't have enough information to speculate on what Subject is up to with these meetings, but I know that she's ambitious enough that whatever it is, it's going to shake up Eden. I'm telling you – a bloodbath is imminent.)

9:00 PM – Subject returns to residence, and prepares a light meal before reading.

11:00 PM – Subject falls asleep.

LEGAL NAME: RICHTER, JOHAN

KNOWN ALIAS(ES): J0hk3r (Hacker's online history confirmed with the assistance of Southwest Branch Field Agent James Miller, Badge No. [REDACTED])

BIRTH DATE: 13 SEPTEMBER 1983
STATE/NATION OF ORIGIN: Baltimore, MD
HEIGHT/WEIGHT: 5' 9", 180 LBS
OCCUPATION: Evidence suggests that MAYOR SHIFFRON pays Johan directly for his technological servies

PRIOR OFFENSES: Murder in the First Degree (Acquitted)

KNOWN CRIMINAL AFFILIATIONS: Anonymous

KNOWN NONCRIMINAL AFFILIATIONS: Best Buy Corporation – "Geek Squad"

PSYCHOLOGICAL PROFILE: Johan's life appears very straightforward to me.
Here is a boy who never really became a man. He was picked on in school, probably bullied relentlessly, and, after graduating, he assuredly retreated into a wholly introverted lifestyle. There were online exploits, and like many shy, awkward boys, he may have found some solace there. But all of that changed when they found the girl's body.
And yes, he was acquitted, and, yes, it's entirely possible that Johan Richter was innocent of the heinous crimes perpetuated on that child. But as far as the public was concerned? As far as the general population of a federal prison would be concerned? Guilty. And you know how they treat pedophiles in general pop. So somewhere along the line, Laura Shiffron found him, and picked him up, and hid him away. Another asset gathered. And here is, as far as I can tell, a spineless worm of man with the technological skill to help take down infrastructures vastly superior to Eden's own…and Shiffron's got him in her pocket.
See why I'm worried?

SURVEILLANCE LOG (SEPTEMBER 28th, 2015):

11:30 AM – MAYOR SHIFFRON arrives at Subject's trailer. SHIFFRON seems unwilling to enter the dwelling, and the two discuss terms outside.

12:45 PM – A short while after SHIFFRON leaves, Subject exits his trailer, carrying several large duffel bags. Later surveillance determines these bags to be full of tech.

1:30 – 4:00 PM – Subject travels from location to location throughout the town, examining power lines, testing areas with various meters, and examining outlets.

8:00 PM – Subject returns to trailer and rendezvous with an UNIDENTIFIED WOMAN. The two enter, and she leaves 30 min later. I suspect this woman was a prostitute, based on her dress and the timing of their visit, but I cannot confirm.

LEGAL NAME: EARLE, DAVID F.

KNOWN ALIAS(ES): "Early"

BIRTH DATE: 12 FEBRUARY 1990
STATE/NATION OF ORIGIN: EDEN, WY
HEIGHT/WEIGHT: 5' 11", 175 LBS
OCCUPATION: Sheriff's Deputy

PRIOR OFFENSES: N/A

KNOWN CRIMINAL AFFILIATIONS: N/A

KNOWN NONCRIMINAL AFFILIATIONS: N/A

PSYCHOLOGICAL PROFILE: If this were any other small town in America, Earle would be the squeaky clean town darling. Young, not brilliant but not dumb, not ugly, not fat – the fellow who spent his entire life in Eden. Just another yokel.

Except, of course, for the fact that his parents, who brought him here as an infant, were convicts on the run, and much like Mark Shiffron, he was raised by murderers, con men, and criminals.

He grew up idolizing SHERIFF MAGNUM – his own father was out of the picture pretty early on, and I think, in a place where order is the only thing that keeps the wolves at bay, MAGNUM must've looked like a powerful, respectable man (even if, realistically, it's LAURA SHIFFRON who commands all the power and respect.)

I don't want to discount or write-off anyone in this unlikely place, but if I had to choose a weak link – a simple man – it'd be Earle. I don't believe he has a hidden agenda, or any grand plans; he's just your stereotypical, townie Deputy-Dawg-type.

SURVEILLANCE LOG (OCTOBER 1st, 2015):

9:05 AM – Subject rushes out of home, disheveled in appearance. Late for work, Subject is clearly in a hurry, and spills coffee on himself several times.

9:25 AM – Subject arrives at the EDEN CIVIC CENTER.

11:00 AM – Subject and SHERIFF MAGNUM leave office, to investigate what appears to be a domestic disturbance. As Magnum attempts to placate her partner, an African-American woman throws a mug at Subject, who tried to enter their home.

12:30 PM – SHERIFF MAGNUM and Subject eat lunch at the EDEN DINER.

3:00 – 4:30 PM – Subject washes windows at the EDEN CIVIC CENTER

5:00 PM – SHERIFF MAGNUM and Subject hold detailed, heated discussion.

6:00 PM – Subject attends late services at the EDEN CONGREGATIONAL CHURCH.

7:00 PM – Subject purchases takeout meal from the EDEN DINER, takes it with him to the town's playground, and eats it, watching the sunset while seated on a swing.

8:00 PM – Subject returns home. Loud rock music can be heard from Subject's dwelling.

LEGAL NAME: NIXON, ATTICUS F.

KNOWN ALIAS(ES): ATTICUS WHITE, "The White Power Preacher"

BIRTH DATE: 9 FEBRUARY 1969
STATE/NATION OF ORIGIN: LOUISIANA (City/County Unknown)
HEIGHT/WEIGHT: 5' 10", 180 LBS
OCCUPATION: Pastor, First Congregational Church of Eden

PRIOR OFFENSES: Disturbing the Peace, Destruction of Public Property, Vandalism, Hate Speech, Conspiracy to Commit Murder, Assault and Battery (Acquitted)

KNOWN CRIMINAL AFFILIATIONS: The Aryan Brotherhood, The Ku Klux Klan

KNOWN NONCRIMINAL AFFILIATIONS: Southern Baptist Church

PSYCHOLOGICAL PROFILE: Nixon was raised a racist, in the Deep South. That kind of hate was in his blood. But he was bright, for a good ol' boy, and somehow ended up learning how to preach from some of those hateful old revival types that travel around the Baptist circuit.
I watched Nixon closely when I first came to Eden – he appeared to have no intention on altering his identity or appearance, and seemed intent on staying in the town. I couldn't find any records of his time in federal, but somewhere along the line he appears to have genuinely dislodged his ethnocentric beliefs. Eden's no stranger to white supremacists (see: the "boxer," BRAD MULVEY), or to former white supremacists (see: the recent addition, ROWAN).
He answers to SHIFFRON, sure enough, and he seems to hold some sway over the town – criminals always seem to find God once they've been caught – but I think SHIFFRON exploits what is clearly latent Narcissism (see: Nixon's flamboyant, theatrical sermons, and his insistence that town hall meetings occur at the church) to ensure Nixon stays under her thumb.

SURVEILLANCE LOG (OCTOBER 3rd, 2015):

7:00 AM – Subject rises early, and following a shower and breakfast, Subject goes for a short walk around the Church grounds, near the town limits.

8:00 AM – Early Service. No one of significance in attendance.

10:00 AM – Several residents arrive, and Reverend Nixon conducts individual confessions. (Surveillance note: Nixon has never worked within a church or congregation that conducts formal confession. I've checked his history. A fascinating appropriation of the Catholic tradition, where it appears to be necessary.)

12:00 – 5:00 PM – Subject remains within church. No one visits.

6:00 PM – Late service. DEPUTY EARLE, and a slightly greater crowd, attends.

8:00 PM – MAYOR SHIFFRON, SHERIFF MAGNUM, and Subject meet.

9:00 PM – Subject retires to apartment attached to rectory.

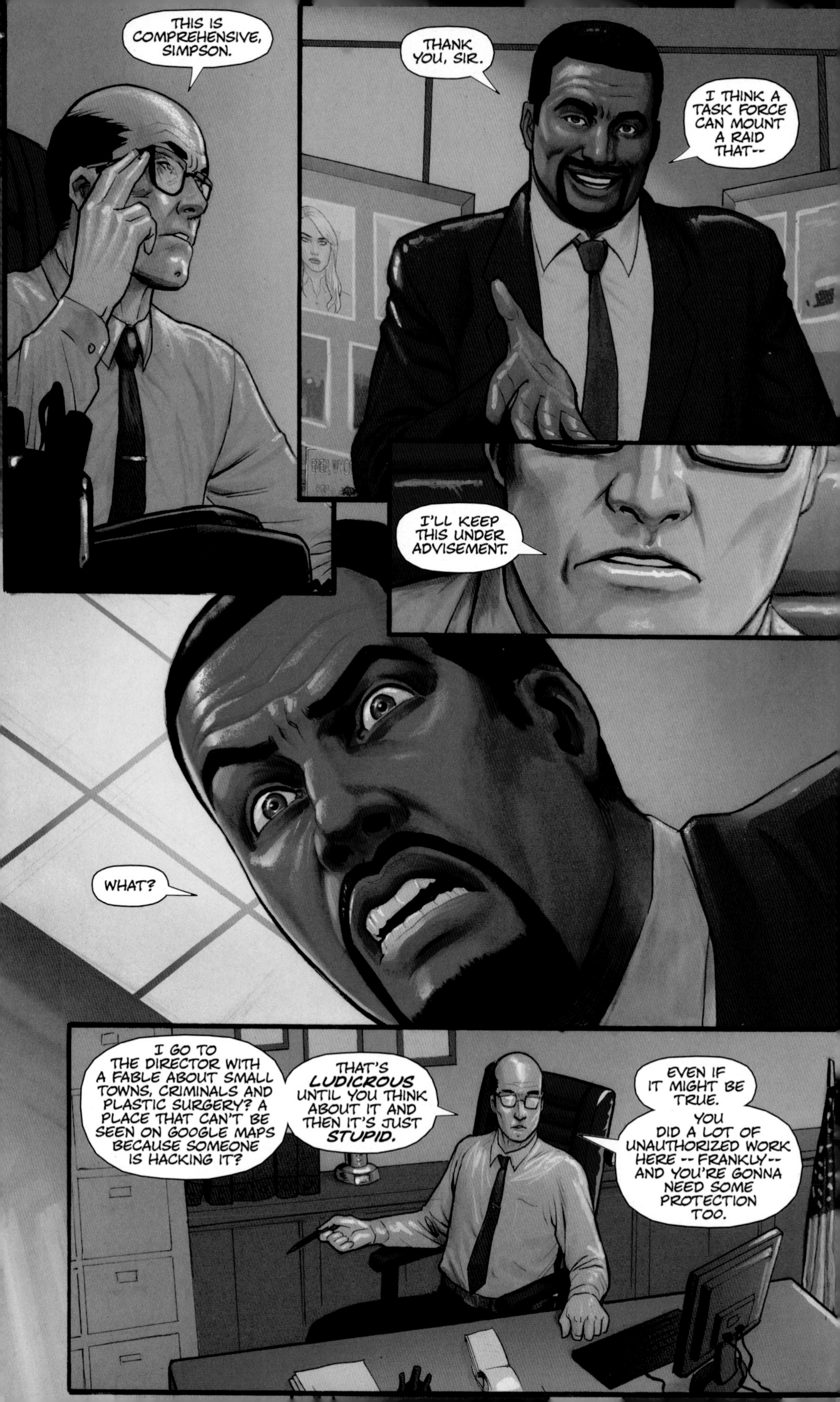
THIS IS COMPREHENSIVE, SIMPSON.
THANK YOU, SIR.
I THINK A TASK FORCE CAN MOUNT A RAID THAT--
I'LL KEEP THIS UNDER ADVISEMENT.
WHAT?
I GO TO THE DIRECTOR WITH A FABLE ABOUT SMALL TOWNS, CRIMINALS AND PLASTIC SURGERY? A PLACE THAT CAN'T BE SEEN ON GOOGLE MAPS BECAUSE SOMEONE IS HACKING IT?
THAT'S *LUDICROUS* UNTIL YOU THINK ABOUT IT AND THEN IT'S JUST *STUPID.*
EVEN IF IT MIGHT BE TRUE.
YOU DID A LOT OF UNAUTHORIZED WORK HERE -- FRANKLY-- AND YOU'RE GONNA NEED SOME PROTECTION TOO.

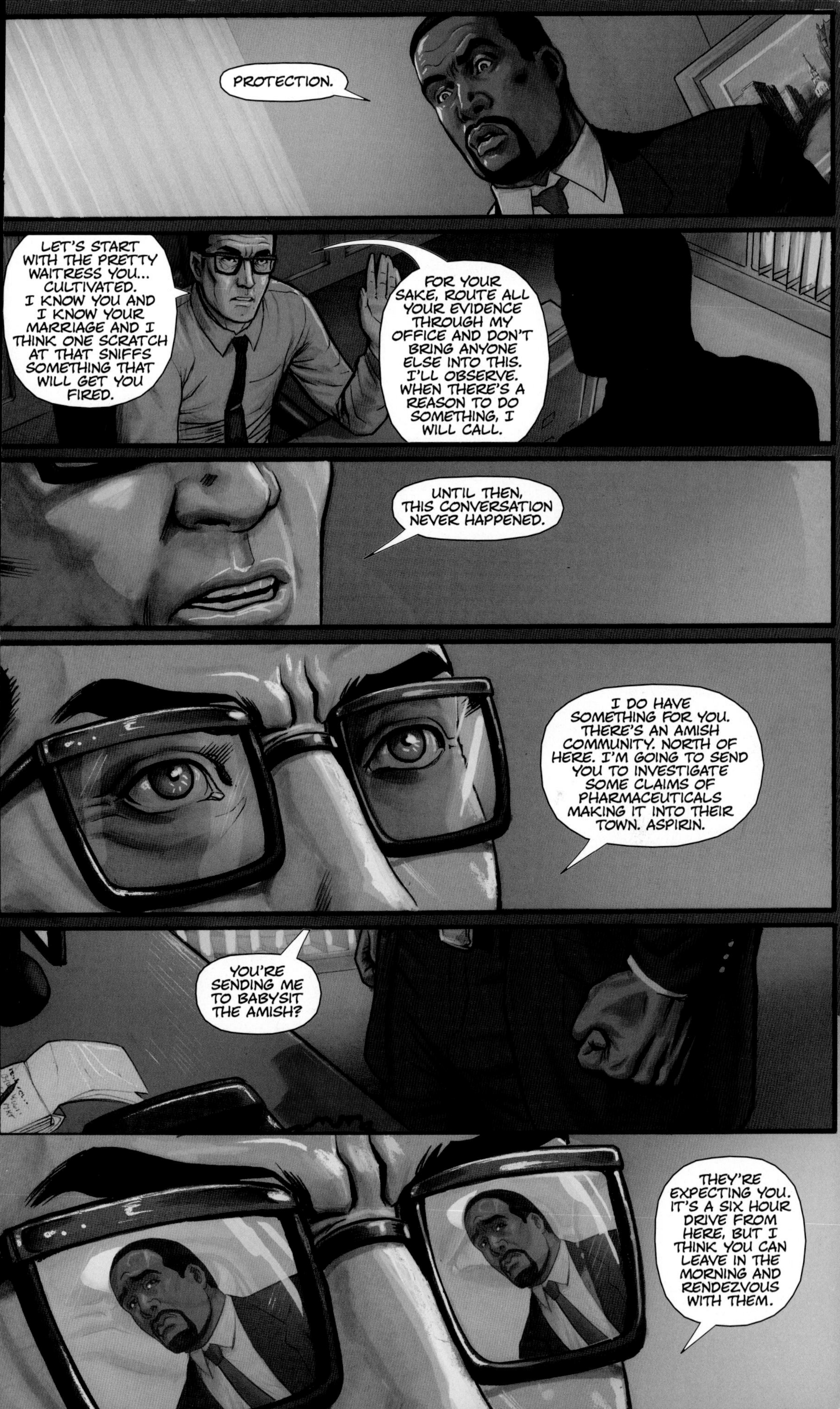
PROTECTION.
LET'S START WITH THE PRETTY WAITRESS YOU... CULTIVATED. I KNOW YOU AND I KNOW YOUR MARRIAGE AND I THINK ONE SCRATCH AT THAT SNIFFS SOMETHING THAT WILL GET YOU FIRED.
FOR YOUR SAKE, ROUTE ALL YOUR EVIDENCE THROUGH MY OFFICE AND DON'T BRING ANYONE ELSE INTO THIS. I'LL OBSERVE. WHEN THERE'S A REASON TO DO SOMETHING, I WILL CALL.
UNTIL THEN, THIS CONVERSATION NEVER HAPPENED.
I DO HAVE SOMETHING FOR YOU. THERE'S AN AMISH COMMUNITY. NORTH OF HERE. I'M GOING TO SEND YOU TO INVESTIGATE SOME CLAIMS OF PHARMACEUTICALS MAKING IT INTO THEIR TOWN. ASPIRIN.
YOU'RE SENDING ME TO BABYSIT THE AMISH?
THEY'RE EXPECTING YOU. IT'S A SIX HOUR DRIVE FROM HERE, BUT I THINK YOU CAN LEAVE IN THE MORNING AND RENDEZVOUS WITH THEM.

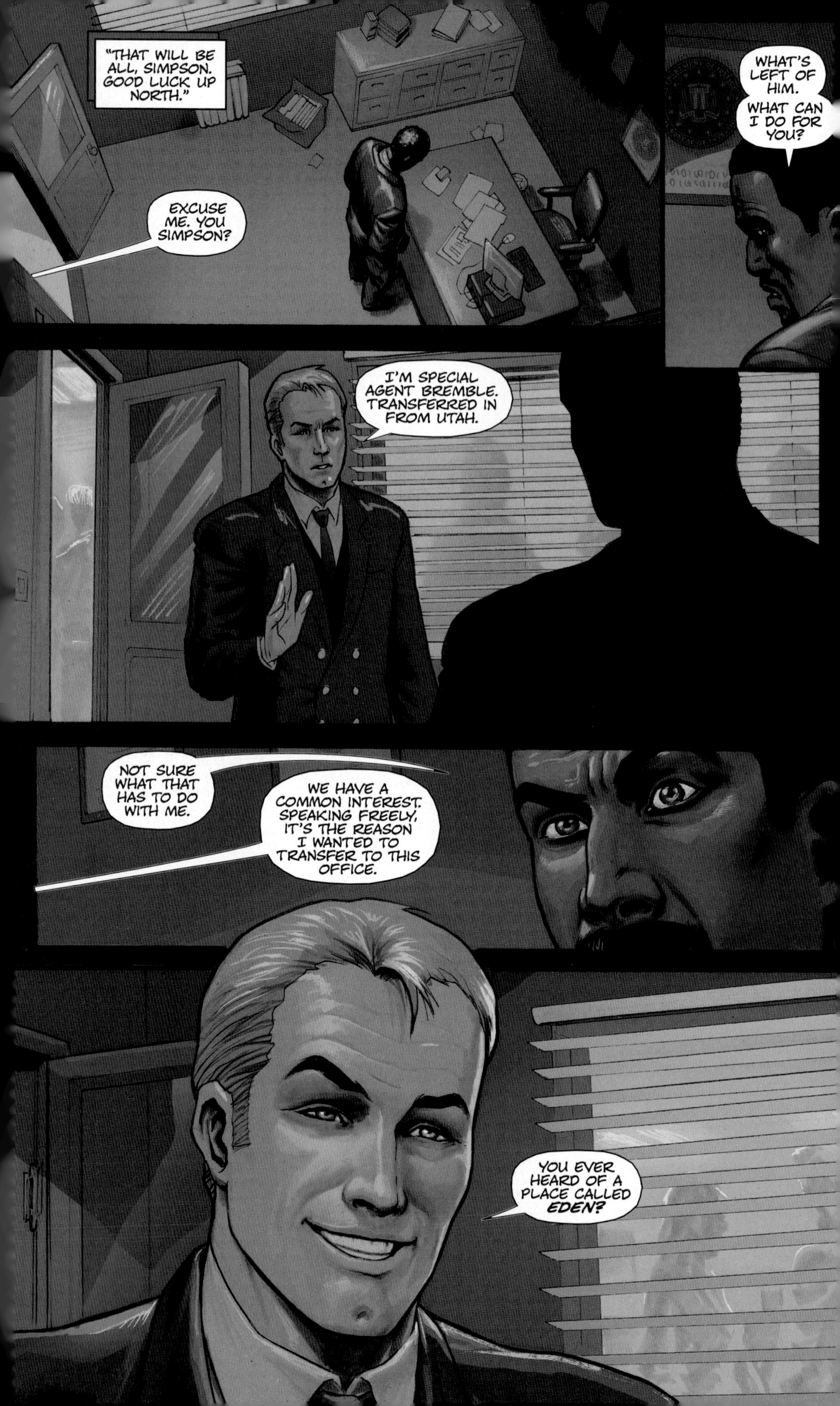

"THAT WILL BE ALL, SIMPSON. GOOD LUCK UP NORTH."
EXCUSE ME. YOU SIMPSON?
WHAT'S LEFT OF HIM.
WHAT CAN I DO FOR YOU?
I'M SPECIAL AGENT BREMBLE. TRANSFERRED IN FROM UTAH.
NOT SURE WHAT THAT HAS TO DO WITH ME.
WE HAVE A COMMON INTEREST. SPEAKING FREELY, IT'S THE REASON I WANTED TO TRANSFER TO THIS OFFICE.
YOU EVER HEARD OF A PLACE CALLED *EDEN?*

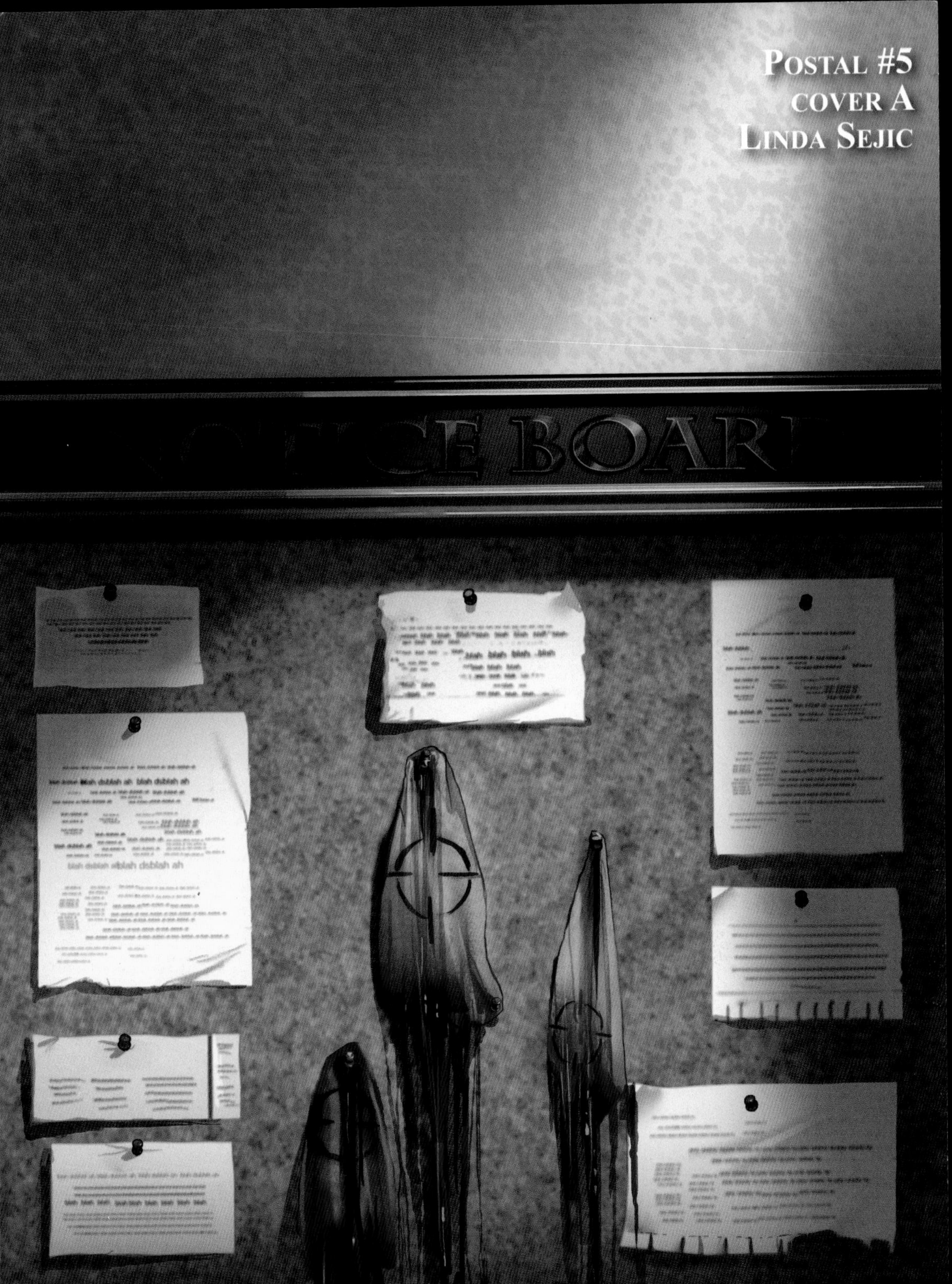

POSTAL #5
COVER A
LINDA SEJIC

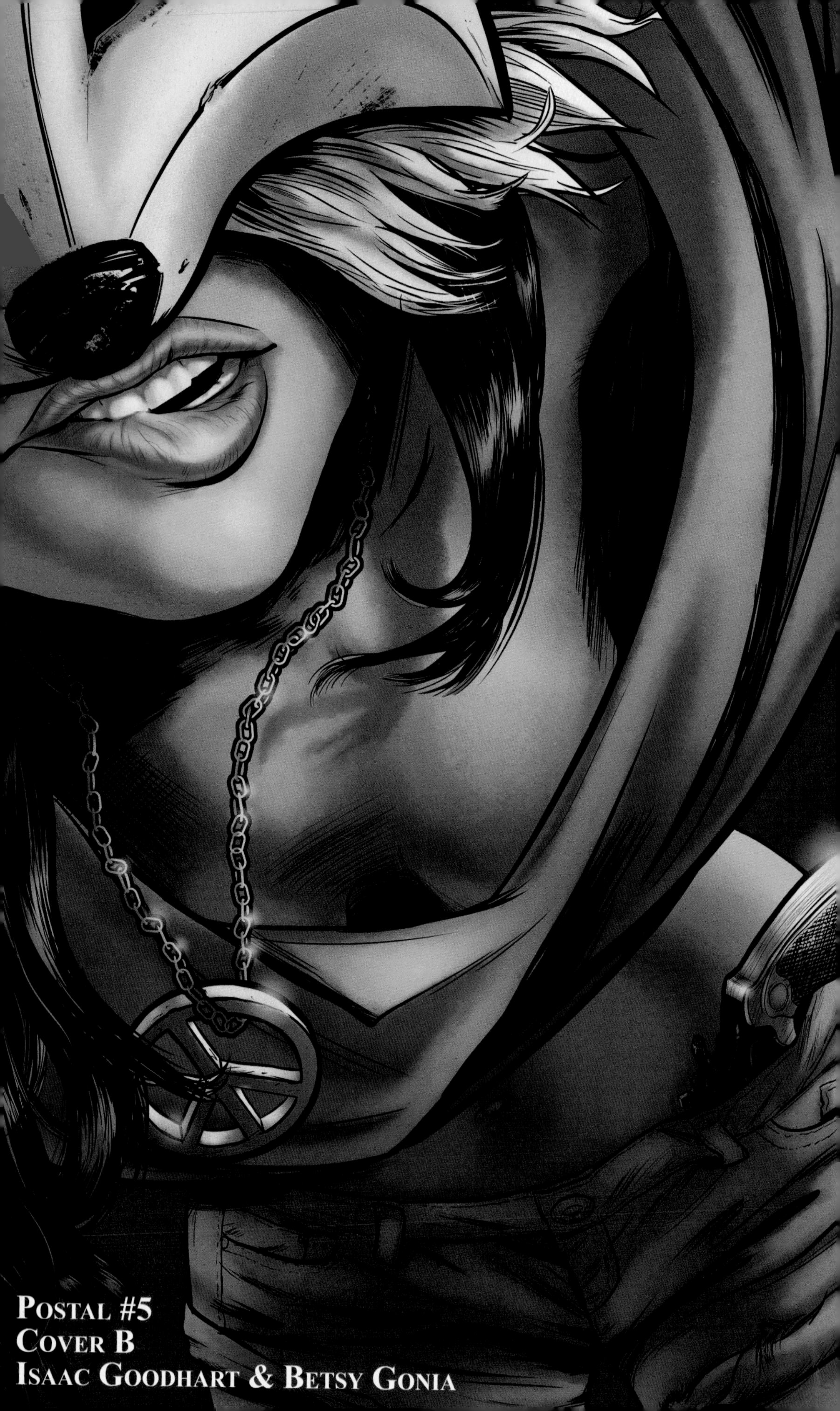

POSTAL #5
COVER B
ISAAC GOODHART & BETSY GONIA

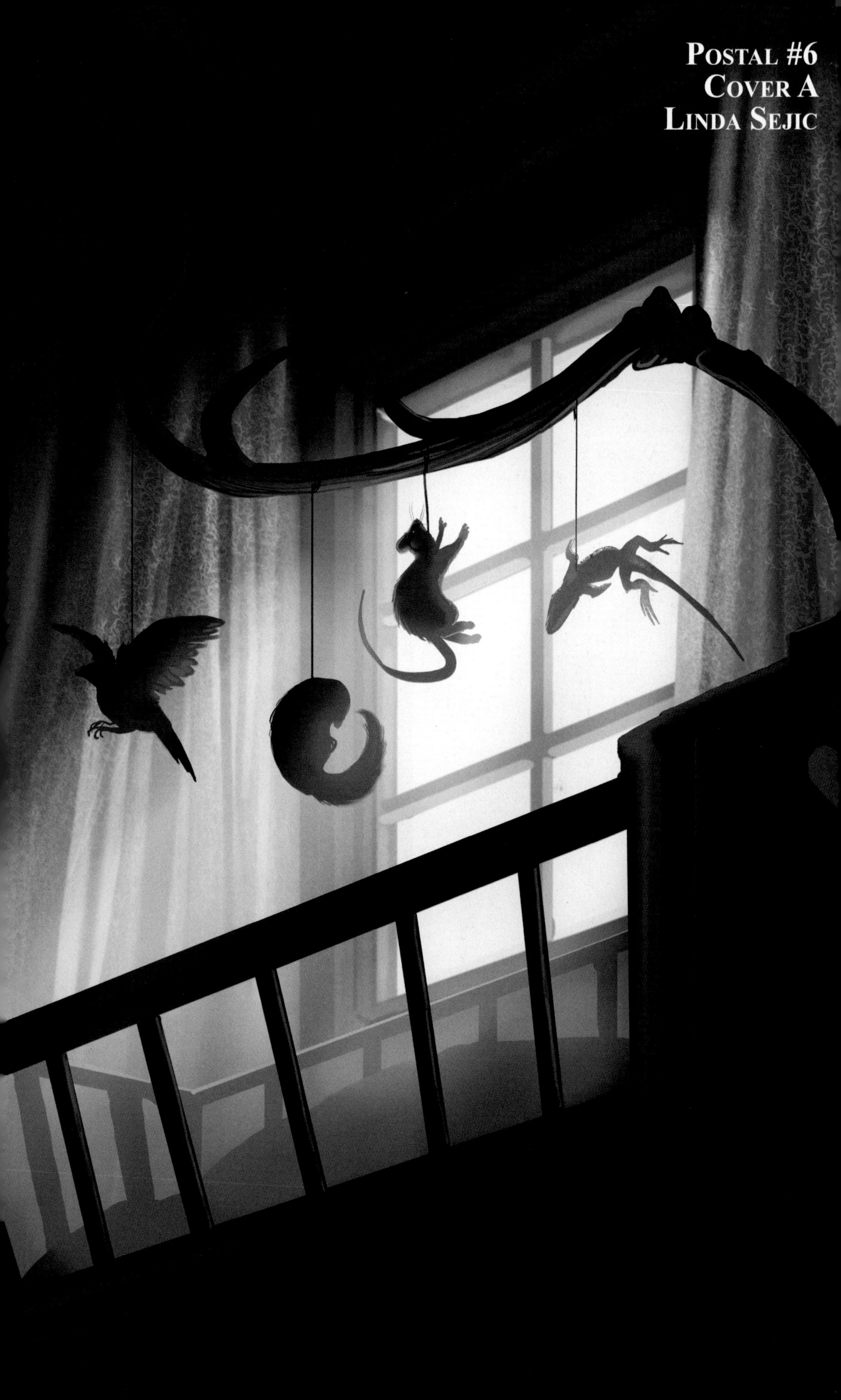

POSTAL #6
COVER A
LINDA SEJIC

Postal #6
Cover B
Isaac Goodhart & Betsy Gonia

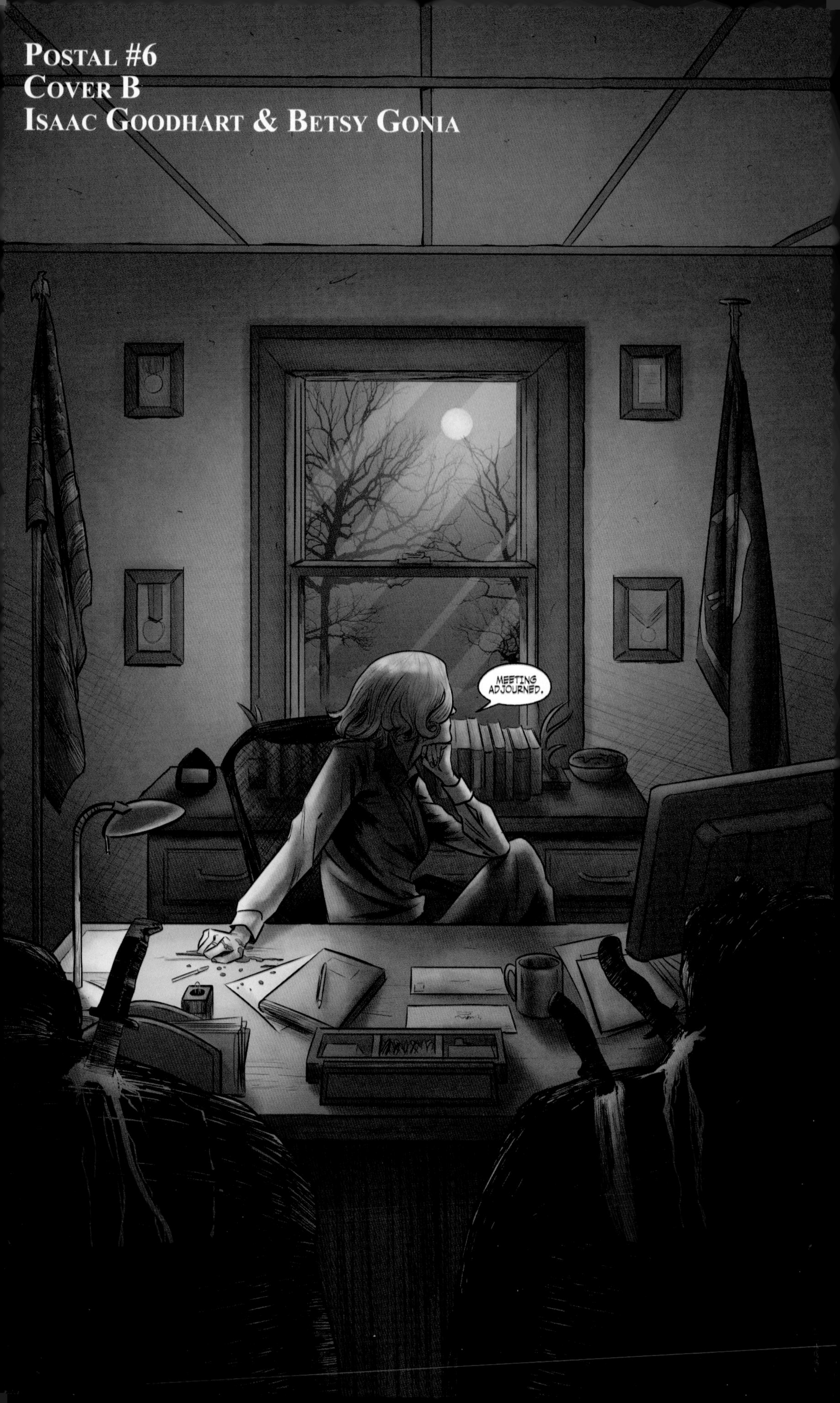
MEETING ADJOURNED.

Postal #7
Cover A
Linda Sejic

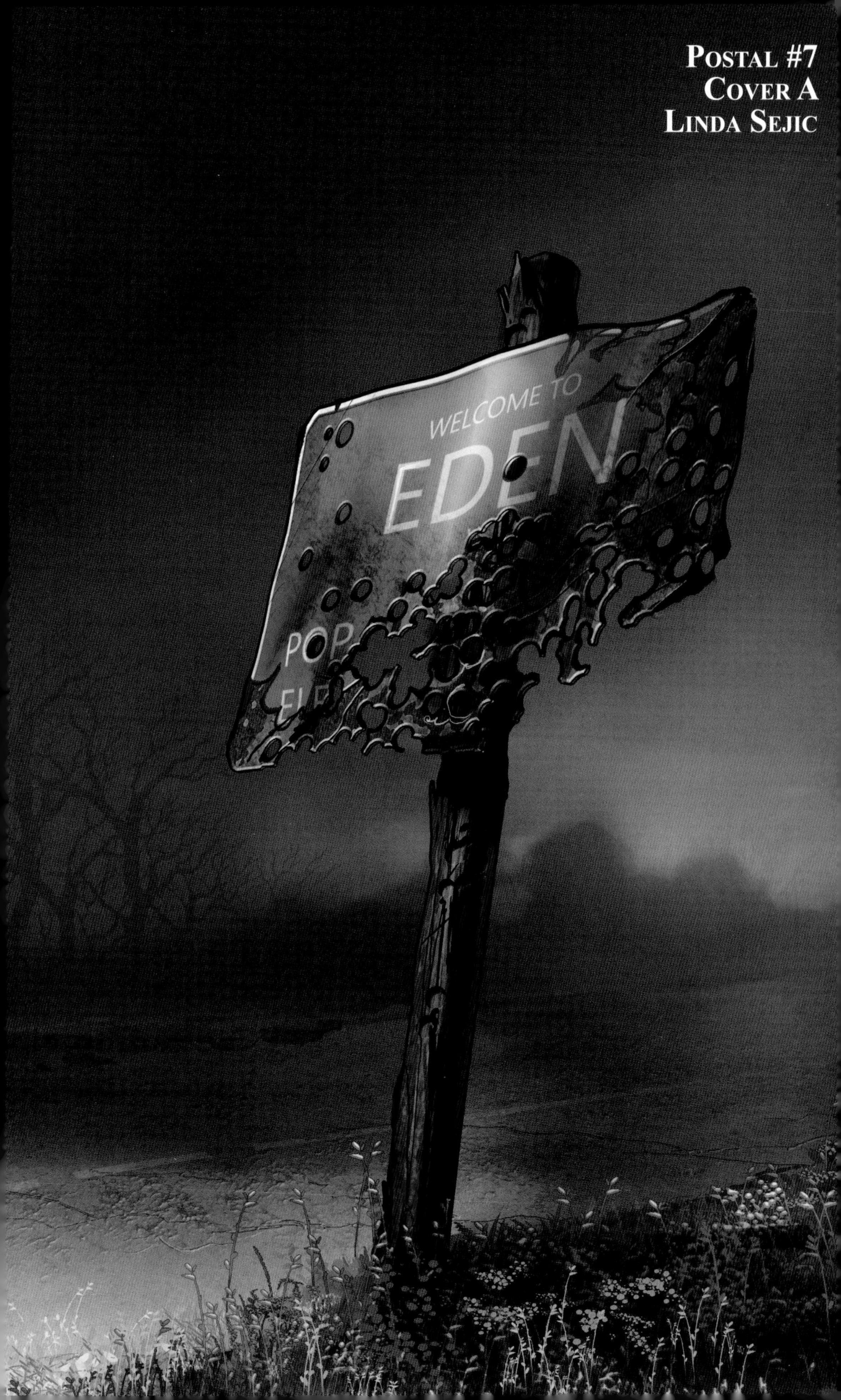
WELCOME TO
EDEN
POP

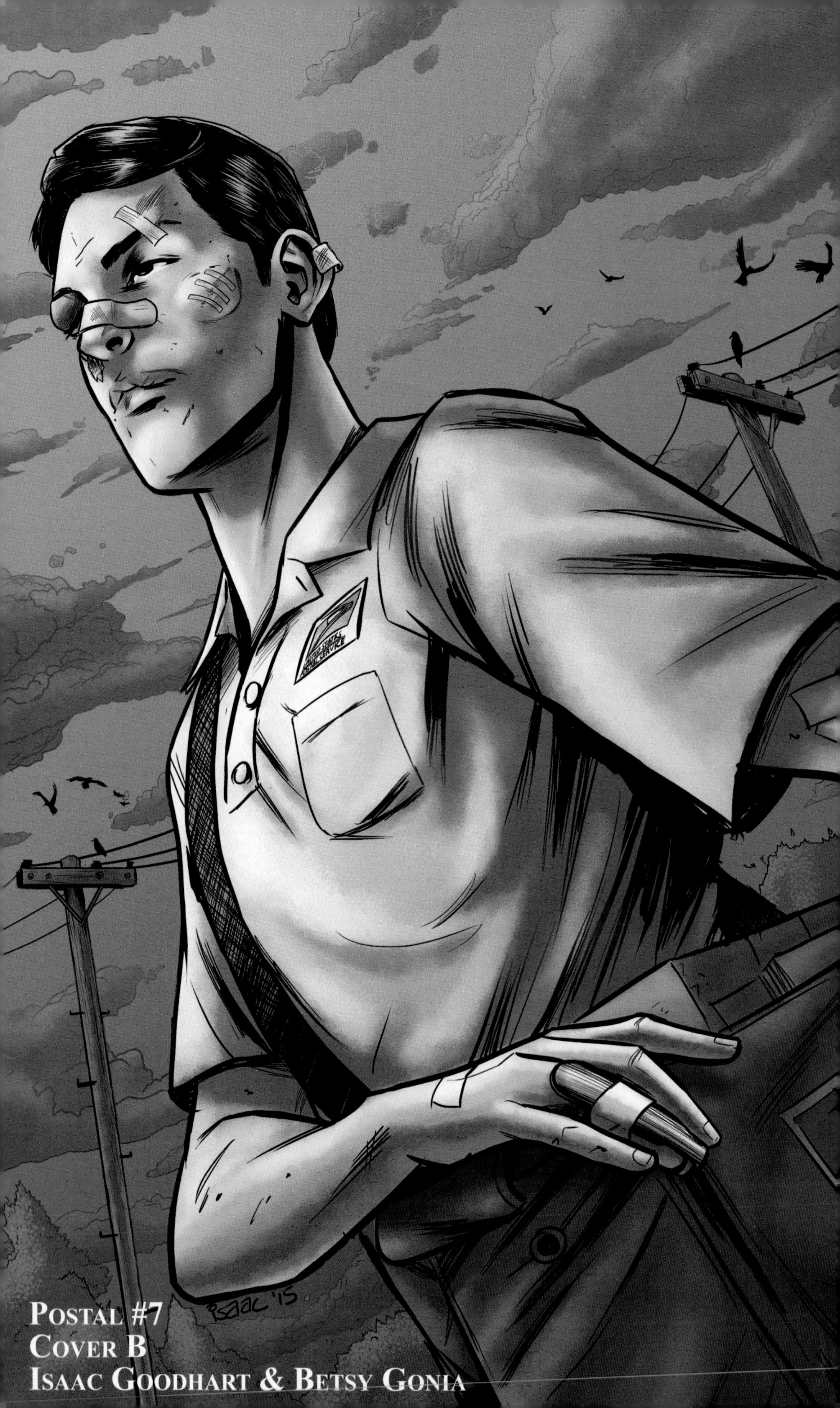
Isaac '15

Postal #7
Cover B
Isaac Goodhart & Betsy Gonia

Postal #8
Cover A
Linda Sejic

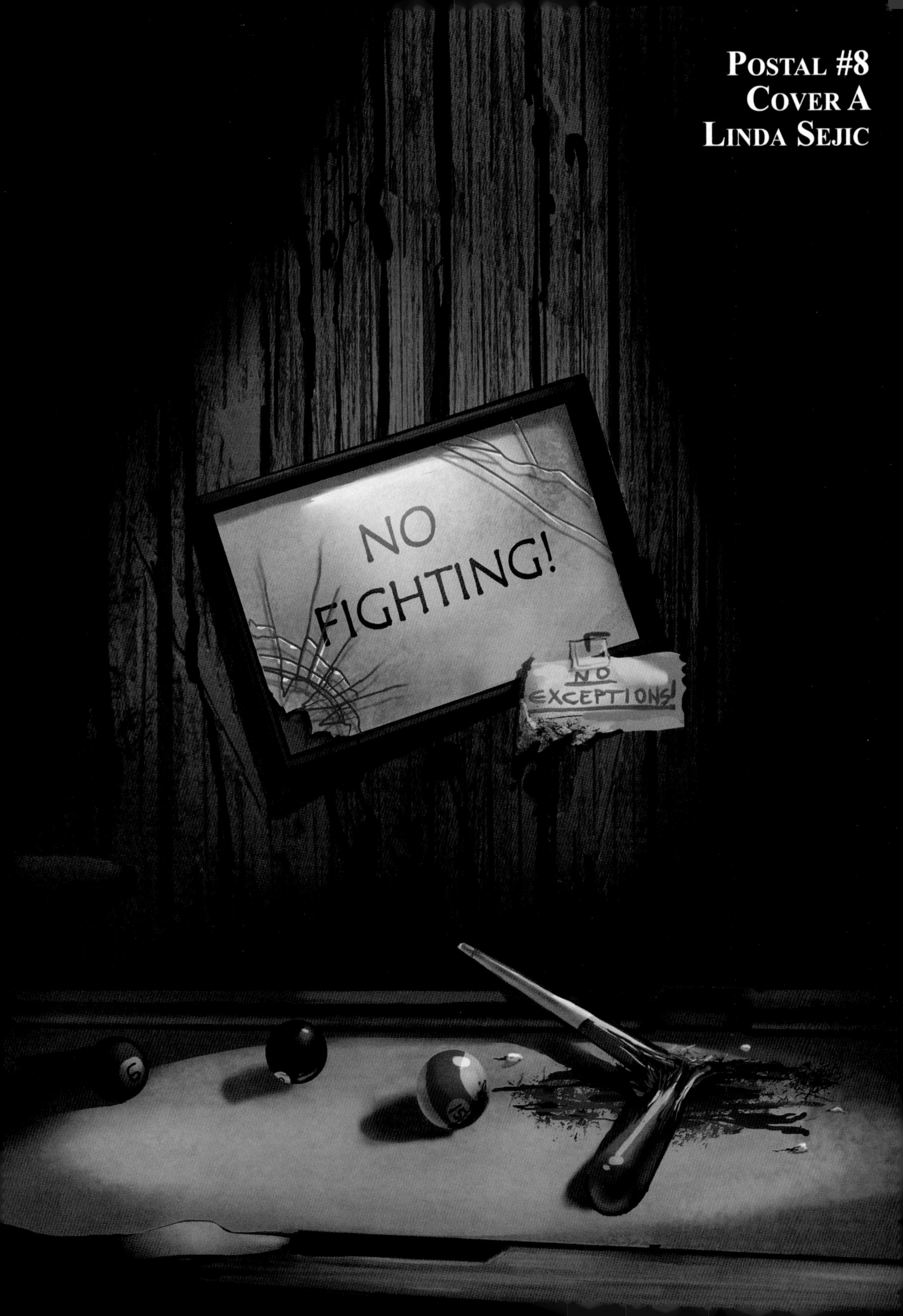
NO FIGHTING!
NO EXCEPTIONS!

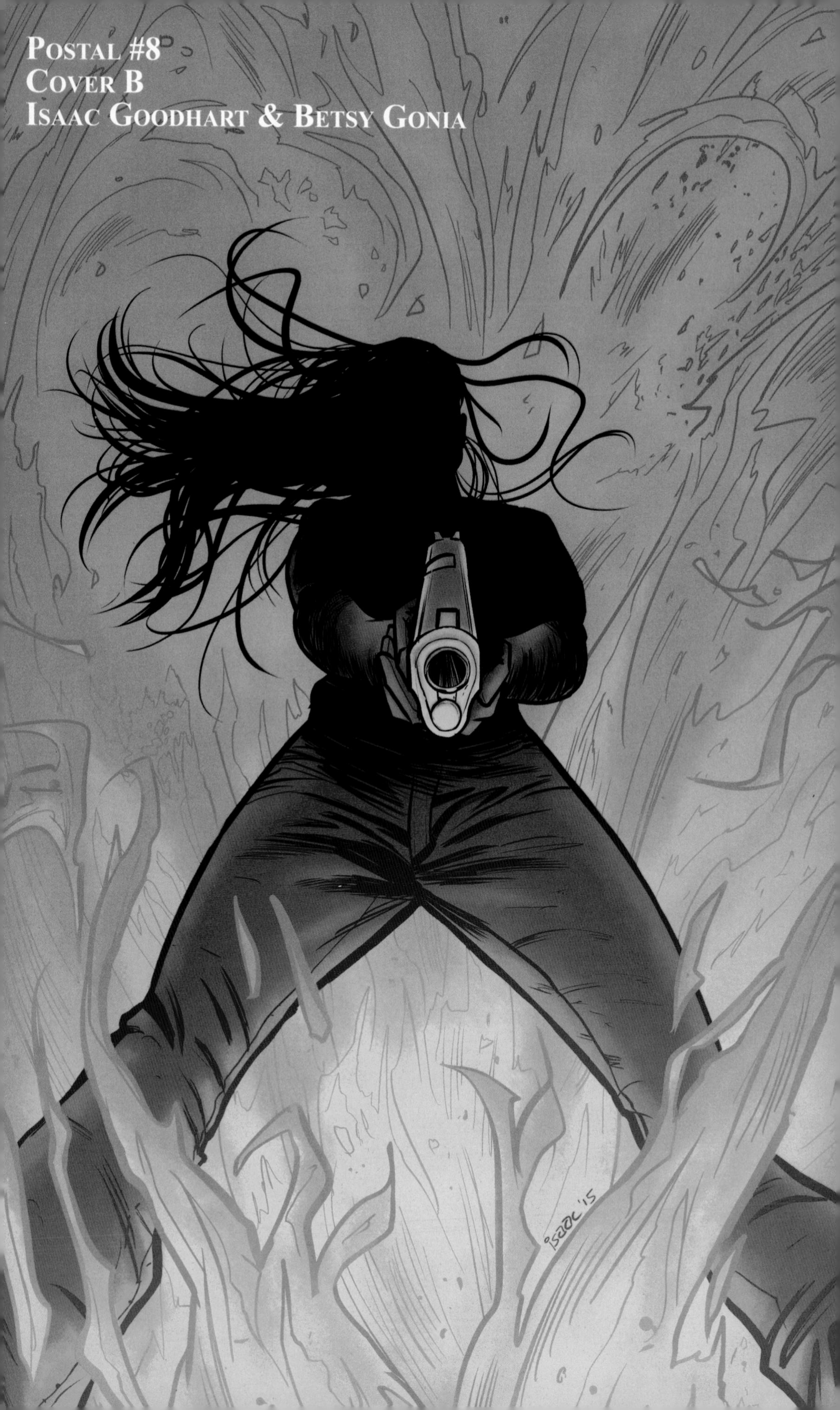
POSTAL #8
COVER B
ISAAC GOODHART & BETSY GONIA
isaac '15

Postal Dossier #1
Cover A
Linda Sejic

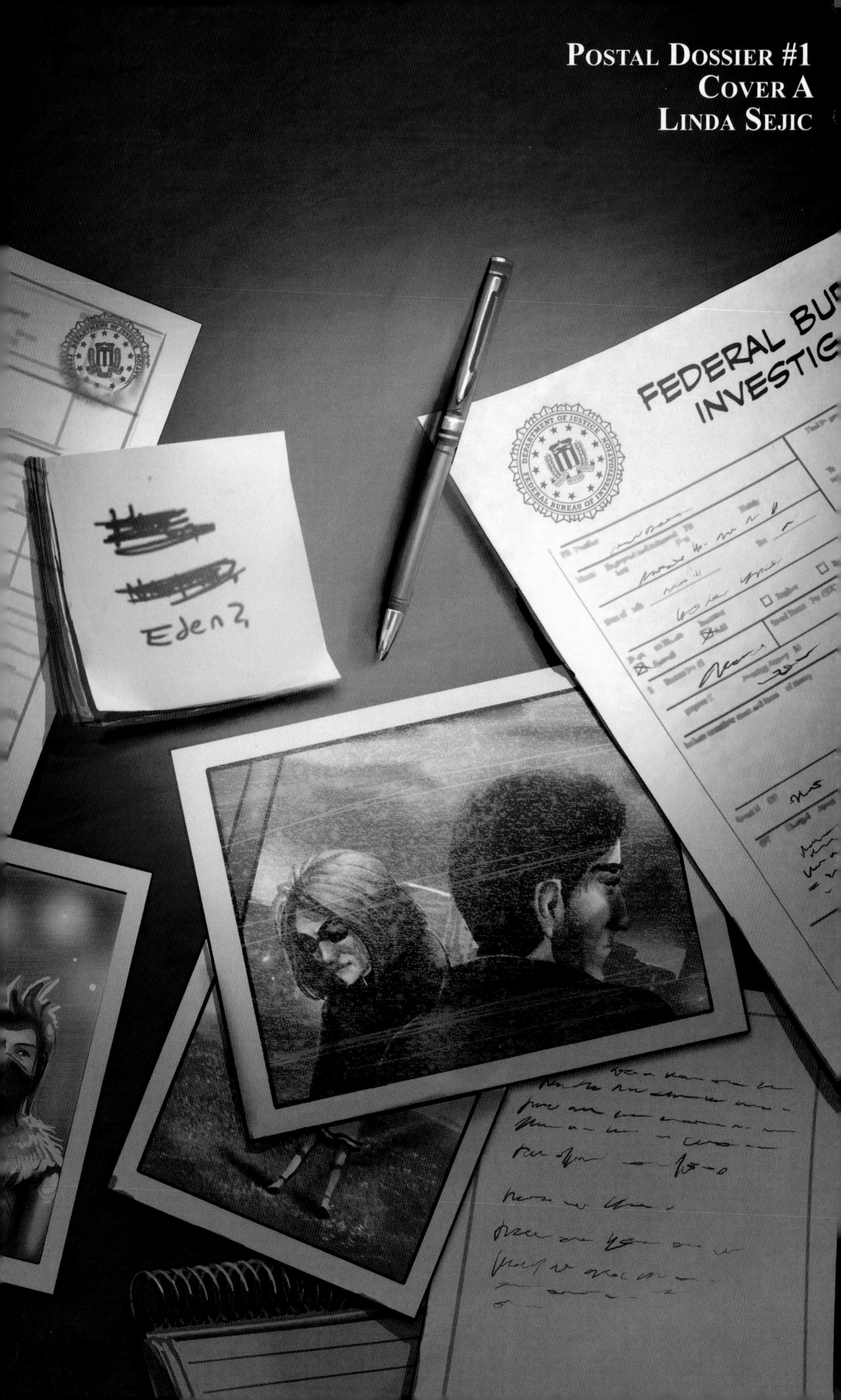
FEDERAL
Eden?
DEPARTMENT OF JUSTICE
FEDERAL BUREAU OF INVESTIGATION

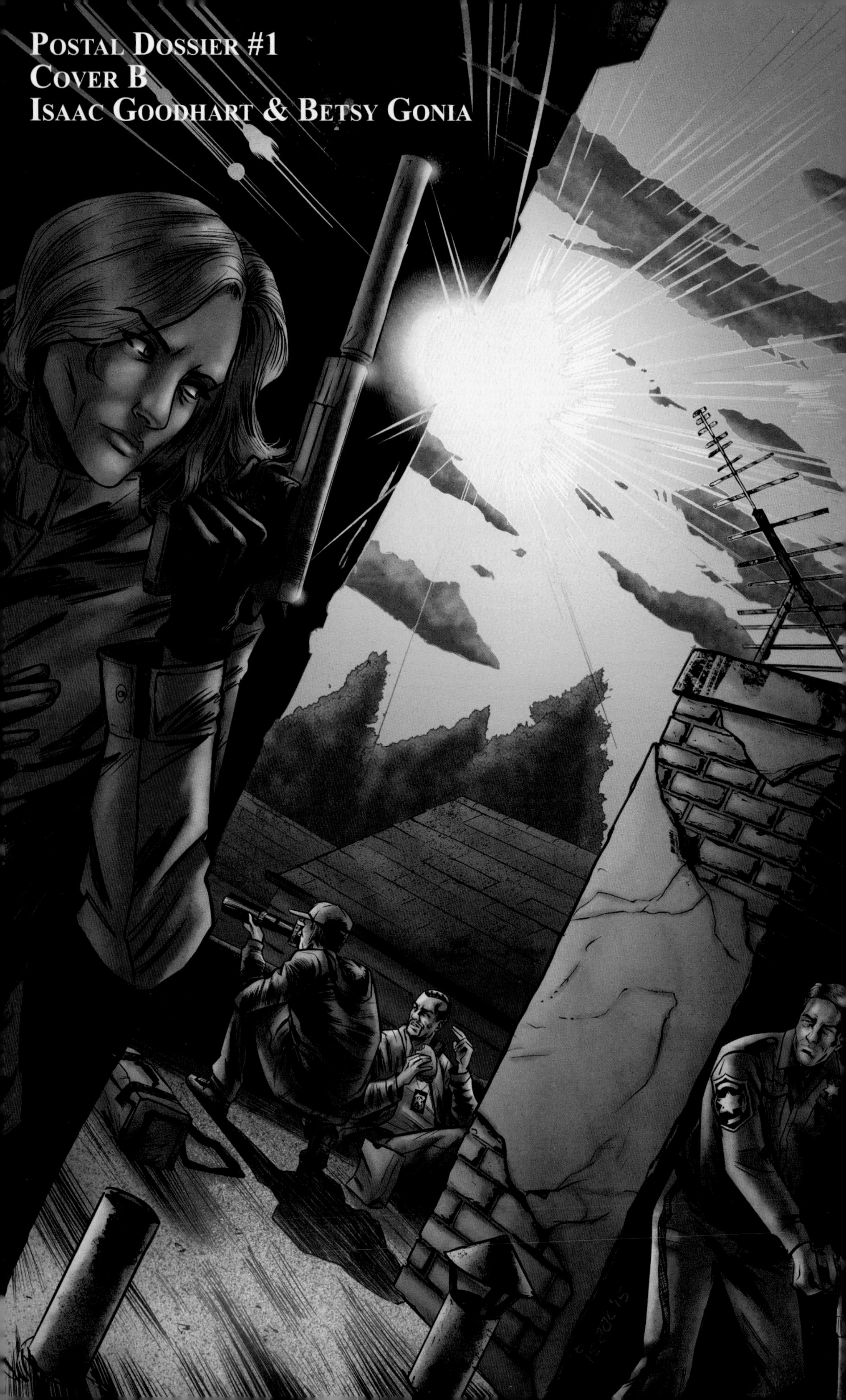

Postal Dossier #1
Cover B
Isaac Goodhart & Betsy Gonia

MEET THE CREATORS

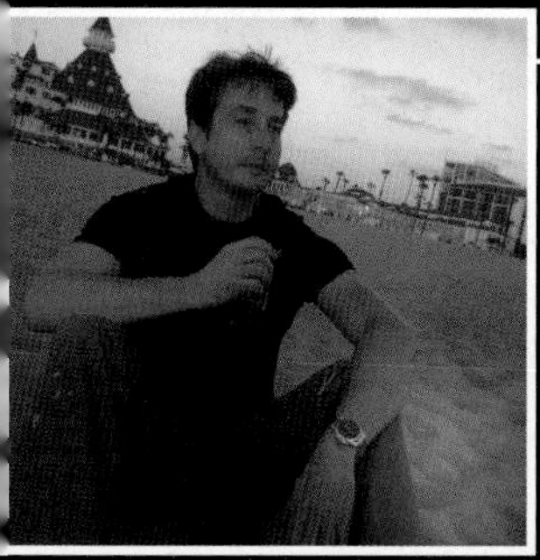

MATT HAWKINS

A veteran of the initial Image Comics launch, Matt started his career in comic book publishing in 1993 and has been working with Image as a creator, writer, and executive for over twenty years. President/ COO of Top Cow since 1998, Matt has created and written over thirty new franchises for Top Cow and Image including *Think Tank, Necromancer, VICE, Lady Pendragon,* and *Aphrodite IX* as well as handling the company's business affairs.

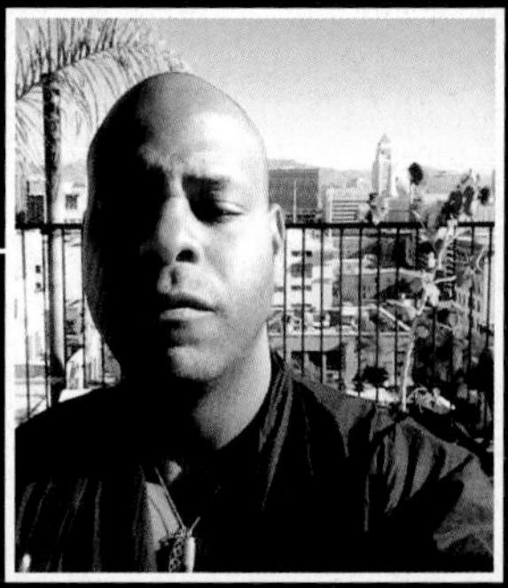

BRYAN HILL

Writes comics, writes movies, and makes films. He lives and works in Los Angeles. @bryanedwardhill | Instagram/bryanehill

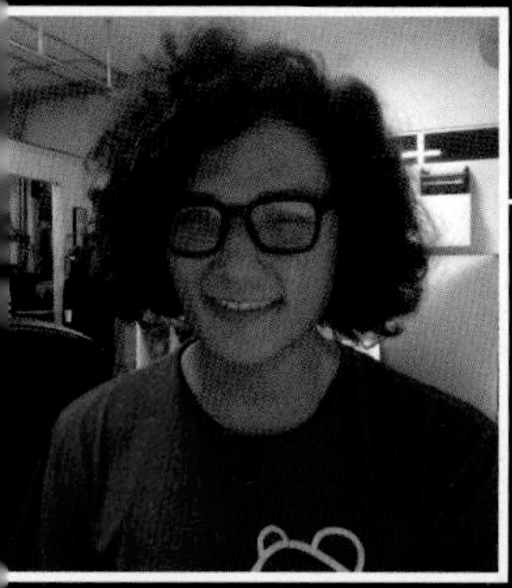

ISAAC GOODHART

A life-long comics fan, Isaac graduated from the School of Visual Arts in New York in 2010. In 2014, he was one of the winners for Top Cow's annual talent hunt. He currently lives in Los Angeles where he storyboards and draws comics.

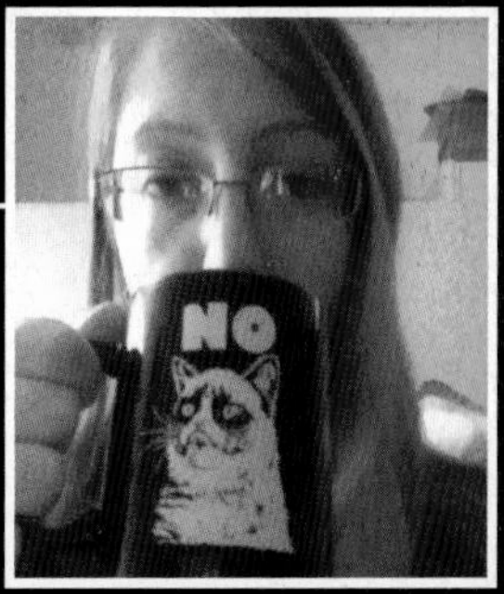
NO

BETSY GONIA

After graduating from the Savannah College of Art & Design in 2012, Betsy began working at Top Cow Productions. Now editing for the company, she also colors a few of their titles to actively partake in her favorite part of comic book creation.

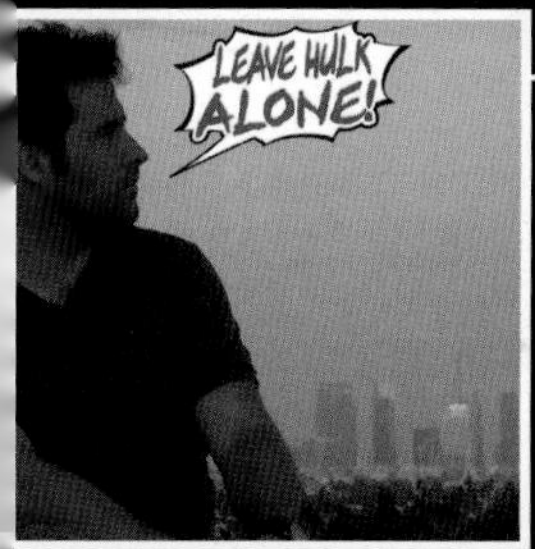
LEAVE HULK ALONE!

TROY PETERI

Starting his career at Comicraft, Troy Peteri lettered titles such as *Iron Man*, *Wolverine*, and *Amazing Spider-Man*, among many others. He's been lettering roughly 97% of all Top Cow titles since 2005. In addition to Top Cow, he currently letters comics from multiple publishers and websites, such as Image Comics, Dynamite, and Archaia. He (along with co-writer Tom Martin and artist Dave Lanphear) is currently writing (and lettering) *Tales of Equinox*, a webcomic of his own creation for www.Thrillbent.com. (Once again, www.Thrillbent.com.) He's still bitter about no longer lettering *The Darkness* and wants it back on stands immediately.

The Top Cow essentials checklist:

Aphrodite IX: Complete Series
(ISBN: 978-1-63215-368-5)

Artifacts Origins: First Born
(ISBN: 978-1-60706-506-7)

Broken Trinity Volume 1
(ISBN: 978-1-60706-051-2)

Cyber Force: Rebirth, Volume 1
(ISBN: 978-1-60706-671-2)

The Darkness: Accursed, Volume 1
(ISBN: 978-1-58240-958-0)

The Darkness: Rebirth, Volume 1
(ISBN: 978-1-60706-585-2)

Death Vigil, Volume 1
(ISBN: 978-1-63215-278-27

Impaler, Volume 1
(ISBN: 978-1-58240-757-9)

Postal, Volume 1
(ISBN: 978-1-63215-342-5)

Rising Stars Compendium
(ISBN: 978-1-63215-246-6)

Sunstone, Volume 1
(ISBN: 978-1-63215-212-1)

Think Tank, Volume 1
(ISBN: 978-1-60706-660-6)

Wanted
(ISBN: 978-1-58240-497-4)

Wildfire, Volume 1
(ISBN: 978-1-63215-024-0)

Witchblade: Redemption, Volume
(ISBN: 978-1-60706-193-9)

Witchblade: Rebirth, Volume 1
(ISBN: 978-1-60706-532-6)

Witchblade: Borne Again, Volume
(ISBN: 978-1-63215-025-7)

For more ISBN and ordering information on our latest collections go to:
www.topcow.com
Ask your retailer about our catalogue of collected editions,
digests, and hard covers or check the listings at:
Barnes and Noble, Amazon.com,
and other fine retailers.

To find your nearest comic shop go to:
www.comicshoplocator.com